THE FIRE IN THE FROST

THE NINE WORLDS RISING
BOOK 4

LYRA WOLF

RAVENWELL PRESS

To Jenn, who weathered every draft, championed every chapter, and made me solemnly swear not to let any harm come to Fenrir (don't read chapter five...or twenty-seven...or, well, this is getting awkward now).

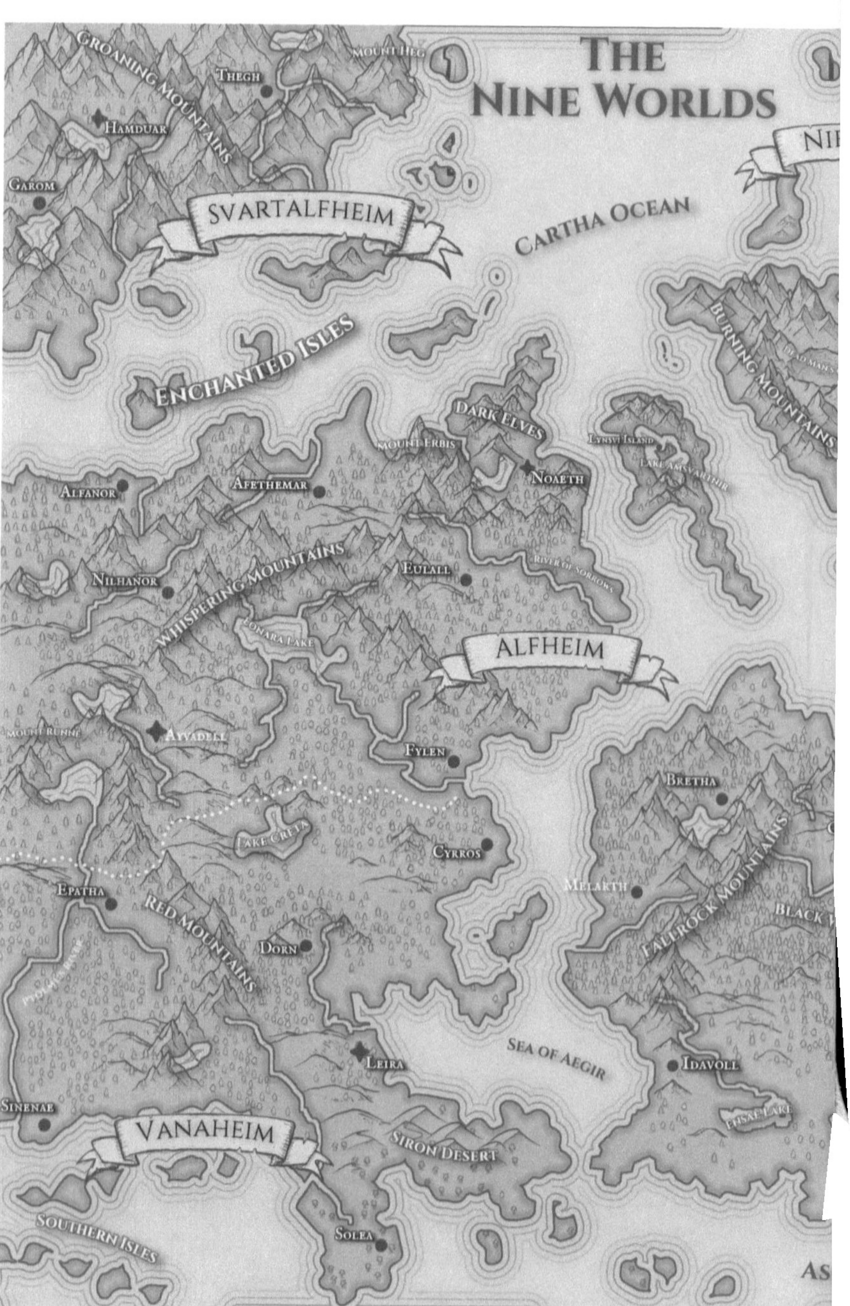

THE NINE WORLDS
SVARTALFHEIM
ENCHANTED ISLES
CARTHA OCEAN
NIF
GROANING MOUNTAINS
MOUNT HEG
THEGH
HAMDUAR
GAROM
BURNING MOUNTAINS
DEAD MAN'S
DARK ELVES
MOUNT ERBIS
LYNSVI ISLAND
LAKE AMSVARTHIR
NOAETH
ALFANOR
AFETHEMAR
WHISPERING MOUNTAINS
NILHANOR
EULALL
RIVER OF SORROWS
ALFHEIM
LONARA LAKE
MOUNT RUNNE
ARVADELL
FYLEN
BRETHA
LAKE CRETA
CYRROS
FALLROCK MOUNTAINS
BLACK
EPATHA
MELARTH
RED MOUNTAINS
DORN
SEA OF AEGIR
LEIRA
IDAVOLL
SINENAE
EHSAE LAKE
VANAHEIM
SIRON DESERT
SOUTHERN ISLES
SOLEA
AS

ELIVAGAR RIVER
SHADOW LANDS
SHORE OF CORPSES
ELJUDNIR
HEL
MIST AND ICE
BAY OF SERPENTS
GJOLL RIVER
BOILING TIDES
S EYE
VEILED SEA
FROST GIANTS
LAVA FIELDS
MUSPELHEIM
JOTUNHEIM
AEG-T
DEEPTOLD MOUNTAINS
MOUNT GLOKE
THRYMHEIM
VIMUR RIVER
UTGARD
GEIRSA
GULF
OF
THIEVES
IFINGR RIVER
GRAY MOUNTAINS
BEAU LAKE
SPRITE LAKE
RANDIR
KORMT RIVER
ASGARD
HOWLING SUMMITS
MOUNT KASTEN
DYRDAL
ORMT RIVER
MYRFELL
KRET
IRONWOOD
UEM LAKE
MIDGARD
CITY OF ASGARD
WILD BLUFF
AN SEA

"In the midst of winter, I found there was, within me, an invincible summer."

— Albert Camus

A NOTE FROM LOKI

I am Loki.

The God of Chaos, the God of Mischief, and I suppose that lying bit holds some truth as well. Depending on who you ask.

Before you crack open the mead and snuggle beneath your quilts to begin this newest adventure of mine, I feel compelled to have a little chat. You see, the author of this particular work, in their questionable wisdom, has taken certain, shall we say liberties, with the myth of *Grimnismál*. Now, in the original tale, Frigg, who has always had a delightfully vindictive streak, made a wager with her husband. She bet that Odin's favorite mortal king, Geirröðr, wasn't quite the gracious host the Alfather believed him to be. Surprise surprise. Odin always was rubbish at judging character.

Well, except for me, but that's another story.

Anyway, our "wise" Odin couldn't resist proving her wrong. So, off he went, disguised as a wanderer called Griming, straight into Frigg's carefully laid trap. See, she'd already sent word ahead to Geirröðr, warning him about a dangerous sorcerer coming to bewitch him. Geirröðr didn't much like the thought of being bewitched, which led to Odin being strung up between two massive fires for eight days and nights, without food or drink, until he was nearly dead. Rather dramatic, really.

In the version contained within these pages, however, let's just say while Frigg's revenge takes a different form, she's no less creative in her methods of teaching her husband a lesson. The author has kept the spirit of a wife's vengeance, just with slightly fewer third-degree burns. Sadly.

More pressingly, I've been instructed—rather firmly, I might add—to warn you about certain elements you'll encounter in this book. Consider this your formal notice that this tale contains:

Abusive relationship

Emotional abuse

Use of alcohol

Psychological manipulation

Cigarettes

Mentions of child death/infanticide

Domestic Violence

Sex

Gaslighting

Torture

Parental Abandonment

Familial trauma/abuse

Violence

Blood

BDSM

Emesis

Profanity

Hospitalisation

Discussions of death/grief/loss

Physical abuse

Poisoning

Imprisonment

Body horror elements

PTSD

Oh goody for me.

Now, there's another matter I simply must address. One that has me rather vexed because it's put me in a rather awkward position.

You see that magnificent eight-legged stallion on the cover? My dear Sleipnir? Well...

While yes, the tale of how Asgard got its wall is woven through these pages, Sleipnir himself doesn't actually, well... appear. I KNOW.

I've already had several strongly-worded conversations with our dear author about this grievous oversight. However, she assures me it's "all for the betterment of the plot." Whatever that means. She wants me to tell you that Sleipnir is perfectly content, happily eating all the carrots and sugar cubes his little magical eight-legged horsey heart ever wanted in his cushy stable back in Asgard.

In fact, out of all of us in this messy, wheel of perpetual pain, Sleipnir might have the best deal of all. Peacefully dozing on fresh straw, blissfully unbothered by something Lyra refers to as "story development."

I must admit, I am a little jealous.

But enough. You've been warned, you've been informed, and now you're as ready as you'll ever be to dive into this particular catastrophe.

Glorious.

PROLOGUE, OR WHY IT DOESN'T PAY TO ACCEPT BRIBES FROM TRICKSTER GODS—EVEN FORMER ONES

Midgard

"Do you ever talk about your feelings?"

"I honestly find it easier to have sex about my feelings."

My pen didn't waver as I made my notes, and kept my shoulders squared, my face neutral, just as I had for thousands of sessions before. But twenty years of practicing hadn't prepared me for the man sprawled across my couch, one leg draped over its arm, casually explaining how he'd lost his immortality after being banished from Asgard.

Just as it hadn't prepared me for the gigantic duffle bag he'd casually dropped on my office floor, filled with gold coins marked with symbols I'd never seen before.

Unethical to usher poor Mr. Jenkins out mid-session, watching him shuffle down the hall, still clutching his tissue box? Definitely.

But I'd finally be able to fund my real passion project: a therapeutic board game where players battle their inner demons with actual tiny plastic demons. It was ingenious.

His copper hair looked almost like flames against the cream walls, which were unusually cool despite the autumn warmth outside.

He shifted on my couch, wearing what had to be ten thousand dollars' worth of black leather and silk. The jacket alone probably cost more than my monthly mortgage. Silver rings glinted on his long fingers, each one looking ancient enough to belong in a museum. My eye lingered for a moment on how his silk shirt clung to his lean frame before I caught myself and looked away. Inappropriate. Unprofessional. And yet...

A faint whisper, like distant thunder, caught my attention. I glanced at my window, but it was firmly shut. Odd. I could have sworn I heard...No. No, it was just my mind playing tricks on me, just like how it kept having me imagine his fingers trail down my thigh.

I adjusted my sweater against the room's chill and forced myself to focus.

"Wh—Why are you here?"

He stretched, each movement fluid and precise. Silver chains at his throat caught the light, and I had to drag my focus back to my notes. This was getting ridiculous.

You can do this. You are a professional. And you are going to get "Battle Your Demons!" on store shelves.

"I suppose..." Something old and wounded flickered behind his sharp features. "I suppose I want to get better."

I made a note, trying not to notice how his lips curved into something between a smile and a dare.

"Better? In what way?"

"I may have a temper."

"Many do."

"That made me start Ragnarok," he said, as if

mentioning he'd started a minor kitchen fire. "Though I only take partial blame."

I wrote 'possible schizophrenia' in my notes, trying to ignore how the ink seemed to solidify on the page for a split second before drying.

"Ragnarok?" I gripped my pen tighter.

"Yes, the end of the worlds. I was in a bad place, but I think anyone would feel that way being imprisoned for 500 years after seeing your two infants murdered all while losing the love of your life and—" Loss consumed his expression. "Of course, that was just the start of it. After I started Ragnarok, I found out Sigyn was still alive, and well, she helped me see destroying everything wasn't the best way to deal with my anger."

Just think of the Kickstarter campaign.

"Destroy?" I managed, adding 'grandiose delusions' to my notes.

Just focus on the gold and get through this session of whatever this is.

"Yes, please keep up." He leaned forward, silver chains sliding against skin where his silk shirt had fallen open at the throat. My gaze fell to the buttons still fastened below. How many would it take to—No. Absolutely not.

I forced my attention back to my notepad.

"Fenrir told me you were good at listening, but you seem to have trouble understanding," he said. "It's not like I'm speaking Elvish to you."

I was definitely beginning to understand Fenrir better...

Loki drummed his fingers against the leather armrest, and that whisper came again, like far away voices carried on winter wind. I looked out my window. Still firmly shut, but was that frost gathering at its edges?

I cleared my throat.

"Let me get this straight," I said, working to keep my voice professional as the temperature seemed to drop another degree. "You started Ragnarok, the literal end of the worlds?"

"Yep, but then I tried to stop it, don't forget that bit." He flashed me a grin. "My chaos, my godhood. Well, it all slipped away faster than Thor's dignity at a drinking contest —" He flexed his hand. "Do you feel that?"

"Feel what?" But I did feel it. A pressure building in the room, like the moment before a storm breaks. I pushed away the questions that rose with that acknowledgment, the implications of actually sensing something my rational mind said couldn't exist, even though he sat on my couch.

There would be time to question my sanity later.

The leather of his jacket creaked as he shifted, and I caught notes of cinnamon and black pepper.

"Something's wrong." His fingers went to one of his silver rings, turning it. "I heard Thor's thunder last week. All the way here in Midgard. When that hammer-happy oaf makes himself heard across the realms, it's never good news."

He sat up, and for a heartbeat, I'm positive the air itself moved aside to make room for him.

"You believe I'm mad, don't you? Sitting here talking about thunder gods and realms? I don't blame you. It's a perfectly reasonable response as a human."

"It seems you're experiencing some significant—"

"Oh, spare me the DSM whatever-number-you're-on diagnosis," he interrupted. The temperature dropped enough that I saw his breath mist. "That's not why I've come to chat."

A thin layer of ice crept across the surface of my coffee. Right...

One nervous breakdown at a time.

The gold. Just think of the pile of gold sitting on your floor. A few minutes more and he will be gone, and the money is all yours.

"Yes, of course, my apologies. You said you wanted to get better," I said, clinging to the familiar script of therapy like a lifeline. "What does 'better' look like to you?"

His shoulders seemed to deflate slightly.

"Everything I touch turns to catastrophe. To shit, really." His smile faltered, and I saw past the dangerous beauty to something wounded beneath. "But I do what I must to keep everyone safe."

"What are your children's thoughts on that statement?" I asked. "Do you think they agree?"

Frost patterns bloomed across my window. That far off whisper became clearer. Voices, laughing, crying, screaming.

"What is that?" I asked, spinning in my chair, heart hammering.

"So you hear it too now?" Loki's lip twisted into a grimace. "Fantastic. Whatever Thor's trying to warn about must be getting worse."

"Worse? What is getting worse?" My voice rose an octave despite my attempts to control it.

"Pay it no mind," he said, waving his hand dismissively. "Shouldn't affect you mortals. Yet, anyway. I think."

"You think?"

He sighed.

"Let's, uh...let's talk about family," I said, though every instinct screamed at me to stop. "You mentioned Fenrir earlier. Your son cares about you."

"Ah yes. He's been quite insistent about this therapy business." Loki's voice grew distant. "Always trying to fix things, that one. Takes after his mother's stubborn determination. Though the gods never saw that part of him, did they? Only saw the monster they feared he'd become." He paused, fingers tracing one of his rings. "But he asked, so here I am. Making an effort."

He must have noticed my unease, because he fixed his green eyes on mine again.

And again, something in that gaze caught and held me, and the tension in my shoulders eased despite my better judgement. The whispers faded to background noise.

"Tell me about your relationship with your children," I said, finding my voice.

He laughed, but it was a broken sound.

"Which version would you like? The myths? The lies? The truths that hurt worse than either?" He stood, pacing to my window. Where his fingers touched the glass, the frost recoiled. "Every time I reach out to help, I leave scars on those I love most. My wife Sigyn, my children...they've all paid the price for my good intentions." He swallowed hard. "I want to stop hurting the people I care about, but I don't know how. Or if I even can."

A woman's voice joined the whispers now, speaking words that made my teeth ache.

Shit. Shit, shit, shit.

I focused harder on his gaze, as if he could somehow erase the impossible things happening around me.

"You coming here at all is progress," I managed, though my voice shook.

"Yes, I know. Now, cure me."

"That's not how therapy works."

He scoffed.

"Then what good are you? I better not be wasting my own time." He ran a hand through his copper hair. "You know what's truly maddening? I used to think I could fix everything with a bit of fire, a touch of chaos. A trick here, a transformation there, thinking if I could just reshape reality enough, everything would work out. Now?" He snapped his fingers. "Nothing. Not even enough chaos left to warm a cup of coffee. And maybe that's for the best."

"You miss your powers?"

"I miss the idea of them being able to protect," he said. "Though I suppose I never really could. Not in the ways that mattered."

He looked down at his rings, breaking our eye contact. The whispers rushed back in like a tide, and the frost spread faster.

Just think of the gold. This is just your imagination getting the better of you.

"What scares you more, that you failed to protect your children, or that deep down, you knew exactly what you were doing when you handed them over?"

He moved like liquid shadow, and a blade pressed against the tip of my nose. His green eyes blazed with something dangerous and terrible, and I finally, truly understood what he was. What he had been.

"Careful, doctor," he whispered, his breath feathering over my cheeks. "Even fallen gods have teeth."

Something shifted in his expression. He lowered the blade.

"Apologies. Old habits. As I mentioned earlier, bad temper I'm trying to work on."

The whispers grew louder, and that woman's voice—sharp, cold, triumphant—spoke words that made reality itself seem to shiver.

Frost cracked across my windows.

Loki crossed to the window in three fluid strides and

pressed his palm against the glass. The frost spread between his splayed fingers like dark veins.

"Well, that's not good." He scratched the back of his head. "I know how earlier I said not to worry about all this. But, I think if I were you, I might start getting my affairs in order."

"What?" My voice cracked embarrassingly high. I jumped to the gold, sweeping the coins into my briefcase. Some spilled onto the floor, and I dropped to my knees to gather them.

"I best be going." He straightened his leather jacket. "I trust you have a will? Well, that won't do much good if everyone is dead, I suppose."

"Dead?" I stuffed another handful of coins into my sweater pockets. "What do you mean, dead? Like everyone-everyone?"

"Good point. Here. Take this." He handed his blade to me. Sleek steel with a handle wrapped in well-worn black leather.

"No, thanks." My hands shook as I tried to zip my over-stuffed briefcase, the coins threatening to spill onto the floor. I needed to get these somewhere safe, needed to think.

"No, no, you definitely need this," he insisted, pressing the dagger into my trembling grip. "The balance is quite lovely, and it's excellent for both ceremonial and practical stabbing. Very versatile."

I stared at the weapon, now sharing space with my client notes and scattered coins.

"I should really get these deposited before—"

"Actually, I think you should head straight home." He was already at the door, fingers curled around the handle with a casualness that didn't match the tension in his shoulders. "Lock your doors. Not that it will help much if what I think may be coming to Midgard is true, but..." He shrugged, a smile still playing on his lips. "It might make you feel better."

"Coming? What's coming?"

"Something old," he said. "Something that shouldn't have been able to reach this realm at all, unless...gods, I hope it's not that. Now, look, I really must be going."

"You can't just say something like that and leave!" I lunged forward, grabbing his sleeve. The leather was impossibly smooth under my fingers, and just as impossibly cold.

He looked down at my hand with an expression caught between amusement and pity. He peeled my fingers from his jacket.

"You humans never do well with divine happenings," he said. "Always so many questions." He flashed that dangerous grin. "Let me rephrase so you might better understand: I'm sure it's nothing. Just the potential end of your realm. Again. Probably won't happen. Maybe. Good session, though. Very illuminating."

He vanished down the hall, leaving me with a churning stomach and the distinct feeling that pushing Mr. Jenkins out the door for a bag of gold had been the worst mistake of my life, which, it seemed, might not last much longer.

1

———

MOOSE ON THE LOOSE

LOKI

Midgard

Durango, Colorado

I kissed Sigyn's neck and trailed my lips down her hot skin towards her collarbone. Pulling her closer, I slipped my hand into her cream blouse and slid over her right breast.

My hunger deepened with every inch of her I touched.

"This isn't working for me," Sigyn said.

"Would you prefer I nibble your ear instead? I'm more than happy to accommodate."

Abandoning her neck, I tugged softly at her earlobe with my teeth in that teasing way I knew she liked.

She pressed her hand against my chest, stopping me.

"No, it's not that," she said. "I'm not comfortable. The edge of the sink is grinding into my lower back. Plus, that stupid moose is staring at me."

I opened my eyes and regretted my decision immediately. A wooden sign of a moose sitting in a bath leered at me in the mirror's reflection. I sighed at the words "wash your hooves" above its antlers that dripped with soap suds.

Why could Fenrir not have a proper bathroom?

Aggressively cute decor cluttered every surface and hung from every rod and peg. Thick towels embossed with playful deer. Soap dispensers shaped like grinning squirrels. Porcelain hedgehogs holding mushroom cap bowls full of cotton balls. It was enough to make you hurl rainbows.

But I would not let a few woodland creatures stop me from enjoying my stolen minutes with Sigyn.

"I know this isn't exactly the most conducive of bathrooms for this," I said. "But we can't let the moose win."

She laughed, the timbre of her voice sparking a fresh thrill of heat through my bones.

"Let's try over there." She pried my hand out of her blouse. I frowned at the loss of her breast in my open palm.

She directed me to the tub and propped up her right leg on the porcelain edge. I grimaced harder at the shower curtain of two black bears roasting marshmallows over a campfire. Fenrir assured me they were vegan marshmallows.

Sigyn wrapped her arms around my slender frame and pulled me against her, exploding the bears and the marshmallows into a thousand pieces and out of my mind. Now this was more like it.

I smiled with a touch of evil in the corners and nestled my hips between Sigyn's thighs, causing her to gasp. Her brown eyes darkened as I pressed myself firmly against her, cradling my body in her curves.

Tucking a lock of her honied ginger hair behind her ear,

I grazed her round cheeks with my fingertips. I loved how her face of soft arcs flushed beneath my touch.

"Now, where were we? Ah yes. I remember. I was about to do this." I kissed the length of her neck again, while I worked at undoing more of those dreadful buttons of her blouse.

"What's gotten into you to...to..." her breath hitched as I suckled at her pulse, "...to sneak me away in here?"

Her skin prickled as I drifted towards her shoulder, leaving hot, open mouth kisses in my wake. Sigyn's pulse quickened against my lips as I crept my hand beneath her blouse again.

"You gave me that look when we were setting the table for dinner."

"What look?" she asked.

I pulled back and stared into her brown eyes that feigned innocence. The saucy little vixen.

"You know the one," I said. "It's the one you make when you want me to do *this*."

I slid my hand between her legs and relished the whimper that rolled out of her throat as I stroked her.

"Besides." I worked her slowly, building the agony. "Now that I've had the stitches removed from my chest wound, and my shoulder is all better—"

She pursed her lips, telling me she was not convinced with that last one. The twinge radiating in my sore muscle confirmed my lie.

"—I mean, my shoulder is *mostly* better. I think we should focus on making up for lost time."

She rocked against my fingers, trying to urge me to quicken the pace. She never was the patient sort.

I kept steady. Slow.

Cruel.

"And how much time do we have left?" she asked. "I don't want Fenrir to know what we're doing."

I shirked.

"You worry too much. Trust me, he wouldn't be shocked. He's found me in way more precarious positions than a simple bathroom quickie."

I deepened my exploration of her.

"We can't have him wait at the table all by himself," she said, each word losing breath. "It would be rude."

"We have at least ten minutes," I said, my voice low and saturated with silk and honey. "Fenrir insists on grating the carrots by hand for that salad of his, which will take him a while. But, if you prefer I stop..."

I slowed even more. She grasped my wrist and put my hand back, urging me faster.

"You better not."

I smiled.

Our mouths met in a kiss and I quickened my pace, finally allowing her to chase that edge she teetered on.

She groaned again.

The more we collapsed into fire, the more my footing wobbled, trying to keep us balanced. Maybe if I moved her this way—

My elbow struck a wall. Damn this small bathroom. But I'd never let any tight space beat me before, and I refused for this to be the first.

I regrouped and increased my speed again. She dug her fingers into the waves of my hair. I kissed her deeper. Harder.

She shuddered with her release, and I drew out her pleasure, relishing each flutter of bliss and whimper in my ear. And as that exquisite relaxed stillness washed over her face, I started working her again, stoking and building that heat in her core.

Once would never do.

Gripping her hips, I hoisted her against the wall, rattling the framed cross stitch picture of dancing field mice.

I shoved her black skirt above her thighs and unzipped my trousers. Everything in me ached to bury myself in her. To be home.

A blender went off, sawing through our heated breaths and sighs.

Damn. I'd have to hurry. Fenrir was already preparing the smoothies. I guess I underestimated how long it took him to grate those stupid orange sticks.

Just as I underestimated my right shoulder.

A spasm twisted sharp in the muscles, cutting through my tendons and stinging into my neck and back.

"Gah!"

All the strength drained from my arm, and I almost dropped her.

"What's wrong—oh." She gulped in air. "It's your shoulder, isn't it?"

I nodded, anger and embarrassment flushing through me. I was so tired of this. I was so tired of the pain. The weakness. I never thought this lovely little souvenir from Surtr burying his sword in my shoulder would continually get in my way. But then, I was also mortal now, and that didn't help much when trying to heal from wounds inflicted by celestial weapons.

She grimaced

"I hate this pain you're always in." She massaged my shoulder, melting the tension into a dull roar. But the anger remained.

"I can bear it." I moved her hand away, and I shook the

residual pain from my arm, turning the sensation of a thousand knives stabbing me all at once into a paltry five hundred.

I sucked in a breath, regrouping myself. Pushing my feelings of uselessness deep down and away. The shoulder pain was bad enough without dwelling on all the weirdness happening ever since we heard Thor's thunder all the way from Asgard. The fact Dr. Thorne heard it too wasn't great either, and—no. I was going to enjoy *not* thinking of any of it right now. I wanted my time with my wife. No prophecies, no elves with impeccable bone structure, and no Surtr.

I smiled at her, as reassuringly as I could muster.

"How about we try the floor?"

She stopped me from tugging her down onto the rug in the shape of a smiling raccoon.

"Fenrir sounds ready for dinner," she said. "I promised him I'd help set out the food once he was done. Besides, it's hard to enjoy *alone time* with that bear looking at me."

She pointed down at a statue of a bear in a corner, holding a roll of toilet paper and looking semi-possessed.

Perhaps she had a point.

2

PEPPER

Fenrir placed a smoothie on the thick oak table that took up most of the dining room—everything rustic and natural. Fenrir explained to me in excruciating detail how every piece in his cabin was either reclaimed, recycled, or, as it pertained to the oak used to make the table, fell in his backyard during the last storm.

His open red flannel shirt covered a dark green waffle knit henley that stretched across his broad chest. He kept his long, dark hair swept up into a bun, which only made his green eyes all the brighter. Green eyes he inherited from me. However, whereas mischief flickered in mine—Sigyn's words—only kindness beamed from his.

Fenrir looked as if he belonged to the wild Colorado terrain that stretched beyond the massive windows behind us, where pine forests marched up rocky slopes until they gave way to snow-capped peaks.

"Where have you two been?" Fenrir asked. "And why is your shirt all miss buttoned?"

I looked down at my black silk Versace shirt screaming with gold Barocco print. The fabric hung crooked off my frame thanks to me slipping the fourth button in the second button slot.

"You know how these things happen when you're in a hurry," I said, popping the missed buttons in their correct holes.

"I knew you'd warm up to the idea of the carrot salad, and...wait," Fenrir scratched his thick stubble and annoyance twisted his softly angled face as his gaze filled with knowing. "Oh...don't you dare tell me. Not again." His expression cycled through denial, horror, and the dawning realization of which room I'd used. "Not in my bathroom."

I shrugged.

"Well, Fenrir, when the mood strikes—"

Sigyn cleared her throat.

"Did I tell you how much I love your handmade ceramic dishes, Fenrir?" Sigyn interrupted, straightening her skirt, ensuring all evidence of our attempted tryst was smoothed away. "I'll get the rest of the food. Loki. Come and help me."

She squeezed out those last words through a strained smile, telling me I was close to trouble.

She hurried into the adjacent kitchen that gleamed with quartz countertops and stainless steel eco friendly appliances.

I took a step to follow and stopped and winced as my shoulder flared again, thanks to me having made the mistake of looking to the right, trying to avoid one of Fenrir's overly large indoor plants.

Why he thought a fiddle leaf tree twice as tall as me, and seven times as wide belonged in his cramped dining room...

Fenrir laid a hand on my arm, directing me to the table instead, making sure the monstera in the corner didn't fondle me too aggressively.

Most of the dinner already covered the table, a feast of vegetables and beans in various sad combinations.

Not that I'd be able to eat much, anyway.

"If you didn't indulge in all those bathroom acrobatics, your shoulder would have a better chance of healing," he said.

He arched an eyebrow, a bit of laughter behind his eyes.

"I'm about to saw the entire arm off. Maybe then it will finally be happy," I snapped, all at my pain and not at him.

I plopped onto the pine bench. A fire roared in the stone fireplace in the living room, adding another layer of cozy to the cabin along with the flannel blankets draped over the hemp fabric couch and chairs. A vase of wildflowers he picked that morning sat on the coffee table. Everything homey and warm and clean.

Fenrir smiled, and a spark I didn't much like flashed in his eyes.

"Or...you could try this," he said. "This is guaranteed to help your shoulder."

He slid the smoothie in a tall glass towards me. Bubbles gurgled to the surface.

"It's green."

He grinned.

"That's the spirulina. I'm going to serve this at *Kalehalla* starting next week. It's a super smoothie that fights inflammation. Now, try it. The avocado gives it a nice, silky texture."

I cursed Surtr harder than ever.

"I'm good." I tried to move my shoulder, proving how limber I was. A burning stiff sensation locked the joint up instead.

Fenrir's smile flattened.

"Papa..." Fenrir said. "The healthiest things are green."

I narrowed my eyes at him.

"You know my opinion on eating what my food eats," I said. "Vegetables are only good for filling holes in the ground."

He held my gaze, refusing to back down.

"Don't be a baby," he said. "Drink."

I sighed and lifted the glass. The chill of the smoothie stung my fingertips.

His smile widened.

I said a prayer and took a sip.

Banana and swamp filled my mouth, followed by something shockingly hot.

I choked and spit the slurry back into the glass.

He frowned.

"What did you put in this sludge?" I pushed the smoothie away. "Is that black pepper?"

Fenrir chuckled and slid the smoothie back to me. The smoothie gurgled.

"Of course," he said. "It helps the turmeric better absorb."

Gods.

Sigyn walked in carrying a blue ceramic bowl heaped with carrot salad and sat the dish in the center of the table. When would these torments end?

"Loki, drink the smoothie," she said. "The antioxidants will help you recover faster. And..." She lowered her voice so only I could hear. I closed my eyes as her breath skated over the skin on my cheek. "Then you can enjoy *other* things again, too."

Heat rushed between my legs.

Perhaps I was too hasty to discount the spirulina.

She slid next to me on the bench. Fenrir plonked himself in the chair across from us.

I picked up the smoothie, and they both watched me take a second sip.

Fishy banana flooded my mouth again. I forced the pond scum down, fighting against gagging the entire time. That oh so delightful bite of pepper burned my gums.

Was sex really worth this?

Fenrir piled his plate with sautéed mushrooms and took a scoop of whole wheat spaghetti he drenched in a vegan avocado Alfredo sauce. Sigyn spooned the carrot salad mixed with raisins into her bowl.

Hunger rumbled in my stomach.

I never knew I'd wish for carrot salad, but ever since I lost my godhood, I developed reactions to almost everything that touched my tongue. Dairy was the first to declare war on my guts. All tree nuts revolted next, followed by cumin, strawberries, sesame seeds, pears, lamb, lettuce, salmon, and asparagus.

I took another drink of the smoothie. My dinner.

"Are you really going to make all your patrons drink this sludge?" I asked.

Why can't I be allergic to spirulina?

"Some people do enjoy foods that are healthy, Papa," he said. "My *Fields of Green* spinach smoothie was a huge hit with the bee pollen booster."

I raised my eyebrow, and not because of the bee pollen. Why was Fenrir chattering away about smoothies nearly as much as Idunn did about botany? He'd always been focused on his health and diet, but not to the extent of giving the equivalent of a sales pitch.

Sigyn plopped a baked sweet potato stuffed with roasted chickpeas on her plate.

"It really is impressive what you've built with *Kale-halla*," Sigyn said. "Now you're voted the number one smoothie and juice bar in Colorado. We are so proud of you."

Fenrir grinned, a touch of red flushing his cheeks. I eyed him. Something was definitely going on with my son.

"The support the community of Durango has given me is overwhelming. Business couldn't be better, and my newest employee, Jenn, is the best at helping me create different smoothie combinations, along with Tyr. She actually helped develop the one you're drinking now, Papa. Tyr gave it his approval and said it helped soothe his sore muscles after leg day. The only problem is what to call it. We've been going back and forth—"

"Oh, I have a name for it," I interrupted after choking down another swallow of slime.

"*Pumpkins Loki*," Sigyn warned me beneath her breath. Her secret word she used for those times when I got a bit *too* honest.

I forced a smile, hoping he didn't notice my eye twitch and—hold on...Jenn? Tyr? Did he just blush at the mention of their names? Was this what was going on?

"I'm sure you'll think of something most appropriate for this *creation*. One that doesn't at all bring about images of vomit."

Sigyn sighed.

Questions sizzled my tongue about this little trio, especially if they were the ones encouraging this creative side of him.

"And how about you, Papa?" Fenrir swirled the spaghetti around his fork. Spaghetti that had no right being that green. "What do you do now to keep busy while Sigyn attends her lectures?"

My questions, it seemed, would have to wait. I never could pass up a chance to talk about myself.

I placed the smoothie on the table. Maybe if I let it rest a bit the taste would improve? I laughed internally at that absurdity, because if I didn't laugh, I'd cry.

"I dabbled in cooking for a spell until every ingredient broke me out with a topography of hives that rivaled most maps," I said. "Currently, I'm a nude model. It's important to support the arts."

"And how do you find the art students?" Fenrir asked.

"They try, the dears, but then it's hardly fair. No human can ever truly capture my sensational calves."

He smiled and tossed the salad bursting with cherry tomatoes, dandelion greens, and radicchio. My stomach twisted at the scent of the apple cider vinegar. I swallowed the sensation of sick down.

Knives and forks scraped plates as conversation bubbled over the crunch of celery and cucumber. I took another sip of my smoothie, and I couldn't help the warmth coursing in my chest at the pride shining through Fenrir's eyes when I forced out a "yummy" sound.

Even though he tortured me with his love, joy filled me that Fenrir finally seemed happy with his life in Durango. Even though he was banished to Midgard like me, he thrived in his new surroundings. And, at least there was no shortage of nature in Colorado, unlike his time confined to the diesel and cement of Vienna.

I tapped the side of the smoothie glass and frowned. A nice head of foam topped the mixture now. I just wanted to eat something that wasn't bland or puréed again. I just wanted the sensation of rats gnawing at my insides to go away.

Fenrir touched my arm.

"If you really hate the smoothie, I'll make you a different

one," he said. "How about blueberry with hemp milk? I just want you to feel better."

Feel better. That was a laugh.

"I wish you wouldn't make such a fuss." I forced another gulp. My stomach flipped. "Just because I'm not a god anymore doesn't mean I'm some weakly human. I'm still half Jotnar and half Aesir—urgh!" My insides made an unholy sound. "Did you put mango in this, by chance?"

He scratched behind his ear.

"Pineapple," he said. "Sigyn said it was a safe food for you."

Another gurgle and a twinge in my bowels told me it was not safe anymore.

Sigyn grimaced.

"You may not be human, but you're also no longer *immortal*," she said. "And your body is all in knots after you ripped out your chaos for me, and—"

She grew silent and looked down at her lap, where she picked at her fingers.

Sadness gripped me that she continued to suffer from the guilt of me giving up my godhood for her. And even though the emptiness of no longer having my chaos sometimes threatened to defeat me, I still did not regret what I did. I never would.

"I will be fine." I wanted her reassured. "My body is still just adjusting to the new me. I just have to push through these lovely *side effects* until..." Fenrir eyed me, but then tossed the next salad. I lowered my voice to Sigyn. "Until Odin can get me a golden apple. That should fix me up, plus give me a boost of about ten thousand years, give or take. I'd like to see spirulina do *that*."

"If Odin can even get you the apple," she whispered. "I'm worried."

My lips thinned with this conversation, because worry buzzed in the back of my mind, too.

I looked out the window at a blue sky dappled by clouds that resembled brush strokes. Everything appeared perfectly serene, but there was a coldness in the air that shouldn't be there. The worlds were vibrating with a frequency that set my teeth on edge. Something fundamental had changed, had broken, and I had no idea what.

All of my messages to Odin remained unanswered. For half a minute I considered sneaking into Asgard, but being mortal made the journey difficult. That, and, I suppose, I knew the price if I got caught breaking my banishment again. Gods. Who was I becoming? Responsible? Disgusting.

"Yes, Dr. Thorne didn't exactly handle the oddities happening in his office well," I said louder, for Fenrir to hear. So he knew I made the effort. Even if it meant traumatizing one more mortal medical professional.

"Oh! You actually went to talk with him. I'm so happy!"

"Well, I don't think he shares your enthusiasm. Mortals can be so closed minded."

He started to ask, and I moved the conversation on.

"There's always drama in Asgard," I said, though the memory of that frost at Dr. Thorne's window nagged at me —how it had spread faster than it should. How it looked like dark veins between my fingers when I touched the glass. "It's probably just one of their usual squabbles with Jotunheim. Skadi is always causing some spectacle, wanting to take over lands she feels owed. Wanting Midgard. And wanting to tickle Balder's feet. *It's a whole thing.* But it will blow over like all the other three thousand Skadi incidents."

Truth was, I wasn't so sure. The walls Odin built between realms shouldn't allow this much cold to seep through. If they were fracturing...well, Skadi would be the least of our problems. Frost Giants had been waiting centuries for such a weakness. And if it wasn't Skadi, but someone else...

Bly's warning about Frigg lived in a dark space within me. If she learned I was mortal...Well, I really preferred she not break my neck. Her killing me would really piss me off.

"You heard that thunder last week," Sigyn said. "And you know Thor. He wouldn't do that unless something was very, *very* wrong."

Fenrir's shoulders slumped.

"Tyr promised he'd visit me last week," Fenrir said. "Jenn and I—" He caught my curious gaze. "He never showed. Tyr doesn't break promises."

He didn't.

And that's when I booked plane tickets for Sigyn and me to be with Fenrir. I wouldn't let him be alone until I knew what was happening in Asgard.

An awful gurgle rumbled from my intestines. A cramping rush followed that forced me to bend forward and clamp my hand over my stomach.

Yes. That's who would protect Fenrir best. Me. A broken down, ex-god with a bad shoulder and twisting guts.

"Just get me a bottle of Pepto-Bismol with a straw. Or a gun. I don't care which," I said.

Sigyn rubbed my back as I cradled my head in my hands, sinking my fingers into my hair.

"I'm afraid I don't have either," Fenrir said. "I tend to stick with more natural and herbal remedies, and you know my stance on solving problems with guns."

"You're making me wish I had a gun right now."

"Show me what you have." Sigyn stood from the table. "I'm sure I can find something that will help."

Fenrir nodded and escorted Sigyn down a hall plastered with paintings of mountains and frolicking deer.

I needed fresh air.

Grabbing the smoothie, I dragged myself outside onto the deck.

Ponderosa pines spread across the Animas Valley, the La Plata Mountains rising jagged against the western sky while the San Juans dominated the east. Fenrir said Colorado reminded him of the wilds of Jotunheim, but with a far warmer climate. Still, as much as he raved about the mountains, brewpubs, and the outdoorsy community, Durango wasn't *home*. I wished he could see the Ironwood again.

But his own banishment wouldn't allow it.

Bitter coated my mouth at that thought.

And speaking of bitter...

I leaned over the railing and poured the smoothie out, smiling as an arc of green splattered into the bushes below where it belonged.

A hot knife cut into my shoulder, as I made a second mistake of moving too fast. Damn. I couldn't enjoy myself one bit.

I reached into my pocket and pulled out a bottle of some over-the-counter painkiller. Over-the-counter because Sigyn took away the Vicodin after she found me crushing it and snorting it with pop rocks. Apparently, that wasn't the "prescribed method."

I shook four white tablets into my palm and swallowed them. I reached across my chest and gave my muscles a gentle pull, stretching my shoulder, coaxing the ache to dull. But it never left completely. Some pain always remained in the joint, making every movement stiff and difficult.

A gust of stiff wind full of salt blew from the East,

tinkling the wind chimes hanging from a nearby maple that burst with autumn colors.

The caw of a raven cut through the metallic jingle.

A large, black bird barreled towards me, swooping and tumbling as it fell from the sky.

My veins iced. This wasn't any raven. This was Hugin.

And Hugin only.

A squawk and a flurry of feathers erupted from him as he crashed onto the deck, and toppled head over tail three times before coming to a stop at my feet.

Why couldn't Odin's damn birds ever leave me in peace?

"Hugin, if you don't fly back to Asgard right now and tell that eavesdropping asshole to leave me alone, I will impale you on a spit."

He croaked and clucked a string of raven obscenities at me and popped onto his feet, feathers poking out raggedly from his usually pristine plumage. His voice didn't have the strength I was used to, his clicks hollow.

Alright, this was all rather odd.

He glared at me, and concern hit me with how sunken his eyes were in their sockets, as if he hadn't had a drink in days.

But why would he not have had water?

This was seriously annoying that I now had to take care of Odin's stray pets.

I picked him up and placed him in the concrete bird-bath. He gave a small trill of thanks and drank greedily. The times I fantasized about having the chance to drown him and Munin—

Munin.

Wait.

Hugin and Munin were never separated.

My breath clouded in front of me, though it wasn't

nearly cold enough for that. Frost crackled across the water in the birdbath, spreading like spider webs from where Hugin's beak touched the surface. The raven jerked back, feathers ruffling.

Alright, this was getting significantly more alarming now.

"Where's Munin?" I asked.

He nuzzled my hand, as if urging me to go. To flee.

"Did Odin send you?"

He clicked and hopped, as if calling me a fool.

I'd call him something far worse if he kept this up.

Sigyn's and Fenrir's screams split the air from inside the house.

3

THE REVENGE OF LARS

The crack of chairs and dishes bursting against walls and the floor shredded my eardrums.

I ran into the house, unsheathing *Laevateinn* from its leather holster at my hip, my heart pounding harder in my throat at the rattle of chainmail and armor.

My guts twisted.

Sigyn and Fenrir stood with their hands bound behind their backs, with nearly two dozen Aesir guards crammed into the living room surrounding them.

Shit.

I charged, but the guards held short swords at Sigyn's and Fenrir's throats, thin smiles promising blood, forcing me to stand my ground.

"I'd put that away if you don't want their throats slit," said a guard in High Asgardian.

His sharp cheekbones might have been handsome if not for the cruel glint in his amber eyes.

With a curse, I slid *Laevateinn* back into its holster.

"Touch them, and I'll make sure those pretty features of yours end up rearranged. Permanently." I forced myself to stand taller. Stronger. Even though every bone in my body hurt.

Fenrir's guard, the one with a jagged scar splitting his upper lip, laughed and cinched his bonds tighter around his wrists.

No. *All* the guards laughed. To my face.

Three marched towards me, one with a broad, red nose, another with an eye milky from an old wound, and a third whose beard was braided with golden rings. They carried chains and irons made of Dwarven steel in their rough hands. None of them looked overly friendly, and this lack of fear confused me, and frankly, made me absolutely furious.

Witnessing a god's anger always inspired a little terror in them, but they seemed as unconcerned as if I were a naughty kitten.

The nerve.

"Loki Laufeyjarson, you are to come with us," said a square-faced guard whose left cheek bore a puckered burn scar like a splash of wax. Ah. The captain of this darling little band of Asgard's finest failures.

He dropped his hand to the hilt of his sword at his hip.

I opened my hand, flexing my fingers in that way I always did when threatening to call up my fire.

"Are you sure you want to do this?" I asked. "You know who I am, and what I can do. And if you don't release my wife and my son, I'm going to sear off your entire face."

Not that I had any fire left in me, but they didn't know that. And the dregs of magic remaining in me might cause some pain if I really put my heart into it.

That was, if I could get it to work. It had been ages since I was forced to rely on basic magic, without the godhood-powered boost.

They laughed again. Louder than the first time.

The guards stepped closer, the one with the red mark across his face leading the charge, while the two dozen others walked behind him, their armor gleaming. A flash of magic flickered in each link of the Dwarven steel cuffs they carried, and their odd sense of security finally made sense. This was magic meant to render any god they ensnared powerless.

Great.

A guard with a face full of pockmarks kept his blade at Sigyn's throat while the one with the split lip held Fenrir. The milky-eyed one pressed his sword harder against my son's spine.

Shit.

"Are you going to give us a little ouchie booboo?" sneered the guard with the red nose, his thick eyebrows drawing together in mock concern.

"Alright. Obviously you want to die today," I said.

Sigyn mouthed "shut up" to me, as if I was going to make things worse. I didn't think that was possible.

The guard with the split lip cleared phlegm from his throat, that particular hack and wheeze scratching the back of my mind. I'd heard that disgusting rasp before—oh. Right. So, this actually could get worse.

"You three will face punishment for your crimes," Lars said, a bit too much enjoyment in his gruff voice. He stared at me. "And as for you, I say it's a long time coming. After what you did to me."

"Please don't tell me this is all because you're still upset about that time I accidentally got sick in your helmet?" I asked.

His face reddened.

"You could have at least warned me first before I put it back on my head," he said.

Snickering from the other guards filled the room.

"Look, I apologized," I said.

"Actually, you didn't," he snapped.

"Well, I just hadn't gotten around to posting the sorry note in the mail—"

"What is the accusation against us?" Sigyn interrupted.

The square-faced captain stepped towards her, the puckered burn scar on his left cheek catching the light as he crunched one of Fenrir's ceramic dishes beneath his heel. The waxy, twisted flesh pulled at his smile.

"You and your compatriots are dangerous fugitives for crimes committed against Asgard and the Nine Worlds," he said.

"What crimes?" she asked.

"As much as this gives me personal pleasure to bring you all in," he continued, not answering her, the scar tissue distorting as his smile widened. "This is simply about cleaning up the garbage that should have been disposed of centuries ago," he stated.

Now it was my turn to laugh. This was a capital joke.

"You have no jurisdiction in Midgard," I said. "You can't do anything to us."

"You aren't even allowed on Midgard," Fenrir added. "Odin decreed it five millennia back after that unicorn incident."

"Look," I said. "I suggest you run along back through the Bifrost before Odin finds out and has you all thrown into the dungeons for this overstep. I hear the fleas in the straw mats are particularly ravenous. I'd absolutely hate that for you."

My lips pulled into a grin.

"She warned us you'd use his name to intimidate us," he said. "But there's a problem with all your bluster."

"Which is?" I asked.

"We no longer answer to Odin." Lars's face split into a grin like a child who'd just gotten away with stealing sweets from the palace kitchen.

"Then who do you answer to?" Sigyn asked.

"Clap them in irons," the captain commanded.

The room exploded into motion.

A wall of armored bodies surged towards me, sword points flashing in the late afternoon light. Two guards, one with a crooked nose that had ben broken too many times, the other sporting a fresh red welt across his temple, pinned Sigyn against the wall. She trashed as they wrestled her wrists into the glowing bonds.

Fenrir's roar turned to a sharp cry as five guards attacked. Three grabbed his arms while two more, built like oxen with arms thick as tree trunks, seized his legs.

His boots skidded against the floor as they dragged him, their chainmail rattling with each of his kicks. The shackles gleamed in their hands as they fought to trap his limbs.

I lunged towards them, but the other guards hemmed me in at every turn. Each time I tried to break through, another stepped into my path, their armor clanking as they shifted.

How thoughtful of them to pack themselves so tightly together. It would make demolishing the lot of them much more efficient.

Shattered porcelain crunched under boots as I grabbed a dining chair, buying me seconds to reach my daggers. But as I hurled the chair at the guards flooding towards me, forcing three of them to step back and knock over Fenrir's prized collection of Fabergé eggs, my shoulder ignited as if stabbed by a hot poker. I choked back a grunt and blinked away the water filling my eyes. Alright, definitely not how I expected that to turn out.

Even if I could draw *Laevateinn*, my useless right arm would probably betray me. The last thing I needed was to fumble with my blade in front of these idiots. Nothing quite ruined an intimidating presence quite like dropping your own weapon. I could do without that embarrassment.

"Those were gifts from the Romanovs!" Fenrir yelled at me, slamming his elbow into a guard's nose while another tried to get him in a headlock. His foot caught a third guard in the chest, sending the man staggering back into the second display case. More eggs shattered.

"This is hardly the time," I shouted, grabbing for another chair. I found empty air. Damn, apparently I'd run out of furniture to throw. "But now that you're done mourning your gaudy egg collection, maybe you want to turn into the wolf? I think that may be a better use of your time, don't you think?"

I reached deep in myself for my magic, grasping at the thin wisps of my power, trying to harness what I could. The familiar emerald glow flickered and died at my fingertips. I hated how my magic was different now in a mortal body. Weak and unstable.

Endlessly annoying.

"But I've been actively trying not to turn into the wolf." Fenrir twisted free of two guards' grip and wrenched a sword from a third. The blade skidded across the pine floorboards with a rasping screech. "What if I squash someone? I couldn't live with myself."

Seriously?

Green flames flickered at my fingertips again...and sputtered out again. I cursed, anger burning through me. With a dash of shame.

"That's the entire bloody point," I said. "I think we could do with a little help from squashing right now."

"I'll only knock them over. I will not shed blood—"

"Just do it!" Sigyn cried, twisting her wrists in the glowing bonds. The magic flickered as she worked her hands free. A trick she'd learned from me. Two guards rushed at her, but she ducked under their grasp, leaving them to collide with each other in a clatter of armor.

Fenrir grimaced, but closed his eyes. A heartbeat and he opened them, his irises the brightest gold.

"Fenrir! Behind you!" Sigyn shouted, straining against the pockmarked guard's grip.

The gold faded back to his usual emerald.

He turned. Two guards lassoed his legs in glimmering silver rope. The cords hummed with magic, and something about their silver gleam sparked a terrible memory. No. These weren't ordinary restraints. These were like the bindings of Gleipnir. The same kind of rope they'd used to take Fenrir from the Ironwood.

My blood turned to ice.

And these damn brutes kept pushing me back...

Fine. The old fashioned way, then. And, I couldn't deny the satisfaction that only feeling tibias break beneath your own hands could give. Magic could do much, but not that.

I fixed my gaze on the split-lipped guard holding Fenrir, marking him as my first target.

I would not let them take my son. I would not let them harm my wife.

Not again.

"Sigyn, you're closer. Protect him until I make it to you. If they bind him with that rope he won't be able to shift into the wolf..." The words stuck in my throat like shards of glass. "They'll take him where I can't follow."

She nodded and drove her heel down on the pockmarked guard's boot with crushing force. He howled, the sound cut short as she slammed her elbow up under his chin, cracking his head back.

Sigyn bolted for Fenrir.

His muscles bunched, veins cording as he thrashed against the biting ropes, trying to shift into his wolf. His blunt nails lengthened into claws, dark fur rippling up his arms. Fangs pushed from his elongating jaw as a snarl tore from his throat. For a breath the wolf blazed in gold through his eyes again.

A guard snatched Sigyn's arms, wrenching her away. Back.

And that silver cord flung around Fenrir's neck and cinched into his muscle. Cinched into his wrists. The magic thrumming through the ropes severed his connection with the wolf, forcing the transformation back. The wolf receded, leaving the man panting and trapped.

The split-lipped guard's fingers on him tightened.

"NO!" The scream tore from my throat. Not again. Not my son.

Two guards lunged for my wrists with their enchanted shackles and cuffs.

I grabbed Fenrir's cast-iron kettle from the stove with my left hand knowing I could never lift it with my right. Scalding water sprayed as I swung it in a wide arc. Three guards went down howling, clutching their steam-burned faces. Another came at me with bonds outstretched—I smashed the kettle into his temple. Snatching up the iron poker from the hearth, again with my left hand, I drove the glowing tip into the chest plate of the next guard. The metal sizzled as he staggered back, screaming.

Gods, I loved that sound.

Sigyn pushed the guard off of her and kicked him through a window, a yelp screaming out of his lungs as his side careened with the birdbath on the deck. Glass showered the garden like ice.

Fenrir slammed his hip into the dining table, throwing his weight against the split-lipped guard's grip. The table flipped with a thunderous crack, sending splinters and carrot salad flying.

I took three steps towards Fenrir—the butt of a sword smashed into my back, pain spearing down my spine and through my shoulder. Stars burst behind my eyes. My knees buckled, the floor rushing up to meet me.

No. Not now.

Stay on your feet.

I locked my legs beneath me, forcing myself upright even as my vision swam. One step. Then another. I wouldn't fall. I couldn't fall.

I turned and shoved my elbow into the guard's nostrils, a nice crack of cartilage ringing out, and a flood of hot blood following.

I staggered towards Fenrir and took out my throwing knives. Not as impressive as *Laevateinn*, but these little blades had their uses. They were smaller, lighter, and with my aim, I could make these work without giving away my weakness.

As I drew back to throw, pain exploded in my side as some bastard struck me with their sword pommel.

Sigyn was faster. She flung out her arm, and blue light erupted from her palms, blasting the guards off Fenrir. Their armored bodies crashed into his wall of Rembrandts, shredding the canvases.

"Good one," I said, ducking under a guard's sword swing.

She flashed me that fierce smile I adored.

The blue glow lingered on her fingertips. Her magic was

a rare kind, and honestly, a little fickle. The magic only flared up when someone she loved was threatened.

I spun around another guard trying to grab me as Sigyn sprinted to Fenrir. She drove her heel into the guard holding the binding cord, sending him sprawling. She snatched up the gleaming rope and snapped it between her hands. The magical bindings crackled and died, fragments falling to the floor.

Fur rippled over Fenrir's taut muscle as the wolf stirred inside him again.

Three guards seized Sigyn. The Dwarven steel cuffs snapped shut around her wrists with a fatal click. The blue glow at her fingertips sputtered and died.

"Get away from her!" The scream ripped out of me as I hurled my knives. The first found its mark in a guard's shoulder with a wet thunk. I missed with my next throw thanks to my right arm, hitting a cake Fenrir claimed was made entirely out of vegetables. Agony ripped down my arm.

I didn't care.

Swords glinted as they surrounded her. Sigyn struggled against their grasp. The milky-eyed guard advanced. The magic-killing cuffs gleamed on her wrists. I had to reach her. Had to reach Fenrir.

I patted for more knives but found nothing. My gaze darted around the wrecked cabin, desperate for anything to use as a weapon.

"Get him down!" the captain barked. "Now!"

The guards surged forward. I grabbed for Fenrir's porcelain rabbits, and hurled them. A rabbit wearing a straw hat shattered against a thick-necked guard's helmet. A rabbit eating a carrot exploded across another's breastplate. They didn't even flinch.

I snatched up a heavy iron skillet, striking one guard across the face. That was more like it.

"Take that you piece of—"

A gauntleted fist cracked against my temple. The cabin tilted sideways. I staggered, fighting to stay conscious.

"The cuffs!" the captain shouted. "Get those cuffs on him!"

My eyesight shuddered as another guard drove his helmet into my jaw. Through blurring vision, I saw them forcing Dwarven steel around Fenrir's wrists.

"Don't worry about the broken cord. It did its intended job of keeping the monster from shifting so we could get the cuffs on him," the captain said to his soldiers, his burned face twisting with cruel promise. "She has something better waiting for him in Asgard."

Asgard?

They slammed my face into the floor. Across the bloodied floorboards, I saw Sigyn pinned down too, her cheek pressed against the pine. I stretched my arm towards her, our fingertips almost touching. Her terrified eyes locked with mine. Rough hands wrenched my arms behind my back, and the cold bite of Dwarven steel snapped around my wrists. I felt what little magic I had wither.

I thrashed against their grip as they hauled us up, my shoulder screaming. They held tighter.

The bitter cold of the Bifrost swallowed our screams as they dragged us from the warmth of the cabin.

4

KISS AND TELL

Asgard

Guards marched through the halls of Asgard, filling the buttresses with thunder, and shouted commands. We hurried down a corridor covered in frescoes of garden parties and feasts, the clap of our own heels joining the continual pounding of metal and stone and leather.

Around a corner, a cluster of soldiers huddled like gossiping maidens at the market.

"...and the biscuits! Fresh every morning with our tea now," one guard practically swooned. "Better than that stale bread we used to get under Odin. Lost two teeth to those hard lumps."

"Aye," another agreed. "And proper toilet breaks, too. And a toilet."

"I will never miss that bucket in the corner and the communal sponge," the third guard added.

What in the Nine Worlds was happening?

"You have no right to take us," Sigyn said. "We've done nothing wrong."

The guards on either side of her clutched her upper arms tighter, causing her soles to slip on the flagstones. She jerked and tugged to loosen their grip.

"Shut up," the man on her right barked, firming his hold, fingers digging into Sigyn's arm. His face was a roadmap of old scars, each one likely a testament to someone who'd fought back and lost. But those marks would be nothing compared to what I'd do to him.

I'd cut out a pound of his flesh for each indent his fingers left on Sigyn's skin.

"You will not speak to my wife like that." I rammed my elbow into the gut of the guard on my left, twisted, and hurled the one gripping my right side to the ground. His armor clanged against stone with a metallic *CRACK* that bounced from wall to wall.

I turned towards the scarred bastard. I was going to savor every scream.

I summoned my fire, ready to blast his greasy nose off his face. Nothing came.

Oh. Right. Cuffs.

And no element.

Great.

Laughter erupted from their guts as I struggled and yanked at my bonds. Each tug tightened the cuffs, making them bite deeper. Panic clawed at my throat, which really annoyed me.

"Give me a minute...your blood is still mine, and..." I wrenched harder, and stumbled sideways like a drunken court jester, which only made their bellowing louder. Ah. Well. This was going splendidly.

The full weight of it all crashed down on my shoulders

with the grace of a dying salamander. I hated this...this *weakness*. This disgusting mortal fragility that left me at their mercy. I was wholly unused to the sensation, and I despised it almost as much as I despised the guards' continuing laughter.

"You are beaten, Trickster." Egil gripped my arm and spun me around. "These bonds are enchanted to stop your elements and magic."

The other guard kicked his boot into my backside with such force that my teeth rattled. Pain bloomed across my lower back as he prodded me forward again, the metal tip of his spear digging between my shoulder blades.

"Power or not, don't think I still can't gouge out your eye," I said. "Give me a spoon and I'll show you. Or better yet, I'll claw them out with my fingers and eat them like jellied eels."

Fenrir groaned.

"Don't give them more to use against us," Fenrir muttered under his breath. "We don't even know what this is about yet. I'm sure it's all just some big misunderstanding. Right?"

"Whatever this is, Odin will get everything all resolved," Sigyn whispered, although her tone wavered like a candle flame. She wasn't so sure.

Nor was I.

And why was there a smell of cat in the halls? The scent of feline lingered in the air, quite out of place from the usual stone and oleander.

The guards jerked us right, pushing us through the gallery. A cold prickle crept down my spine as we passed the heavy oak door with the iron hinges.

"I believe you were supposed to take the door to the left for the dungeons," I said. "Unless you're all new here? The dungeons are that way. Though I must say, this is a refreshing change of scenery."

Please...Please...Don't take us to the north wing.

The north wing was *her* domain. My throat dried as we continued our march towards that section of the palace.

"Disappointed?" Egil said, continuing to steer us down the corridor lined in tapestries of ships and oceans.

A servant girl scrubbed blood off a bronze boar statue's snout. A black cat wearing an overly ornate diamond collar leapt off the head, its yellow eyes fixing on me with a warning of a thousand scratch marks in my future.

"Well, since you asked, yes," I said, trying to focus on anything but the growing list of weird goings on in the halls. "I thought you said we were dangerous criminals. I'm rather offended you think so little of me. I expected at least triple the amount of guards for starters."

"Dangerous?" Egil scoffed. "You're no more dangerous than pond scum now."

"You are quite impolite," I said. "I've done you no wrong. This rudeness is rather uncalled for."

His laughter evaporated into the roar of Vanir soldiers stomping past, their sun emblems glinting in the torchlight. A dozen guards carried one cat each on a velvet pillow. One guard's face turned an interesting shade of purple as he maintained perfect posture, despite the snow-white cat latched onto his forearm like a furry leech.

Freya never brought these cats here. Her precious felines had always stayed in Vanaheim, far from Odin's halls. But then why—

The pieces began clicking together in my mind, each one worse than the last.

"I got twenty lashes because of you," Egil snarled, his

fingers digging deeper into my arm until I could feel the bruises forming. "And Haldor still cleans the privy."

"Ah!" I said. "Now I remember you. You're the one who fell for the old 'but Odin said so' trick. Hilarious! So, how have you been, I mean, apart from the twenty lashes?"

His lower lip trembled. If I didn't know better, I'd say those were tears welling up in his eyes. Oh dear. This was just getting awkward for everyone.

Today just wasn't my day with guards, or their apparently excellent memories. Though in my defense, how was I supposed to keep track of every guard I'd tricked? It wasn't my fault they made it so easy, letting me in to Balder's rooms that night I essentially returned from the dead and slightly murdered him.

"You better start taking things more seriously, Trickster," he said, voice wavering between rage and what sounded like a suppressed sob. "Because what she has planned for you will be far worse than scrubbing any toilet."

I opened my mouth to ask for further clarification, but they opened a thick oak door and shoved us into a room bursting with oil paintings, fine furniture, and a raging fire. Another three cats ran past our legs, crystal bells jingling from their collars in discordant chimes that made my skin crawl.

Muffled mumbles followed.

My breath caught seeing him.

Odin.

He sat in a chair, hands behind his back, a white cloth jammed between his teeth and tied tight enough to make the corners of his mouth bleed. Violent splashes of purple and yellow covered his face from bruises and welts. Blood crusted the russet whiskers of his beard, and the corners of his split lips twitched as he tried to speak through the gag.

My stomach churned.

How had this happened? How was it *possible* to have happened? He should heal. Odin's wounds always healed. It was a benefit of being, well, a god. Unless...

Unless another god, one who used Dwarven weapons, inflicted his wounds. Someone had not only managed to injure Odin, but had kept him wounded. Had kept him bound. Had kept him here for use.

"Who did this to you?" My voice came out hoarse with emotion.

After everything, after all the pain and betrayal between us, I shouldn't care. I shouldn't feel this desperate need to help him.

Odin met my gaze, and without thinking, I tried to go to him. To save. To soothe. To clean the cuts on his face—

Egil yanked me back, rasping out a tsk.

But I had gotten close enough to see another reason.

The same enchanted bonds on my wrists also bound his behind his back, the runes glowing with a green light that pulsed like a heartbeat. The enchanted bonds blocked his magic and powers, leaving him nothing but flesh and bone and blood. So much blood.

I cleared the emotion from my throat. I found all those prickling sentiments nearly more horrifying than this entire ordeal.

"Well, there goes the theory of Odin being useful," I said to Sigyn and Fenrir, trying to shove the mix of feelings away. "I don't suppose anyone has a backup plan that doesn't involve the most powerful being in the Nine Worlds actually being, you know, powerful?"

Odin narrowed his gaze into a glare at me. Even bound and gagged, he still conveyed 'insufferable little shit' with remarkable clarity.

"It's always some quip with you," a voice said from beside me. "You are so tiring. If only I could have done this centuries ago."

Her.

Every muscle in my body turned to stone at that voice. We were all in far more danger than I'd imagined.

Frigg emerged from the shadows, crimson skirts cascading down her narrow hips like a river of blood. The fur-lined sleeves of her robe trailed behind, sweeping across the patchwork of ornate rugs. More cats scattered around her.

"Finally the wolf is shackled, as it was always supposed to be." Frigg circled Fenrir, tracing the air inches from his nose, making him bristle. "See, Odin, was capturing this monster really so hard?"

She caught Odin's gaze, his eye burning with a hatred that could have melted Niflheim. A satisfied smile played on her lips as she turned back to us.

Frigg's sharp features, all angles and ice, ignited a seething rage within me. This was the first time I'd laid eyes on her since I buried that mistletoe into Balder the Beautiful's neck. Five hundred years of snake venom burning through my flesh, five centuries bound in that cave while my children suffered and died because of her. The memory of their screams mixed with my own made my vision blur red.

Egil grunted and staggered as Sigyn thrashed against his grip. Her own years of pain and anger still raw as my own in my marrow wanting to claw Frigg's eyes out.

"You murdered my children!" Sigyn's voice cracked with five centuries of grief. "You made me listen to their screams. And you bound Loki with their..." she couldn't say it. "And for what? You sadistic monster!" Sigyn spat, twisting and lunging at Frigg, her nails inches from raking that excruciating face. One of her hairpins clattered to the floor in her struggle.

Frigg's laughter sliced the thousand emotions roiling within me. Rage for my dead children, hatred for the centuries of torture, fear for my son. I stood my ground, though I wanted to scream and drive my fist through her chest and rip out her heart and feast on its chambers.

"The only monster in this room is Fenrir," she said, stepping closer.

"You will not speak to him—"

She struck me, her rings slicing across my cheek with enough force to snap my head sideways. Iron filled my mouth and coated my tongue.

"And the father of monsters," Frigg added with a sneer, her perfect teeth gleaming.

"At least I'm not a witch," I said.

Frigg seized my jaw, nails breaking skin as she wrenched my face towards hers. Her grip forced me to meet her eyes, to remember the sear of her needle as she sewed my lips shut, thread pulling through flesh again and again and again.

"If I were you, I would mind that razor tongue of yours, World Breaker," she said. "We both know what happened the last time you spoke so freely to me. Although nothing would delight me more than to have your blood."

Well, since she asked so nicely.

I spat the blood pooling in my mouth into her face, taking pleasure in watching the red droplets speckle her cheeks.

"Why wait? There. Have it."

Her lips curled into a grin as she wiped the red splattered across her face with her sleeve.

"Stop this." Fenrir strained against his bonds. "You've no right to imprison us."

Frigg sneered.

"Oh, I have every right," she said. "I'm doing what should have happened a long time ago. I'm ending Odin's incompetent rule."

"And how will you do that?" I asked. "Who would possibly side with you?"

"Me."

There had been few sights that split terror through me. This was definitely in the top three. Freya sauntered in the door, dressed in the armor she only wore when she was about to gut someone with a fishhook. My stomach dropped to somewhere around my ankles.

Gleaming steel shielded her forearms and calves, her breastplate emblazoned with the same sun emblem on the Vanir warriors' shields. Intricate braids twisted with silver bells wove throughout her black hair.

Retribution burned in her eyes as she stroked her favorite cat, Mr. Ragnar, whose whiskers looked a little on the charred side. Gods. If Freya forced me to ask Mr. Ragnar how his rectal prolapse was progressing, that would be a spectacular new kind of torture.

Yes. This was definitely a worse case scenario.

The one benefit now was that Freya could not sing at us. She couldn't direct her voice at only one person. And Frigg would not take too kindly to being entranced along with her prisoners.

"Freya. Please don't tell me you've joined forces with ice queen here all because of a few singed cats?" I asked.

A rage full of a thousand knives blazed in her eyes as if I'd suggested we turn Mr. Ragnar into mittens.

"Mr. Ragnar's fur may never recover its luster," she said.

"And let me remind you that you and Odin also burnt my palace, stole my two best race horses, and destroyed my favorite gowns. I want recompense."

Frigg's laughter chilled the room.

"You and Odin really are the two biggest idiots in the entire Nine Worlds," Frigg said. "Although, I suppose I should thank you, in a way. It's your actions in Vanaheim that finally proved to Freya how serious things had gotten with Odin's continued lax attitude with you."

"You can't just walk into someone's summer palace expecting to be fed dinner—"

"You did insist," I said. Odin made a muffled sound that might have been agreement. Or choking. Hard to tell with the gag.

"—and then steal their property." Freya's fingers tightened in Mr. Ragnar's fur. "My beautiful necklace! My Brisingamen. My radiance has never fully recovered. So, when Frigg asked me my thoughts on imagining Asgard with Odin deposed, well..." she smiled, and a small, satisfied sigh escaped from between her lips. "I was more than eager to provide her with a paltry 25 legions of Vanir soldiers."

I swallowed as the implications sank in. Freya had effectively handed over her entire Vanir army—nearly 250,000 strong—to Frigg. With Frigg now controlling both these forces and Asgard's own military, her power was overwhelming. The Vanir and Asgard's military combined would vastly outnumber any remaining Aesir soldier loyal to Odin. In this new reality, continued allegiance to Odin was suicide.

That, and Odin really couldn't compete with Frigg removing the communal sponge.

"I couldn't do this coup without her support or her

army," Frigg said, placing a hand on Freya's armored shoulder.

Freya smiled.

"And I made sure each is well endowed, because you never know when an orgy can happen."

A tabby cat leapt onto Odin's lap, its collar all pearl and gold. He shifted, trying to move the animal. The cat responded by stroking harder against his chest, leaving a trail of white fur sticking to the dark navy of his ratted tunic.

"Her soldiers allowed us to finally make a change," Frigg said.

"Excuse me, did you say coup?" Fenrir asked, blinking rapidly.

"It's my turn now, Wolf," Frigg said, her fingers trailing along the back of Odin's chair. "Asgard is under my control."

I snorted.

She walked towards me, silk skirts snapping.

"You find this funny, Trickster?"

"You mean to tell me every god has pledged loyalty to you? That Thor has pledged his loyalty to you?" A grin spread across my face. "Yes. I find this hilarious. Because you need them all to actually succeed in this madness, don't you? Every last one."

"I don't need their—"

"Oh, but you do," I said. "What's your brilliant plan when the Jotnar come knocking? Who's going to maintain Odin's barriers now that you've got him trussed up like a Yuletide boar? And what happens when Thor isn't there to send those Frost Giants running with Mjolnir? Or have you forgotten our charming neighbors to the east?"

Frigg's right eye twitched. I loved when I hit a nerve, especially with her.

"Thor just needs time," she said, but uncertainty played

across her face like shadow. That told me everything about the situation.

I snorted louder.

"The only thing he needs time for is deciding which mead barrel to empty next. Face it, Frigg. You're sitting on a throne of twigs. One good Frost Giant sneeze and it all comes tumbling down."

"If you're waiting for Thor to engage in political intrigue, you'll be waiting until Mjolnir sprouts wings and flies south for the winter," Fenrir said. "And without Odin's barriers... the wall can only protect Asgard so much."

A familiar tightness coiled in my chest at the mention of the wall, old memories threatening to surface. I swallowed hard, forcing my voice to remain steady.

"Without all the gods united," I pressed, "you're just an island. A very fragile one. I don't know how I'm supposed to be impressed by this little takeover of yours. You are nothing."

"Am I?" she asked. "How can I be nothing, when I've made all the gods rather inconsequential? Just like I'm going to do to you."

"What are you intending?" Sigyn asked.

That...was a good question, and I didn't like how it made my insides coil, because I doubted I would like the answer.

A smirk played across Frigg's lips, as if Sigyn's question was precisely the opening she'd been waiting for.

"The Salvation Weave." Frigg dug her hand into the small leather pouch at her hip that was filled with all her most dangerous runes and pulled out a carved, bone tile. I recognized the sigils. Curses. Extremely dark curses. Darker than even Odin would touch. The kind that left stains on your soul just from looking at them.

"A curse?" I asked.

"Even you will be impressed, Destroyer," Frigg said to me, the firelight catching the rune's etched surface like blood in water. "This is beautiful magic. Only a curse is powerful enough to stop a god, and I stopped all the gods." She twirled the rune. "You see, that's the fun of the Salvation Weave. I write everyone's stories, and each god has their own tailored prison. Same with Thor and Odin. That curse keeps them chained where I wish."

So she had Thor confined somewhere in Asgard as well, probably just like Odin. That certainly answered some of the questions stacking in my head.

"That's definitely how you win loyalty. By force." Tension tightened Sigyn's shoulders. "You've weakened Asgard trying to save it."

"You misunderstand," Frigg said. "This is transient. A necessary restructuring. Yes, Asgard may be slightly more vulnerable with Thor and Odin and the others *momentarily* engaged. But what's a minor, temporary risk compared to eliminating the eternal threat of Ragnarok? When I'm done, Asgard will be strong again. Safe again. Sometimes you have to crack a few skulls to build a better kingdom."

"And now you bring Ragnarok into this? Really? You have to know when to let things go. I've quite moved on from my world ending days," I said. "Though I suppose that's why you waited until now, isn't it? Until Freya joined your little crusade?"

Frigg's eyes gleamed.

"Oh, that was kismet timing that you and Odin set in motion," Frigg said, her voice rich with satisfaction.

"You see," Freya interjected, stroking Mr. Ragnar's singed fur. "Frigg and I have always been close, and only growing closer over the millennia of yours and Odin's constant shenanigans. But burning my palace—"

"Yes, you mentioned that already," I said, rolling my eyes.

"—and Odin allowing you to break your banishment without punishment?" Frigg asked. "You both believed you could get away with it. And that was the straw that broke the camel's back, because it proved Odin would always aid the Destroyer and endanger us."

Freya nodded in agreement.

"I suppose we really should thank you for making this happen. It was the culmination of eons of frustration," she said. "Your actions pushed us together, finally giving us the resolve to take matters into our own hands."

I sighed.

Why did the ramifications of my actions continually come back to bite me in the ass?

"Besides, we understand each other," Freya said.

I scoffed.

"This is absurd," I said.

"No, this is finally extinguishing the danger of Ragnarok," Frigg snapped, her composure cracking. "This is protecting all of us."

"If you've not realized, Ragnarok already happened. It's over. No more. Passé. Finis. Finito. Est acta."

She shook her head, laughing as if I'd said the most ridiculous thing she'd ever heard.

"While the pieces all remain, Ragnarok can always restart. The other gods didn't understand either," she said. "Chaos shouldn't have been permitted in Asgard. That wolf should never have been allowed to leave his island. And you..." She pointed at Sigyn. "You bore the sign of Ragnarok—"

"My children, you mean?" Sigyn asked. "The ones you murdered."

Something like genuine hurt flickered across Frigg's face, which somehow only angered me further.

"I am the goddess of family. I understand the pain I inflicted," she said. "And had Odin stopped Loki from the start, we both would have been spared that anguish. But now, I can finally clean up Odin's mess. I can finally bring true safety to Asgard and the entire Nine Worlds. This isn't about power. It's about protection. About doing what must be done. I will finally eliminate the danger of Ragnarok and obey Yggdrasil's instructions."

I scoffed.

"You always were full of shit," I said.

Her lips quirked. Like I had said exactly what she wanted to hear.

"Maybe you'd like a demonstration?"

She gripped the curse tight. Magic coated her knuckles in a green smoke that slipped between her fingers. It pooled at her feet, writhing and whispering secrets I didn't want to hear.

Frigg hurled the curse at Sigyn's feet.

"No!"

I screamed and lunged forward, trying to pull Sigyn behind me, to block the curse from touching her. To do anything but watch as the curse reached for my wife.

The guards wrenched my chains back, links biting deep into my wrists. Beside me, Fenrir strained against his own bonds, muscles bunching beneath his flannel shirt as he tried to reach her.

Sigyn's eyes went wide as the smoke curled around her ankles.

I thrashed against my bonds, writhing and twisting as the green light and smoke engulfed her like a hungry beast. My throat burned from screaming her name over and over.

In seconds of absolute terror, the smoke cleared, leaving nothing behind. Sigyn was gone, vanished as if she'd never existed at all. Only the hairpin on the floor proved she had ever been there.

Fear and fury churned in me like poison, threatening to tear me apart from the inside.

"Where did you send her?" I snarled. I pulled harder on my bonds, not caring that the steel ate into my skin. Blood dripped warm down my wrists.

Frigg tilted her head, studying me like how Freya's cats would watch wounded birds.

"Sorry, not telling," she said. "She should be quite cozy where I've locked her away. It shouldn't be anything too unfamiliar to her...well, actually—" her words melted into laughter.

Something hot rushed through my veins at that sound, a strength I didn't know I had anymore. I ripped the chains from the guard's grasp and lunged at her. I would get Sigyn back. I would stop Frigg from carrying out her twisted plans.

I was a breath from digging my nails into her back and tearing out her spine in pieces—she spun around and pressed a razor-sharp Dwarven steel dagger against the trashing pulse in my neck, freezing me in place.

My heart thundered in my chest as I stared into Frigg's eyes, that glinted with enjoyment. She leaned closer, breath hot in my ear.

"I could do it." She squeezed the blade deeper, biting my skin. "Gods. I want to do it. To slit your throat and watch the life drain from your eyes. Nothing would give me greater pleasure than killing you."

I swallowed hard, throat dry, feeling the blade bob against my skin with each movement.

"Then what's stopping you?" I asked. Dared.

"Well, see, that's the thing," she said, running the flat of the blade along my jaw. "If I kill you, the chaos inside you will simply reincarnate elsewhere, slipping through my grasp. The threat of Ragnarok would be as real as ever. I can't risk losing your element. So, sadly, you have to stay alive so I can keep you contained." A cruel smile played at the corners of her lips. "You're sweating. I thought you liked the sensation of steel against your throat."

She eased off the blade, and I hated the relief washing over me. I hated she actually achieved in making me afraid. It highly irritated me. But I was mortal now. And we played a very different game.

If she ever discovered that my chaos was actually gone...

That she could kill me and risk nothing...

She'd do it in a blink. My life was her greatest desire.

She removed her dagger from my throat and I stumbled back, chains rattling. I rubbed my throat, hot slick coating my fingertips where she'd broken skin.

"Don't worry, you get to join in the curse too, Loki," she said, wiping my blood from her blade. "And that leaves the wolf and his brother, and one, last ingredient to seal my curse."

Ingredient?

She turned to Fenrir. "The Great Wolf. Destined to eat the sun and the moon." Her eyes gleamed with a determination that made even Freya shift uncomfortably. "I know exactly what fate I will write for you. I will finally imprison you on Lyngvi, bound with ropes woven from my curse, stronger than Gleipnir ever was. And this time..."

She reached out as if to touch his face, making him flinch.

"This time, I'll drive a sword through your jaw, pinning you to the bedrock itself. The blade will rust there for eternity, while you strain against it, unable to close your mouth, unable to eat, unable to howl. You'll only have the taste of your own blood as it drips down your throat." Her voice dropped. "Perhaps then you'll finally stop dreaming of devouring our sun and moon."

Fenrir's eyes went wide with terror, and I saw my son, my child, trembling.

"No. Please," he whispered. "Not Lyngvi."

She gripped the curse again. That green smoke curled between her fingers, and my stomach lurched.

"Don't you touch him!"

I yanked against my chains until my shoulders threatened to pop from their sockets, thrashing and twisting, trying desperately to reach my son. Blood ran freely down my wrists now, but I didn't care. Every instinct screamed at me to protect him, to throw myself between them, to do something. Anything.

Lyngvi was an island in the center of Lake Amsvartnir. No light touched that place. No warmth. No life. Just endless gray waters lapping at black shores. Lyngvi was as dead a place as a tomb. And she would bury my son there, alone in the dark, while I could do nothing but watch. Again.

"Please," Fenrir said, the word cracking my heart further into pieces. "I promise to be good."

She chuckled.

"I don't trust promises." She ran her fingers through the green smoke. "They never seem to stick."

Anger rushed through me, and heat rose in my cheeks. I pulled against my chains again, feeling something in my shoulder tear. The pain barely registered. I wouldn't allow her to rip my family apart twice. I wouldn't let her send Fenrir to that...that *place*.

I turned to Odin, the cat making his lap its personal

cushion. Our eyes met, and I saw my desperation mirrored in his face. My anger strengthened, even though it all threatened to crush me.

Was this really how it all ended? With all of us cursed? Sigyn vanished to some horror I couldn't even imagine, my son was about to be bound in a pit of endless darkness, Odin batted by cats, and me...

What about me?

That question hung in the air like a blade waiting to fall.

I imagined the fate Frigg had planned for me with her curse. How she'd slowly chip away at my sanity, torture after exquisite torture. And then Freya would come, shoving Mr. Ragnar in my face and—

Wait.

A plan burst in my mind. Dangerous. Chaotic. The kind of plan that would probably get us all killed, but then again, death would be preferable to this curse.

And it was all I had.

She lifted her hand and aimed the curse of the Salvation Weave at Fenrir.

My pulse pounded as I sucked in a breath. Time to see if I still had any trick left in me.

"Stop," I said. "I want one last goodbye with Fenrir—" I looked at Freya, fully knowing what I was doing. "—and Odin. I think I am owed at least that since we are about to be cursed for eternity."

Freya's eyes lit with a lust only what I offered her could illicit. She practically vibrated with excitement, nearly dropping poor Mr. Ragnar.

Frigg paused, the smoke retracting into her palm. Her eyes narrowed into pure suspicion.

"What in Ymir's eyelashes makes you think I would ever allow—"

"Oh! Let it be a last goodbye with Odin first," Freya said. Actually, more like squealed, really. She stepped forward, clutching Mr. Ragnar to her chest.

Frigg glared at her with all the warmth of a Jotunheim winter.

"If you are suggesting—"

"Oh Frigg. Don't be such a stick in the mud," Freya said, practically dancing in place. "Where's the harm in a little tragic romance? Especially the delicious heartache that their last goodbye would drip with."

She bit her lower lip, eyes glazing over.

Frigg sighed as Freya's cheeks flushed deeper, no doubt imagining scenarios that would make even *me* blush.

"This isn't a game," Frigg said. "Their tortured pining isn't for your amusement. If there are any goodbyes, it can be with the wolf—"

Freya scrunched up her face and huffed.

"Mr. Ragnar wants to enjoy their humiliation *now*." She squished her cheek into the cat's fur, making baby noises. "Don't you Mr. Ragnar? Don't you want to watch the Trickster drown in exquisite suffering?"

"Freya, we've talked about this before—"

Freya let out an irritated breath.

"You will not stop me from having this," Freya said.

I smiled.

Just as I'd hoped. Freya's obsession with romance and drama was as predictable as Mr. Ragnar's next health crisis.

As they bickered, I lifted my hands to my lips and whispered a few charms over my rings. The metal glowed faintly blue and...it extinguished. Damn. This would all be a lot easier if I wasn't mortal. I spoke again, hoping no one noticed me squinting in concentration and finally the ring pulsed with the hum of power again.

I glanced up. Freya stomped her feet, holding her breath in a tantrum. Excellent.

I sucked my thumb, and carefully slipped off a ring and tucked it under my tongue, feeling its cool weight. Fenrir shot me a curious look.

If only he knew my next move...

This was about to get real awkward, real fast for all of us.

"He is not entitled to any favors," Frigg said, interrupting Freya's outburst. "Especially not from us. We are his captors, not his friends."

"I perfectly understand that he's not entitled to a proper farewell, I agree, but *I* am," Freya said, stepping closer, clutching Mr. Ragnar until I thought his yellow eyes would pop out of his sockets. "And I won't let you rob me of all this delectable drama."

"You're being ridiculous, Freya. We can't afford to waste any more time on your particular desires." She picked cat hair off of her sleeve. "I've already permitted your cats."

Freya's expression hardened. That did it. Frigg walked right into Freya's breaking point.

This friendship of theirs definitely would not last. They were both two narcissists with big personalities who thought they were both right. I'm surprised they made it this far without killing each other.

"If you're inferring my cats are anything less than my babies..." Freya's voice plunged. "If you don't let me see Loki's goodbye to him, then I won't be able to vouch for your safety in future dealings with the other gods. Remember whose army is helping make this all possible."

Frigg's eyes narrowed.

"Fine," she squeezed out through clenched teeth. "Ten seconds."

Freya grinned and skipped to Odin, humming a Vanir

love song. Her cheeks flushed a hotter pink as she untied his gag, letting out little sighs of pleasure. She didn't remove the cat from his lap. It blinked at me. Gods. This was going to be the worst.

Pain contorted Odin's face, making his bloodshot eye seem heavier with guilt and regret.

"I'm sorry," Odin rasped. "I should have listened to you when you warned me..."

Freya's breathing grew heavier as I met Odin's gaze. I forced a stiff smile, trying not to choke on the ring in my mouth.

I wanted to tell him everything would be alright. Like I always used to, back when we shared more than just betrayal and broken promises. But that was hardly true now.

"And what do you have to reply, Loki?" Freya asked, her impatience growing along with her obvious arousal. A flush had crept up her neck, and she swayed slightly on her feet.

My muscles tensed. Leave it to Freya to add complications.

"I'm waiting, Loki," Freya prodded. "I want angst. I want pain. Hurt me with your yearning."

A bitter ache rose in my chest that I quickly squashed down. I did not yearn for him. I wasn't some lovesick fool like Freya imagined. This was about survival, nothing more.

The cat in his lap looked between us.

"Can you ever forgive me?" Odin asked. "This is all my fault."

I nodded. I mean, I couldn't deny that.

"I'm so sorry."

My smile turned pained, waiting for him to shut up.

I marched up to him, holding his gaze, hoping he could see what I wanted him to know. That I was giving us all a chance.

"Loki, please tell me you forgive me," he said.

And as usual, he wasn't getting the message.

"I'm sorry—"

Bloody hell.

I crushed my lips to his in a kiss. He stiffened in surprise, his entire body going rigid beneath me. I was surprised too. We hadn't been this close since...since before everything fell apart. I deepened our kiss until he relaxed under me, muscle memory betraying us both. I slid my tongue between his lips, pushing the ring into the heat of his mouth, trying desperately to ignore how naturally we still fit together. The scratch of his beard against my skin, the taste of mead and memories on his tongue, the ghost of centuries' worth of love threatening to drown me. Each sensation sparked echoes of what we'd once been, what we'd lost, what we'd destroyed.

But, hopefully, now we could use this moment to save us all.

I pulled back before it could pull me under.

Freya squealed and clapped in delight, bouncing on her toes. Mr. Ragnar dangled precariously from her arms, looking thoroughly unimpressed with the whole display.

"This is even better than I ever hoped," she said, voice breathy. "I didn't expect them to kiss! With tongue!"

Frigg shrieked. She dug her fingers into my clothes and ripped me away from Odin. But before she could break my gaze from his, I caught a flicker in his eye—understanding, then the smallest hint of that clever spark I remembered from centuries of shared schemes. A ghost of a smile touched the corner of his mouth.

Her magic crackled around us as she flung me to the ground, and a cry escaped my lips as my shoulder hit the floor, pain bursting in my joints like fireworks. Behind me,

Freya hummed happily as she tied his mouth shut again, unknowingly securing the ring inside.

All I could do now was hope.

Especially that he wouldn't swallow it accidentally.

Fenrir moved to rush over, but I signaled him back with a shake of my head. I forced myself to laugh through the pain. I wanted her anger to remain on me. Needed her focused on my defiance rather than what I'd just given Odin.

Frigg stood over me and glared, her lips pressed into a thin line, and I felt as though I stared into the eyes of death itself.

I think she tried to intimidate me. I hated she succeeded.

But I kept laughing.

Also, because I now understood why frost had been creeping through realms it shouldn't reach. Her curse wasn't just affecting the gods, it was weakening Odin's barriers between worlds. The walls were fracturing, letting the cold seep through. And it was going to let a lot more come with it...

"Skadi must be salivating with your curse...oh! She doesn't know that bit yet, does she?" I asked. "What a pity for you when she finds out Asgard is no longer a threat to Jotunheim. You won't win against her, and the Vanir soldiers you have are nothing against Skadi. Jotunheim will devour Asgard now you've removed the only thing stopping them."

I pointed at Odin.

I loved the fear igniting in her eyes at the mention of the Giantess's name. Skadi was a warlord and as beautiful as a butterfly...if that butterfly ate two dozen eggs for breakfast, and could smash your face in for disagreeing with her over foot creams.

Fury overtook it in a heartbeat, transforming her face

into something terrible. She grabbed my collar, fingers curling, nails scraping my skin. She hauled me towards her.

"Enjoy your fate." She flung me away from her and reached for her curse. The Salvation Weave left her fingers with force, exploding at my feet in a burst of light. Emerald and sapphire and violet twisted together like living things. The color seared my retinas, burning into my sockets until tears streamed down my face.

The curse latched onto me like thousands of needle-sharp teeth burrowing through cloth and skin. Ice spread across my body, replacing blood with frost. Each heartbeat pushed the cold deeper until even my bones ached with it. The magic wrapped around me like chains, pulling, dragging, demanding.

A rumble filled my ears like the quake of Yggdrasil's branches. The floor bucked beneath me, marble tiles splitting with sounds like breaking bones. Cracks raced across the floor, spreading and spreading.

I stumbled, arms flailing, as the floor collapsed. And I fell. I fell into darkness.

"No!" Fenrir shouted.

Fenrir leapt towards me, reaching out even as Frigg's shouts blared, commanding her guards to pull him away.

He grabbed at my shirt, and he tried to pull me back from the abyss. The fabric strained and tore, but held.

The floor continued to crumble and crack, chunks of marble falling around us. The soldiers retreated, boots scraping against stone as they scrambled backwards, not wanting to fall in.

The curse tugged at my ankles, ice trailing up my veins, trying to pull me in. Under.

Down.

"Fenrir, let me go," I said, meeting his eyes. "It's ok." I

tried to smile through the biting cold that had reached my chest.

He only strengthened his grip.

"I'm not letting go."

A cry battered my eardrums as everything went dark, the sound of Frigg's anger following us down.

I was falling.

I was falling and Fenrir's grip was still tight on my clothes as we plummeted together into the endless black.

5
———————

HEL HATH NO FURY

Hel

The steady crash of waves replaced the ringing in my ears. The brine of the sea flooded my nose, cutting through the metallic tang the curse had left coating my tongue. Home. I was home. But the waves sounded hollow. And the air was too still. My mind focused, piecing together the jumbled fragments of memory scrambled by Frigg's curse.

No, I wasn't home.

Sigyn. I had to find Sigyn.

And Fenrir...

The chill seeped into my bones, followed by the gritty scrape of sand on my skin. I tried opening my eyes, fighting the heaviness weighing my lids down.

This was all extremely unpleasant.

My muscles ached as I sat up, waves of pain pounding my stiff body. I felt raw and oversensitive, as if the curse had scraped my skin with steel wool. I blinked, my eyes still unfocused. I blinked again through blurred vision at the broken chains dangling from my wrists. We'd hit the ground hard enough to shatter enchanted metal. That explained why I felt like someone had thrown my body off the top of Yggdrasil. Curses were always rather on the brutal side, and a bit rough on the stomach.

Fenrir retched his guts out beside me.

"Are you alright?" I asked.

"Yes," he rasped. "Is it always so jarring, traveling with curse magic? That was unpleasant."

"Not as unpleasant as that smoothie you made me drink."

He glared at me as he wiped his mouth with the sleeve of his flannel shirt, his form sharpening from a blur of red and black plaid into familiar features.

I rubbed my palms over my eyes, trying to scrub away the remaining fog.

The world slowly focused. A black sand beach stretched before me, scattered with the twisted remains of warriors. Cracked shields jutted from the obsidian sand next to swords snapped mid-blade. Crushed helmets dotted the beach, their metal caved in by killing blows.

Shit.

So, she condemned me to Hel? Frigg knew the cold and humidity would vex me every excruciating, clammy second —wait.

Oh. This was bad.

While humidity definitely ranked as one of my top ten most hated things, Frigg's plan wasn't just about trapping me somewhere mildewy. This was far too tolerable. Nothing chained me to a rock. I could roam the underworld freely. I could even bear the cloudy weather. Most importantly, I wasn't alone. I had the souls of the dead to chat with, not that they were great at conversation. And I had my daughter,

Hel...even if she would crush my larynx on sight. But I'd talked my way out of worse situations before, so I liked my odds.

No, this place was a temporary holding area. A waiting room for something more.

And one last ingredient to seal my curse...

A frigid, creeping suspicion slithered down my spine. Frigg had emphasized how crucial Fenrir, Jormungand, and I were to The Salvation Weave. But why hadn't she mentioned Hel?

Frigg wouldn't trap both Hel and me down here together for shits and giggles. Whatever she had planned for us both, it would be far worse.

But what?

The creeping sensation worsened as I looked at Fenrir.

And then my thoughts turned to Jormungand. He was banished here after Ragnarok.

Oh. Fuck.

It was too perfect, too convenient. All her pieces arranged just so. Me trapped in Hel with both Hel and Jorg already here. That wasn't a coincidence. She wanted the three of us together for something. And now Fenrir, who'd just slipped free of her curse, had trapped himself with us. She could easily curse him and drag him to Lyngvi.

Fuck fuck fuck fuck fuck!

"Why did you do that?" I asked Fenrir, my voice cracking with fear I couldn't quite hide. "Why did you follow me? You should have let me go and saved yourself."

A small smile quirked his lips. Sand speckled his eyelashes and flecked the stubble on his cheeks and chin.

"I couldn't let you go alone. Not with you so weakened and hurt," Fenrir said.

He worked, freeing himself from the broken chains

around his wrists. They clattered as he tossed them aside with a growl. I hated the bruises and scrapes covering his knuckles.

Guilt clawed my chest, watching Fenrir brush sand from his matted hair. He was only in this mess now because of me. Another son I'd failed to protect, another child I'd led into danger. And now he sat here in Hel, sand in his hair like he was a boy again playing on a beach, not realizing the trap that was slowly closing around us all.

"Fenrir, I'm grateful you came with me. That you want to help," I said, meeting his green eyes, so like mine, gods help him. "But there will be consequences."

He tilted his head, his face pinching with concern.

"Frigg, you mean?"

I nodded, still trying to shake off that phantom sensation of her curse crawling over my skin.

"By ending up here together in Hel, we've handed you to her on a silver platter. Now she just needs to stroll in and curse you to Lyngvi. Gods. Curses are so unpleasant."

I wiped what felt like cold webs off of my skin, even though nothing was there. Curses were icky things.

Understanding lit Fenrir's face. He nodded slowly, jaw tightening until the muscle jumped there.

"She'll track me here. Chain me again."

"Yes. And she will be displeased that she has to come here to get you. Can't blame her for that one, really. It's colder than a witch's tit in this realm."

I gestured at the gray landscape, the clouds so heavy and thick and threatening to swallow us in gloom.

I stood, the sand shifting beneath my Gucci loafers, not helping my already wobbly legs. I rubbed the stiffness from my shoulder and shook off the grit clinging to the barocco print of my shirt. Versace was not meant for the underworld.

Fenrir surveyed our bleak surroundings, lips curling.

"Where exactly is 'here'?"

His voice wavered in my still-ringing ears. I grasped his hand, hoisting him up. Mist slithered across my skin and plastered Fenrir's hair to his forehead, each droplet gleaming like tiny pearls in the dim light.

"That's right, you've never had the pleasure of being in this place." I spread my arms wide. "Welcome to Hel, realm of the dishonorable dead."

Fenrir froze, muscles tensing under his flannel shirt.

"Wait. This doesn't mean we're dead, does it? This isn't what I would expect dead to feel like," he said, fingers flexing as if testing they still worked.

"No," I said. "We aren't dead."

Fenrir exhaled, breath rolling out from between his lips in the frigid air.

"For now, anyway," I added. "Frigg still believes she can't kill me. A blessing that better persist. For our sakes, and especially Sigyn's." Her name spiked fresh fear through my heart. I had to get out and to her, curse or not.

"SIGYN!"

Gods. Where had Frigg sent her? What if Frigg harmed her? She'd do that. She'd hurt Sigyn just to watch me break.

"Sigyn! Where are you?" I shouted, the words shredding my throat.

Only the churning ocean answered, waves crashing against black sand with hollow thunder.

I sprinted along the beach, dodging rusted weapons and leaping over fallen warriors, scanning the horizon for any flicker of movement or life. My soles slipped and slid on the obsidian grains, each step threatening to send me sprawling.

Every shout of her name grew hoarser until the roaring surf and gusting wind stole my voice entirely.

Sigyn wasn't here.

I knew better than to hope she would be, but the realization still hit like a punch to the sternum, driving the air from my lungs.

But where had The Salvation Weave sent Sigyn? More importantly, *how* was she cursed? Curses meant a million possibilities. I, for one, was grateful I wasn't sprouting daffodils from my ears. Other than being stuck in Hel for eternity, I appeared unscathed.

Fear clawed my insides, twisting deeper with each passing second. I had to reach Sigyn. I had to find her.

Now.

My heart pounding in my chest, I raced along the shoreline towards the nearest coffin. I flung open the lid, hurled out the skeleton, and pounded on the bottom, waiting for the familiar ripple of a doorway opening beneath my touch. Nothing. The wood remained solid, unyielding.

"Why isn't this working?" I asked.

Panic clawing up my throat, I slammed my fists against the sides of the coffin, ready to tear my way through if necessary. The one time I wasn't a god...

"What do you mean by 'isn't working'?" Fenrir asked.

I dashed to the following coffin, lungs burning. Skidding to a stop, I yanked open the lid, shoved aside a yellowed femur, and pressed my palm against the wood, praying the doorway would open.

"Coffins and graves are the only way in and out of Hel," I said. "But none of them are opening for me. I have to get out of here and find Sigyn."

I kicked and clawed at the bottom, hating the despair bearing down on me.

Fenrir scanned the shoreline, his jaw set in a grim line.

Sand clung to his tangled hair as the wind whipped it across his face. He rubbed his rough stubble.

I snatched a small axe from a nearby skeleton's bony grip and hacked at the coffin bottom, ignoring how each blow sent pain sawing through the tendons in my shoulder.

"That reminds me," he said. "What did you pass to Odin?"

Was he serious?

"Is now really the time?"

The memory of Odin's lips against mine, familiar yet wrong now, made me want to scrub my mouth clean. Worse was the unexpected surge of anger at seeing what Frigg had done to him. His face beaten, his body broken. I pushed the thought away. I didn't want to care for him anymore. I shouldn't care anymore.

But I did care. Each bruise on Odin's face had cut deeper than I wanted to acknowledge, even to myself.

Fenrir's eyes bored into mine, telling me he was as serious as a heart attack, which I felt on the verge of.

"I saw you remove your ring, before you went and...well, I just don't like when you involve yourself with Odin." Suspicion filled each word. "Especially when I'm also involved. Anytime you two plot something, it doesn't turn out too well for me."

Fair.

"If you must know, I ensured we have a chance," I huffed. "You're welcome."

Fenrir's expression dissolved into utter bafflement, as if I told him I was going to open a cabbage farm. Why was that always the reaction I got when I said I did something helpful?

"Chance? How?" he asked. "I'm sorry, but I'm going to need a little more information."

I tossed the axe aside and ran to the next coffin. My chest heaved as I pounded across the sand, each footfall sending small explosions of obsidian grains into the air.

"Well, having an ally on the inside will improve our odds of escaping this madness," I said between labored breaths. "I enchanted the ring to communicate secretly with Odin. That's what I passed to him. Now we can exchange information without detection. And I was told learning seidr magic was a waste of my time."

Fenrir's eyebrows knitted together. He didn't seem fully convinced.

"Seidr?" he asked. "Can you even still do magic without—"

"Without being a god?" I finished. "Again, I'm mortal, not human. I'm still capable of some magic, thank-you-very-much, even though it may not have quite the same *kick* it used to with my chaos and godhood."

I paused, hating the emptiness inside of my chest where my element used to burn. The emptiness ached like a missing limb.

I kicked my heel into a skull, a sharp crack echoing out as bone fragments scattered across the black sand.

"Now, if you'll excuse me." I placed my hand over my heart. "I'm a little busy trying to get back to my wife."

I took a deep breath and slammed my foot down, bracing for impact.

"Stop," he said. "We must find my sister. Hel can help us."

Gods, no. Not her. Anyone but her.

I kicked harder, welcoming the pain that jolted up my leg. These Gucci loafers weren't made for smashing ancient bones, but then again, nothing about this day was going according to plan. Better than thinking about facing my daughter.

"You can't be serious," I said. "Hel won't lift a finger to help me, not after everything that happened between us, especially after Ragnarok."

The wood splintered and cracked under my foot. On the third kick, the bottom collapsed, and I stumbled forward, catching myself before face planting into splinters and beach.

I fell to my knees, the coarse sand biting my skin. I clawed at the wood, ignoring how splinters drove under my nails and blood smeared the broken planks.

I had to reach Sigyn. Every second crawled by like an eternity, and I knew each wasted moment could mean life or death. I kept scratching and digging, staring at the broken bottom of the coffin, willing it to open into something, anything but this endless beach.

Why isn't it letting me through?

Fenrir's rough grip encircled my waist, yanking me back with enough force that nearly knocked the breath out of me.

"Stop!" he shouted. "This is fruitless. You're cursed here, remember? You cannot leave this place. That seals every door out to you. And Sigyn's clearly not in Hel."

I looked around, the towering cliffs and jagged rocks pressing closer, squeezing the breath from my body. Fenrir's tight grip barely registered over a thousand monsters nibbling at my mind.

"What if Sigyn's hurt, or in a worse place?" I hated that thought. It gutted me. Tears spilled hot down my cheeks. "I have to find her. And I can't find her because of this bloody curse keeping me here."

Fenrir pulled me against him, wrapping me in his arms.

His steady heartbeat drummed against my back as he held me close.

"We *will* find her," he said. "I understand being trapped in a place very well, having had centuries of the experience. And I've learned in my own captivity that cracks exist in every magic. There may be an override."

"Override?"

He nodded.

"You know, a loophole. Magic. Why am I telling you this? I thought loopholes and tricks were your expertise?"

"Well, I am rather stressed," I squeezed out. "And this damn shoulder makes it hard to concentrate."

Fenrir let go of my shoulder. I pulled my bottle of pain tablets from my pocket, the cap clicking as I shook four tablets into my palm and swallowed them dry.

Regardless, Fenrir was right, and I berated myself for not thinking of this already.

A little sorcery could always find weak spots in a curse. Places where the magic thinned enough to slip through. The respite wouldn't last long, but even a temporary escape might be enough time to find Sigyn.

Now, did that type of magic also come with unpleasant prices, ramifications, and the potential for severed limbs?

It was best not to dwell on that.

But I'd never let a curse beat me yet, and I didn't intend to start now. Especially if it was one of Frigg's curses. The thought of her smug satisfaction at trapping me here made my blood boil.

Fenrir sniffed the air, his head tilting like a wolf catching a scent on the wind.

"Our time together is short." His voice hardened. "Papa, if there's a way out of this mess, of finding Sigyn, she will know. Hel is our only hope."

6

TURNING TABLES

Taking those pain tablets on a stomach still full of Fenrir's spirulina smoothie was a mistake. As the pills slithered down my throat, the texture of swamp rose, flooding my sinus cavities with overripe banana and the tang of pineapple.

The air sharpened into icy daggers as we crossed the bridge, our boots sliding on the slick obsidian. The guardian of Eljudnir, Modgur the Very Cranky, hunched at the main gate. Her face twisted from its usual glower into an even deeper scowl at our approach.

I stifled a groan. Convincing Modgur to let me in would be a bitch.

Clearing my throat, I squared my shoulders, preparing to give her a long soliloquy about how lovely the wart on her nose had grown, anything it took to persuade her to allow us entry.

But Modgur stepped aside, her cloak dragging across the stone as she yanked the gates open. No argument, no demands, not even a chance to compliment that lovely shade of yellow of her tooth.

At least one thing was easy.

Actually, suspiciously easy…

Whatever. The palace consumed my thoughts as it rose before us, its walls of black glass reflecting our distorted shapes. Spires clawed at the sky, their tips vanishing into clouds thick with bruised purples and greens.

And those monsters that nibbled at my mind earlier, now feasted on it. Even if Hel agreed and assisted us in finding Sigyn, even if I discovered some enchantment to bypass the curse chaining me here, we wouldn't achieve the future we dreamed of. With Odin otherwise engaged for what appeared to be a very long time, any chance of that promised golden apple had slipped away like smoke between my fingers. My mortality pressed down harder now, each heartbeat a reminder of what I couldn't give her— forever.

That was the problem with curses. They aways tended to get in the way of happily ever afters. And I couldn't bear the thought of her watching me grow old while she stayed frozen in time.

"This won't be easy, will it?" Fenrir asked.

Won't be easy? I snorted. This reunion with Hel was going to be about as pleasant as gargling razor blades.

"Ever since I triggered Ragnarok and convinced her to lend me her army, she's not been overly pleased with me. She vowed that if she ever got her hands on me again, she would impale me through the backside to the roots of Yggdrasil. So, no. I don't suspect this will be easy at all."

Shadows dripped down the slick walls of the foyer. Flames guttered in hollowed femurs that jutted from iron sconces. I could have done without the skulls grinning at me from alcoves, withered flowers stuffed in their sockets.

"You are the reason she is now banished," he said. "If

you had just considered the consequences of dragging her into your 'let's end the worlds bender, maybe this wouldn't have been so bad."

The stench of decay clung to the damp air, thick enough to taste.

"Yes, I'm well aware."

"And now everything is worse for her after Ragnarok. The punishment the gods gave her—"

"Well, I hardly had any sway with punishments—"

"When she described what would happen to her if she ever left the underworld..." His voice cracked. "I can't have my sister chopped up into a thousand pieces and spread across the surface of a thousand suns."

His words struck me like a blade of ice to the heart and guilt clawed at my edges, almost as cold and damning as the surrounding chill numbing my fingertips.

I swallowed the bites of emotion prickling my throat.

Wind shrieked down the corridors, carrying the wails of the battle-slain. The roots of Yggdrasil punched through the walls, creaking and groaning with every twist and bend through the stone. Lovely.

"Perhaps..." I lowered my voice. "Perhaps it would be best if you speak to Hel first? Appeal to her sense of family."

"Me?" Skepticism tightened Fenrir's features. "You know how stubborn she is. What makes you think she'll listen to me?"

"You're her brother. She lov...loves you...in her own little, morbid way." I squeezed his shoulder, feeling tension coiled beneath flannel.

Fenrir's sigh misted in the frigid air.

"I'll try my best, but no promises. When Hel sets her mind to something, she rarely changes course. Best prepare yourself for the tree roots."

I rubbed my backside, wincing at the thought. I really could do without that experience.

The temperature plunged as we neared the sitting room. Our breaths puffed out in clouds, and frost crackled beneath our boots.

"Where is everyone?" Fenrir turned, studying the tapestries woven with scenes of warriors falling in battle and sailors sinking beneath waves. "Is it always so empty here?"

There was an odd lack of half-rotting servants scuttling about, adjusting the cobwebs on spinal column candelabras, or stoking fires to more than glowing embers. Curious.

"This must be Frigg's work," I said. "She's already stripping away Hel's power, her servants, her army. Making sure when she comes for us, there's no one left to stand in her way."

The sitting-room door groaned open. A dying fire sputtered in the stone hearth, casting more shadows than warmth. Green silk wallpaper peeled from stone like dead skin, while a purple velvet sofa squatted in the center—the only splash of color in a room that had all the coziness of a bottle of arsenic.

A pencil scratched against paper, the sound harsh in the silence. Perhaps Hel had finally adopted a new, less grim hobby after all.

My hopes crumbled as Jormungand lounged on the thick cushions, sketchbook balanced on his knees. Perfect. Just what I needed. Another surly child who made Hel look positively cheerful in comparison.

Locks of Jorg's cropped blonde hair fell across his green eyes as he hunched over his work. A cigarette dangled between his lips, smoke coiling up to the black tin ceiling tiles.

His scowl deepened with each stroke of the pencil. The fact his drawing depicted me with a knife buried in my eye socket didn't exactly fill me with confidence about this reunion.

"Jorg?" Fenrir asked.

Jormungand's head snapped up from his sketchbook, firelight playing across sharp cheekbones and the black tunic that clung to his slender frame. He removed the cigarette from his lips and crushed it into the porcelain dish on the coffee table.

"Brother," he said. "I'm happy to see you."

Jormungand's smile split his face as he launched himself at Fenrir, wrapping him in an embrace.

And then his gaze found me.

His smile died like a snuffed candle.

He untangled himself from Fenrir and dropped back onto the sofa, reaching for the teapot.

"I had hoped the benefit of being exiled with the dead would mean not having to see you again." He spoke in the rough words of the Jotnar language, which made his meaning all the more harsh. "But now those hopes lie crushed."

He never would speak Asgardian if he could help it.

"You don't seem very surprised to see me here," I said.

He shrugged.

"Why should I be surprised?" Amusement slithered through his voice. "With the thousands you've pissed off across the Nine Worlds, one of them was bound to send you down here, dead or alive."

Along with my green eyes, Jorg also appeared to have inherited my sharp tongue.

"You must flee," Fenrir said. "Frigg is coming, and she is going to curse you."

The thought of us gathered here like birds waiting for Frigg's stone nagged at me again. This was exceedingly bad.

He shrugged, the black silk of his tunic rippling. I couldn't help but envy how his leather trousers hugged his calves like a second skin.

"I know," he said.

"You know? How?" I asked.

"I've heard whispers," he said.

"Then why are you waiting around here drawing?"

"Uhhh, banished?" Bitterness dripped from his voice as he poured black tea into a gold-rimmed demitasse cup. "Not all of us had the luxury of being exiled to small town Midgard like Fenrir." He passed the cup to his brother.

He refilled his own cup, set the teapot down with a sharp click, and ignored my existence entirely.

"Well, you were a bit more aggressive than Fenrir," I said. "You held Sigyn hostage and forced me to unleash Surtr from Gullveig's heart. Remember?"

Jorg's expression cracked, his mouth falling open.

"Ok, I'll give you that," he said. "But only because *The Call* drove me to madness."

"Look, regardless, I don't like that we have all ended up here," I said. "And that Frigg hasn't cursed you yet. I would have thought you'd be first. You are a rather easy target."

"Am I?" he snarled, teeth flashing. "In case you've forgotten, I can turn into a rather large snake and—" He snapped his jaws wide, then clicked them shut with the force of a steel trap, mimicking the bite of a massive serpent.

He was right. Even Frigg wouldn't have wanted to deal with his prickly mood until the last second. He had all the ease of barbed wire, and getting cursed wouldn't improve his disposition.

"The fact remains her curse will send you back into the

ocean, I assume. Since she is doing what Yggdrasil commanded," I said. "I have a terrible feeling about all this."

"And I'm not impressed with her curse after I studied the mechanics of the magic she used," he said, drumming against his cup. "I have no concerns. In fact, I think I'll enjoy the sport of watching her try to bind me back in the triangle. See how well that works for her when I coil around that thin waist of hers and *SNAP*."

"Curses are faster than we can both shift," Fenrir said. "I've seen it with my own eyes. I'm afraid."

Jorg's shoulders softened.

"It will be alright, Fen," he said. "You have me to protect you."

My mind kept bubbling with thoughts and reasons and suspicions.

"Something's not right. This shows too much orchestration. And why is Hel the only one of us not caught in Frigg's curse? Actually, where is your sister? I need—I mean, Fenrir needs—to talk to her."

He tossed a wedge of lemon into his tea, delicate wisps of steam curling from the surface.

I longed to hold the cup, to have the warmth seep into my frozen fingers.

"Entertaining again," he replied with a slight groan. "I wish they'd be quieter about it. Fenrir, would you care for a slice of lemon?"

"Entertaining? She doesn't entertain," I said.

"Fine, doubt me. She's in her rooms." Irritation sharpened his tone. "Fenrir, stay here and enjoy your tea. Tell me everything about how father looked getting cursed by that witch. Don't leave out a single detail."

Jorg's eyes slid to mine, calculation glinting behind that casual smile.

"I think it's best Fenrir goes," I said.

"I know why you think Fenrir must go, but I'm telling you if you want anything from her, don't be a coward and face your daughter," he said. "Or you can prove me right."

Fine.

I looked at Fenrir and motioned for him to stay.

Fenrir sank into the wingback chair, wood creaking under his bulk. Firelight softened his features as he wrapped his hands around the delicate cup. Jorg sprawled across the sofa, arms stretched wide across the backrest, leather creaking with each shift of his weight.

I turned to leave. Their voices chased me down the empty hall.

"You don't have to be so hard on him," Fenrir said. "Give him a chance. Papa has changed."

Jorg scoffed.

"You're fooling yourself. Father doesn't change."

7

———

THE NIGHTMARE

I couldn't tell who screamed louder.

Hel or me.

"Oh, my gods!" I stumbled backwards, hip cracking against her dressing table.

She leapt off the face of some naked man strapped spread-eagle to her bedposts, leather cuffs biting into his wrists and ankles.

"Why do you always ruin everything? Get out!" Hel shouted, jabbing her finger at the door.

She snatched a black silk robe from the floor and whirled it around her shoulders, the fabric clinging to sweat-slicked skin. Her black hair tumbled wild down her back, framing her split features. One side blue-tinged decay with flesh peeling from bone, the other hauntingly beautiful with my green eyes.

"I'm sorry for interrupting, but..." Gods, I doubted if I'd ever emotionally recover from this. "I must speak with you. Urgently."

She stormed to the bed, grabbed an armful of scheele's green bedding and hurled it over her lover's face. She tugged the black lace canopy shut, hiding him beneath murals of dark forests and white stags that prowled her coffered ceiling.

"I'm rather busy."

"I can see that," I said. "But I'm afraid this is rather important."

Hel stalked across herringbone floors, her bare feet silent on crimson rugs. She yanked open a wardrobe stuffed with silk and velvet, sending books and candles clattering from its top while she reached behind the clothes.

"It would have to be important for you to continue standing here when I've told you to get out!" she snarled. "I hope it's worth me impaling you."

She spun, spear leveled at my chest. Lovely. Getting skewered by my daughter while her naked lover watched wasn't quite how I'd pictured this day going.

"Hel, please." I held up my hands, palms out. "Let's discuss this rationally."

"If by rationally you mean me impaling you through the arse, then that's fine by me."

She jabbed the spearpoint against my ribs.

Despite the murder screaming behind her eyes, a rumpled purple tunic dangling from one of the beaded chandeliers snagged my attention. The embroidery was exquisite, definitely Asgardian, though the cat hair rather ruined the effect. I'd seen this particular pattern before. Which god was it that always wore grape vines? Very obnoxious—

A stone dropped into my gut.

Horror clawed up my throat.

"Hel. Please. Please, please, *please*. Don't tell me what I am thinking is true," I begged, pressing my hands together.

Her spear lowered, the fight draining from her stance as

she caught my gaze on the tunic. She propped the weapon against an alcoved shelf, candlelight dancing across brass bowls and apothecary bottles and books.

"Father, don't overreact." Hel slid between me and the bed. "I think you had a brilliant idea earlier. Let's discuss all of this rationally." Her voice stayed steady, but sweat glistened on her brow.

Rationally?

I sprang for the curtains, ripping them aside and yanking away the blanket and—

The room wobbled. Spun. Pirouetted with sconces, and lace, and brass.

A demented carnival waltz shrieked through my skull.

He thrashed against his bonds, terror etched across features as he stared up at me.

Balder.

My eyes were lying. They had to be. The candlelight was playing tricks. This wasn't real. This was all just one big, horrible, practical joke.

I laughed.

"Father?"

"You are such a prankster, Hel," I said. "You really fooled me with this one. You and Balder? Hilarious!"

My smile spread wider, pain needling my cheekbones.

"This is a prank, right?" I asked. "Tell me it's a prank. Say it."

"No, Father," she said. "This isn't a prank."

I didn't think it was possible for my day to get worse, but Balder always managed to find a way.

However, as he trembled beneath my eyes like a wet field mouse, a rush of dark delight washed over me. And, I admit, a touch of arousal.

Perhaps I had been shortsighted. No, the more I considered it, the more I saw how this horrible, horrible thing may end up being the best day of my life.

I grinned, a smidge of evil curling the corners of my mouth.

"Please!" he squealed. "Don't hurt me!"

I slipped my dagger from my hip and pressed the blade to the tip of his nose. He screamed, the noise piercing enough to crack glass.

"I'm going to really enjoy killing you a second time," I said. "And now, you can't wiggle away from me like you did in that whorehouse."

He shivered harder.

"I swear if you just let me go—" he launched into a stream of promises and pleas, each more pathetic than the last.

Now, could I interrogate Balder about where his mother's curse had sent Sigyn? Of course. But I knew it would be a waste of time. His mother was many things, but dumb was not one of them. She knew Balder was rubbish with keeping secrets.

I pressed my dagger closer to his flesh.

"No, no, no, no, no," he whimpered, his limbs still stretched out in a grotesque star shape.

Hel stepped between us, wrenching the dagger from my grip and sending it skittering beneath the armoire.

I moved to retrieve it, but she blocked my path, her shoulders squared. She reminded me very much of Angrboda, who could make you feel a head shorter with a glance, and would *make* you a head shorter if you continued to annoy her.

"You will not hurt him," Hel said.

"Hel, you don't understand who he is," I said over Balder's whining and sniffling. "He's...he's...Hel, please...

just let me kill him. I'd love to kill him. Gods, I *want* to kill him."

My gaze drifted to the tapestry above the bed, moths and moon phases stitched across the weave. I could stuff it down his throat, watch him choke slowly—

"No." She curled her fingers, her pointed red nails digging into the bottom of her palms.

If this wasn't a prank, then surely it was part of some grander scheme? A calculated ruse. Yes. That was it. She was simply using him, luring him into an intricate trap.

Of course, she had made him that altar...

"I don't understand you Hel," I said. "Balder is as charming as what runs in the gutters."

"I love him," she said with far more calm and conviction than I liked.

Behind her eyes, I glimpsed something unexpected that melted their usual frost. I knew that look all too well.

Oh no.

No, no, no.

I'd find it easier to accept Hel being in love with a tapeworm, or even Thor. But Balder?

This was utterly incomprehensible.

Unacceptable.

Hel turned and unbound Balder's restraints. He sat upright, incredibly naked, and hurriedly clutched a satin pillow to his lap to cover himself. Gods, he was a joke.

"Love him?" I choked out. "Why? What is there to love? I genuinely do not understand."

"You need to give him more credit."

"CREDIT?" I shrieked.

Hel took Balder's hands in hers, and he gazed into her eyes with a tenderness that made my stomach heave.

"Yes. Credit," she said. "He's been the only one ever kind

to me in Asgard. He's been the only one ever kind to me, well, *ever*."

Balder laced his fingers with her skeletal ones, and a small smile played on his lips.

Sweet.

Sincere.

Absolutely disgusting.

"He sees me," she said.

"And Hel sees me," Balder added.

Could Balder actually be capable of love?

Hmmm...

I studied him, considering.

No way.

"Fine," I said. "You may love him, but you can't convince me he loves *you*."

Balder's face flashed with that pristine irate rage I was incredibly familiar with, having found personal pleasure in stoking it to inferno countless times. The way he'd scrunch his face and look like a little chipmunk never failed to amuse me.

His fingers raked through short, blonde hair as his jaw tensed. Candlelight carved his face into planes of light and shadow, causing him to resemble one of the marble statues Asgard frequently had made in his honor. His blue eyes narrowed to ice chips, full lips pressing into a grim line. Gods. Why did his anger always make him more attractive? I felt like punching him across the face for it.

"But I do love her," he said, each word daring me to challenge him. "I love Hel. She's the most incredible woman I've ever known, and I want to be her husband."

"HUSBAND?" The word exploded out of me.

Just when I believed things were as bad as possible.

Hold on...

A grin spread across my face. Again.

"Balder," I said. "Dear, dear Balder...don't you, oh... already have a wife? Or did you forget all about Nanna? What a shame. I guess the wedding has to be called off now."

My smile stretched wider.

Truth was, there was as much to love about Nanna as there was a wet napkin. Though she was rather good at choosing party decor, I'd give her that.

I didn't like how Balder's smile mirrored mine in that "gotcha" signature smirk.

"Well," he said. "Ironically, when you killed me the first time," his glare could have frozen flame, "you released me from that marriage, and she's since run off with some giant-ess. Anyway, point is, I'm now free to marry whom I like."

He squeezed Hel's hands tighter.

Damn. Why did murder always have to come with consequences?

Hel walked to the chandelier and untangled Balder's tunic from the beads. She handed it to him, and he slipped the silk over his head. I bit back a laugh at the tufts of white cat hair dotting the embroidered grape vines.

"Why are you even here, Father?" Hel asked. "You weren't supposed to arrive in the underworld until half past-two. Wasn't that right, Balder?"

Balder nodded.

"We were supposed to have another hour, at least," he said.

My gaze bounced between them.

"Wait," I said. "Are you saying you *knew* to expect me?"

"Yes," Hel said. "Frigg informed me weeks ago of the Salvation Weave. And her plans with you."

The ground tilted beneath my feet. I couldn't believe what I heard.

"So, let me get this straight." I pressed my thumb against my forehead as a migraine bloomed behind my eyes. "You knew of the coming curse, but didn't think to warn me? A little heads up would have been nice."

Hel must have been the source of the rumors Jorg referred to.

"I don't owe you a thing," she said. "I rather like the idea of you cursed. I find it more than fair. In fact, I'm sending you to one of the shacks lining the marshes. I think you'll appreciate the varied toad population. They *croak* the entire night."

She chuckled at her own joke.

I guess I couldn't blame her for some retribution after all of my own betrayals. Perhaps this was only fair. At least she hadn't impaled me to Yggdrasil's roots. Yet.

"Why aren't *you* cursed?" I asked.

She walked to a lacquered table, crystal goblets clinking as she reached for a bottle of port.

"I'm protecting her," Balder said.

"No, that's not it," I said, shaking my head at the thought of him being able to protect anything. "There's something more here to all of this."

I dropped into a chair, purple velvet cushions swallowing me as my mind raced through possibilities.

"And so you have nothing else to say to me?" She splashed port into two goblets. "There's nothing else you can possibly think of? Father, are you even listening to me?"

Her sharp tone yanked me from my tangle of theories about Frigg's schemes.

"What? Oh. Look, Hel, I'm really trying to think this all through—"

"Forget it."

"No, what is it you want me to say, right now, during this wonderful timing before you throw me to the toads?"

She handed Balder a goblet and drained her own in one swift motion. What was it with my children offering me no hospitality?

"To start, how about an apology for what you put me through with Ragnarok."

I pushed my face in my hands.

"Hel, I understand your anger about the whole banishment thing, but I've had a horrible day. First with losing Sigyn, then getting cursed, and now finding you two—"

"Why am I not surprised?" she asked. "Focusing only on everything that's about you."

I looked up at her. If she could have pinned me to the wall for display like her moths and butterflies hanging over the fireplace, I think she would have.

"What are you trying to say?"

She sighed, port sloshing into her glass for a second round.

"You've not come to find me just to chat," she said. "After Ragnarok...I almost lost my kingdom, my life, because of you. I won't risk it for you again just so you can play the hero. Losers don't fight battles."

"That sounds very defeatist, which isn't you."

Hel's spine stiffened at my accusation.

"Things have changed since Frigg took Asgard," she said. "Since my banishment from ever rising above the surface. I don't have quite the same freedoms and power anymore. Now I must answer to Asgard fully and wholly. You wish to understand my silence in warning you? She made it clear she'd view my insubordination as a breaking of my banishment, treason, if I didn't agree to you being cursed here."

Balder crossed to Hel and touched her shoulder.

"I won't let her harm you," he said. "Mother promised me as long as you do what is required—"

I laughed.

Cackled, actually.

"Yes," I said. "Because your mother always keeps her promises. You're still such a boy."

Anger blazed in his eyes, carrying an edge I hadn't seen in him before. Interesting. Was this the beginning of a backbone?

I wiped tears from my eyes at the notion.

"That doesn't matter. What does matter is Mother seeing that Hel is on our side," he snapped. "If Hel proves loyalty—"

I laughed louder. He was serious.

"Frigg is unaware of your marriage plans yet, is she?" I asked. "Oh. Don't tell me. Is Hel proving her loyalty to your mother how you plan to get Frigg to bless your marriage?"

Balder twisted the goblet in his hands.

His stupidity astounded me more each time.

"True, Mother needs time to see the benefits of our union," he said. "She needs time to understand."

"At least you understand how she will react to your wedding," I said.

Balder's face darkened, and he slammed his goblet on the table rough enough to jolt the other goblets. One clattered to the ground. His hands flexed. I think he wanted to strike me.

I smiled.

"She will accept us," he said. "Mother will see the advantage of my marriage to Hel. And with you now gone...*well.*"

Anger cracked through me.

I shot up from the chair and faced him, fighting the urge

to hurl him into the settee covered in porcelain dolls. It felt odd speaking Jotnar with Balder, though I appreciated how effectively its rolling Rs and rhythm conveyed rage.

"You're a mouse, Balder," I said. "And you understand who your mother is. What she's...what she's done." I forced my nails out of my palms. "You once said you deserved recompense for the role you played in what happened to me five hundred years ago. And what did you do instead? Stood by and let her take Asgard like she takes everything. Your father—"

"Father is unfit to rule," he cut me off, voice rising to fill the room. "Now she can clean up all he destroyed and weakened. We can bring true safety to Asgard and the entire Nine Worlds. Mother will finally do what Yggdrasil commanded and rid everyone of the risk of Ragnarok for good."

My gods. Balder had turned into a parrot, spouting his mother's words—hold on.

I didn't like that.

What Yggdrasil commanded.

This was worse than bad.

"I didn't realize I'd be getting a matinee of your mother's little monologue before she cursed me," I said, pressing fingers to my throbbing temples. "I never thought Fenrir would be the lucky one having tea with Jormungand."

"Wait, Fenrir is here?" Shock filled Hel's voice. "Frigg said nothing about sending Fen here too when she spoke of her plans with me."

"Well, his being here is more of an accident, really—"

"Jormungand warned me she might do something, but I didn't think it would involve Fenrir."

And that itch in my brain grew sharper as more puzzle pieces snapped together.

"Perhaps your fiancé would care to elaborate?" I asked

Hel, arching an eyebrow at Balder. "Especially about how the curse would bind Fenrir on Lyngvi. And then he'd have a sword rammed through the bottom of his jaw to pin him to the bedrock."

Her mouth dropped open.

"Balder..." Hel turned to him. "Were you aware of her intentions with Fenrir? He doesn't deserve to be cursed to that island. And Jormungand..."

"I thought she was cursing Fenrir and Jorg like your father. Like the other gods so they couldn't interfere. Just...to a place."

"To a place?" I sneered. "You really are useless. Do you never consider asking more questions? Seek specifics? But then why would you, when you've always just followed along with whatever mummy wants?"

His eyes stayed locked on Hel, pleading.

"I...I didn't know about Lyngvi, I swear. I would have told you," he said. "You know my mother..."

I did, and that is why I, sadly, trusted him when he claimed to be ignorant of the matter. Because his mother wasn't a moron like him. She knew when to keep her cards close.

"How could you turn your back on your father like this?" I asked. "You are endangering the woman you claim to love by following Frigg."

He shook his head, jaw clenching.

"It's because of Father never taking the necessary measures that we are here discussing this at all."

"Oh, you mean the measures of locking me in a cave with snake venom searing off my face for eternity? And I'm suspecting there is more waiting for me than just being condemned to the underworld to live my days out in a marsh with toads."

His eye twitched.

"I made her promise me you wouldn't suffer a fate like that again. She is only—"

I laughed.

"Doing what Yggdrasil commanded?" I asked. "You and I both understand what that means. What she plans with Fenrir and Jormungand proves it. And you want me to believe you are not naïve?"

He swallowed hard.

"None of this changes the fact that Father is inadequate to rule. He is a menace. Like you."

"Your father is a stubborn asshole, I'll give you that. But he made his choice to follow what he thought was the right path. One day, you'll face a similar fork in the road, and you'll have to pick between doing what's right and doing what's selfish. I have my doubts you'll be able to muster the same backbone your father had." I stepped closer. "Because right now, all I see standing before me is a coward."

Balder's shock dissolved into that familiar, simmering hatred for me. Again.

"I'm no coward."

I smiled.

"That remains to be seen," I said. "Now, for the love of all the gods, make the choice to put on some trousers and leave. I need to speak with Hel. Alone."

He glanced down at his bare legs, face flushing crimson.

Gods. He was more pathetic than I remembered.

"Finding a way out of here and going after Sigyn, you mean?" Hel asked, plucking Balder's trousers from the gilded mirror and passing them over with her skeletal fingers.

"I really don't want to discuss this in front of golden boy."

Balder almost stumbled next to her as he tried to dress. His face reddened further with embarrassment as he fumbled with buttons and belts.

"You're after some magical item that can help you, aren't you?" she asked.

Balder grabbed his overly polished boots from behind the brocade curtains, nearly toppling over as he shoved them on.

I suppose I didn't need to fear him reporting all this to Frigg. What more could she do to me?

Actually, I didn't want to know the answer to that.

"I mean," I said. "I was rather hoping you may have some enchanted talisman, or arcane bauble, a minor trinket that is capable of piercing through curses. You wouldn't happen to have anything like that laying around, do you?"

She sighed.

"No, I don't. And even if I did, I'd not give it to you."

"What about a magical snail?"

Her sigh could have collapsed mountains.

"I have no idea what you intend to achieve by leaving the underworld, but it's quite impossible. There is no way out. That's how curses work."

"And your brother?" I asked. "Fenrir doesn't deserve this."

Sadness creased her brow.

"No, he doesn't," she said. "Look, even if there was a way to override the curse, if Frigg found out..."

My heart splintered into shards, jagged pieces tearing at my insides. I couldn't watch Fenrir suffer from my mistakes. Not again. Not like this. And Sigyn...Sigyn was somewhere out there alone, probably wondering why I hadn't found her yet. The thought of her waiting, hoping, trusting me to come...it hollowed out my chest until breathing hurt.

Balder straightened his tunic, smoothing out the wrinkles and picking at the cat hair with fastidious disgust. For once, we shared a sentiment. That tunic didn't deserve the indignity of tabby fur marring its silk.

"What's your purpose here, Balder?" I asked, ignoring the bitter taste of spirulina sizzling my tongue again. "I'm surprised mummy dearest and Freya would even allow you out of their sights to dally in the underworld."

He fixed me with a look that begged for a broken nose. Or femur. I hadn't decided which yet.

"I don't have to tell you that," he said.

I raised an eyebrow.

"Ah, the messenger. As I said, you're a boy. And furthermore—"

The room lurched sideways. Cramps followed, knife-sharp and vicious.

My knees folded, and I stumbled forward, clutching my roiling stomach. The spasms intensified until I doubled over.

"What's wrong?" Hel's living hand pressed against my shoulder.

"Nothing," I lied, fighting back the acid climbing my throat. "I'm totally fine—"

Pain twisted through my abdomen like a dagger being turned. My hand clamped over my mouth as nausea crashed over me in waves.

I lunged for the chamber pot beneath her bed, barely getting my head over it before Fenrir's smoothie rocketed back into my mouth.

Sadly, the chamber pot was no match for the smoothie.

I looked down at the resulting carnage splattered across my shirt.

Not the Versace.

Hel rolled her eyes.

"Drunk again?" Hel's gaze hardened with annoyance.

I couldn't let her learn the truth. That a stupid piece of pineapple had done this. She'd know instantly about my mortality, and that was one secret I couldn't let Balder discover.

"Must be just an extra fun torture of the curse," I said, my voice more like a whimper. "That's all. Obviously not anything else."

Her expression turned calculating, like a cat spotting a mouse's poor attempt at hiding.

"I know for a fact the Salvation Weave does not cause vomiting as a side effect," she said.

She yanked a black shirt from her wardrobe and tossed it to me—silk, lace cuffs, a touch too low cut, but absolutely divine.

Balder's eyes dropped to my chest as I peeled off my stained shirt and slipped on this new beauty. I supposed I couldn't fault him for looking. The definition of my lean muscle was exquisite. And my pectorals—

"Why do you have a scar on your chest? And on your shoulder?" Suspicion sharpened his tone.

Before I could spin an excuse, Hel pressed her hands against my skin. Her cold touch stole my breath.

"These are wounds caused by divine weapons." She traced the scars, fingers ice. "A Muspel Blade. I recognize the etching of the teeth. And the other, Dwarven. Your dagger, Father."

"Your point?" I asked, willing my breathing steady.

"They're wounds that should have healed completely, even for a god. One would expect a thin scar, but these?"

"I'm telling you, it's nothing."

"These look like what you'd see on a human...oh my gods...Father, are you mortal?"

I scoffed, but my heart raced.

"No, of course not. Why would you say something so silly?" I asked.

My stomach gurgled again, louder. I clutched my abdomen as an invisible drill bored through my insides. My shoulder blazed with fresh pain, making me wince.

Hel's eyes widened.

"You *are* mortal!" she said. "That explains the vomiting. But how is this even possible?"

Her eyes searched mine, confused and seeking an answer to a question she didn't even know how to ask. I guess my secret was out.

"Doesn't matter," I said.

"That means your chaos is gone as well," she said.

I stared at my feet, avoiding Hel's gaze. The truth of her words hung heavy in the air.

"Does Mother know this?" Balder asked, shattering the tension.

I closed the distance between us until I could count his eyelashes, pouring every ounce of threat I had left into my glare. Why did Hel have to toss my dagger under the armoire?

"And she better never find out," I said through gritted teeth.

Hel wouldn't betray my secret, bound by godly rules as death's keeper. But Balder...I wouldn't trust him as far as I could throw him. And I'd tried that once. It hadn't gone well.

"You will keep this secret, Balder, if you know what's good for you," I said. "You allege to love my daughter, but if you breathe a word of this to anyone, you'll be showing her the ultimate betrayal."

"I will," he said, wilting under my gaze. Mortal or not, I wanted him to know I could still destroy him.

"Swear it to Hel. Make an oath."

I seized his shoulders and spun him towards Hel, forcing his hand into hers. His fingers trembled slightly. Good.

"I swear to keep this secret," he said, meeting her eyes. "I swear on my life, on my love for you, and on my loyalty to you."

Hel nodded, iron in her grip. A ghost of a smile touched her lips.

"I accept your oath," she said.

I watched them, satisfied. A solemn oath was one of the most powerful bonds among gods. But just to be sure...

"And remember, Balder," I said, my voice dropping to a silky purr that promised violence. "If you ever betray this family, if you ever break your oath, I will hunt you down to the ends of the Nine Worlds and bleed you out slowly. And unlike the last time I killed you, I'll make sure it's exceptionally painful."

Balder's face went the shade of old porridge. He nodded, swallowing hard enough I could hear it.

"Good...then—"

Another cramp punched through my gut, my insides writhing for round two. This time, I wasn't sure which end. Or if it would be both.

8

ENEMIES WITH BENEFITS

I wiped bile from my mouth and walked down a hall, desperate to get as far away from the scene as possible. Fenrir's blasted spirulina powder had turned my stomach into a battlefield. I guess I got my wish, and it could join the growing list of foods I couldn't eat. Applesauce, or worse, rye crackers, would soon be all that was left.

Sigyn would know how to settle my stomach, how to remove this swamp from my tongue.

Reality slammed me hard. Sigyn wasn't here.

I was alone.

Trapped in this pit.

And I was a weak, mortal sack of nothing. How was I going to get out of here with this curse from that witch? And what about Fenrir and Jorg? And Sigyn...Sigyn could be anywhere.

Anywhere.

I slumped against the stairwell wall. Mildew soaked through my clothes as decay filled my shuddering breaths. Only the rhythmic drip of water from the damp ceiling broke the silence.

My mind raced.

Visions tore through me.

Her curse could be worse than mine. Her prison deeper.

Fear gripped my chest.

She could be afraid.

The thought of her alone and terrified and me unable to do anything about it spiraled me deeper into my mind that screamed with beasts.

I might never see her again.

Each breath burned hotter than the last.

And then Fenrir and Jorg. Frigg would hunt them down and curse them, too. The certainty of it gnawed at my bones.

My boys didn't deserve to be hurt.

I buried my head between my knees, tears dripping onto stone as the underworld's weight crushed my joints, as if wanting to grind me back into dust.

For a heartbeat, I wanted to surrender to the quiet. To the end of pain.

No.

These chains, this curse, wouldn't hold me.

I would escape Hel. I would hide my children somewhere safe. I would find Sigyn.

Swallowing down my emotions, I lifted my head, swiped at my wet cheeks, and began the long, *long* climb up the worn, winding steps.

Why did Hel have to love spiraling and gothic architecture? The atmosphere was divine, but all the stairs were murder.

The tower room's door screeched open, and must and mildew struck me in the face. Floorboards creaked under each step as I walked past trunks and creepy portraits of women veiled in lace standing on storm-swept shores. I ignored the shelves lined with specimens floating in murky jars or stuffed with sawdust.

Of course, where I headed wouldn't be any less sinister.

I lowered myself to the floor, crossing legs and placing palms on knees. Closing my eyes, I sucked in a deep breath —and spent the next minute coughing thanks to the dust surging into my sinuses.

I cleared my throat and tried again, taking in a smaller breath that wasn't so chocked full of rot.

I found the silver ring, each circle around the metal gathering intention, seeking its twin. To achieve seidr, you had to sink into a trance, a state between waking and dreams. Not easy without my godhood, and after eons of disuse. One wrong step in the dream-walking and I'd turn inside out. Seriously annoying.

Odin better be waiting on the other side. The cuffs blocked his magic, yes, but seidr was different, more trance than spell. While Frigg's bindings could stop him from wielding power, they couldn't prevent him from slipping into the dream-walking state that seidr required. A loophole that made my plan brilliant.

I glided my finger over the warming silver band, runes pulsing beneath my touch as I willed myself to sink deeper into another world. A damp one, where moisture clung to every breath.

Each step through the thick mist echoed, my muscles straining as if wading through mud. Tendrils of vapor coiled around my ankles.

The ring seared my flesh, metal branding deep into bone. I gritted my teeth until my jaw ached and clenched the band tighter, speaking the words with conviction. The syllables scraped my throat as I forced them to take shape, even as mist and magic writhed against my presence here, hooks of power tugging at my essence, threatening to hurl me back through the void. The seidr realm didn't like me here.

The curse binding me to the underworld also didn't help. But what was the point of astral projection if not to bypass these little thorns?

Molars ground together. I would reach him, so help me—

A silhouette materialized in the murk, edges bleeding into shadow. My concentration narrowed on the form. The outline crystallized until a man's figure emerged from the haze.

Sweat beaded on my brow as I squinted, straining to make him out as his form flashed in and out of focus. Seidr was a bitch. His projection sharpened, strengthened—the short russet beard, the broad shoulders. The only difference was that both his eyes fixed on me, the missing one restored in this soul-state. A very naked soul-state. Afraid the price of projecting into the seidr realm was leaving your clothes behind with your physical form. Souls came as they were made.

I swallowed hard, trying not to notice the perfect shape of his biceps. Though I definitely still had the better legs.

"Loki?" Odin's voice sliced through the vapor. "Hel hasn't sent you to the toad hut yet, has she?"

Mist coiled around our torsos and calves, while absolute darkness pressed against us like a living thing. Our bare feet splashed across the thin water film stretching into infinity.

"Wait, how do you know I'm in Hel?"

I didn't like when he already knew things. That was always bad, and usually meant things were about to get much worse for me.

"Get out of the underworld as fast as you can."

Ice-needles of cold pierced my skin with each step as we approached one another.

"I appreciate the concern, but I'm already doing all I can to protect my backside from Hel's spear," I said.

"There is more at stake than your arse," he snapped. His features hardened into a look I recognized well. It was a look that told me everything I feared was right.

That sinking feeling I couldn't shake hardened. Perfect. Wonderful. Just the added dose of stress I needed.

"This is about what Frigg said, isn't it?" I asked. "About Fenrir and Jormungand being the last pieces to allow her to seal the Salvation Weave."

Sadness tightened the lines at the corners of his eyes further. A clammy cold slithered along my vertebrae.

"It's more than needing only them," he said. "She needs all of you to complete what Yggdrasil commanded. She's using the Salvation Weave to finally bind you three."

Cold tingled where the entrails of my children once bit into my wrists. And now, she wanted to bind my children.

She wanted to bind *me*.

Again.

"Bind us? Where?" My voice cracked on the words.

"The location isn't certain, but I know this…" He floated his hands over my shoulders. "She plans to bind you with Hel's guts. Unlike last time, when mere humans could break your bonds, these will be forged from a goddess's own entrails. No mortal tool, no wandering human, or being could ever sever them. This time, it's truly forever."

My stomach lurched. And now I saw why Frigg had left Hel out of any mention of her curse.

"How sure are you about this?" The words tumbled out as panic clawed up my throat. "No. It can't be true. Hel is a goddess—"

"Yes, that's right," he said, forcing his hands back at his sides. "And what could be stronger than the entrails of a goddess? The magic required to bind you must be of your blood. She thinks the others failed because of their fragility, but with Hel's..."

His words sat like poison in my mind as I thought of Hel, my daughter, being gutted like a fish. Memory flashed. Blood on Frigg's hands, tiny bodies, her calm expression as she worked. I swallowed back acid. Not again. I wouldn't watch another child's entrails spill across stone.

"She's going to butcher my daughter," I said through my rising panic. "But why am I here, in this holding place, if she's not ready for me yet?"

None of it made sense. But then, neither had her calm that day in the cave, hands painted red with my children's—no. Focus. I had to focus.

Odin drifted closer through the mist.

"Fenrir was meant to be first, remember? Until you made her snap with that kiss..." Something raw crossed his features. "But, after that trick, well, you forced her to adjust. So, now you're cursed to Hel until she has them all secured. Her plan requires a specific order of binding, because each builds upon the last, creating an unbreakable chain of curses, and you're the last piece."

Well, that was just splendid news. Really, fantastic.

"How considerate of her to save me for last."

Vapor swirled between us as I stepped back.

"She learned from your last escape. Each curse is a chain in her trap. The gods' stolen power fuels it. Fenrir's rage anchors it. Jormungand's binding nature tightens it. Think of it like forging a chain. Each curse adds another unbreakable link, each one drawing power from what makes them strong. The gods' magic sparks the forge. Fenrir's strength becomes the foundation. Jormungand's world-encircling power makes it constrict ever tighter."

I swallowed hard.

"There is one irony in all this," Odin said, a grim smile playing at his lips. "You have no element to drain, since you gave up your chaos to Surtr. So while she can curse you to the underworld, her curse can't feed on you like it does the rest of us gods. We will soon be turned into husks."

"Oh, lucky me." I forced a bitter laugh. "Stuck in the underworld, but at least I get to keep my sparkling personality."

Odin's form wavered as he paced through the darkness.

"With the combined power of the gods and your children, she'll seal you away. And Hel—" His words settled like lead. "Her entrails will bind you, but it's her essence as Death itself that makes the curse eternal, unbreakable across all realms. And once we gods are drained completely, there'll be no one left to protect the Nine Worlds. No Thor guarding Midgard, no Heimdall watching the Bifrost. Everything will crumble."

I forced my projection steady, even as memories of screams echoed in my mind. My daughter's guts. The curse. The worlds falling. I swallowed it all down with a smirk.

And one last ingredient to seal my curse...

"So, what's her brilliant plan for keeping the Nine Worlds running without us? Put up a 'Help Wanted' sign?"

"Something like that." His mouth twisted. "She's already searching for replacements. But creating gods isn't as simple as handing out name tags and powers. Trust me, I made all of you and it takes time, knowledge, power."

I thought back to that day on the banks of the Ifingr, when he shaped my chaos into godhood. It wasn't the most pleasant of experiences of my life...

"And she doesn't have the strength to create full gods," he continued. "She'll be stuck with half-powered fledglings, minor spirits. Imagine a sprite trying to do Thor's job." He shook his head. "By the time she manages to replace even one of us, the damage will be done."

"But why risk it? Why destroy everything we've built?"

Odin's form stilled, features softening.

"Because to her, you're the greater risk. Frigg has always been a fanatic when it comes to Yggdrasil. She won't listen about how this will weaken Asgard. All she sees is the prophecy. That once you and your children are bound, once she's completed what Yggdrasil commanded, Ragnarok can never come. The Destroyer and his offspring chained forever." His voice dropped. "She thinks she's saving the Nine Worlds. She's going to destroy them instead."

His eyes met mine, and for the first time, I saw genuine fear there.

And I knew.

The truth hit me like ice in my chambers. Without Thor, giants would raid Midgard. Without Odin's power, ancient things that should never wake from slumber would rise. Even Braggi had his uses, though I'd never tell him that. Poets would be stuck rhyming 'moon' with 'June' without his inspiration. Frigg would destroy everything we'd spent millennia protecting, all to stop me.

"The fights Frigg and I had over this..." Odin said. "She always pushed me to do what the tree commanded, and I always tried to find the loopholes because I...I couldn't do that to you."

The cave's darkness crashed back, bonds slicing to bone, blood slicking stone as my screams shattered against rock walls. Venom seared through eye sockets, melted throat flesh, stripped skin from muscle. The snake's fangs gleamed above, dripping death onto my face, each drop burning deeper until my world narrowed to acid and agony.

"I can't go back..." My voice splintered. "I can't watch my children die again..."

My heart slammed my ribs like a caged beast. And Sigyn. Gods, what would become of her this time?

"Sigyn. What about Sigyn?" My projection flickered as fear gnawed on my bones.

His lips thinned.

"Well...thing is...she's on Midgard," he said. "I've heard Frigg's guards whisper in the halls after too much drink. That's where Frigg sent her, though they didn't mention exactly *where*." He paused. "But *where* won't matter for what's coming, because she'll be...be..."

"Be what? Tell me."

"She will be eaten."

"Eaten?" I asked. "What do you mean by 'eaten'? She's a goddess—"

He sucked in a breath, his image wavering.

"Plenty a god has gotten eaten by Frost Giants," he said. "Of course, once the curse is sealed, the curse will drain Sigyn's power until she's practically mortal. That will make her a little easier for them to catch."

My projection stilled.

"I'm sorry, did you say Frost Giants?"

"And that's not all I've caught from those drunken gossips. Skadi is banding together the Jotnar clans. They've sensed the weakening borders. The weakening protections. They already march towards Asgard, and without Thor's full power, without *me* on the throne..." He let the implication hang heavy in the air. "They mean to take everything while we're vulnerable, while our powers are being drained. And they'll..."

"—They'll finally sweep through Midgard." I scrubbed my face. "The Frost Giants must be salivating already."

Asgard was Midgard's only protection from Jotunheim, and especially from the Frost Giants. While Skadi's clan practiced a more *traditional* diet—beets, cabbage, goat cheese—The Frost Giants in the far North quite enjoyed Midgardians ground into their bread. For the extra protein.

"Ever since that episode where we slightly murdered Skadi's father, Thiazi, she has been wanting vengeance," I said. "Won't shut up about her oath to take Asgard."

"No thanks to you. You're the one that led him right through that bonfire that killed him."

If I could have slapped him without my hand flying through his jaw, I would have.

"You're the ones that listened to me and built the bonfire. I think the guilt here is fifty-fifty," I said. "Besides, he tried to steal Idunn's apples every other century. His schemes got worse each time, too. First it was disguising himself as a merchant, then that eagle, then...gods, he tried dressing as Freya once." I shuddered at the memory. "What were we supposed to do, let him have immortality and suffer through another thousand years of his terrible theft attempts? The bonfire was a mercy, really. Saved us all from more awful disguises."

"And now, because of Frigg's cruse, Skadi could actually take Asgard. No, she *will* take Asgard. This is the war she's threatened for eons." His projection darkened. "Skadi also wants your head to satisfy her vengeance for her father."

I rolled my eyes.

"Why is it always my head?" I threw up my hands. "Thor breaks twice as many peace treaties as I do, but no one ever demands his head on a platter."

I saw how it would all play out. Asgard would fall, and

without my head to offer, Frigg would bargain with the next best thing—her precious Balder. She'd offer her own son to Skadi to save herself. And Balder would agree to spare his mother's life. Pathetic.

Of course, the thought of Balder married to the fiercest Jotnar War Chief almost made this worth it. At least he'd be away from Hel. I smiled, imagining Skadi's massive hunting dogs, Leif and Frode, each the size of a baby mammoth, slobbering up his legs as they begged for pats.

Marvelous.

"Skadi is smart," Odin said, pacing through the mist. "She will soon figure out that I no longer rule Asgard. And without me and the other gods, without Thor and Mjolnir to fight, Frigg is no threat by herself. She's opened something she can't put back, and she'll keep denying it even as Skadi drives a blade through her heart."

"This will be like piranhas devouring a leg of mutton," I said.

"And when they win because Frigg cursed all the gods, Jotunheim will devour Midgard." His projection dimmed. "I wish that could be just a metaphor, but all humans—eaten. And that includes Sigyn."

My stomach churned as his words sank in. The image of Sigyn, alone in Midgard, Frost Giants advancing across the realm, their hunger echoing in their footsteps...

"So what do we do?" I asked. "I know I'd love to avoid being tied to a rock with another child's entrails again. I want our lives back from this curse and the resulting mess."

9

IT'S ALWAYS THE APPLE

"There are two things we must do to get our lives back," he said.

"Great," I said. "Let's hear them."

"First, we break the curse. It's the only way to stop Frigg, and for us gods to be free and have our powers back, and you all to not get bound."

My face flattened.

"When I asked what do we do, I didn't mean you state the most obvious answer in the entire Nine Worlds. Care to give some specifics? Like, oh, I don't know...let's start with *how*?"

He let out a deep sigh.

"Look, an act of love can break any curse," he said. "But we don't have the luxury of time to just hopefully fall into the right combination of whatever that act could be. We need a more straightforward way. And this is what will work."

He carved his finger through the mist, leaving ribbons of golden light hanging in the void. The symbol bloomed outwards of two serpents devouring each other's tails. Runes speared through the coiled snakes, each character sharp as thorns, written in a language that made my temples throb.

"This incantation will let me break the Salvation Weave and free us all."

"You really must have oatmeal for brains if you think these squiggly lines are our salvation."

"Are you seriously doubting me?"

"I thought that obvious."

"I've broken countless dark curses before," he said.

"True, however—"

"I exorcised Surtr, pure dark matter, out of Sigyn."

"Yes, but—"

"I think that more than qualifies to break Frigg's curse, and this symbol is how I will achieve destroying it."

"I just find it awfully ballsy of you to assume you should be the one to break the Salvation Weave. Why not *me* break it?"

He laughed. The bastard.

"You?"

"This affects my family. Sorry to say, but I don't like putting my faith and life in your hands if I can help it."

He narrowed his gaze at me.

"Now, who came to me to rescue their girlfriend because they couldn't do it, as they lacked the understanding of dark magic?" he asked. "Oh, that's right, *you*."

"That was different." I waved my hand through his symbol, scattering light like shattered glass. But the golden lines twisted back together, serpents reforming as if I'd never touched them.

"Was it?"

The memory of Sigyn writhing as Surtr possessed her flashed through my mind. And Odin had been the only one capable of of saving her...

Damn him.

"Would you also like me to bring up the last time you tried to break a curse?" he asked. "Ivar's village was reduced to ashes."

"Fine. I think you've made your point."

"Furthermore, you're mortal now, Loki," he said, grief tugging at his words. "You don't have the strength necessary to perform such a spell."

"Watch your mouth." How dare he call me mortal, even if it was technically true.

That familiar tenderness I used to know crept into his eyes.

"You gave up your chaos, your very godhood, just to make the amulet work…"

He reached towards my face, then stopped. Gods. He'd changed so much since our last conversation in that hospital in Midgard. Even in this void, stripped to the soul, I saw the weight of the curse crushing him. Something in my chest tightened, and that terrified me.

Because of what it meant.

I wasn't supposed to care if he lived or died anymore. Hadn't for centuries. Yet here I was, worry coiling in my gut like an old friend, some ancient reflex refusing to fade. The familiarity of it burned.

"I know my care is intolerable to you, but…I don't want you hurt," he said, mist swirling between us.

I wanted to scoff, to deflect, but the words stuck in my throat. After all, I had grated off my fingertips trying to make a cucumber salad. Things were different now, as much as I hated admitting it. As much as I wanted to deny how easily we fell back into old patterns, like worn paths in old forests.

I sighed, pushing down the ache.

"Let's get back to the subject of breaking Frigg's curse."

"Yes, I'm ninety percent sure I have everything I need," he said, still studying the glowing symbol as if avoiding my gaze.

"Ninety percent? Your confidence is overwhelming."

"I have all the components necessary for the spell. Blood of a star, essence of void, tears of a newt. Everything except for one small detail." His finger traced the thorned runes.

"And that is?"

He cleared his throat, shoulders tensing.

"I don't know what this incantation says."

"Oh, you mean the incantation you just claimed was the key to breaking the curse? Perfect." The serpents coiled through the text. "And here I thought you were the one who understood all the darkest things."

"And this is where, I can't believe I'm going to say it," he muttered, his form dimming like he wished he could disappear into the void. "I have to rely on you accomplishing an extremely important task for me to stop the curse."

I crossed my arms.

"Oh, I can't wait to hear it."

"I need information. Information only Sigyn can provide."

"Sigyn?" Her name caught in my throat. "What does she have to do with this?"

He pointed at the symbol still pulsing in the void, serpents writhing.

"I must have this incantation translated to complete the spell and break the curse. She carries knowledge of the language of Muspel—the dark, primordial tongue of Surtr. That's what these runes are."

The thorned markings seemed to twist and smolder, looking rather creepy.

"You mean you don't speak the language of dark matter incarnate? Shame."

"Only those touched by darkness can understand the tongue," he said. "When Surtr possessed Sigyn, he left an imprint. He branded her, and it's why she now has the ability to speak this language."

I narrowed my eyes.

"And let me guess, I can't just ask her nicely for this translation? What aren't you telling me?"

Odin sighed.

"She can only transmit the translation to me through a willing blood ritual. *Laevateinn* should do the job nicely."

"Of course it's a blood ritual," I said. "Because when isn't it?"

"The stakes are high, Loki. If we don't break this curse, the consequences will be catastrophic, not just for you and those you love, but for all the realms. You must find Sigyn, and you must get her to perform the ritual."

"Oh, is that all? Just convince my wife to participate in a potentially dangerous blood ritual. Just find her. Just escape Hel when I'm cursed here. Should be a walk in the park. Maybe I'll pick up some flowers on the way."

"Once she performs the ritual with *Laevateinn*, and I receive the translation," he said, ignoring me. "Then I can perform the spell to break the curse. But if you fail, if Frigg binds you with Hel's guts...then I cannot break it. The curse is sealed and becomes permanent." His projection flickered. "Which is why we have no time to waste. I've already searched through what dark texts I can access from my chambers. Her mistake, really. She's too lazy to keep walking to the dungeons, so she's confined me to my rooms. Though..." His voice darkened. "That also speaks to her confidence. She isn't worried about what I might do."

"I'll warn Fenrir and Jormungand, and find a way to protect Hel. If we can prevent even one of these bindings."

"There is no way to prevent the bindings except by breaking the curse," he said. "Now, memorize this symbol so you can have Sigyn translate the incantation when you find her."

I stared at the glowing lines, tracing each curve and angle with my eyes. The twin serpents twisted through thorned runes. Each mark burned itself into my mind. The sharp descent of the first rune, the way the second curved like a blade, the third's jagged peaks.

"Do you have it?"

"Give me a minute..." I focused harder, making sure each detail was perfect. One wrong line and the whole ritual might backfire. I didn't want to risk him losing the other eye.

"Do you have it?"

I closed my eyes, seeing the symbol floating in darkness. Every rune, every scale, every twist of serpentine body.

"Yes."

Odin's projection sagged with relief.

"Good, and then after we break the curse—"

"You mean *if* we break the curse."

"The second thing we must do is stop the aftermath."

"Skadi and Jotunehim and protecting Midgard," I said, watching the serpents and symbols fade into vapor.

"Yes, and your children will be how we win this, fighting for Asgard alongside the gods—"

"Wait." My form flickered. "Are you joking?"

"You must convince them to fight beneath our banner," he said. "Under the circumstances, we might sway them to fight and save us from Jotnar expansion."

Laughter burst from my throat, scattering the last traces of his symbol.

"Frigg's curse has left you more demented than you usually are."

"Listen," he said. "You know Asgard's strength at its best. Even after the curse breaks, even with Thor and Mjolnir, even with my throne restored, even with all the gods free, we are not enough to stop what Frigg has unleashed. Her curse has brought both Jotunheim and the Northern Frost Giants to our door." Darkness gathered in his eyes. "You know what that means."

I did know.

Odin's father, Bor, had barely beaten back the combined Jotnar forces and the Frost Giants last time. And Odin himself had spent centuries keeping them from Midgard's borders. It was why he'd enlisted my help in those early days, when Midgard was young and vulnerable...

"Your children are the only chance to win. To protect Asgard, Midgard, and all Nine Worlds. Once the curse breaks and the gods are free, we'll need Fenrir's Wolf, Jormungand's Serpent, and Hel's army of the dead to defeat Jotunheim. With them, I can save Asgard, put back my protections, and clean up Frigg's mess."

"This is rich," I said. "I think you're underestimating Thor, which physically pains me to say. But, he is rather good with that hammer. Just let him loose."

"Let him loose? Even Thor has his limits on how many skulls he can crush," he spat. "It's because of me helping you I'm even in this position."

"Sounds like you made a bad choice and are facing the ramifications. Not my problem," I said.

"Oh, it's not your problem?" His eyes flashed. "Tell me, when the curse is broken and you're forced to return to your exile on Midgard, how long before you become a Jotnar snack? How long before Skadi takes your head?"

"Come again?"

"You know if I'm not on the throne, there's no one in your court. Even with the curse broken, you're still banished to Midgard, and it will become Jotunheim's. And we know what Skadi will do once she finds you, which she will. She'll mount your head above her toilet."

She would. She'd told me as much, right before trying to feed me my own intestines.

"And Fenrir won't fare better. *Kalehalla* will end up in flames. The Jotnar won't allow a single vegetable to stand." His form rippled. "You have a choice. After the curse is lifted, you can either have the life you want, or have your face become a urinal target until the stars burn out."

Well, shit.

If Odin wasn't on the throne, I would be up a very particular creek without a paddle. And a hole in the boat.

The only chance we had was breaking this curse, and the only chance at any kind of life after was if my children helped the gods win the war. Jorg and Fenrir were capable of devastating entire Jotnar battalions in their shifted forms. Hel's army matched that of Odin's warriors of Valhalla.

"This is all easier said than done." Mist curled through my fingers. "I'm a bit mortal. A bit cursed. Oh. And my children have a deep, seething hatred for all of you. And they aren't exactly too fond of me, either."

His projection straightened, and that gleam in his eyes brightened.

"I don't like it when you get that look...the last time was when you suggested that trip to Samsey."

"And, another benefit, since you really seem to need one...If you and your children reinstate me as ruler, I can pardon them for this noble act of saving the gods, and for saving Midgard from becoming a buffet...I can even pardon you," he said.

"Go on..."

"You'd finally give me a valuable advantage to convince the other gods *and* realms to grant your freedom," he said. "No more banishments. No more exiles. No Jotnar tearing you apart. *Think.* You'd all finally have freedom. I promise you this."

Freedom. Hel no longer in fear of her soul being scooped out of her body. Jormungand no longer trapped in the underworld. Fenrir no longer kept from the Ironwood. And as for me...

I envisioned myself drinking Fareth with Sigyn in the Southern Isles, where we'd bring nothing but a toothbrush and sunscreen.

I scratched my nose, sniffing hard.

"The problem is," I said. "My children don't trust your promises. Your *promises* led them to being imprisoned already once before."

The corners of Odin's mouth turned down.

"Don't tell them this promise is from me. Gods. It's not that difficult."

My gaze snapped to his face.

"Let me rephrase that. *I* don't trust your promises. You've broken too many to me."

His left eye twitched. Good.

"How about this," he said. "Without me on my throne, you won't get your golden apple."

Hold on. Now that was interesting...

"Ah, I see that got your attention," he said.

"And what if it did?"

"If you want your golden apple, your *partial* immortality back, I am the only way to have what you want."

Dammit. Now this was a bargain worth considering. The apple was my only hope for years with Sigyn. And only Odin could get it for me. I needed that apple. Another vision floated by—Sigyn and I on the beach, but this time my mortal body wasn't failing, wasn't counting down precious days. With the apple, everything was possible again.

I would not allow anyone to steal my life with Sigyn. And bonus, it would fix my shoulder that screamed every morning, my stomach that rejected everything but bland toast. I could drink my Chateau Haut Brion '61 again without spending three days in agony.

With the apple...

Odin always had a remarkable ability to persuade. I gritted my teeth. Trusting Odin was not something that came easily to me.

Of course, I could never tell my children my personal benefit in this bargain.

I considered his words and all they could mean.

All they could break.

All they could hurt.

10

SWEET SIXTEEN

BALDER

Asgard

I brushed grave dirt from my shoulders as I stared at the door of the War Chamber. Why wasn't I lifting the latch and walking in? Only Mother waited on the other side. But what Mother would I get? She lit up rooms when happy. But when her mood darkened...

Acid burned the base of my throat.

It didn't matter. My news would ensure a smile from her. I completed the task she asked of me, and in half the time she requested. She would praise my good work.

Of course, she would probably follow that praise with some criticism. Point out how I could have been even more efficient with the task she assigned me. Or question my sudden lax attitude with my appearance. My nails were horrifically untidy lately. Removing the grave dirt from beneath my nails was quickly becoming a full-time job thanks to my visits to Hel, of which only two visits had actually been allowed.

Mother didn't need to know about the other twenty-six times.

I scraped off the dirt that still clung to my knuckles, turned the posey ring Hel had given me, sucked in a breath and walked in.

Shelves packed with books on military strategy, siege warfare, and the dark arts towered towards the ceiling. And in the middle of the room, Mother hunched over a large, circular table, the ebony wood disappearing beneath a mess of maps and battle plans. Her expression carved into sharp angles of focus as she studied the maps. The purple silk of her gown draped over her slender frame.

"Damn that wolf." Mother slammed her hand on the table, rattling the war figurines. "He's supposed to be bound right now. What's the point of the Salvation Weave if you can't even get one sun eating wolf on one little island?"

"Are you planning to chain Fenrir to the rock?" I asked. My stomach twisted at the thought of anyone trapped like that, alone forever. "Why can't he and his brother remain locked in the underworld with Loki?"

She sighed, her shoulders dropping.

"Balder, it's what Yggdrasil commanded, and you know this time, I'm not taking any chances. I apologize if I failed to mention this to you, but I thought it obvious."

"Well, change it to something else. Something more humane."

"More humane?" She traced battle lines on the map. "I already have to adjust everything because Loki just had to kiss your father. He knew it would vex me. He's always making things harder." She pinched the bridge of her nose.

"As if I needed Skadi and her Jotnar friends breathing down our necks on top of it all. One peaceful day. That's all I ask. But no. I hope you at least brought me some *good* news, and not *bad* news..."

"I have—wait. Skadi and the clans have moved closer?"

The acid burning in my throat flared up at the mention of her name.

I walked further into the room, my steps echoing against stone floors as I carefully skirted grandfather Bor's spear.

Mother sighed.

"Skadi thinks we are some feast set out for her."

Skadi and I had history.

She once barged into Asgard demanding my hand in marriage as compensation for her father's death. Loki, ever helpful, said she could pick me by my feet in a lineup. Brilliant plan.

Knowing her foot fetish, I'd spent a week in boots so tight my calluses could've made a troll weep. It worked. She chose Njord's dainty toes instead. Called it a scam and swore she'd marry me someday, bunions and all.

And now without Father and the gods to defend us... without Thor crushing a thousand Jotnar skulls with Mjolnir...and even then, would it be enough to stop the hordes if the Frost Giants also started to march?

No. No, it would all be fine. Mother and Freya had it all under control.

"Don't worry, you will get that wolf cursed soon enough," Freya said, stroking Mr. Ragnar. "It actually makes a certain kind of sense, him already down there. After you curse Fenrir, you can easier get his brother. After that, it's just Loki and—"

Mother shot Freya a glare that made her falter.

"—And Skadi has only sent a few scouts," Freya

rushed on, her leather armor creaking as she settled across from Mother. "We will have Thor agree to fight with us long before she tries to cause any trouble." Freya plopped Mr. Ragnar down on an embroidered pillow that partially covered the map of Alfheim. As she spoon fed him bits of raw liver, her nose twitched. She fixed her eyes on me. "Do you smell something? It smells...*loving*. Oh! Balder, do you have a new lover? Do tell us all those filthy little details!"

Not again. As the goddess of love, Freya could smell desire like others sensed rain.

It was hard enough keeping my relationship with Hel secret from Mother, but Freya? I was exhausted.

"No," I said. "No lover. I'm certain the scent you detect is the liver Mr. Ragnar has smeared all over his face."

She pulled a delicate silk kerchief from her sleeve and dabbed at the cat's whiskers, where chunks of raw meat still clung. Gods. Mr. Ragnar looked like he'd been dead for years. She already resuscitated him once at breakfast.

"Doubtful," Freya said, "I only noticed it once you walked in here—"

"Back to my news—" I said, cutting her off.

"Yes, I'm still waiting for you to tell us," Mother said. "And especially why a simple underworld visit took so long —No! Not in the onion tartlets, Mr. Ragnar! Oh, Freya! He is always terrorizing anything he can dig in."

"No matter, those tartlets give one awful goat breath from the cheese," Freya said, scooping up Mr. Ragnar mid-squat over the tartlets.

Cold sweat slicked my palms, while heat crept up my neck.

"You know how traveling to the underworld can be," I said. "Modgur still makes me answer her riddles before I'm allowed to cross the bridge. Last time I spent three hours arguing with her over things that walk on four legs."

Freya flicked a carved Jotnar figurine across the table, sending it skittering over the map's surface to make room for a second course of duck for Mr. Ragnar. The ceramic plate clicked against the wooden table as she set it down.

"Why do I still detect a scent of romance even more, now?"

Freya stood and walked closer to me, silver buckles glinting.

I snatched one of the untouched tartlets and crammed it into my mouth, desperate to drown whatever love-scent clung to me in a fog of goat.

I gulped the pastry down in one swallow. My mouth flooded with layers of caramelized onion, the bite of balsamic, and the overpowering musk of goat cheese that burned the back of my throat.

She wrinkled her nose, nostrils flaring, and retreated to her chair. Mr. Ragnar sprawled across the table, belly exposed to the ceiling.

"Perhaps if you allow Hel more freedom, I can avoid the delay upsetting you, Mother," I said, grasping for any other topic.

Mother chuckled.

"My sweet, Balder," Mother said. "It's not the lack of her freedom that is the issue. I'm afraid the issue is me thinking you experienced enough to confirm that the curse was successful in sending Loki to the underworld. I suppose I shouldn't be surprised—"

And here we tumbled into the familiar list of my short-comings. But what clawed at my gut the most was knowing that if I dared voice my feelings, she'd crumble and tell me how I misunderstood her. Ask me how could I be so hateful as to think she'd ever say such a thing?

No, it was far easier just to listen.

"Now tell me," she said.

"I saw Loki in Hel," I said. "I've confirmed his arrival, as you requested."

Her face softened, sharp angles melting into something as delicate as porcelain.

She smiled, and I felt that familiar rush of warmth, that surge of validation that came with meeting her approval. That precious, rare gift of making her happy. She was wonderful when she was happy.

"This is good news, thank the gods," she said. "I would only trust your eyes. Now step one with that Trickster is complete."

"Step one? I thought that was the only step—"

"Mr. Ragnar, you are the best pussy wussy!" Freya's voice rose to a coo that echoed off the walls.

Mr. Ragnar needed to go.

"Every time I saw Loki, I saw death itself. And your father?" Mother's voice went quiet. "He chose his own cock over our safety. But now, with my curse, we'll finally do what Yggdrasil commanded. Stop Ragnarok for good. There will be no mistakes this time."

A chill crept down my spine at her tone.

"Just to be clear about Loki," I said. "After the misunderstanding with Fenrir, I need to be certain. The plan is still only to trap him in the underworld to rot with the dead, right? Not bind him? You aren't following *all* of Yggdrasil's commands this time?" I held Mother's gaze. "Remember your oath to me."

Mother went still. Her hand jerked to her chest as if I'd stabbed her.

"Balder, are you implying I would break an oath to my son?" she asked, her voice small and hurt. "After everything we've been through? Faced?"

"Well, I suppose—no. No, that's not what I'm saying—"

"You think I would lie to you? I am a good mother—"

"You are. It's just—"

She smiled.

"You are a sweet boy, and I understand your concerns, but believe me when I say they are unnecessary," she said. "And I have not forgotten my oath to you. The underworld will serve as Loki's prison. As for Yggdrasil's commands, well..." She paused, and something unreadable quirked the corners of her mouth. "I have no intention of following its directions to the letter."

That somehow didn't make me feel better.

She pulled me into an embrace, and all my doubts dissolved in her warmth. This was Mother's love, pure and fierce and protective and my fears were foolish.

"We are going to bring such wonderful change." She squeezed me tighter. "All the gods who supported Odin, who let him endanger us all by keeping Loki free—they're finally gone. Now Asgard can be safe. Now Asgard has hope."

I couldn't deny her words. The gods had let Father keep his lover while putting us all at risk. And for what? Because Loki could tell a good joke? Because he could be fun at a party? Talk away what trouble he caused as a little harmless mischief?

I hated Loki. Hated how he turned my father into his fool.

On my sixteenth birthday, on a clear evening, I went to go find Father. He promised me he'd be back in time for my coming of age feast, and I was excited for him to give his blessing on me as his father did him. But he was late. The boar Mother had specially prepared was already being served. Gods were already getting drunk on mead.

Maybe his horse threw a shoe. It happened. Or he just arrived from his summit. *He promised me.*

I walked to the stables. The air was crisp. Perhaps he was still cooling down his horse, unsaddling the gelding and brushing its flanks, checking the hooves for stones before leading it into its stall. Yes. It was all completely reasonable. In fact, it was better this way. We could walk in together for the feast. Father and son. King and prince. The perfect dynasty.

I entered the stables' warm glow, coated in gold and shadow. Metal jingled in the back room for storage and tack.

I smiled and walked closer.

Moans and grunts filled the stillness, mixing with the metallic tinkling.

I reached the edge of the stall, out of sight, and froze.

My smile vanished, finding them together, trousers at their ankles, standing and bracing themselves against a saddle rack. I froze, unable to tear my eyes away.

Their mouths were locked together, Father's knee propped on the saddle and Loki pumping into him from behind.

A line of sweat drenched Loki's tunic on his back as he grasped and pressed Father firmer to him. Loki trailed kisses down his neck.

Father's hands slid behind Loki and gripped the back of his ass, his legs, coated in sweat and oil. Loki wrapped his arms tighter around Father's chest and thrust into him faster.

Blood rushed to my face.

He let out a cry.

I ran back to the feast hall.

My pulse pounded in my ears.

Anger and confusion ate at me.

So, this was why he was late for his own son's birthday. Because rutting in the stables was more important than spending time with me.

When he finally arrived an hour late, cheeks still flushed, he apologized, offered some bullshit excuse I would have accepted if I didn't already know the truth.

He gave me his blessing.

Loki arrived later in a clean tunic as dessert and wine were served. He drank and laughed as if nothing was amiss.

As if he didn't hold responsibility for breaking my family apart a little more that night.

He promised me.

I woke myself from the memory, rage still burning in my gut after all this time.

And that was Father's great leadership in a nutshell. He rather fuck the monster destined to fuck the entire Nine Worlds than protect his own family and people. The familiar rage burned through me, but this time it felt righteous. Mother was fixing everything Father had broken.

I released her hand and reached for the crystal decanter, inhaling notes of summer berries and oak before pouring the wine into silver goblets. Yes, her curse would cleanse Asgard of father's mistakes.

"To all our futures," I said, raising my glass in a toast. "We should never have brought chaos to Asgard. And now, it's finally gone thanks to the Salvation Weave."

The wine slid down my throat like velvet. But Mother set her glass down, untouched. Worry carved lines between her brows as her gaze drifted to some distant point beyond the chamber walls.

"What's wrong?" Concern rose in my chest, along with something else. Something I didn't want to name.

"I want Loki dead." She stood and stepped to me. "He deserves worse than this curse. Worse than that cave. One day, I will learn how to kill him without releasing that chaos of his. Only then will we truly be free of him."

She snatched her goblet and drained it in three swallows.

And I kept my mouth shut about Loki's *lack* of chaos. I wouldn't break my oath to Hel. And, though the wine's warmth still told me Mother was right, I refused to believe Loki deserved death.

Even at my angriest, I never wished Mother's blade for Loki's throat. Ever. As much as he filled me with rage, execution was too harsh a price. Just as he never deserved to be bound and tortured in that cave. The screams still echoed in my nightmares. Not just Loki's, but Sigyn's. And their infants...they were innocent.

"It was for the greater good," Mother had told me the next morning, when I was still heaving with regret and guilt and shock. *"The alternative would have been our own lives."*

The horror of that day would never leave me. The sounds...from children who moments before had been sleeping in their mother's arms.

And that's why I forced her to make an oath to me. My hands trembled as I gripped hers, but my voice remained steady. Each word tasted like iron on my tongue. She tried to soothe me, to mother me, but I wouldn't let her deflect or soften what needed to be done. For once in my life, I made her listen. Made her swear in the old way, with binding words that even a goddess couldn't break. I ensured that no soul would ever again be sacrificed for her *beliefs*.

This oath was also how I got her to agree to curse Loki to

the underworld, instead of doing the horror again. I pressured her into finding another way, one that didn't require entrails or suffering. The curse was clean. Simple. Just magic and intention, not blood and screams. At least, that's what I kept telling myself.

"There is no need to kill him," I said. "His danger is gone now."

Mother laughed. Cold. Hard.

"I can't believe what I'm hearing. You're actually defending him? Loki murdered you."

My cheeks burned, and I instinctively touched my throat. No, I hadn't forgotten the mistletoe tearing into my jugular. How could I?

"I understand, Mother."

She arched an eyebrow.

"He killed you, Balder," she repeated. "How can you not see the danger?"

"I said you're right."

Her smile faded as she inspected me closer, sniffing my hair and examining my hands, gaze lingering on the dirt beneath my nails.

I hoped she didn't notice me stiffen.

"I appreciate you being willing to go to the underworld on behalf of Asgard," she said. "I know it's odious work, but remember, this is temporary."

Her earlier words echoed in my mind.

"It has to be you, Balder. You're the only one she tolerates."

If only Mother knew why.

"Your role will be strictly at my side once this coup is completed, and the curse sealed," Mother continued. "You won't have to see that creature again. Think of it, Balder. You and I, rebuilding Asgard together. Making it pure again, safe again. Remember how you used to help me in my garden?

How we would plan the spring plantings?" She reached for my cheek. "We can do that with all the realms. Plant something new from the ashes of the old. You and your mother, the way it should have been before Odin let chaos poison everything."

I clenched my fists.

"I truly don't mind going to the underworld. It's good to monitor things there."

Her brow raised.

"Surely you don't enjoy visiting that ghoul? And to think she actually thought she'd win your love." Mother cackled. "She is not fit for you. Nanna was a far better match, even if your father disagreed."

Her words sliced through me like a blade between my ribs.

"Don't speak that way of her. Hel is a strong woman and—"

"She's a monster," she spat, venom dripping from each syllable. "But don't worry, she won't be a threat to you once this is all finished."

Thunder rolled through my chest.

"Hel is not a monster," I said, anger breaking through. "She rules her own realm. Being Loki's child doesn't make her evil."

Mother's eyes narrowed. I'd overstepped.

"I'm sorry." I swallowed the rage back down like bitter herbs. "I understand your worries, yet I believe Hel is not like her siblings. She deserves a chance to prove herself."

Her sigh emptied the warmth from the room.

"I know you've always had a soft spot for her, even as a child. Believe me, if there was any other way to negotiate with her, I would never send you. But we have no choice. I'm tortured each time you go." She twisted her fingers in her skirts. "After Hel kept you hostage, I simply can't bear the thought of her setting eyes on you. I won't allow her to keep you again."

Loki's words rang in my ears, their truth burning. I'd known Mother watched Hel and me like a hawk stalking prey, but hearing it spoken so plainly pierced something tender I'd tried to protect. But what burned me was that Mother had proven Loki right.

I could never tell her.

Or Loki.

I hated myself harder.

"Of course, Mother," I said, each word a betrayal.

"Right now, the priority is maintaining the status quo." She turned from me, pacing the length of the war table, fingers trailing over carved battle markers. "As long as Skadi believes your father still rules, that the gods protect Asgard, she will stay away. At least Thor is still of some use. For now."

For now?

Mr. Ragnar lay beside the battle markers, his whiskers glistening with bits of raw duck and liver, snores rumbling like rusted chains.

"Thor would be useful, if he'd fight for us," Freya said. "But he's made his stance clear. Even with my charms, he won't budge. Keeps saying we can burn in Muspelheim for what we've done." Her lips twisted. "If only Odin hadn't warded the gods against my voice."

"Thor refusing us makes no sense," Mother said. "The deal was fair. Swear fealty to me, and even under his curse he could feast in the great hall, keep his titles, his honors. But he'd rather rot in his chambers." Mother dragged her hands down her face, nails leaving red trails on her skin. "Unfortunately, he's the only one who can wield Mjolnir, and is the best giant-killer in the Nine Worlds. We need him to face Skadi before—" She caught herself, lips pressing into a thin line.

"Before what?" I asked.

"Before the situation escalates. He still has enough power left to wield Mjolnir. That will have to be sufficient," she said, repositioning a marker on the map. "Pray he agrees to face Skadi while he can still swing that hammer."

"Left? What do you mean 'still has enough power *left*'?" The wine turned sour in my stomach. "Mother, you said the curse was just to keep the gods from interfering, to banish them. You never mentioned it would drain—"

"It's all temporary, darling," she cut me off. "I better find the replacement quick—" She stopped again, turning away to study the battle plans.

Replacement? Ah. Probably for that servant who kept dropping the wine jugs. Yes. Obviously, that's what she meant.

Five guards marched through the doorway, armor clanking against stone with each step. The commander, muscles straining his breastplate, clutched a rolled parchment in his fist. Freya's gaze trailed from the curve of his jaw to the leather straps crossing his thighs to the tight calves beneath steel greaves. Her tongue darted across wine-stained lips.

Poor bastard. With her brother Frey safely curseless in Vanaheim, Freya had already devoured half the army's ranks.

Mother snatched the note, breaking the crimson seal with her thumbnail. Storm clouds gathered in her expression.

She crushed the parchment in her fist.

I frowned.

"Observers have spotted Skadi's troops setting up camps at the border. Well, as I said, we must maintain appearances for precisely this reason. Come along, Balder. I know just the thing to set this right."

That knot in my stomach twisted tighter.

"Where are we going?" I asked.

Mother smiled in that way that told me I wouldn't like the answer.

11

———

DADDY ISSUES

"**Y**ou wouldn't know where you put my book *Runes of Revelation: A detailed study of the ancient runic alphabet and its mystic applications*?" Father navigated the towering bookcases, his dark gray tunic pulled taut across his shoulders as he reached for higher shelves.

He leaned forward, his good eye scanning title after title while half-formed words tumbled from his mouth.

His chamber remained as I remembered. Star charts and half-translated texts buried his mahogany desk. His leather chair bore the impression of countless nights spent reading. A heavy oak bed layered in wool blankets sat pushed hard against the back wall.

Mother anchored herself in the doorway, arms crossed over her chest. She tapped her heel in an irregular rhythm against the threshold.

"Why would you need that?" The question cut through the scent of beeswax and old leather.

Father traced the worn spines, his tunic riding up with each stretch. The silver cuffs at his wrists dug into his skin, suffocating any wisp of magic, while the curse did the rest.

"And what about *Blood Sorcery Unveiled*?"

Mother's face hardened into carved granite.

"Oh, don't tell me, you're—"

"Seeking to break your curse? Excellent deduction, wife."

"You always had enormous balls."

"At least you remember."

They stared with a thousand darts aimed at the other.

"Whatever you're thinking, it's no use. There's no undoing the Salvation Weave."

She walked to a brass-bound trunk and wrenched out *Runes of Revelation*, sending it spinning towards his chest. Father caught it with both hands, and his mouth twisted into a smile.

"There's no undoing it only after you have the curse sealed, which you've yet to accomplish."

"But I will. Don't you dare doubt that."

He lowered himself into the desk chair, wood creaking beneath him, and spread the thick tome across scattered papers. The spine crackled as he opened it.

"My dear, I doubt you every single day. Especially with how you're running Asgard. How many camps does Skadi have now?" He dragged his finger down the yellowed page, never glancing up.

Her spine straightened.

"Enough to require precautions."

Father's lips curled at one corner, a fox discovering a hole in the henhouse fence.

"And that involves me, I gather?" He thumbed through the index, then flipped to another chapter. His hand darted to a notebook bursting with scraps—diagrams, equations, and observations bleeding onto every margin.

She drifted to the arched window. The setting sun

painted her silhouette in copper and rust, her shadow stretching across the stone floor.

"You will weave—"

"Weave an enchantment to make it seem that all the gods roam free and are not imprisoned? So predictable. You want me to disguise your curse." He chuckled low in his throat. "Did you truly believe you and Freya could rule Asgard without the other gods? Without me? And especially without Thor?"

Mother faced Father, eyes sharp with knives. I knew that look. And I knew what followed. I swallowed.

"Mind your words," she warned. "I can make this much worse for you."

The past surged up uninvited. Each memory struck like an iron spike. The threats, the tension...it all churned my gut into knots.

I was seven and their screaming crashed in my ears.

"Why are you always a stubborn mule?" Mother's voice splintered the air.

"Why are you always a horror?" Father's voice thundered back.

"Thor's daily tantrums stir up thunderstorms by teatime," Mother said, yanking me back to the present. "I think that would be a good start."

Father laughed.

"You really think some dark clouds will make Skadi shake in her ox-skin boots? That the clans will hear a little rumble of thunder and run back into the ice?" He rapped against the book's cover. "She wants Asgard, Frigg."

"They won't dare take one step closer to Asgard if they have the smallest hint that you still rule and that everything remains unchanged. Until I create my new stronghold, it will be enough."

He laughed harder.

"This is a wonderful gift you've given me. Everything you've planned, everything you want, is falling apart."

"Don't be so sure," she said. "And as for Thor, you know I have my ways of motivation."

Father's lips thinned behind his beard.

"The skies remain worryingly clear." She turned to the window, where dusk painted the clouds in bruised purples. "Maybe also include an illusion of Idunn out in her garden. And of Braggi singing one of those annoying ballads."

"You wanted to rule Asgard." Father grasped another weathered, leather-bound book from the desk. "Consult your new Vanir generals. This is not my concern anymore. It's yours. Leave me alone. For once."

"You bastard." Mother's voice ricocheted off the lime-washed walls. "You put me in this position to take Asgard from you. To take the worlds. All because you proved unfit to rule them."

And he had. If he had just left Loki alone in Jotunheim, none of this tragedy would have ever happened.

Mother's heels clicked against stone as she paced.

"I should have done this years ago," she said. "I should have taken the throne the moment you first told me you bound yourself in blood to Loki instead of binding him to rock."

Her words straightened my spine. Finally, someone saying what needed to be said.

Father surged up, sending books tumbling from his desk. They hit the floor with dull thuds as he crossed the space between them in three long strides, his remaining eye burning like a coal in snow. He towered over her, shoulders rigid.

Mother lifted her chin, unmoved.

"Did you ever once think why I did that?" His voice carried the quiet menace of a blade being unsheathed. "Why I thought Loki worth the risk?"

Heat surged through my chest, rising like bile.

"So you admit the risk," I said.

"The blood oath would have worked. It was your mother who forced me to break the oath with Loki, which started Ragnarok in the first place. I am not the one to blame."

Not to blame? The words ignited something in my gut.

"You let a thief into our home, and for what?"

Father's eye snapped to mine. I flinched, but planted my feet wider, meeting his glower.

"Why should I explain to you, when you have no hope to understand," he said.

"I understand plenty." My voice grew stronger. "I was the one that had to comfort her tears you caused."

The memory burned fresh. Mother's shoulders shaking as I held her, watching Father ride to Alfheim with Loki at his side. A journey meant for her. She'd spent months preparing, even practicing Elvish with me late into the night.

As they departed, Loki twisted in his saddle, fixing Mother with a wicked grin.

"It's a wonder Odin didn't choose you this time, being so skilled at deceit and all."

Then his gaze found me, a nine-year-old boy with fists clenched tight, and he chuckled.

"Nice of you to try, little one, but your mother has no honor left to defend."

In those words my hatred for Loki was born.

Father exhaled sharply, and something in his rigid posture crumbled.

"I should have seen how deep your mother's claws dig

into you," he said, voice softened. "I should have protected you better from her."

That flash of sincerity pulled at something inside me, a thread I didn't want tugged.

"You should have protected all of us by obeying Yggdrasil," Mother snapped.

"Before you wrecked everything, I had found another path to prevent Ragnarok." His voice caught like fabric on thorns. "And you murdered them...you massacred those children."

"I..." Mother faltered.

A second. A flash.

Color flooded her cheeks, anger and guilt battling in her expression.

I moved closer to her, fearing she might break down in that second.

"I kept Asgard safe," she said, frost claiming her again. "As I'm doing now. I do not crave blood. I just see when blood is the only way."

"Safe," he spat. "Tell me how safe Asgard is with Jotunheim at our gates. Tell me how Midgard is safe. The Midgardians rely on us to keep them protected, and now...You think some enchantment parading the gods around that all is well will suffice slaking Jotunheim's lust? And you lecture me about safety?"

Their glares locked, the rest of the world falling away, and I became a ghost, watching through glass. Mother lifted her hand, brushing Father's cheek with a tenderness that seemed to belong to another lifetime. His expression melted beneath her touch.

"We were so good in the beginning," she said.

"We were." Father leaned into her palm.

"What kind of fool tears such a thing apart?"

He sighed, the sound weighted with centuries of something bitter.

"How could I tear apart what you already shredded?"

She withdrew her hand as if burned.

"Now tell me, Odin," she said. "Will you obey me or continue starving?"

My stomach dropped to my feet.

What did she say?

"You've starved him?" The words burst from me before I could cage them, my boots shifting against the plush rug.

"Of course," she said. "Starving makes them obedient. You're too good to understand."

My stomach knotted tighter.

Father barked a laugh and collapsed back into his chair, the wood popping. Papers rustled as he shuffled them, shoving vials of ink aside.

"Yes, starvation makes them so very compliant," Father said. "I am so accommodating now you're exploiting my hunger. Truly cunning."

The mockery in his tone drew blood. I rocked back on my heels as Mother's expression darkened.

"You used to admire my cunning." She walked towards him until she loomed over his chair. "You admired my craftiness, my intellect. All qualities you claimed to lack in your brute warrior way. When did my cunning become disgusting in your eyes? When did you stop seeing my ambition as a virtue?" She leaned in, lips curling. "Was it when I dared turn that cunning against you, rather than remain silent by your side?"

She gripped the arms of his chair, her nails digging into the leather. Father held her gaze.

"Besides, you should have enough left for what I need. The others are proving quite...sufficient."

Father's laugh echoed hollow through the room.

"Ah yes, how could I forget? Leaving us weaker each day to power your ambitions. How much more of my power do you require before you're satisfied? Or will you keep feeding until there's nothing left?"

I frowned. How dare he. Mother was an incredible witch. She'd spent years perfecting the Salvation Weave. Of course, it required power, but she wasn't taking all the gods' strength. It was all temporary. I drummed my fingers against my thigh. No, Father was just baiting her again.

"You valued my wits when they were yours to use," she continued as if he hadn't spoken, though something dark writhed behind her eyes. "But the second I used them for myself, they became weapons. Admit it. You only prized my intellect when believing it yours to command."

Mother released the chair and stepped back.

"My mind remains my own, Odin. Don't you dare condemn me for using it to claim what I am owed."

Father shuffled his papers again, pages crumpling under his fingers.

"I never wanted to control your cleverness," he said. "Only to stop the cruelty you use for your own selfish ends."

She chuckled.

"As if you've never been cruel," she sneered.

Father's lips quirked into a small smile. He raised his head, his remaining eye hard as steel.

"The difference is I take no pleasure in cruelty as you do," he said. "Seeing that sickness in your soul is when you became disgusting to me."

Her features fractured and she slammed her fist on the table making me jump.

"You will weave these enchantments, Odin. You will conjure this storm, conjure whatever magic it takes to make it appear that Asgard remains unshaken. If you refuse me, and Skadi brings death to us all, that Midgardian blood you're so worried about spilling will be on your hands."

Father's jaw clenched, muscles fluttering beneath his beard.

For a heartbeat, a battle raged behind his eye. The desperate need to defy warring against the only path forward.

A second longer, and his shoulders sagged.

He cleared his throat, the sound rasping against silence.

"Balder, how many of Skadi's camps have your scouts sighted?"

"Why are you asking him?" Mother snapped.

"Because I know it annoys you," he said. "Now, answer me Balder."

"T-Ten," I forced out, hating this familiar position between hammer and anvil. "And more are being built."

Mother smoldered beside me, and I prayed I'd not have to hear another lecture about undermining her authority. We needed this done, and quickly, and I'd play whatever game necessary to get Asgard protected as fast as possible.

"And where exactly are they located?" He cracked open another book, releasing a cloud of must that tickled my nose.

"You don't require that information, you just need to do what I command—"

"I need to know what direction the storm will come from to make it as realistic as possible," he said. "Knowing Skadi's location is rather important for that purpose, wouldn't you agree?"

Mother fumed.

"Answer me, Balder."

"East of the Ifingr," I mumbled.

He nodded, quill scratching against parchment as he crammed notes into margins. Something caught the candle-light on his desk. A ring I hadn't noticed before. A gaudy garnet that seemed wrong on his finger, more suited to Loki's flashy tastes than Father's usual restraint. Loki always loved to strut around in embroidered silks like a preening peacock. Why would Father wear something like that unless —no, that was absurd.

"I see." He turned the page. "Understand this, wife. The enchantments you want will only buy days at most. Skadi is no fool, unlike you."

I clenched my jaw until pain shot through my temples, swallowing words sharp as broken porcelain. The old familiar rage bubbled up. That need to shield her, protect her, make him see.

"This is only a temporary obstacle," I said, squaring my shoulders, voice steadier than I felt. "Mother will keep the throne, and the Salvation Weave will be sealed."

Father chuckled, that low, knowing sound that had haunted my childhood, the one that made me feel small and foolish no matter my age or conviction.

"Yes, I'm sure you believe that," he said. "Now, remove these cuffs so I can set to work."

12

DINNER IN HEL

LOKI

Hel

The only path to save all our hides was accepting Odin's bargain.

And, I suppose, helping Asgard and protecting Midgard and the Nine Worlds was the right thing to do.

Sigyn always told me that we should help even our enemies, which I always found a damn shame. Nothing beat the satisfaction of stabbing them instead.

I despised how my fingers trembled as I scratched the symbol Odin had shown me onto the parchment. The runes burned black against the yellowed paper, each stroke a reminder of the bargain I'd struck. The corners crackled as I folded it and shoved it deep into my pocket, where it pressed against my thigh.

Gods. Convincing my children was going to be a bitch.

* * *

HEL PRESIDED over our bleak gathering, perched at one end of the ebony table that had been rubbed and rubbed with oil.

My joints ached from the chill that seeped from the stone walls and floor, the kind of cold that could turn marrow to ice. I knew heating such a large space cost a small kingdom's worth of gold, but this went beyond a tad extreme.

I craved nothing more than a sip of the wine in front of me to take the edge off the cold, but I didn't dare touch the goblet. I didn't want any encores of what had happened to me earlier. And then there were the carved figures writhing in agony along the columns, their faces twisted in silent screams as they held up the vaulted ceiling.

Not at all creepy when trying to enjoy dinner, not that there was much for me to enjoy.

Fenrir and Jorg murmured to each other, their conversation a faint buzz in my ears. I stabbed at the bland chicken on my plate, pushing a boiled potato through congealed gravy. My stomach roiled.

"What a wonderful meal you've had prepared, Sister." Jormungand filled Hel's glass with blood-red wine.

"Yes, the lamb is exceptionally rare." Her lips hinted at a fleeting smile before returning to her favorite solemn expression.

Hel curled her rotting fingers around a platter of roasted tomatoes and garlic, passing it to Jormungand. He scooped out a spoonful, then reached across the table to hand it to me. As I stretched out to take it, he stood abruptly and leaned over the table, passing the platter to Fenrir without a word.

I withdrew my outstretched hand, letting it drop to my lap.

Of course.

I twisted my lips through my grimace into what I hoped passed for a smile.

"How nice to be having dinner together again as a family," I said.

Silence hardened the space, broken only by the screech of silver against bone china and the occasional gulp of wine. Hel chewed aggressively. Jorg tilted the crystal decanter, letting claret splash into his glass. Fenrir speared a tomato, its juice bleeding across the black roses painted on his plate.

Well, I suppose I'd rather have silence than having curses shouted in my direction.

"What has it been?" I continued. "Three thousand years?"

Hel twisted her knife and glared at me.

"I lost count after the first five." Hel sliced through the lamb on her plate, crimson juices spilling out.

A second awkward hush fell, punctuated by the steady drip of wax onto the table from the wrought-iron candelabras.

"We just need your mother here to complete the reunion," I said, injecting false cheer into each word at the thought.

Jorg scoffed, his sharp features etched in shadows and shivering golds of candlelight.

"So you two can argue about which is best to serve at Yule, roasted boar or smoked venison?" he asked, rolling his eyes.

Gods. He always brought that up.

"You have the palate of a troll if you think tough old boar compares to the delicate flavor of well-smoked venison," I said. "We had a few differing opinions from time to time —"...*on everything and anything...*"—We got along well."

Fenrir's eyebrow arched, a gesture that reminded me too much of his mother.

"I remember mostly screaming," he said.

"You and mother always were at each other's throats," Hel added.

Fenrir's fork hovered over his poached blue trout. His face twisted as if he'd caught a whiff of the rotting corpses Hel kept in her parlor as conversation pieces.

"What's wrong with your trout, Fenrir?" Hel asked.

His gaze locked onto the fish's glassy eyes staring back at him.

"I don't eat meat."

"That's why I served you fish. Fish is practically a vegetable."

"It has a face."

Hel drummed against the table as she considered this, then seized the crystal dish of caviar.

"Would you rather have caviar, then? No faces!"

Fenrir's nose crinkled as she heaped the black pearls onto his plate, each spoonful landing with a wet splat. His hand shook as he pushed the plate away, nearly toppling his water glass.

"Here." I slid my plate towards him. "Eat this potato. You appreciate these dug up stems more than I do."

Jorg extracted a cigarette from his silver case and touched the flame of a candle to the tip. The paper crackled as he drew deep, his cheeks catching shadows.

"I really must compliment you, Father." Jorg exhaled the words with his smoke. "I assumed your presence here was a mere obligation. That you'd never come to visit of your own free will. But how wrong I was."

Smoke curled from his nostrils.

My jaw set.

"You really know how to compliment," I forced through a stiff smile.

"Now I see," he said. "You got yourself cursed to the underworld on purpose. All because you wanted to enjoy spending some quality time with your family."

He reclined in his chair, drawing slow on his cigarette, the ember burning bright with each pull.

I glared at him and twirled the goblet between my fingers, weighing the risks of drinking it against the satisfaction it would provide.

Keep it together.

"Jorg, you have a right to be angry."

His smug smile curdled like spoiled milk.

"Oh, I am glad to know I have a right to be angry about being abandoned to the gods. Thank you."

He crushed his cigarette into his plate, the ashes mixing with the remnants of the lamb.

"I didn't want to see you taken from the Ironwood, but your mother and I had to give you all the best chance of survival. It was to protect you."

"You let the gods take your children so you could please the *great and mighty* Alfather."

Anger blazed beneath my skin, threatening to burst through.

This conversation was dissolving into vinegar.

"I think we should discuss the more pressing matter at hand," I said, forcing steel into my voice. "We are all at risk with this curse."

Hel lifted a piece of lamb to her lips, savoring the flavor before swallowing. Her black pantsuit embraced every curve as she settled deeper into her velvet chair.

"What more can she do to us?"

"Well, she does want me back on Lyngvi." Fenrir leaned

forward, bracing his hands on the table. "That is definitely a worse fate than being banished to Midgard for me."

"Alright," she said. "Besides that. What more can she do?"

Jorg reached across the table and placed his hand over Fenrir's, giving his knuckles a squeeze.

"Don't let Father scare you, Fen," Jorg said, his expression set in determined lines. "I will protect you."

Hel nodded in agreement.

A pretty thought.

And it was my turn to laugh.

"You can't protect Fenrir from this," I said. "The Salvation Weave is worse than we thought, and it will damn us all, because we are all the key to her sealing the curse."

"All? How so," he said. "This I *must* hear."

I explained everything Odin had told me. How Frigg needed all four of us to seal her curse. How each of us was an integral cog in her wheel of horror. How she would tear out Hel's guts to bind me to the earth for eternity...

"Hel and I are the grand finale. She must have the complete set to finish what Yggdrasil commanded," I said. "And then Ragnarok is no longer a threat."

"Frigg is using blood ties to seal her curse?" Jorg asked. "I didn't realize she put blood ties into the curse. That we'd all —this...this changes things. Blood ties are unbreakable."

I nodded.

"Hence, why it is important she isn't able to seal the curse, because I don't think I need to spell out how very bad that is, not just for us, but for everyone this curse affects."

Hel shrank, the living half of her face draining to match her dead side. Her fingers clutched the armrests as if the chair might swallow her whole. I'd seen my daughter afraid only twice before. This was the first time her hands shook.

"Frigg will rip out my guts?" The words whispered past her lips. "Usually such a grim thought would thrill me, but for them to be used to tie you down?"

"Yes, it's horrifying," I said.

Her initial terror morphed into a different kind of horror entirely.

"Ew. I can't have my innards touching you."

Alright...

"Everyone the curse affects?" Jorg scoffed. "Meaning just the gods. I don't see that being such a bad thing."

"But what is a bad thing is the lovely multitude of disastrous consequences of Frigg's curse," I said. "If the curse remains unbroken, a worse fate awaits, not just for our family, but for all the realms, and especially for the Midgardians, when the Frost Giants eat them."

Fenrir's eyes stretched wide.

"Eat them?" The words tore from his throat.

"Skadi is gathering the Jotnar clans, including the Frost Giants, and marching on Asgard. And you know they will win."

"I remember Skadi at mother's parties," Jorg said. "She has quite the taste for violence. She extinguished her pipe on my newest landscape, burning right through the canvas." Jorg's lips curled. "If she now is going to kill Odin before me..."

Hel turned to Jorg.

"You said we didn't have to worry about this curse," she spat. "And now I find my brothers are going to be bound, and my person is going to be used to bind our father."

"I said we didn't have to worry *too much*," he said. "And let me remind you, my conclusions were only based on the information you gave me from Balder."

"Leave Balder out of this," Hel said. "I can't help his mother kept this from him."

I rather liked the blame sliding onto Balder's shoulders.

"Well, thanks to him, I didn't have all the facts," he said. "And my research has now suffered because of that brat." He put his head in his hands. "I knew there was a piece missing, and it being blood ties explains everything. The magic she used seemed too paltry before."

"And it's very much going to be our ruin if we don't act," I said.

"Wait," Fenrir's voice cut through our bickering. "How do you know all about the curse now? These risks. You didn't when we first arrived."

Dammit. I was hoping to avoid this.

I tapped the edge of the table, the rhythm matching my racing pulse.

"Well, I may have had a little chat with Odin in the seidr realm," I said, trying to sound casual. Calm. As if I spoke of nothing more interesting than the boiled chicken Hel had served me.

They all stared at me as if my head had rolled off.

"You're telling me all this information is from Odin?" Jorg's voice dripped poison. "I'm done."

His chair shrieked against stone as he launched to his feet, crumpling his napkin and hurling it onto the table.

"Jorg," Fenrir's voice softened. "Please stay. Listen to what he has to say. You know this is serious."

"The problem is I *am* listening, and—Look, it is unfortunate about the Midgardians," Jorg said. "Their art and literature weren't bad. Keats was an alright poet. But this is entirely too much."

Fenrir looked at Jorg in that gentle way that only he

could. As if looking at a child who simply couldn't understand.

I stood, drawing to my full height. Without Jorg's help, any hope of putting Odin back on the throne crumbled into dust. Along with my golden apple.

"Look," I said. "You admitted there was a missing vital piece. His words complete the picture. Doesn't that prove his claim?"

Jormungand's lips thinned. He released a long breath, his shoulders sagging. He slumped back into his chair and reached for another cigarette.

"Fine." Smoke coiled from his lips. "From everything you've said, it sounds like we just need to outrun Frigg's curse until Skadi and Jotunheim wins. I'm sure we could work out some deal with them—"

"And how is that better?" Fenrir cut in. "Jotunheim is no friend to us."

I nodded.

"Jotunheim fears you all equally as Frigg," I said. "Your heads will end up impaled on a Jotun spear. Why do you think your Mother and I never slept due to worry about you three?"

"Wait," Hel's voice cracked. "But if Jotunheim takes Asgard, that means Skadi will take Balder." Her nails gouged the table edge. "I cannot allow that to happen."

How the loss of Balder could be so intolerable to her, I couldn't understand.

"This is ridiculous." Jorg slashed his hand through the smoke. "Because of your boyfriend, you expect me to what? Fight Skadi in one-on-one combat while juggling not getting cursed?"

"I will slit her throat," Hel snarled.

"This is all extremely confusing." Fenrir tapped his

fingers against the lacquered table. "I can't even keep straight who is after me at this point. What is the solution? How do we stop Frigg from sealing her curse and us getting bound? What can we do to prevent those poor Midgardians from getting eaten?"

"H—How?" I asked. "Oh, you want to know that bit...I suppose it makes sense. Well, there is a way—we just—would any of you like more wine? I think that may help us all be in a better mood—"

"We *what*?" Hel asked, raising an eyebrow.

"Well." My hand found the back of my neck. "It's actually a very simple solution...we..."

The collar of my shirt seemed to tighten. Braggi better write an entire opera in my honor for this.

"We help Odin break the curse."

"Help Odin?"

Jorg's jaw swung loose, but Hel's gaped wider. Fenrir's groan muffled behind his dragging palms.

"Well, Odin is rather good at breaking curses, and he already has what he needs to enact the spell except for one small part and then—"

"And then?"

"And then, to get our lives back and not all live in a world ruled by the curse's consequences and Jotnar rule, we help the gods fight Skadi and the Frost Giants."

"Help the gods?"

"Yes. You see, Asgard isn't strong enough on their own to fight all of Jotunheim, especially with the Frost Giants. Fenrir and Jorg do their little shifting tricks, and with your army Hel—"

"*My army?*"

"Yes. Your army. And we save all our hides. Easy!"

"I rather die at the end of a Jotun spear than help the

gods," Jorg spat. "Than help Odin back on the throne after what he did to me."

"I'm not denying he is an asshole," I said. "But, there is more to all of this—"

"Yes, Odin dumping me out in the Bermuda Triangle was definitely the act of a stand-up guy."

Jorg's right eye twitched as he took another drag. Even without my chaos to reveal lies, something in his voice rang hollow. But did Jorg's secrets really matter? I wouldn't justify Odin dumping Jorg there. Odin's actions betrayed his promise that Jormungand would roam the seas freely.

I sighed.

Everything would be fine. Totally, totally fine.

"Look, I understand wanting the gods to rot. I started Ragnarok, remember? I was going to burn them all, but things have changed. I have changed. And I highly doubt you would make these jokes if you understood what being bound to the earth meant. Believe me, I was tied to a rock in the darkness, with venom searing my eyes and throat, bound with..." my voice splintered. I met Hel's gaze. "...This is serious, and it will happen, and I am doing everything I can to make sure you do not suffer how I suffered. And, to be frank, it was an experience I really don't want again. I learned the hard way you cannot escape fate, and fate is coming for all of us with this curse."

If crickets had existed in the underworld, their chirps would have been thunderous.

"And how will Odin break the curse?" Hel asked.

I kept my relief hidden behind carved features. Her interest, however slight, was the first crack in the wall.

"He has an incantation that will break the curse and—"

"An act of love can break a curse," Jorg interrupted. "We don't need this incantation."

"Yes, but we don't have the luxury of waiting around, wondering what this act of love could be. That's the problem," I said.

"And even if we knew what it was, that knowledge would corrupt the motivation, and the curse would never be broken," Fenrir added.

"He's right," I said. "No, the only way to break it is with this spell Odin has. There's just one small, insignificant little problem. The final words needed to be said are written in the language of Muspel, and only Sigyn can translate it."

I reached into my pocket and pulled out the folded paper, my fingers smoothing the creases. The symbol's sharp lines seemed to writhe in the candlelight as I held it up.

Jorg leaned across the table, arm stretching past the platters, and plucked it from my grasp with those long, elegant fingers of his. My jaw tightened at his presumption, but at least his eyes had lost that bored glaze.

"And Sigyn can read this?" he asked, turning the paper in his hands as if hoping the runes would suddenly make sense.

"Only one touched by Surtr can read these runes," I said. "Surtr possessed Sigyn. His essence burned through her very soul." My voice caught on the memory. "We must have her translate what's written here, otherwise Odin can't complete the spell to break the curse."

He stretched back across the table and pressed the paper into my palm without a single barbed comment or critique. A miracle in itself.

"Of course, to do that, I have to find her first, which will be its own challenge," I said. "And then she performs a very minor blood ritual with my dagger *Laevateinn*, and bing bang boom, Odin gets the transmission, and we have ourselves a broken curse."

"Say we find Sigyn. Say she reads these runes, does the ritual, and sends the translation to Odin. What if Odin still can't break it?" Fenrir's question hung like an executioner's blade.

I didn't want to think of that possibility. Because it was too likely he'd fail.

"Not a concern," I said. "Focus on the other opportunity this gives."

"Opportunity?"

"After we break the curse, after we ensure that we won't be bound, and Hel keeps her insides, well, inside of her, we will reclaim our lives by fighting alongside the gods against Skadi and Jotunheim. We'd show the worlds we're not enemies, but heroes," I said. "This would provide a hearty reward. Such as Odin pardoning us for returning him to power."

I plastered on my biggest, most sincere smile.

I couldn't tell him about my own opportunity with Odin promising me the apple. Definitely something to mention never.

Jorg laughed again, colder this time.

"How drunk are you?"

"Sadly, very sober," I said.

"Then you're more of a fool than I ever thought, and that's hard to top."

Hel narrowed her eyes and traced the diamond patterns on her shoulders. Doubt etched every line of her face.

"And what makes you think Odin would pardon us?" Hel asked.

"It would only be polite," I said.

"Polite would have been releasing us after Ragnarok when he knew the call drove us to act," Fenrir said.

"It's up to you," I said. "Prove yourself an asset, gain your freedom, or stay in this lovely..." I looked at the pile of bones in the back corner "...place, waiting for Frigg to finish you all off, because she will before Skadi breaks down her doors and takes Balder back to Jotunheim."

"Curses. Frost Giants. I don't care," Jorg said. "This is madness and—"

"Stop it," Hel commanded. She fixed me with her coldest stare. "Father, you swear to me what you say will come to pass?"

I held her gaze.

"It will," I said.

She nodded.

"If translating this incantation is all that stands between us breaking this curse and keeping Balder from becoming Skadi's, if this can save my brothers, can save you and I from becoming Frigg's grand finale..." She heaved a deep breath. "I can't believe I'm doing this, but I know how to find Sigyn."

13
____

BONE VOYAGE

"I cannot believe it's come to this. Me helping you. Again," Hel said, her stiletto heels clicking against stone as she walked down the corridor. The silver buttons on her black suit jacket winked in the torchlight. "I swore I'd rather see you squashed and scraped off my shoe first."

Yes. I suppose I should be grateful she hadn't rammed her spear through my backside as she'd sworn.

The heavy oak door groaned on its hinges, and Hel's rings flashed as she flung it wide to her study. I congratulated myself on not saying a word about the shelves that sagged under leather-bound volumes on embalming, or the specimens that dotted the walls—moths with wings spread like parchment and centipedes frozen mid-crawl along the green silk wallpaper. The beetles' shells gleamed, reflecting the flames that devoured logs in a hearth large enough to roast a boar.

I walked deeper into the room until my gaze snagged on an ornate globe perched atop a desk carved with serpents and wolves. The hairs on the back of my neck bristled. The sphere's surface churned and pulsed with light that seemed to breathe, and I understood what kind of magic Hel possessed.

"I've owned this little beauty for quite a while." Pride threaded through her words as she traced constellations across the globe's surface. "Just in case fate tried to part us again, this would always lead me to Balder."

I'd heard tales of such artifacts that could track beings across the Nine Worlds, but they were quite rare. And if you did find one, it was usually tucked away in some dragon hoard, which didn't make it the most accessible.

"How does it work?" Fenrir leaned forward, loose strands of dark hair falling from his bun. His flannel sleeves pushed up as he reached towards the white sphere.

"Simple." A smile slithered across her lips, the dead side curling back to reveal more teeth.

She clamped around my wrist.

"What are you—"

A small blade flashed in her other hand, and before I could tug back, she jabbed my fingertip.

"Ow!" The sting drew a hiss through my teeth. "That hurt."

Hel's smile widened and she tightened her grip as she squeezed my finger. Blood welled up like a small ruby from the prick.

"A little warning would have been nice. I'm mortal, I could get sepsis now—"

"Shut up about your finger, and watch," she said, yanking my hand over the globe.

The drop of blood struck the swirling surface. A red line flowed and curved across the map, winding through the jagged mountains of Jotunheim, skirting the towers of

Asgard, and plunging straight for Midgard. The trail slowed, pooling in the city where it all began.

My heart hammered against my ribs as memories flooded back. The warmth of Sigyn's smile in that candlelit house in Heuburg, the way sunlight had struck her face through the cathedral's stained glass when I realized I loved her. Basel. Of all places, the curse had sent her there. My mind skittered away from darker memories, where everything had unraveled...

"She's in Basel?" Fenrir tugged at his collar, his whisper rough with disbelief. "Why would Frigg send her there?"

"I don't know," I said, forcing my thoughts back to the present. "But I'm sure it ties into whatever this curse demands."

"Do you think she plays more of a part in this?" Jorg's voice was barely a whisper. "A component like us?"

My stomach turned to ice at the thought.

I pushed the questions away, clinging to the one certain thing I had.

I knew where Sigyn was.

Of course, I still needed magic to bypass my own curse, and claw my way from the depths of Hel before I could reach her. And, with any luck, I'd make it out with all my pieces and parts intact.

Maybe, just maybe, things were finally looking up for me.

"You're helping me...even after I...Why?" I asked Hel, emotion threatening to strangle my words.

Fenrir's boots scuffed across the floor as he pulled Jorg to the corner, where a stone gargoyle crouched with a mouth full of fangs. Their shoulders hunched together, heads bowed as they whispered in hushed tones. Their eyes darted towards me every few seconds.

Hel's shoulders rose and fell, diamonds sparking like stars across her jacket's sharp edges. But her usual hardened expression cracked for a heartbeat.

"Because, probably stupidly, no, it is stupid, I believe you about the curse, about the ramifications," she said. "I've felt Frigg is plotting something darker, and I know Balder means it when he says he will protect me, but...against his mother? His protection only stretches so far. So I must do what I can to protect us both."

Her love for him was almost endearing. If I hadn't found it so disgusting, I would have felt a tug at my heart.

"And does this help also include giving me your army?" My voice steadied as I straightened my spine. "They'd be a real asset. If I could borrow just a few. Preferably the ones who still have all their bones attached."

Hel's lungs emptied in a long exhale, the kind reserved for particularly dense children.

"Always asking for a foot when given an inch," she said, her rings clinking against the carved desk. "And what makes you think I even still have an army to lend? With Frigg's claws sunk into my realm, those soldiers march to her drum now." She arched an eyebrow. "But please, tell me more about how you'd like to borrow them."

I could feel my request crumbling to ash. Of course, she couldn't hand out soldiers like party favors, not with Frigg pulling the strings. Unless some miracle knocked the Queen of Asgard off her throne, that army was out of reach.

"I would have thought me offering you a means of leaving here would be sufficient," she said.

"What about that one skeleton guard who keeps confusing his helmet for a flower pot? Wait. A way out. What are you talking about?"

She dipped her hand into her silk jacket pocket and pulled out a coin. The metal gleamed like polished obsidian. Perfectly round. Intricate runic engravings along the edges. She threw it spinning through the air towards me. I snatched it mid-flight, and the weight settled into my palm, the surface sleek as oil, marbled with threads of silver.

"Magic?" I examined the coin, but as I rolled it between my fingers, something stirred within the metal. A faint vibration that sent electricity crawling up my neck, raising every hair.

"You're the only one that needs it to walk out of here being cursed and all." A smile sliced across her face. "It will let you bypass the Salvation Weave and leave the underworld."

"You said you didn't have any magic." I clenched the coin tighter.

"I know what I said," she replied evenly. "But you aren't the only one capable of telling a lie. And I now stand something to lose if Frigg isn't stopped."

The coin grew warmer in my grasp as the magic intensified its thrum. Power throbbed against my skin, alluring yet unsettling, like a heartbeat in my palm.

"Frigg is oblivious to its existence. And she especially doesn't know that this coin grants passage through the underworld's gates. No matter the circumstance, no matter the magic. As long as you possess the coin, you'll materialize in my throne room whole and unscathed, even if your soul gets blasted into a million pieces."

I twisted the coin between thumb and forefinger, tracing each rune carved into the obsidian surface. The metal warmed further beneath my touch.

"How did you create such a piece?" I asked.

The harsh lines on Hel's face softened.

"There is no stronger magic than true love. You of all should know that," she said. "I harvested the essence of our bond during the blood moon, when Balder and I met in secret. I then fused the magic of our love into the metal."

Oh.

"Are you saying the magic fueling this coin is—"

"Balder and my love for each other? Yes," Ice crystallized in her voice once more. "That's exactly what I'm saying. I created it so if Odin or Frigg ever separated us again, we'd have a way back to each other. One of us could use it to breach the barriers between realms, slip past any magic." Her lips twisted. "Though I never imagined I'd be using it to save your sorry hide, Father. But at least I think of all possibilities, unlike you."

For two agonizing seconds, I considered whether I preferred staying cursed, or using anything fueled by Balder and Hel's *love*.

"I'm allowing you a one day head start before I tell Frigg about your *miraculous* escape from the underworld." Hel leaned back against the desk. The silk shirt beneath her jacket dipped low, exposing the stark line where living flesh met death. "However, there are conditions."

Of course there were. Why would anything ever be easy?

"Alright, how many fingers do you need?" Metal scraped against my knuckles as I twisted off my rings. "Or is this a 'part of my soul' type thing?"

Hel's glare struck like an axe. I shoved my rings back onto my fingers. Alright. No limb sacrifice. That's mildly reassuring.

"You must guard this coin more preciously than your own life," she said. "You cannot separate it from yourself, not even for a moment."

"I'll end up right back in the underworld?" The coin's pulse quickened against my palm while I rotated it.

That didn't seem so bad. I slipped the coin into my pocket, its warmth seeping through the silk lining.

"Yes, you'll end up back here, because you'll lose its protection from the Salvation Weave," she said. "And there will be no second chances. This is the last of my magic, and once it's gone, you're stuck here. Forever." Her eyes narrowed. "So don't lose it if you enjoy breathing surface air. And don't come crawling back if you fail, because if you waste my coin, I'll make sure you beg for Frigg to hurry up and bind you to that rock."

Ah, and there was the catch.

Hel walked over to a satin cord dangling beside the fireplace and gave it a firm pull. The rope creaked under her grip. Gears ground and chains rattled through hidden passages as flames leaped higher in the hearth, their heat battling the bone-deep chill that crept through the chamber.

My hand caught her wrist before she could turn away.

"Hel, come with me," I said. "You can't stay here. You and your brothers need to go into hiding—"

She stilled under my touch, and for a second, I saw not the Queen of the Dead, but my daughter. The child I'd failed to protect so many times before.

"You just have the curse keeping you here, but me..." Fear cracked through her words. "If I would dare step foot out of the underworld and break the terms of my banishment..." She shook her head, silver earrings glinting in the firelight. She pressed the coin harder into my palm. "The price is too great for that risk. Break this curse, Father. That's how you keep me safe."

My chest constricted. Another prison, another banishment. All because of me. My actions during Ragnarok now forced her to wait like prey. Dread coiled in my gut as I watched her straighten her suit jacket, reinforce her walls. I could not fail her. Not this time. Not again.

A servant, well, bones wrapped in paper thin-skin in the appearance of a servant, crossed the flagstones and handed Hel a wool cloak.

"Follow me." The cloak settled across her shoulders. "I'll take you to the secret path, the same one Balder uses. It will keep you hidden from Frigg's sight."

I braced myself, because the way out of Hel was always worse than the way in. If I further scuffed my Gucci loafers...

Fenrir's boots thundered behind us as he yanked Jorg forward, racing to join us.

* * *

I STEPPED on something squishy and tried not to consider what it could be. The silk of my shirt clung to my sweat-dampened back.

Fenrir let out a soft whimper behind me, his flannel sleeve brushing against the wall as he hugged close to it.

Cockroaches scuttled out of our way the deeper we ventured. The plink of water droplets echoed off the slick walls covered in fungi and moss. The underworld pressed down on my shoulders, squeezed my chest, suffocating, as if it wanted to crush me inside itself.

My breath grew harsh and rapid, each inhale choked with mildew and rot.

I licked the condensation from my lips. The taste of venom flooded my mouth. The dark walls melted together until all I saw was the cave's damp stone. My wrists and ankles burned as if the bonds branded my skin. Screams rang in my ears. Shadows pinned me down.

I am safe. I am not in danger.

I breathed the cold air until my racing heart steadied, fingers pressed against the rough wall to ground myself.

The walls came back into focus.

Rats scurried past our feet, their tiny paws scuttling in the gloom. I focused on their squeals, each one bringing me back to reality, each sound an anchor to the now.

I am safe. I am not in danger.

Hel rifled through a ring of rusty keys until one fit the iron door's lock. The gate's shriek pierced the dank hall as she planted her heel and shoved it open, her pantsuit collecting cobwebs.

Bones lay scattered across the ground and withered flesh still clung to several skeletons sprawled against the walls.

"Ah, spinal columns, what every hallway needs for that welcoming touch," I said, brushing dust from my silk shirt. "Really ties the space together."

Fenrir wrinkled his nose and looked away, only to come face to face with a skull rammed into a rusted spike. He covered his mouth with his hand and gagged.

Jorg shook his head, stepping carefully around a pile of femur bones and ribcages.

"This will take you out," Hel said, gesturing at a rickety boat at the lake's edge.

Algae slicked the water's surface.

"If you say the passage is through the sewer, Hel..." I swatted away a writhing maggot clinging to my sleeve.

"No, not the sewer," Hel said, lips curving. "But try not to rouse the kraken who lives at the end of the lake. I'd hate to come back down here to retrieve your corpse."

Lovely.

I suppose it was time to get this show on the road.

I grasped the boat's rough wooden sides and stepped in, nearly losing my footing as it rocked beneath me. My shoulder sent sharp stabs of pain through me with each jolt.

These risks would have absolutely delighted me before. Death on the line gave everything more of a thrill.

But this was about more than me now. This was about all of us.

And the odds were definitely not in my favor.

Fenrir reached out and steadied me, his warm hand gripping my arm.

"I'm coming with you," he said, eyes meeting mine.

"No, Fenrir," I said, water taping against the boat. "You and your brother must go into hiding before Frigg finds you. If she curses you and Jorg, there will be no breaking the Salvation Weave, ever. All hope will be completely and utterly lost. Together we are at greater risk—"

He clasped his hand over mine, gripping.

"Stop," he said. "We are at risk regardless where we go, and you should know better than anyone. There is no hiding from the Aesir for long. At least this way, I can be with you and help find Sigyn and stop this curse. If I can ensure even one Midgardian avoids being eaten because of Frigg's actions..." He shuddered. "Then I will do my best to save lives. Including yours."

"I'm fit as a fiddle!" I said, waving my hand and—I winced as another jab tore through my muscle.

Fenrir's gaze dropped to my shoulder, his jaw tightening.

"A piece of cheese can finish you off," he said, fingers tightening on mine. "I will stay with you, until the end, whatever the end may be."

I searched his expression, seeing resolution as hard as iron there.

"Are you sure?"

He nodded, a faint smile tugging at the corner of his lips.

"I'm very sure," Jorg said. "I'm very sure this is complete suicide, but I suppose it's best to see Midgard now, before it's destroyed. I may never get the chance again."

"Wait, you are also coming?" I blurted in surprise.

"I'm only coming to protect Fenrir from Frigg. And from you," he said. "I told him I wouldn't let him get cursed, and I won't. I don't trust you to do that for a myriad of reasons."

Jorg hopped into the boat, splashing water over, and into my Gucci loafers.

My eye twitched, and I fought back a comment about the cost of Italian leather.

Fenrir grabbed the weathered oars, his muscles flexing beneath his flannel as he settled them into the rusted locks. He rowed, each stroke sending ripples across the dark water. The boat groaned as we pulled away from the shore.

"Maybe it would be better you stay here, after all, Jorg," I said, wiping off what water I could with my sleeve. "If you get caught breaking your banishment, I just couldn't live with myself, even though I'd truly miss your supportive nature."

Jorg smirked, shifting his weight in the rocking boat. A cruel glint lit his eyes that mirrored my own far too closely.

"And pass up such a good wager? Watching you fail is worth the price of returning to the sea."

"What wager?" The boat creaked beneath us as I turned to face them fully.

A faint blush tinged Fenrir's rough stubble as he glanced between us.

"I want him to see what I know to be true about you," Fenrir mumbled, keeping a steady rhythm with the oars.

Jorg shot me a nasty grin.

"Yes, I want to see if Fenrir's right that you've changed." His tone dripped with skepticism. "I bet him you haven't. Don't let me down."

14

A THOR(NY) CONVERSATION

BALDER

Asgard

Thor towered over me, his frame a muscular mountain compared to mine. A smile hid behind a tangle of red whiskers. Mead sloshed in the clay jug he gripped, while mischief glinted in his small eyes.

"Return Mjolnir and rid me of this filthy curse—" He clawed at his chest with his free hand as if trying to tear away an invisible web. "—and I may start thinking about considering accepting Frigg's rule."

His voice rumbled like thunder through the hall, rattling shields from their hooks and shuddering the flagstones beneath our boots. The coffered ceilings vaulted far overhead, where centuries of smoke from the immense hearth had blackened the oak beams.

"The best I can do is remove the binding cuffs," I said, trying to sound reassuring. "Once you agree to help Mother, I can free what power you still have."

His shoulders sagged.

"I want more than just these damn cuffs off," he said. "This curse...it's feeding on me. Drains me day by day." He flexed his hands, covered in calluses. "Even my thunder feels distant."

"I assure you, the draining is all a temporary...uh...side-effect," I stammered, though uncertainty prickled in my gut. "This is why, I beg you Thor, please pledge to Mother, and I'm sure after you prove your loyalty by helping us against Skadi, she will return your powers."

Thor's stare intensified, his bushy eyebrows pinching together.

"Will she?" he asked. "In my experience, things that feed off of you never end well."

His words carried a weight I chose to ignore.

He tilted the jug to his lips and guzzled it down, mead flowing through his beard and soaking his already stained tunic. He flung the ceramic behind his shoulder. The jug exploded against a pillar, shards skittering across stone and bearskin rugs.

"Now, give me Mjolnir." His smile vanished, teeth baring. Even without his full power, his presence filled the chamber like an approaching storm. I took a step back.

Thankfully, they removed his battle-axes, along with every other weapon that usually littered the walls and corners of his chambers. Only the heads of stags and moose remained hanging over the crackling fire.

"As I've already told you a hundred times," I said, my patience fraying. "Mjolnir is yours once you pledge yourself to Mother and agree to defend Asgard beneath her banner. Make this promise and she will keep hers."

I craned my neck to meet his gaze, stifling a wince as my toes squished in my new boots, made from the stiffest, most unforgiving leather I could find. Just in case Skadi would—well, the trick worked once before.

He harrumphed and crossed his arms over his broad chest.

"Then where's my roasted ox?" His breath wafted across the space between us, heavy with mead and meat. "I requested it an hour ago. You aren't doing a good job of convincing me she keeps her promises."

He was exhausting me.

I collapsed into the leather chair by the fire, the cushion covered in animal skins sagging under me. I threaded my fingers through my hair, fighting the urge to tear it out by the roots. But Mother told me to indulge him. We needed him to win against Skadi, though I wasn't sure Thor alone would be enough to save us anymore.

Frost Giants had been spotted marching towards Asgard, and all beneath Skadi's flag. This changed everything.

With a thump and a creak, Thor's bulk dropped into a massive wingback chair across from me. He pulled out a ham hock from somewhere in his tunic and tore into it.

"The kitchen cannot cook an entire ox in an hour," I said, pinching the bridge of my nose. "Be reasonable."

He ripped flesh off the bone with his teeth and sucked his fingers clean, each smack of his lips grating.

"You promised me anything, and I said I wanted ox with my tea." Cartilage crunched between his molars as he stripped the last bits of meat. "I'm starving."

He tossed the cleaned bone into a growing pile of ribs and legs. Patting his large stomach, he produced a belch that rattled the antlers on the wall. Yes, I saw how much he 'starved.'

Thor walked over to the feast table, his boots crushing breadcrumbs and vegetable scraps. Servants darted around him, snatching half-eaten Monte Cristo sandwiches and congealed venison pies from the floor. Fresh platters clattered onto the oak table—Thor's fourth feast that day—while bowls of mashed potatoes steamed in the afternoon light.

He picked up another bottle of mead, bringing it to his nose. The corners of his mouth twisted downward.

"What's wrong this time?" I asked.

"I hate to be a bother," he said.

"Thor, if you're about to request a peacock pie—"

"This mead isn't the good stuff," he said. "Where's the orange blossom?"

I raised an eyebrow.

"You seriously expect Midsomer mead? Impossible. That's months out of season."

He let out a deep sigh and gave a slight shrug, his eyes fixing on me with a gaze that said I was the idiot in this conversation.

Gods. I should have insisted Mother send Freya instead, but she believed our shared blood gave me an advantage. I was his half-brother. That carried some weight.

"More unfulfilled promises," he said. "You really aren't succeeding at this convincing thing."

He slammed the bottle against wood, making the table shudder. A tower of meat pies swayed, gravy oozing from their crusts.

I heaved a sigh that felt dragged from my bones. Even without his weapons, Thor was grinding my resolve to dust faster than if he had his seax at my throat.

"Tell me what you want," I said, leaning close enough to smell the mead on his breath. "We need you on our side if —"...*if we have any hope of winning the war...*"—if...Look, I'm sure I could convince Mother to make you a general. Give you your own army. Think of all the Jotnar you could slay. This battle will be glorious, and I know how grumpy you'd be to miss that."

Please, please, please just accept and help...

Thor scoffed.

"Father let me knock out trouble on my own, *un-cursed*," he said, cracking his knuckles. "He gave me one job. Protect the realms from the Jotnar, especially those damned hungry Frost Giants terrorizing Midgard. And that's what I did until now. Being a general?" He snorted. "Sitting in stuffy war rooms, moving tiny flags across maps while others get to swing their weapons? No thank you. A warrior's place is in the thick of battle, where Mjolnir can crack Jotnar bones."

Now I understood why Loki found Thor so irritating.

"Thor, tell me what will change your mind," I said. "I will make sure you get what you want."

That twinkle of amusement sparked in his eyes again.

"You sound desperate, brother," he said. "However, as I said, I will pledge to Frigg if you meet my demands."

Parchment crinkled as Thor yanked a tattered scroll from his belt. He handed me the paper, and I unrolled yards of demands scrawled in his rough hand.

He had to be joking.

"An entire tavern built in your quarters? With a mead fountain?" I crumpled the list into a tight little ball and threw it at his chest. "This list is ridiculous."

Thor picked a silver cat hair from his red beard.

"Let's start with ridiculous." He threw the wadded parchment back at me, the paper striking my forehead before tumbling into my lap. "It can't be any more ridiculous than this entire curse nonsense."

I understood his game now. He wanted to be difficult. He wasn't as stupid as people believed.

"I see what you're doing," I said. "You're mocking us. You're abusing my Mother's generosity with no intention of ever oathing to her."

His amusement vanished into rage. He surged to his feet, lightning crackling in his eyes, but with his curse and cuffs, his fury was all sound and no strike.

"And what you're doing isn't mocking?" His bellow shook dust from the rafters. "You think food and drink is enough to sway me to betray Father? Especially food full of Freya's cat hair. Your mother—" His chest heaved as he sucked in a breath. "Your mother could have spared Loki's children, but instead here we are, not because of Father allowing the Destroyer to wander around freely, but because *she* ignited the torch of Ragnarok by killing innocents. She made the prophecy come to pass with her actions."

"Shut up," I said. "I don't need to hear all this again—"

"You know it's true."

"No. I mean. Well...it's...it's complicated."

The memories from that night tore at my mind like hungry wolves, and I fought to cage them. And the thousand *what ifs* followed.

What if she faced such a choice again? Would she...

No. She wouldn't.

She promised me.

I was sure of it.

"Complicated," he repeated, the word dripping with contempt. "It's actually not complicated at all. Your mother is the worst. No person should ever have endured what Loki endured that night. What Sigyn endured...And still Frigg didn't leave that poor girl alone. After, when your mother..." His words trailed into silence.

After?

I leaned forward in my chair, leather creaking beneath

me. The fire spit and popped in the hearth, filling the silence.

"When my mother what?"

His gaze settled on his hands.

"I won't turn on Father for her," he said. "She can't ever leave well enough alone."

Anger flooded me. My fingernails bit crescents into my palms as I clenched my fists. I wasn't sure which infuriated me more. His stupid, stupid lies, or my gnawing envy at his freedom to choose.

"I don't know what you're going on about, but I'm sure it's all the result of too much mead," I snapped. "Father is the one who oath bound himself to Loki. To chaos. To the Destroyer. But yes, blame my Mother."

Thor laughed, filling the room with summer thunder again, rattling the plates across the table.

"Your mother deserves every bit of blame she receives." His fist struck the chair arm. "For all of it."

I lunged forward, seizing his prized drinking horn from his belt. Before he could react, I hurled it into the fire. The horn crackled and popped as flames licked its surface, the same horn Father had gifted him after his first giant-slaying.

"Now you've done it!" he roared, shooting to his feet, his face flushing crimson beneath his beard.

"Mother watched her husband choose the Destroyer over Asgard. Over her," I said, standing my ground despite my racing heart. "Father harbored chaos within our walls. And you all accepted it. You stood aside while Father abandoned his duties as Alfather. While he neglected the safety of the entire Nine Worlds. If he had obeyed Yggdrasil's commands, Mother wouldn't have needed to act. But I shouldn't be surprised," I spat, bitterness lacing each word. "Father betrayed Asgard, like he betrayed Mother. He abandoned us for Loki's bed. At least he was consistent in his unfaithfulness."

Thor's face scrunched in confusion.

"Father was faithful to your mother," he said. "Always. Because she made sure he had no choice."

I rolled my eyes.

"What's that supposed to mean?"

He hesitated for a second.

"He exiled my mother at Frigg's command in order to wed her. Just one of her many...conditions." Bitterness crept into his voice. "My mother was no threat, but Frigg saw rivals everywhere."

I recalled Thor's rare mentions of Jörd. She was a giantess, an earth goddess. Mother said she was a whore. I suppose I hadn't ever seen Jörd at court, though. It never occurred to me to ask why.

"As a goddess of family, Mother takes marriage seriously," I said. "I'm sure she had reason to bar Jörd from court. Any wife would want—"

"Want?" Thor laughed as he walked to the table, his heavy footsteps echoing on the stone floor. His gaze swept over the ornate silver bowls filled with exotic fruits, five-tiered cakes, and an entire roasted boar. He grabbed a loaf of bread filled with grains, drew a knife, and split the bread. "Your mother didn't just want—she demanded. She took."

He stuffed the bread with layers and layers of boar meat, dark juices soaking into the grain and dripping onto the polished table.

"Father had ended things with my mother long before Frigg started throwing her weight around," he said. "There was no lingering romance between them. But Frigg couldn't stand that my mother existed at all. Before Frigg took control of court matters, my mother's presence had never been an issue. Then suddenly I'm sneaking around like a thief just to see my own mother, all because Frigg decided she couldn't bear the sight of her in the halls."

"Mother wouldn't—"

"Wouldn't what? Control? Manipulate?" He spread mustard across the meat in thick swaths, its sharp scent sparking the air. "She enforced Father's absolute faithfulness while she flirted with every charming face at feast. And if Father so much as looked at another..." he trailed off, shaking his head.

"I won't have you speak more lies about her," I said through teeth clenched tight enough to crack. But doubt still took root.

He took a large bite of his sandwich, savoring the flavors as his body relaxed into the chair, a contented hum escaping his lips. Crumbs scattered across his beard as he chewed.

"Lies?" He sprayed breadcrumbs across my lap. "You weren't even born for most of it, and then too small to remember the rest. But I was there. I saw it all. The way she held things over Father's head. The threats. The conditions. Like a scorpion spinning her web tighter and tighter."

Spider. He meant spider.

I shifted in my seat, the wooden chair creaking beneath me.

I'm sure he *saw*, and I'm sure he was probably too full of mead to notice the truth. Just like whatever "after" he referenced concerning Mother and Sigyn.

He had to be wrong. I was certain of it.

Wasn't I?

Mother wasn't controlling. She just cared. Deeply.

But still...the thought burrowed deeper as I snatched a goblet from the table, filling it with mead. The honey-sweet liquid burned down my throat, but couldn't wash away Thor's words.

Thor decimated half the sandwich in three massive bites, crumbs pattering onto the flagstone around his boots.

"The years when Father was bound to their marriage were pure misery. Constant shifts between fighting and apologizing and promises to change. Made life right awful for everyone around them," he said, washing down his words with a swig of mead. "It was like watching someone dance with a knife to their throat."

A scoff escaped me as I shook my head, trying to dismiss the unease creeping up my spine.

"I'm sure it wasn't that bad," I said.

"Bah!" His fist crashed against the table, sending plates dancing and mead sloshing in goblets. "Screaming matches at dinner, where she'd threaten him with gods know what. Then suddenly they'd be all over each other, like she was marking her territory. No one could sleep with their fights or their very loud...*reconciliations*." He grimaced. "I missed killing Thiazi because I was so exhausted from their drama. Try sleeping with your father and stepmother's 'marriage' playing out over your head every night."

Heat flooded my cheeks as my gut twisted. More lies. They had to be lies. But they explained so much—No. No. They explained nothing.

"The particulars of their relationship isn't the issue," I said. "The issue is...is..."

"The issue is you don't know what she's capable of," Thor said softly. "You never saw."

"The issue is the neglect," I snapped, grasping for solid ground. "His absence. His selfishness. He never even took me on the yearly camping trips with you both."

Thor raked his fingers through his beard, his eyes

suddenly full of pity. The fire snapped behind him like breaking bones.

"What are you talking about? Father begged Frigg every Midsommer to let you come. He tried everything. Bargaining, promising, pleading. But she always found some reason to keep you close. Too many allergies, too dangerous, too far from her watch. Just another way to keep her hooks in him."

My body tensed as I met Thor's gaze. The mead in my cup rippled, betraying a shake in my hand.

"Mother said he didn't...she told me he didn't want me there."

Thor scoffed.

"Like I said, scorpion," he said. "She kept you close because you were her favorite leash. It drove Father to madness. He'd sit by the campfire, drinking and ranting about how she used you against him, how she threatened to keep you from him entirely if he stepped out of line."

Rage surged through me, hot as molten iron, but beneath it writhed something worse—doubt.

"How could she stop him?" I spat, but my voice shook. "No. He made a choice to leave me behind. He made a choice—" The words failed in my throat as memories began to shift, realigning themselves into darker patterns.

Thor's eyes narrowed, his jaw set in a hard line.

"Frigg left him no choice if he wanted to see you at all," he said, leaning forward. "Father tried everything to appease her, but it was never enough. She always wanted more control, more submission. Used every weapon she had, including you. She twisted him tighter than I twisted Hrimgrimnir's head off in Utgard."

My stomach knotted itself into rope.

"Meaning?"

"She used you to keep Father on her leash," Thor said.

"A tool to keep him in line. She hid her cruelty behind motherly concern, behind protection, behind love. Look, everyone feared Loki, but at least you could have a drink with him, and his jokes weren't bad." His voice dropped to a whisper. "And Loki was never capable of what she was capable of."

The fire's crackling grew louder, each pop and snap like accusations.

"Like in the cave," I murmured, the words escaping before I could stop them.

Thor lifted his drink with fingers that trembled almost imperceptibly, his eyes growing distant as if seeing horrors painted on the air. The haunted look aged him a century.

"Father commanded me to ensure Sigyn's safety, to keep her protected after...after that night in the cave. But the poor lass attempted to slip across the borders from Alfheim." He shook his head slowly. "I suspect she meant to return to Midgard and release Loki."

His gaze snapped back to mine.

"And then what Frigg did to Sigyn in the forests of Vanaheim..." The words died in his throat as he turned to stare into the flames. "Frigg never knew I saw her. If she had..."

My body went rigid. Wait.

"Vanaheim? Is this the *after* you spoke of earlier? You really must be drunk. Mother never crossed paths with Sigyn again after the cave."

His massive frame shifted in the creaking chair as his eyes darted away from mine. Sweat beaded on his brow as he reached for his mead, knocking it over in his uncharacteristic nervousness. The amber liquid spread across the table like a tide.

"Oh. I shouldn't have said that," he muttered. "I swore to Father never to tell you about it."

"Tell me what?" I asked, my heart pounding as I leaned forward, gripping the arms of my chair.

His mouth opened and closed like a fish gasping for air.

"No," he said, though his tone wavered. "I've said too much already. I won't break my promise to Father."

"Thor, what happened between my mother and Sigyn in Vanaheim?"

The hinges of the door screamed open. A guard's boots struck the floor in a sharp, urgent rhythm as he marched towards us.

"Leave us!" I snapped at the guard. "We are not to be disturbed—"

"Apologies, my Lord. But Loki has escaped Hel."

Shit.

15

JUICE CLEANSE

Loki escaped Hel.

The words punched into my stomach.

Loki ran the worlds free...

...and I was sleeping with his daughter.

Blood pounded in my temples at the thought.

I was as good as dead. A second time.

For a good fifteen minutes, I drummed the windowsill as I toyed with the idea of telling Mother about Loki's mortality, anything to save my throat from his blade. A god might cheat death once, but twice?

Rain hammered the conservatory's glass panes, each drop a tiny spear in the downpour that matched the storm in my chest.

Mother hunched over the oak table, staring at a patchwork of maps and battle plans, monstera leaves brushing her elbows. A tabby cat licked its back leg beside her porcelain teacup.

Freya stood behind Mother, her polished nails digging into Mother's shoulders as she kneaded the knots there. The sharp scent of Freya's celery juice with lemon and cayenne cut through the fragrance of soil and flowers. She claimed it was for her complexion.

"He's going to ruin everything," Mother mumbled repeatedly, crumpling Captain Geirr's report in her fist. "Ragnarok can't happen again."

"The curse should have chained him there," I said, shoving my terror into the darkest corner of my mind. No matter my fear, I would not break my oath to Hel about keeping her father's mortality secret.

Mother's neck creaked as she lifted her face from her palms, eyes boring into the second piece of parchment on the table, the one bearing Hel's handwriting in precise, needle-thin letters.

"First, my finest guards report total failure in their note yesterday," she spat. "'Mission compromised. Wolf missing. Will continue searching.' And then this morning, I receive this note from that ghoul saying: 'Loki is out.' No explanation. Just 'Loki is out.' My guards are still searching for Fenrir, and now his father is gone. This is why I warned you. Loki remains a danger. I needed that wolf first—had to have him first. The binding must be performed in the correct order to..."

She stopped herself, knuckles white against the parchment.

"To what?" I asked.

Her fingers tightened until the parchment nearly tore.

"The wolf is key. Once I have him, the rest will follow. His brother will be next, and everything will proceed as it must. At least Jormungand remains trapped in the underworld."

Freya, who had been reading over Mother's shoulder, made a sound like she'd swallowed her celery juice down the wrong pipe.

"Um, actually..." Freya tapped a perfectly manicured nail at the bottom of Hel's letter. "There's a postscript. 'P.S. Fenrir and Jormungand have escaped too. Sorry about that.'"

Mother snatched the letter back, squinting at the tiny text.

"Ymir's eyelashes, how did I miss—" She slumped back. "See how addled this is making me? I'm missing postscripts now. I am extremely put out!" She heaved in a breath. "I should have chained that snake to Yggdrasil's roots myself. I thought his prison in the underworld would hold while I dealt with Fenrir. I wasn't in the mood to face a big, nasty, scaly snake. This proves I'm right. That whole family is like holding onto oil."

The parchment crackled as her fist crushed it into a ball.

"What's the point of sending guards if they can't even secure one wolf?" Mother snapped. "What's the point of a curse if people continually interfere?"

Freya pushed mother's teacup aside, nearly toppling a glazed ceramic vase overflowing with ferns. She poured rich garnet wine into a silver goblet and pressed the cup into Mother's hand.

"Drink this instead of that lukewarm tea. It will help," she said. "I'd join, but I'm in the juice phase of my cleanse, and my complexion is finally glowing instead of only dewy."

Freya sipped her celery juice by the bird of paradise plants, their leaves dark against the glass wall.

Mother lifted the wine to her lips and took a long, *long* drink.

Mr. Ragnar jumped onto Mother's desk and sniffed her tea, whiskers twitching.

Freya refilled the goblet and worked her hands over Mother's shoulders while Mother stared at the maps and plans.

The cat stretched forward to her wine and dipped his pink tongue into the goblet. I wasn't sure how much more of this I could stand.

I walked closer to the windows, swerving past the cats lounging on plush pillows and rugs between the jungle of passion flowers, yucca, and palms. Tails lashed as several cats hissed, their ears flattening against their skulls as I passed by.

Clouds, thick and gray and dense, strangled the sky. Rain battered the windowpanes, carving jagged rivers down the glass. Thunder growled in the distance.

Thor's voice boomed in my mind, matching the rumble outside.

"I swore to Father never to tell you about it."

What didn't Father want me to know? And what happened between my mother and Sigyn in Vanaheim?

"We'll get through this," Freya said, breaking me from my thoughts. "Together. As we always have. I will eagerly await crushing Loki's balls. It's been ages since I twisted off a good set."

Mother nodded, steadied. She lifted the wine goblet and met my gaze, oblivious to the wine dripping off Mr. Ragnar's chin and whiskers.

Words rose to my throat—

"I can't tolerate incompetence," steel crept into her voice. "Hel had one job, and look where we are now."

My stomach twisted as that familiar harshness I despised in her surfaced.

Mother downed her wine in a sharp gulp. She slammed the empty goblet back onto the table.

And I was five years old again. My feet pounded the palace floors as I bolted for my hiding spot in the old gallery. No one ventured there in centuries, leaving it choked with dust and grime and memories. I was always hiding in rooms and passages. I knew the palace better than anyone. When Mother's warmth turned angry or harsh, I'd burrow beneath tables or behind drapes, waiting for the storms to pass. I'd wait with the cobwebs until her anger turned into warmth and hugs again.

Maybe Thor had a point...

No. He was dead wrong.

"The blame falls solely on Loki," I said, the lie bitter on my tongue. How could I blame only him when I knew, or at least strongly suspected, Hel had helped him escape? When I was keeping his mortality secret? "Not Hel. She's loyal to you."

She laughed.

"Loyal? The fact Loki is free proves her treachery. This is what I've been cautioning you against, Balder. You can't trust her."

"Why do you say that?" My heart thundered.

She gave me a bewildered look as if my brains had transformed into toads and someone had been dropping those toads on their heads repeatedly.

"Loki had to have gotten some magic from Hel, some help to let him bypass his curse. It's the only explanation for how this could have happened," she said. "And I hope whatever magic she provided cost him all of his fingers and half of his soul."

She stood and walked to my side, shoulders rigid as she glared through the water-whipped glass. I could almost see the punishments forming behind her eyes, and my stomach churned at the thought of what she might do to Hel.

"I swear to you Hel had no part in this," I said, clinging to the technical truth that I didn't know for certain. But gods, it felt hollow even to my own ears.

"And how can you swear what you don't know? Why are you defending her?" Each word probed for weakness.

Sweat prickled the small of my back.

"Well, I—I suppose I just..." Heat crawled up my neck, strangling my words. I had to throw her off this scent before she started digging deeper and found not just Hel's betrayal, but mine as well.

Freya's nostrils flared as she scooped one of her prized sphinx cats from its velvet throne, cradling its wrinkled flesh against her chest. My pulse spiked.

Every. Time.

"There's that smell again," her eyes narrowed. "Love. And it always comes from you, Balder. Are you quite sure you don't have a new lover? I could swear I detect it."

Dammit.

I lunged for Mr. Ragnar, dropping to my knees beside him as his rough tongue lapped at the dregs of Mother's wine. The cat's rancid milk-and-decay stench punched my nose as I scratched his matted ears.

"I think what you're smelling is the bath blend you use for Mr. Ragnar," I said, trying my best not to gag as the overwhelming stink filled my lungs. "What is that? Vanilla?"

Her lips curved up.

"Vanir Vanilla, but just a drop."

I thrust Mr. Ragnar into Freya's waiting arms, where she immediately nestled him against her sphinx, her voice climbing octaves.

"Who is a nice smelling, boy? You are!"

I turned my attention back to Mother, one fire seemingly out, only to contend with a second, far more dangerous blaze.

"I think you're overreacting, Mother."

My hands found her shoulders, steering her back to her chair. She collapsed into it, her chest rising and falling.

"This proves weakness, Balder," she said. "You don't understand. But, how could you?"

I ignored the sting of her barbed words. She was just in one of her volatile states again. Nothing I hadn't weathered before.

"I'm trying to say that all will be well, Mother," I said. "We'll find a way through this."

She managed a faint smile.

"My sweet boy." She squeezed my palms with her thumbs, almost bruising. "In what way will all be well? When Fenrir slips further from my grasp? When I lose my chance to—" She caught herself, jaw tightening. "When he joins Loki, the Destroyer, and Ragnarok starts again? And now with Jormungand loose...they ruined the order. Every action must be performed with precision, and now they are scattering like roaches in the light. Or, perhaps all will be well when Skadi takes you as her husband? This will all happen if you don't handle things exactly as required."

My skin crawled, but I pushed the feeling aside. She only wanted to protect us all.

Pulling out of her grasp, I poured wine into Mother's goblet. Was it the same goblet Mr. Ragnar had stuck his gunk encrusted eyes and tongue into earlier? Possibly. A slight twinge of guilt tugged at me as I pressed it into her hand, but a whisper of satisfaction curled through my chest along with it.

"Fenrir is priority," she muttered, more to herself than to me. "The wolf first, then his serpent brother. Only then can we..." Her words trailed into silence as she stared into her wine, lost in calculations I couldn't begin to guess at.

"What if..." Freya's fingers combed through Mr. Ragnar's

reeking fur. "What if you turned to an old, reliable solution to capture them?"

Mother's smile stretched like a blade being drawn.

"You mean the one I used on Astrid when we took Dyrdrall?" Mother's eyes gleamed.

I didn't like the expression blossoming on Freya's face.

It was the same look she gave when she crushed Holgar's balls in the feast hall for laughing at her newest hairstyle. In Holgar's defense, the miniature longboat set atop her chignon had been a bit lopsided...

"Precisely," Freya's purr harmonized with Mr. Ragnar's rumbling chest.

This was all spiraling towards disaster.

16

OUT OF THE CRYPT

LOKI

Midgard

Basel, Switzerland

"She had to send us through the juicy corpses," I muttered, scraping at the gore that had embedded itself into the fibers of Hel's silk shirt. Blood and viscera had transformed the fabric into a canvas of horror. No amount of bleach would ever be enough.

People parted around us as we trudged through the morning bustle of Marktplatz. A mother yanked her daughter behind her, both clamping their hands over their noses. The cheese seller stumbled backwards, eyes watering as he frantically waved a hand before his face. Even the chestnut roaster and sausage griller paused, nostrils flaring as we passed. I believe someone somewhere screamed.

"Keep walking," Fenrir said, his shoulders hunched against dozens of horrified stares.

Grave muck caked Fenrir's trousers, the fabric crackling with every step as the mud dried. Jorg grimaced as he plucked a yellowed molar from his matted hair.

The kiosk owner's newspaper slipped from trembling fingers as his jaw swung open.

I waved and gave a small grin, my cheeks burning against the autumn chill.

Green trams clattered and jolted along their tracks, their mechanical rhythm pulsing through the bones of Basel like a heartbeat.

Basel.

I dragged my hand across my neck, fingers gliding over a cold film of sweat. The ghosts of this place still hungered, and they devoured me whole.

Venom coated my mouth, bitter and burning.

Flashes of the cave hacked through my head like a rusted blade, the same cave miles from here, where I had spent 500 years. Lost 500 years of my life. Stolen. Taken. Ripped away, while I lay bound in darkness, feeling my sanity crack drop by drop...

It was all so close I could taste the limestone walls. Feel the cords biting into my wrists.

My lungs squeezed the air out of me, just as they had done every time I screamed, begging for death. And death never came.

A firm hand on my shoulder anchored me back to reality, Fenrir's fingers digging into my skin.

"Are you alright?" He searched my face, seeing too much.

I cleared my throat, trying to swallow back centuries of horror. Worry lines carved deep valleys across his forehead.

"Of course," I lied, stretching my lips into what I hoped resembled a smile. "I'm just...I'm fine."

I took off at a clipped pace, my heels striking the slick cobblestones. Anything to distance myself from the phantoms chasing me, from the memories that threatened to drag me back into that endless dark.

"Fenrir, can't your wolf senses detect Sigyn?" My words tumbled out in a rush. "She wears a lovely, subtle vanilla perfume, and—"

"This is the tenth time you've asked me, and once again, my senses have their limits. Especially with these overwhelming smells choking the air."

He shrugged.

I narrowed my eyes at the half wheels of cheese bubbling beneath heat lamps, each breath full of the stench of stinky cow, armpits, and cigarettes.

"I suggest we find a less crowded spot," I said.

Jorg snorted and plucked a shriveled finger off his shoulder, and flicked it away.

"No," he said. "Fenrir means *us*. As in, pieces of rotting flesh and gore glued to one's shirt are not exactly conducive to tracking anything."

"It's just a slight hint of corpse." I frowned, touching a gelatinous glob of something in my hair. "I'm sure we don't smell *that* bad."

A severed hand tumbled from my pocket and landed on the cobblestones with a wet smack.

Jorg's eyebrows arched towards his hairline, his expression screaming 'you absolute idiot' louder than words ever could.

"Whatever," I huffed, kicking the hand into the storm drain. "Let's keep going. I'm not wasting anymore time."

Sigyn was here, breathing the same air, walking these same streets. The thought burned in my chest like swallowed fire.

I plowed through the maze of stalls and crowds, shoulders battering aside tourists and locals. It might not be so dreadful if the Frost Giants ate half of the people. It would definitely make this task simpler.

"Papa, slow down," Fenrir called after me, trying to keep pace without bumping the tourists out of the way. "Do you honestly believe you'll just stumble upon Sigyn by aimlessly wandering around the city scaring half the humans to death?"

"They'll recover," I snarled over my shoulder, not breaking stride, hearing the distinct sound of someone fainting into a flower cart.

"Let's take a moment and a breath," Fenrir's heavy footfalls thundered closer, sweat beading on his flushed face. "We need a plan."

"Plan? I'm not wasting time on a plan—"

I stopped mid-sentence, an uncomfortable thought slithering through my mind. The same nagging doubt that had plagued me since learning of Sigyn's location resurfaced. Why had Frigg sent Sigyn here, of all places? So close to where I'd been bound...

I knew Frigg too well. Nothing she did was without careful calculation. What role did my wife play in all this? There was something I was missing, some crucial piece of Frigg's elaborate game...

"Papa?" Fenrir's voice pulled me back from the fog.

I shook my head, forcing the thoughts aside. The priority was locating Sigyn. I could unravel Frigg's schemes later.

My shoes left the cobblestones for smooth asphalt as I stepped into the street. A bell's sharp cry split the air. Metal wheels screamed against rails as a tram hurtled towards me, sparks showering from its emergency brakes.

I leapt back, and my heel caught the curb's edge. The world tilted as I crashed backwards, my spine connecting with the lovely soft sensation of cobblestone. Hel's coin leapt from my pocket like a living thing and twirled across the stones before diving into a murky puddle.

Shit.

A deeply unpleasant slipping sensation trailed through my veins like tendrils of ice as the curse gripped me. My fingertips faded, transparency creeping up my hands. The underworld pulled at me, hungry, eager to reclaim its prisoner. I could already taste the ash on my tongue.

No.

I lunged forward, muscles screaming, heart thundering against my ribs. Water soaked my sleeve as I snatched the coin from the puddle. The slipping sensation stopped, retreating like a tide. The cold withdrew, reality solidifying around me as I laid back sprawled on the cobblestones, clutching the coin.

Fenrir clamped onto my arm, yanking me back to my feet with a grunt. My heels grated against stone as I found my footing.

"Are you alright?" His eyes widened, pupils dilating with shock. "That was freaky to witness. You got all see-through for a moment there."

A dark chuckle bubbled from Jorg's throat.

"Of course he's fine," Jorg said. "He's not a severed head shorter, and not dragged back to Hel. It's actually a little disappointing."

I shot him a glare as I clutched the coin so tightly the engraved runes dug into my palm. Each ridge and valley of the metal was a reminder of how fragile my freedom truly was. I almost dissolved into nothing.

The thought of no more me in the land of the living was enough to make me almost need a new pair of trousers.

"Right," I said, throat dry. "I'll admit I did not expect... *that.*"

"Perhaps if you swallowed it for safer keeping?" Jorg's words dripped with barely contained laughter.

I tightened my grip further as my particular predicament fully sank in. Any mugger, loose thread, or torn pocket and it would be bon voyage, Loki, enjoy eternity in the underworld. I knew Hel awaited me, and that meant her impaling me.

"Perhaps you're right to take a breath first," I said, hating how my voice wavered. "And make a—" I gagged on the word and the entire concept. "—a plan."

I shoved the coin deep into my other pocket, pushing it down as far as the fabric allowed.

Don't think about how many ways this could go sour. Don't think about what awaits you if it does.

A rumbling growl erupted from Fenrir's stomach.

"You're hungry," I said.

Fenrir raked through his matted hair, gore and grave dirt raining down as he scratched his scalp.

"Well, yes...I wasn't able to eat anything much at Hel's. That boiled potato only went so far." Exhaustion carved deep lines around his eyes, his frame seeming to shrink with hunger.

I wouldn't watch my son starve.

"Then finding food is where we start." I dove into pocket after pocket, each search more frantic than the last, disturbing clumps of grave dirt and worse things. "Let me buy you something to eat...I have...wait...dammit. My wallet is still back at your cabin in Colorado. Of course. Perfect."

I had no money.

I turned to Jorg, who stared transfixed at one of the historical fountains of a basilisk. Water cascaded from its weathered beak, the spray shimmering in the weak autumn light.

"Jorg, do you have any money in that bag of yours?"

"What? Oh. Nothing but a sketchbook and some charcoal in here." His right shoulder lifted in a half-shrug, the small backpack shifting against his tunic.

"Really? That's all you thought to take with you on this adventure? Drawing supplies?" My voice rose with each word. "You don't even have your wallet, or coin pouch somewhere else on you?"

He shot me that snarly look once more, the kind that conveyed his opinion of my intelligence in no uncertain terms.

"You expect me to have a coin pouch wearing these leather trousers?" His palm skimmed the smooth surface of his skin-tight leather. "I don't even have pockets."

Fenrir pressed against his temples, massaging in slow circles as if warding off a headache.

"And I can't access any of my accounts," Fenrir added. "Freya's guards took everything from us so fast. Even my mobile is gone."

I didn't have my mobile either. We had nothing but the clothes on our backs. Sadly disgusting clothes. And clothes not at all suitable for this cold weather.

A gust of autumn chill sliced through the air, accompanied by the sting of raindrops. Silk was a wonderful fabric, but what I'd give for a proper cloak...

Jorg shivered, his teeth chattering as the icy rain began soaking his shirt.

"This is what I'm trying to tell you." Fenrir's words turned into clouds of frost. "We need to pause, for a moment, and think about how we accomplish all we must. Please."

I didn't want to take a moment. I didn't want any moments without Sigyn.

I wanted to keep scouring every inch of the city, but the gnawing hunger in Fenrir's belly and the shivers racking Jorg's body gave me pause. Basel was immense, a sprawling mesh of winding streets and alleys.

They were tired, and I hated admitting that I was tired, too. My body ached, as if it had been torn apart and put back together wrong. Mortality was quickly losing its charm.

And then there was the matter of Fenrir and Jorg being the top of Frigg's curse priority list. If we were going to be exposed like this, we had to be smart about how we'd keep out of Frigg's grasp.

I pressed my lips together and nodded.

"Fine," I said. "So, what do you recommend we do?"

A spark flickered in Fenrir's tired eyes, a glimmer that made my stomach sink.

This would not be good for me.

"We could find work," Fenrir said.

"Work?" I asked, tilting my head. "Did you just say *work*? As in doing physical labor?"

"I have the smoothie shop," he continued. "I'm familiar with washing dishes. Although Jenn tends to fuss that I'm doing it wrong, so maybe that's not the best idea. Oh, we could be street performers. Sing a song, and if someone has pity on us..." His voice faded as he watched our expressions curdle.

Jorg's eyebrows knitted together, his face contorting as if he'd bitten into something rotten.

"Are you suggesting we resort to panhandling?" He folded his arms across his chest.

"What other choice do we have?" Fenrir spread his hands wide, flecks of grave dirt falling from his fingers. "I've been told my voice is good. If we collect enough money, we could afford some fruit or a granola bar to share, and if we are lucky, a bunk in a hostel where we can rest for a few moments. It would be honest work. Money earned nobly."

"*Honest*?" Jorg's upper lip curled back.

"*Hostel*?" The word exploded from my mouth.

"I said hostel only 'if we are lucky'," he said. "We'll likely be huddled together on a park bench to escape the worst of the cold."

I envisioned the night ahead—a sleepless night in a park on damp grass, chilled to the bone, while Fenrir and Jorg grew increasingly irritated from sharing an apple for a meal, and fighting over who got to be in the middle.

Fat raindrops pelted my cheeks, the cold droplets sliding down my face.

No, this plan was absolute bullshit.

Especially when there was a third option. Now, was that option slightly on the villainous side? Perhaps. But I would not let my children starve and freeze on a park bench because of some pesky morals.

Besides, once Frigg discovered our predicament, we couldn't risk being easily discovered in the open.

My shoes splashed through puddles as I marched towards a line of gleaming vehicles, their chrome and glass glinting in the rain.

"Oh my gods, what are you doing now?" Jorg asked over the patter of rain.

Acting as casual as could be, I let my fingers do all the work and reached for the handle of a sleek BMW.

Locked. No matter. I'd have preferred the XM model, anyway.

"You better not be doing what I think you're doing," Fenrir said, his words carrying a sharp edge of warning.

I continued down the row, water streaming down my neck as I tested the handle of a sturdy VW—damn, locked again.

"Stop," Fenrir's voice cut through the air filled with the rumble of trams and people.

"Stop what? Finding a solution to our problem?" I asked, jostling the handle of a red Fiat 500. "Does no one in this city trust anyone that they keep everything locked—ah! Finally. A moron."

I slid into the Fiat, folding my frame to fit into the cramped space. My knees smashed against the dashboard. The leather seat squeaked beneath my gore-crusted clothes.

"Get out of the car," Fenrir said through the rain-spattered window.

'Car' seemed generous.

"No, *you* get in." I fished through the tangled web of wires beneath the steering column.

Horror bloomed across Fenrir's face, his rain-soaked features twisting as understanding dawned.

"I won't let you steal this car," he said.

Now that was a rather rude presumption.

The accusation made me click my tongue as I separated the ignition wires.

"Why are you so pessimistic?" I worked the copper free of the plastic. "I'm not stealing, I am only borrowing the car. It can't be theft if the owner gets it back...eventually. It's all perfectly ethical."

"A lecture from you on ethics is something I must hear." Jorg's laughter cut through the rain like a knife. "Please. Tell me more about how hot-wiring a car that doesn't belong to you is *ethical*."

The wires sparked beneath my fingers, and the engine coughed to life with a triumphant purr. The tiny car vibrated around me like a content cat. Perfect.

Fenrir's gaze narrowed, boring directly into mine. His frame tensed as if preparing to physically remove me from the vehicle.

I maintained eye contact as my palm found the steering wheel's center, poised over the horn.

"Now Fenrir, if you won't get in, I'm afraid you leave me no choice."

"You wouldn't dare," he said.

I slammed my palm on the horn. Daring. The sharp blast shattered the afternoon calm.

People walking along the sidewalk glanced our way.

"The longer you gape like a landed fish, the more likely we are to attract unwanted attention, like the authorities," I said, finger hovering over the horn. "In fact, maybe I'll lay on this horn until they come to investigate, if that's what it'll take to get you both in the car already."

A thin sheen of sweat glistened on Fenrir's forehead as he clenched and unclenched his fists.

Good. I was getting through.

"Typical drama from you, Father," Jorg said, rain dripping from his nose. "Always making a scene. Just like that one time we went to the beach."

He always loved bringing that up. Many people bring cocaine to the beach.

"I'm only solving our dilemma." I shifted in the cramped seat. "You said you were hungry and cold. So I'm going to get you both fed, find a change of clothes, and get us all cleaned up. We won't be sleeping on any damn bench in the damn rain, leaving ourselves vulnerable to Frigg."

I slammed the horn again, making sure the shrill sound pierced every eardrum in the vicinity. Several bystanders drew closer. Including a police officer. He walked towards us from the far end of the street.

"Stop this and get out of the car." Fenrir growled, arms crossed. "You're going to get us arrested."

"Only if you don't get in the car with me," I said.

I honked again, tapping out an obnoxious rhythm, making a statement with each blaring burst.

"No." Fenrir planted his feet wider, jaw set like stone.

Apparently, he had inherited my stubbornness. This could take ages.

"Look," I said, the last shreds of my patience snapping. "I've had a very rough day. Do not test me, Fenrir. Now get in this vehicle, or I swear to you I will physically throw you into the trunk."

Jorg's laughter grated my nerves thinner.

I blared the horn again, and once more for good measure.

A muscle twitched beneath Fenrir's right eye.

Jorg leaned against a lamppost, that insufferable grin splitting his face as if I was proving some grand point to his brother.

More and more heads turned in our direction. The police officer's steps clicked closer, his radio crackling at his hip.

"You know he won't budge on this, Fen," Jorg said, that smile still carving his mouth. "It's almost as if Father is still a major dick."

Fenrir's shoulders slumped as he shook his head, droplets flying from his hair.

"No," Fenrir said. "He's not still a dick. Only his manner is dickish."

"It doesn't look that way to me." Jorg's smirk widened. "I think I'm already winning my bet, and we haven't even been here for five minutes."

"Just...just..." Fenrir dragged his palms down his face, smearing grave dirt across his skin. His chest expanded with a deep breath as he squared his shoulders like a man surrendering his last shred of common sense.

He locked his eyes on mine through the rain-streaked glass.

"Swear to me we return the car—*undamaged, mind you*—once we're done with...whatever this is," he said.

"Of course," I said. "I'll return it and fill the gas tank completely. How's that for a deal?"

I patted the vacant passenger seat.

Fenrir held my gaze, rain streaming down his face, before offering a sharp nod of surrender.

"You're taking decades off my life," Fenrir grumbled. We waited as Jorg twisted his tall frame into the back seat, cramming himself into the space behind my seat. Fenrir dropped into the passenger side, each motion a statement of disapproval.

"You aren't going to move the seat up at all, will you?" Jorg asked me as Fenrir shut the door.

I hope he didn't notice me grin. The little shit.

"No."

Knuckles rapped against my window, the police officer's face staring through the glass.

"Hey, what's going on?" he said in Swiss German.

Gripping the steering wheel, I shifted the car into gear,

loving the surge of adrenaline racing through me. I slammed the pedal to the floor and jerked forward, the front bumper crumpling against the parked car in front with a sickening crunch. Fenrir let out a startled shriek from the passenger seat.

"Papa, what are you doing? Gently push down the gas, don't slam!" His palm slapped against the dashboard, bracing for impact.

"Sorry, sorry!" I said, throwing the car into reverse. Tires screamed against wet pavement as we shot backwards, metal shrieking as we scraped the car behind us. Fenrir kept muttering about liability and other boring drivel.

I cut the wheel hard, trying to wiggle out of the tight spot. The car rocked back and forth as I alternated between gas and brake, each movement punctuated by the sound of scraping paint and Fenrir's increasingly panicked protests.

"Are you trying to kill us?" Jorg yelled, his knuckles white as he clutched the back of my seat. "Or destroy every car on this street?"

The officer dove for safety as I finally broke free. I sped off probably a touch faster than I should have, leaving the policeman and a trail of dented cars far behind as I careened through the city streets. Fenrir's ragged breathing filled the car.

"I swear, Papa," Fenrir said between gasps, "if we survive this, I'm never getting in a car with you again—AHHH!"

Fenrir's voice erupted with a mix of terror and pleading as I whipped around a corner, tires howling. The screech of the rubber drowned out his wailing and prayers as I threaded between a bus and a row of parked cars.

This was such fun!

Pure exhilaration coursed through my veins as I yanked the wheel, narrowly missing a pedestrian who had stepped off the curb because that silly little green crossing light told them it was safe. Now where was the...ah! Here we were. The bank.

"What's the plan now with this car theft?" Jorg gripped the back of my seat harder. "You're really off to a smashing start—"

I slammed on the breaks and Jorg's face smacked the back of my chair.

"I have an errand to run," I said.

Rain drummed against the windshield, distorting the view as I studied the building's layout. Especially the exits.

"Errand? What possible errand could you have at a bank?" Fenrir asked. "Oh, you mean that dry cleaner over there on the corner. For your shirt, right? It looks awful...bits are getting all over the leather. Gods, how will we ever get this clean for the poor person we stole this from?

I rummaged through the glove compartment barely listening, brushing past papers and receipts. I closed my fingers around a pair of sunglasses. Excellent. I settled them on my nose. Not my usual *Persol*, but they'd do.

"Wait here. Oh. Fenrir, can you drive?"

I reached back and upended Jorg's backpack, which did contain more than just a sketchbook and some charcoals. A mess of pencils, charcoals, a leather journal, a sketchbook, and multiple packs of cigarettes spilled over Jorg's lap and onto the floor.

"Do you know how expensive that charcoal set is you just flung out of my bag?" Jorg asked.

Gods.

"I've not had my Austrian license renewed since I let it lapse in 1951," Fenrir said.

The seatbelt clicked free as I stepped out, my gore-crusted Gucci loafers splashing in a puddle.

"Good enough," I said. "Get in the driver's seat and be ready."

I marched towards the glass entrance doors.

"Ready for what, exactly?" Fenrir's panicked voice carried over Jorg's dark laughter and muttered comments about his brother's naivety.

But I was already walking through the revolving doors.

CRIME AND DINE

My business at the bank didn't take long.

I flung open the passenger door and wedged myself in the small seat, crushing the backpack against my chest with one arm. Leather squeaked beneath me.

"Were they able to help you with your shirt?" Fenrir asked. "Wait, why are you still wearing it? And Jorg's back-pack...why is it bulging?"

Laughter rumbled from the backseat as Jorg's boots kicked against the upholstery.

"Just hit the gas," I said, metal slamming as I yanked the door shut.

Fenrir nodded. The engine whined as he pressed the pedal—and the Fiat crawled forward at precisely thirty-five miles per hour.

I exhaled. Sharply.

"So, Father, do enlighten us," Jorg said as we pulled away from the curb. "What all did you do in the bank? Make a deposit into your savings? I'm sure you have so many to make these days."

"No, it wasn't a deposit." I dug into the canvas of the bag.

"Bank?" Confusion crackled in Fenrir's voice. "I thought you were going to the dry cleaner."

The car puttered along while bicycles and joggers breezed past our windows. At the crosswalk, Fenrir stomped the brake despite the empty sidewalks. The sudden lurch sent the backpack tumbling. Canvas split against the floorboard and stacks and stacks of bills spread across the footwell.

Fenrir's jaw fell. I wanted to say it was from surprise, but horror was probably the more accurate emotion.

"No, please, no..." the words rasped from his throat.

Howls of laughter erupted from Jorg as tears streamed down his cheeks.

"Ah, I see it was actually a rather sizable withdrawal." His cackling filled the car. "Told you he hasn't changed one bit, Fen."

Fenrir's right eye twitched as a groan rattled from his chest.

"Papa, please tell me you didn't actually rob that bank," he said, a pleading edge in his words.

Now that offended me.

"Rob?" Indignation prickled across my skin. "I asked for this money, thank-you-very-much. Now, can you possibly drive this infernal car any faster than a sulking tortoise's pace?"

"I am driving the posted speed limit," Fenrir said. "And I will not be breaking any more laws today." He cut his eyes towards me, mouth compressing into a tight line. "And what precisely do you mean by 'asked' for the money?"

I swallowed back my annoyance. Really. He was making a bigger deal over this than was necessary.

"Yes, asked," I said. "Firmly."

Fenrir's mouth dropped so low I feared it might fall to the floor entirely.

"This is unbelievable." Fenrir shook his head.

"What's unbelievable is how slowly you drive away from a bank robbery."

"So you admit robbing that bank?!" Fenrir slammed his fist against the steering wheel. "We are going back…"

How about no.

I clamped my hand onto his knee. Muscle and bone shifted under my grip as I forced his leg down, jamming the pedal to the floor. The engine screamed as we raced forward, buildings blurring past our windows. Anything to put a bit more distance between us and the sirens blaring behind in the distance.

"Keep driving!" I shouted over the squeal of the engine and roar of his extremely loud lecturing about moral codes. "Try to think about all the excitement we're sharing right now as a family!"

Jorg's laughter boomed from the backseat, his breath fogging the window.

"*Excitement*?" Fenrir's voice cracked like splitting ice. "No. This is wrong, on so many levels. Gods." His shoulders hunched as he clutched his midsection with one hand. "My stomach hurts."

That twisted something deep inside me. Guilt flared in my own bowels now. But I didn't want him and Jorg hungry and cold. How was I supposed to care for them with no money? This was the only way.

I uncurled my grip on Fenrir's knee, letting the car settle back into his preferred snail crawl.

"Look, I know you aren't used to this *lifestyle*," I said, massaging my throbbing shoulder. "But we are facing a very particular dilemma, one that may occasionally require drastic action. Can't you understand that, even if only this once?"

Fenrir's brows knotted like tangled rope. The steering wheel creaked under his grip.

"I can understand the reasoning," he said, shadows rippling across his face as we passed under streetlights that had flickered on early against the bruised sky. "But there are always other ways. Ethical ways."

"You're right," I said. "But we don't have the luxury of time for any of them. Your sister has given us one day before informing Frigg of our escape, and most of those hours are already gone."

Silence crashed over the car, broken only by the engine's steady pulse and the crunch of tires on asphalt.

A metallic click echoed as Jorg flicked open his Zippo, the flame wavering in the rearview mirror before touching the cigarette's tip. Smoke ribbons twisted towards the ceiling, carrying the sharp scent of tobacco.

"I'm sorry to pull you both into this mess," I said, barely hiding a wince as my right shoulder flared with a stab of pain thanks to the cramped seat. "And I'm sorry I cannot find more noble means to provide you with food, shelter, and the basics to live."

"Don't worry about it, Father." Jorg's words rode out on a cloud of smoke. "You're providing all I expect from you."

"Jorg, please, not now." Fenrir's eyes flashed in the mirror before swinging back to me, his mouth carved into a grim line. "I'm wrestling with the ethics of this entire situation here. I...I don't know if I can go on this way. I don't know if I can accept any of this money, even for food and shelter."

I reached across the console, settling my hand on

Fenrir's arm where muscles tensed beneath his sleeve. I squeezed gently, feeling his pulse hammer beneath my fingers.

"Fenrir, please. Have faith in me. I will make everything right in the end. You have my word."

In the backseat, Jorg sank deeper into the leather, a smirk blooming across his face.

"*Your word*," Jorg repeated. "And what exactly is that worth these days, Father? Less than the exhaust spewing from this hunk of stolen metal, I'd wager."

Lamplight caught his eyes in the rearview mirror, turning them to molten gold filled with centuries of resentment. Smoke curled from his nostrils.

"You actually expect us to have faith you'll make things right?" The cigarette trembled between his fingers, ash spilling onto the upholstery. "Just like all those other empty promises you've made us you've broken over the centuries?" A bark of laughter. "I would sooner trust a cat to properly prepare a gourmet seafood dinner."

I THOUGHT my hair would sprout silver before Fenrir agreed —extremely reluctantly, he kept repeating—to use the stolen money. However, his agreement finally came, and it came wrapped in a long, *long* list of conditions.

For starters, any funds we used must align with sustainability principles. Clothes would be thrifted, reducing waste and our carbon footprint. Fine. Surely, some excellent vintage Armani waited in some secondhand store.

Five minutes in the fluorescent lit store told me I would not be that lucky. The racks were an endless hellscape of polyester and something called "fleece."

After some time rifling through the mountains of discarded clothing, we found some weather appropriate pieces that would keep us from freezing, and most importantly, were devoid of corpse. Fenrir smiled, collecting his predictable favorites. Plaid flannel shirts, sturdy corduroy trousers, and lace-up high tops made from recycled plastic bottles.

Jormungand and I, cursed with identical tall and lean frames, waged silent warfare through the racks. Hangers clattered as we hunted for anything that might fit. He shot me a challenging look as we both reached for the same pair of slim fit black jeans. I let him have them. And the black t-shirt. And the only not wholly hideous denim jacket.

I wasn't completely selfish, shocking as I knew he'd find that thought.

This left me with graphic tees suggesting a midlife crisis, jeans hanging like potato sacks, and a faux leather jacket instead of a genuine one, because I did not want to burden Fenrir's conscience further. Worse still, the only footwear that accommodated my size were hideous orange foam monstrosities riddled with holes. Fenrir informed me they were named after some crocodile. And his grin only widened when he spotted my purple shirt, which featured a cartoon duck in a fedora who, he said, fought crime nocturnally on a formerly popular children's show.

As I said, I was a beacon of selflessness.

After even more hours of searching for an "eco" hotel to satisfy Fenrir's second stipulation, we finally found one in a not-at-all inconvenient location on the outskirts of town. Fenrir beamed, his eyes crinkling at the corners as we entered the modest lobby. He pointed at a sign describing their water conservation measures, which meant I would get the absolute joy of a low pressure, trickling shower. Perfect.

At least I could finally sit, even though the room was twenty years out of date. We took out the ironing board and made it a makeshift table, setting everything out we had purchased at the local grocery store—containers of hummus, crisp salads, and sandwiches stacked like small mountains.

Fenrir and Jorg sat on their beds, attacking their food like wolves breaking a winter fast, color flooding back into their cheeks.

I wished I could say the same for myself. I sat on my corner cot next to an ugly laminate wardrobe, wiggling my toes in these ridiculous perforated orange horrors that somehow made my foul mood even fouler. The springs creaked and poked into my backside, the littlest movement making the entire damn thing rattle and threaten to snap back in half with me in it. I picked at rice crackers and applesauce, which didn't help my mood as I chewed over Fenrir's third and final condition.

That once our ordeal was over, I make an extraordinarily big, fat, generous donation to a charity of his choice, doubling what I took from the bank.

The scratch of Fenrir's pen on paper snapped me out of the thousand voice choir singing of rage and creative profanity that filled my mind. I glanced at him, hunched over the bed's edge, his hair twisted into a messy bun. Paper fragments accumulated beside him.

"What are you doing?" I asked, watching another sheet tear free.

He didn't lift his eyes from his furious scribbling.

"Making a list of IOUs for everything we've spent. I want it all accounted for and returned."

I frowned, running my fingers through my still damp hair after the worst shower of my life. A dripping faucet could have produced more water pressure. Hell, a mouse sneezing would have had more force.

"Fenrir, this is survival," I said. "We had no choice."

His pen never stopped as he shook his head, loose strands escaping his bun.

"Actually, there is always another choice," Jorg said. He glanced up from his sketchpad, charcoal staining his fingertips black. "Although, I know saying there was 'no other choice' is your favorite excuse."

Jorg reclined on the bed, propped up by a huge pile of pillows behind his narrow shoulders. The charcoal scored against paper with vengeful strokes. I could almost see the violence taking shape beneath his hands, likely another artistic rendering of my face meeting his fist.

My cot groaned as I stood and crossed to Fenrir and his small forest worth of paper notes. The IOU stack crinkled beneath my fingers as I lifted it. His green eyes met mine, a storm of guilt and uncertainty swirling in their depths.

"Look, the guilt is purely all on my shoulders for the stealing. Your conscience is clear, Fenrir. You tried to stop me, but I was not to be reasoned with." I held his gaze, willing him to believe me. "You tried your best, so, please, the blame is all mine. Don't worry anymore. I don't want you to keep suffering over this."

I crammed the pile of IOU's into the cavernous pockets of my jeans. I guess they had one redeeming feature.

A glimmer of a smile tugged at the corners of his lips as some of the tension left his shoulders.

"I'm not sure," Fenrir said.

"Well, I am," I said.

Charcoal scratched louder as Jorg scoffed. His mouth twisted into a bitter line while he methodically cleaned his blackened fingers, each swipe of the napkin deliberate and harsh.

"What consideration, Father." The words dripped acid. He folded the stained napkin. "Was this the same care and consideration you had when you made your deal with the gods to take us from the Ironwood?"

Fenrir winced at his words.

"Jorg, please stop." Fenrir raised his hand to his brother. "Now is not the time. I can't take any more stress. My ability to meditate is already being impacted by all of this negative energy."

Jorg rolled his eyes and reached into his pocket, sliding out a cigarette. Metal clicked as he sparked his lighter, the flame briefly illuminating the face that could have been my reflection from centuries past. Those same high cheekbones, that identical knife-edge nose I'd given him. Fenrir's disapproving frown deepened as smoke began coiling towards the water-stained ceiling.

"I already told you," I said, forcing my tone to stay even. Calm. "I did what I thought was best for your safety, as I am doing now what's best to provide you both with what you need. We have a long road ahead of us."

A laugh burst from Jorg as smoke streamed from his nostrils.

"Yes, Fenrir is so much happier now," he sneered, lips curling around the cigarette.

Frustration boiled up from my gut. I sucked in a breath, trying to picture my anger dissolving, melting away from my clenched jaw, floating off like a red balloon into the sky of absolute bullshit.

Gods. This never worked.

"What do you want from me, Jorg? For me to have let you starve this entire time? I can't allow that. Not when it affects my sons. Not when I know what it's like to go hungry."

His eyes locked onto mine, as he drew deep on the cigarette.

A wet coughed punctuated the tension.

"Must you smoke those cancer sticks indoors?" Fenrir's nose wrinkled.

"And when did you ever starve except from lack of attention?" Jorg's words sliced Fenrir's complaint. "You always stuffed your gob at every feast in Asgard, like you competed with some gluttonous pig, or fire itself."

Something dark and ancient stirred in my chest.

"There were no feasts when I lived in Jotunheim during the wars," I snarled, memories rising like corpses from frozen ground. "I endured the harshest winters back in those early days, when the worlds were young. Many starved, and I was among them. One winter was so cruel we had to stuff our shoes with paper from father's books to stop frostbite. Of course, when Father found out what I had done to his encyclopedia…"

Cotton sheets rustled against wool blankets as Fenrir shifted, his eyes wide with a child's curiosity.

"You've never told us this story," he said.

No. I hadn't. Because it wasn't something I particularly liked remembering, let alone speaking of aloud. The words scraped my throat like frozen razors as they emerged. Speaking in Jotnar again only made the memories sharper, more immediate.

I plunged back in time, into the ice. I was there again, frost needling my cheeks and cold searing my fingertips. But worse was the hollow ache in my belly, a hunger so deep it felt like my stomach was consuming itself.

"Father stole the chicken off the table of the neighbor," I

said, my voice distant as I stared out into fragments of the past. "I can still taste the crisp skin. Juice ran down my chin. It was one of the rare, useful things my father did for us. I suppose even he drew the line at letting his children starve."

Although, an extra log on the fire to fight off the chill, or shoes without holes, would have been equally welcome. But he always was tight as a duck's arse with his coin. Miserable, stingy bastard. He was the reason I could never abide being close-fisted.

"This is the first time you've spoken about our grandfather," Fenrir's words cut through the fog of memory.

"Haven't I?" I asked, lost somewhere between past and present.

"What was he like?" Jorg's voice carried an unfamiliar weight, the sneer replaced with genuine interest. The mattress creaked as he leaned forward, crushing his cigarette into the ashtray.

My feet shifted in my shoes, gaze fixed on some point far beyond the hotel's peeling wallpaper.

"He was..." the words came slow. "He was strong. Fierce. Never touched a drop of ale. Which made his words cut deeper because you knew he meant them, and...and..."

More memories sawed through my mind, barbed and poisonous.

I didn't think father would notice the missing pages. The book had sat untouched on his shelf, gathering dust since before I was born. The book's paper crinkled in my shoes, guilt warring with the need to stop my toes from freezing in that drafty hovel. Father found out. Said the holes in my shoes were my fault for not taking better care of them. That the frostbite would teach me my lesson to respect my belongings.

I lifted my hand to my face, rubbing away the phantom sting of his calloused palm striking my cheek.

The clock's red digits blazed 7:00 PM. The walls seemed to inch closer, the ceiling dropping lower with each breath. I couldn't stay here. Here was suffocating. I had to go.

I had to leave.

Run.

I shoved the ice and the hunger and the tears back into their vault, locking them in where I never dared visit.

"I'm going out to look for Sigyn."

I found Hel's coin through the fabric of my pocket, tracing its edges for the hundredth time since the *incident* this afternoon. The memory of that pulling sensation, that void trying to drag me back to the underworld, still made my skin crawl.

"Go?" Alarm cracked Fenrir's voice. "The plan was to rest a couple hours first, and *then* go. Together. You're exhausted. We all are."

"I'll rest once I know where she is, that...that she is safe." I turned at the door, meeting his eyes swimming with worry. "I'm fine."

My shoulder screamed as I tried to roll it, pain shooting across my back like lightning. A grunt escaped through clenched teeth.

Dammit.

"I'm fine after I take more pain tablets," I said, snatching the bottle from the dresser's scarred surface.

Before I could twist the cap, Fenrir's fingers locked around my wrist. His gaze bored into mine, searching for something I wasn't sure was there anymore.

"You're no use to anyone if you push yourself past your limits," he said. "And what if you lose your coin again? That curse will take you back to Hel quicker than a whirlpool at sea. You saw what happened earlier."

Springs creaked as Jorg melted back into his mountain of pillows. The sharp click of his lighter cut through the tension, followed by the familiar hiss of tobacco igniting. Fenrir batted at the smoke drifting towards his face, his nose crinkling like paper.

"Just let him go, Fenrir," he said, exhaling smoke. "Leaving is what he does best, anyway."

18

AIN'T THAT A KICK IN THE...

Just let him go, Fenrir. That's what he does best, anyway.

Jorg's words cut deeper each time they replayed in my head, like picking at a wound that wouldn't heal.

And, if I wasn't already depressed enough, these foam shoes hugged my feet with infuriating perfection. I wanted to hate them. I needed to hate them. But with every cushioned step, my fury only grew at how gloriously they supported my arches. I didn't want to like sensible shoes. I didn't want to be the sort of person who prioritized comfort over dignity.

I didn't want my son to hate me.

The way I hated my father.

Just let him go...

The cobblestones glowed amber under the street lamps as I walked, not caring where I ended up. I wound through steep alleyways and climbed worn steps, shouldering past crowds of festival-goers who packed the narrow streets.

Ferris wheels and spinning carnival rides lit up the squares. I searched every face in the crowd for Sigyn, my ears playing tricks on me, catching whispers that sounded like her voice in the noise.

I slipped away from the glittering squares into the darker streets, letting the shadows swallow me whole. The solitude hit me harder than I expected.

Venom coated my tongue, seared my skin. Each cobblestone, fountain, and shop front forced me to remember, to face my losses carved into Basel's bones. The pressure of five hundred years pressed against my chest.

I sucked in a sharp breath of cold night air that stung my lungs. I focused on the new structures, the steel and glass that hadn't witnessed the pain. I breathed in diesel fumes and coffee shop aromas, anything to stay anchored. But I couldn't escape the truth that rattled in my marrow like chains. That somehow, I was destined to be alone, forever reaching for happiness, only to watch it crumble. To keep losing until nothing remained but echoes.

The Rhine River wasn't far now. Part of me itched to shift into falcon form for a better view, but I didn't have the energy for it anymore, not since becoming mortal. Gods, I was so useless in this weakened state.

I clenched my fists and kicked the side of a sputtering basilisk fountain. These damn things were all over the city. Pain shot through my foot and I swore under my breath.

I couldn't wait for that apple to give me even a fraction of my former self back.

The fragility of mortality gnawed at my insides, along with all the tasks ahead. Finding Sigyn, performing this blood ritual, breaking this curse...it all threatened to snap my spine. Not a god, what was I now? I was weak. That's what I was. Weak. Broken. Falling apart at the seams.

Jorg's hatred festered in my chest, and Fenrir's trust was as thin as a strand of hair, and just as brittle. And if Fenrir ever discovered the deal I'd struck with Odin in exchange for that apple...

That last thread of trust would snap.

I hobbled on along the Rhine's river walk, my black mood growing blacker. Moonlight shimmered across the dark water and drenched the roofs and spires of the old city in silver. Rotting leaves squelched beneath my feet, still slick from the afternoon rain.

My shoulders hunched against the autumn wind as I thrust my hands deeper into my pockets, and—

"Oof!"

I collided with someone. Pastries launched skyward as two cremeschnitte cartwheeled from a small box clutched in her hand. The first pastry plunged into a puddle, its layers dissolving into a milky swirl. The second smashed onto the pavement, cream oozing between sheets of pastry.

A woman in a baseball cap and trench coat dropped to her knees, her purse spilling its contents over the walkway. A lanyard with an ID badge skittered across wet stone, keys jangled into the shadows, lipstick rolled towards the river's edge. Her fingers scrabbled over the pavement, snatching at her belongings as they scattered.

She lunged for her phone, pulling it out of the melting cremeschnitte. She wiped at the screen with her sleeve.

"I'm sorry," I said, crouching beside her to help—and my foot crushed her lipstick, grinding it into the mess of cream and pastry. The tube crackled under my weight.

Oops.

A defeated sigh escaped her as I peeled the mangled lipstick from my sole. Grit and pastry fragments clung to the fractured plastic as I offered it back. She snatched it away, stuffing it into her purse with the other salvaged possessions.

"Of course," she said, smearing cream from her fingers on her coat. "Four tries at these stupid pastries, and I finally thought I'd gotten lucky. Special-ordered and everything." She glared at her phone, pastry oozing from its charging port. "I really am cursed."

The voice froze my lungs mid-breath.

Her voice.

"Sigyn?" The name escaped my lips, nearly lost beneath the rumble of passing cars and echoing footsteps.

I lifted her work badge from the wet pavement, carefully avoiding the battlefield of destroyed pastry.

She raised her head, and those familiar brown eyes locked with mine. Surprise rippled across her face, transforming the soft arcs and curves of her features. But something else played behind her expression. An emotion I couldn't quite place. Was it confusion?

It didn't matter.

I had found her. Now, she only had to perform one little blood ritual, and we would all be saved.

This was definitely easier than I expected.

Joy surged through my veins as I lunged forward, capturing her cream-sticky hands in mine.

"Sigyn, thank gods! Are you alright? Are you hurt?" My words spilled out over each other as I checked her arms, her face, her wrists for any injuries or abuse. "I know curses can make you feel icky—"

She wrenched her hands from my grasp, taking a stumbling step backwards. That confusion transformed into something harder as she studied my face like a stranger's.

"Who are you?" she asked. "Get away from me. I don't know you."

Her words hit me like a strike, but the way she stared through me drew blood.

"Sigyn. It's me. It's Loki." My voice splintered around her name as I searched her face for any flicker of recognition.

"Why do the drunks always find me?" She grumbled beneath her breath, in that way of hers that told me she was extremely done with my nonsense.

"I'm not drunk," I said, fighting to keep my voice steady as dread crept up my spine.

She laughed, and I knew from the tone she didn't believe me.

"Regardless," she said. "You must have me confused for someone else. I'm not this *Sigyn* person. I've never seen you before in my life."

My words died on my lips as understanding punched through my chest. Each breath turned to ice as the truth crystallized with a clarity that made me want to vomit.

Because I knew exactly what Frigg had done.

Frigg hadn't just cursed Sigyn to be imprisoned in Basel, like she chained me to the underworld. No, she'd crafted something far more vicious. She had carved out Sigyn's memories and stuffed the void with false ones.

A pristine rage ignited in my gut, red and vicious and howling for blood.

I'd kill Frigg for this.

Fury pulsed behind my eyes as I watched Sigyn flick globs of cream from her fingers onto the pavement. Moonlight caught her wedding band on her finger, and reality slammed into me with the force of Mjolnir breaking my face. Everything we were, everything we'd built across centuries, gone. As if it had never existed at all.

We hadn't just lost our chance to break the Salvation Weave. Frigg had gouged out every moment we'd shared. The midnight talks in her study in Hueburg, the wine-soaked laughter on Malibu beaches, the promises whispered against skin. All of it cut away, leaving nothing but scar tissue where our life had been.

Frigg had taken away hope—Sigyn's hope.

And with it, our salvation from what was to come.

"Damn it," she muttered, pulling me back as she gathered the rest of her belongings. "I really thought special ordering those pastries would mean I finally got to eat them this time. Now they're nothing but mush, just like the last time."

"This has happened before?" My voice rasped, emotions clawing to get out.

"Multiple times," she said. "It's like the universe is trying to destroy anything that remotely gives me joy."

With an exhausted sigh, she slung her pastry-smeared purse over her shoulder, cream leaving streaks across the leather.

"If I don't eat something with sugar, or something with caffeine soon, I don't know how much more I can take."

I didn't care about the bloody pastries. The world splintered and unraveled around me. All I had fought for, bled for, lost—

I latched onto Sigyn's arms, hauling her up to face me. I had to crack through this fog clouding her mind.

"Sigyn, please. You must remember me. Remember us."

If I could just touch her, forge any sort of connection, perhaps I could jar loose her memories...

"Get your hands off me, you creep!" She twisted away, but I clutched tighter, praying the contact would be enough to shake the spell's latch on her mind.

"Let me go!" She thrashed against my grip, nearly wrenching my shoulders from their sockets.

I yanked her closer still, panic drowning out reason. I

needed to get her back to the hotel. I needed to get her somewhere safe until I could figure this out.

"Sigyn, please trust me," I pleaded, my heart hammering against my ribs. "I know you're confused, but...Come with me and I'll make everything alright. I'll explain everything."

I pulled her harder, trying to guide her steps. Strands of her honey-ginger curls spilled from her cap, cascading in gentle waves around her face.

"Sigyn, let me help you, please..."

Something flickered behind her eyes, a spark I desperately hoped was recognition. A small smile curved her lips.

My shoulders relaxed.

This was the crack I needed...

"Help me?" she asked. "Oh, I'll let you help me."

Her knee rocketed upwards, slamming directly into my groin. White hot agony exploded between my legs, devouring every thought. Twinkling stars burst across my vision as my lungs forgot how to function.

The world lurched sideways. My knees buckled, and I collapsed onto the wet cobblestones, rainwater seeping through my jeans.

"Handsy bastard," she spat, glaring at me.

"Sigyn!" I wheezed, barely able to force the words past my constricted throat as she turned and stormed away.

19

———

THE KISS

The faint hum of the television and the scratch of Jorg's pencil filled the stale air as I hobbled through the door. Pain knifed between my legs with each step. Gods. Mortality really was the worst. I silently prayed for relief in the form of ice tucked away in the mini fridge.

"What's happened to you?" Fenrir's brows knotted as his gaze raked over my crooked form. "And why are you limping?"

I rummaged through the fridge and grasped a small bottle of orange juice wedged in the corner. Not ice, but it would have to do.

Wincing, I eased myself onto the cot's edge, pressing the chilled bottle against my throbbing groin. Finding Sigyn was great news, fantastic even, but at this particular moment, the searing, throbbing agony was making it *really* hard to celebrate.

"I ran into Sigyn along the river," I said.

Fenrir's eyes snapped wide. Even Jorg's pencil froze mid-stroke, hovering above his paper.

"You found her?" Fenrir bolted upright, his chair screeching against the threadbare carpet. "Where is she?"

"Yes, I'd also like to know why you didn't bring her back." Jorg's eyes narrowed.

"I tried to bring her back," I snapped, the pain making my patience thin. "Why do you think I'm icing my balls?"

Fenrir planted himself in front of the television, blocking a prince whose shoulder pads threatened to devour his grinning face.

"I don't understand..." Fenrir said.

"Frigg didn't just curse her, she threw in a spell as well that erased her memories," I spat, my anger boiling fresh and wicked. "Frigg is a heartless viper—"

"Erased her memories? How?" Fenrir asked.

"—I will make her pay dearly for this." My fist smashed into the table lamp, sending jagged fragments shooting across the floor.

Jorg flinched, his pencil clattering to the carpet.

I inhaled slowly, wrestling the rage back into its cage before the beasts in my head could pull me under.

"I apologize," I murmured, messaging my temples. "My anger is not at either of you. But what Frigg has done to Sigyn is just...it's beyond wicked."

"If she is under a memory spell, that means...oh gods." Jorg bent to retrieve his fallen pencil, then slumped forward onto the edge of his bed, the pencil dangling limply between coal-stained fingers. "Without the translation of that incantation, we can't complete the blood ritual. And without the ritual..." The words withered, leaving the unspoken threat to coil around us like a noose.

We would all be bound, and she would seal the curse.

"What? No," Fenrir paced the worn carpet. "But she still has her powers beneath the spell, right?"

"I suppose," I said, pressing the cold bottle harder against my aching groin.

"What if we convince her about this being real? Make her believe so she will translate those scary runes. So she will be willing to do the blood ritual." His words tumbled out, desperate. "Surely that would work."

"And how would you go about starting that conversation? 'Oh Sigyn, can you please give us some of your blood? Why? Oh, no reason other than to break a curse.' She'd sooner have me committed," I said.

"Yeah, people get real weird real fast with blood stuff," Jorg muttered, gnawing his pencil.

"Even if we could convince her about magic and curses being real, there's no way for her to translate the Muspel runes during the ritual," I said. "Without her memories, that knowledge remains trapped within her mind. We need those memories back."

Jorg twisted his pencil between his fingers, teeth marks carved into the wood.

"We have no chance of breaking the curse without her knowledge." The admission burned like acid on my tongue, and not knowing killed me. "We are done."

I buried my face in my hands.

The television's chatter clawed at my thoughts. Through my fingers, I glimpsed the screen where some idiot prince knelt beside a glass coffin to kiss a cursed, sleeping princess. Gods. This was absurd. Who trampled around a forest kissing random, dead women?

The prince cupped the woman's face, eyes brimming with devotion as he leaned in. His lips met her in a gentle kiss and—

A ripple of pure white light emanated outwards from

their kiss and washed over the woman's body in a pulsing wave down to her fingertips and toes.

Her eyes fluttered open, clarity and recognition dawning on her face, the curse imprisoning her shattered.

I rolled my eyes. What an overdone cliché, and—*hold on.* Something clicked into place.

"Of course," I said, lifting my head as hope stirred in my chest for the first time since Sigyn's knee had connected with my groin.

"What?" Jorg asked, his pencil stilling once more on the sketchpad in his lap.

A grin stretched across my face as the spark of a brilliant idea took root.

"Oh, don't you dare say it," Jorg warned, recognition darkening his features. "That is old, archaic magic."

"Old, archaic magic that will *work*," I said, the words electric on my tongue. "Think about it. We need her memories, her knowledge, her willing participation. We can't force it, we can't teach it, and we can't trick her into it. But if we break Frigg's memory spell..." I let the implications sink in. "The curse may be too powerful for me to break, but a memory spell? That I can handle."

"What are you talking about?" Fenrir's features twisted with suspicion. "This is like that time you said you knew a shortcut through Jotunheim and we spent a week being chased by Frost Giants."

I turned to him, excitement swelling in my chest. Why hadn't I seen this before?

And finally, *finally*, I could prove myself useful.

I might not be able to break a big bad curse like Odin, but I COULD break a spell, and in so doing, save all of us.

"Sigyn and I need to share true love's kiss." The words

tumbled out in a breathless rush. "That's how we break the spell. And that's how we get her memories back, and then she can translate the incantation and perform the blood ritual."

As comprehension lit Fenrir's face, Jorg stared at me as if I'd sprouted a second head. He pushed off the bed and leaned against the wall, muscles coiled tight.

I raked my hands through my hair, fingers snagging on tangles thanks to Fenrir's brilliant idea about Castile soap being good enough for everything.

"Naturally," I responded, words tumbling faster with each breath. "It will take a little romancing on my part, and perhaps a touch of seduction. But it will work. This is all giving me quite the rush!"

Energy thrummed through my veins. I stood, but my battered groin screamed a sharp reminder of Sigyn's earlier ass kicking she gave me. But that still wasn't enough to squash my surging excitement.

"Wait, wait, wait." Jorg shot up his hand, stopping me. "It will work, only if you can get *Sigyn* to fall in love with you again. The real Sigyn, buried under Frigg's spell. And right now, you're dealing with..." He waved his hand vaguely. "Someone else entirely. The spell has created its own version of her. You might get this new version to fall for you, but that's not enough. True love's kiss only works if it reaches the real person beneath."

"But it's all we have," I said. "Breaking the spell is the only option."

And how did you come to this conclusion?" Fenrir's voice dropped into skepticism.

"Where an act of love can break any curse, true love's kiss can break any spell," Jorg recited, like a boring professor. "But you need to reach the real person first. Sometimes...sometimes the buried self shows through in places that matter to them. Where memories run deep. But it's still risky, and it's slow. Which is why I think we need to find a different, speedier approach. Time is not something we have much of, and I'm still not convinced you can break this spell. Having true love's kiss with Sigyn when she's trapped behind this other version of herself? That's not just starting from scratch. It's trying to reach someone through a wall."

"There is no other approach," I said.

Jorg's mouth snapped shut, weighing my words.

"Why would Frigg take her memories away and no one else's?" Fenrir asked.

"Well, I...hmmm." I snapped my fingers, finally understanding. "Because she knew of Sigyn's possession by Surtr. She knew that left her with certain knowledge. Knowledge she doesn't want us to have access to, which explains why she cursed her first, and added this delightful spell to the mix. Which also means Odin's plan to break the curse must be genuine. That bastard."

However, it still didn't explain why Frigg had sent Sigyn to Basel of all places. It was far too kind.

Jorg scoffed, head shaking, as he slumped against the wall.

"I'm still not fully convinced about all this 'true love's kiss' stuff being the best solution," he said, but..." He sighed, dragging his hand over his jaw. "But, since we've no time for alternative theories at the moment—and I can't believe I'm saying this—how do you propose to start?"

"Obviously, I start by taking her somewhere nice for dinner. Candles. Tablecloths—"

"Yes, I got that part," Jorg cut in. "What I want to know is, did you actually do something useful, like getting her information so you can contact her again?"

Leave it to him to always ruin the fun with practicalities. I was working on it.

"Afraid I didn't get the chance to enquire between her not remembering me and, oh, that's right, kicking me in the balls," I said.

He shook his head, mouth flattening into a disapproving line.

"Typical you," Jorg said. "So we're just back where we started, without the faintest idea of where Sigyn is, or even her new name, because I'm assuming she has a false one."

Well, when he said it like that...

I brushed something hard in my pocket, coated in wet goo and pastry crust. A smile tugged at my lips as I pulled out Sigyn's work badge. The one I'd forgotten to return, probably because she'd incapacitated me and stormed off before I had the chance.

I straightened, extending the cream-smeared badge to Jorg with a triumphant grin. Finally, something was going our way.

"Why is this smeared in pastry?" he asked, squinting at the ID.

Fenrir leaned forward and snatched it from his grasp.

His eyes widened.

"That's her!" he said. "But why is her name Ida Wechsler?"

"That's the new identity Frigg gave her. Sigyn dropped this when I...that doesn't matter. What does matter is that thanks to this badge, we know her curse name, and more importantly, where to find her."

Jorg studied the badge behind Fenrir's shoulder, his eyes narrowing in concentration.

"The Basel Historical Museum?" he asked. "That means

we will have to wait until morning...Frigg will know by that time..."

She would, and it would make everything harder. Which suited me fine.

"A kiss with Sigyn is all that now stands between us and any hope of getting our lives back," I said. "We must take this opportunity. Without Sigyn's memories, we are fucked, and time is running out. If Frigg finds us and curses you two, and binds me with Hel's...it will be the end. For all of us. This may be our only chance."

Jorg's frown deepened as he exchanged an uncertain look with Fenrir. Fenrir's shoulders sagged in response.

"I realize Sigyn's lack of memories will make achieving true love's kiss harder, but we've already gotten past the first challenge of even finding her. I'm thinking three days for the kiss part, give or take. And then, poof, the Salvation Weave is broken. Easy."

Jorg pointed at the frosted bottle of orange juice nestled between my legs.

"Except for the part where you two didn't get off to a good start, judging by her reaction," he said. "She clearly hates you. That could pose an issue."

"And I doubt we have three days. I think we will be lucky to have one," Fenrir added.

I waved away their concerns as if irritating flies.

"Not important," I said. "I may not be a god anymore, but I still have my charms. She'll be powerless to resist. We already know I'm her type."

Jorg leaned against the desk, arms crossed over his chest.

"Yes, but that was pre-curse Sigyn. Cursed Sigyn seems to feel differently about you," he said. "And your *charms*."

"A minor detail."

Fenrir's sigh filled the room. He slumped onto the bed's edge, burying his face in his hands.

"Gods," Fenrir groaned. "We're all going to die."

20

THE RAVEN

BALDER

"I will not allow Loki to cause Ragnarok again." Mother latched onto a tower of astrology books perched on the mantel in Father's study. "If only it were as simple as taking his head. Skadi would certainly appreciate that gift." With a grunt, she hurled them to the floor, leather covers cracking against the wood, pages spiraling through the air. "But, since I can't kill him, at least I have something equally permanent to look forward to when I finally corner that monster."

"Permanent? You mean the curse we agreed on...right, Mother?"

"—where does your father keep that damned spell book?"

Leather-bound books cluttered the room, their spines forming mountains on shelves, desks, and the floor. And those were the ones not wedged between scattered notes, trinkets, and emptied wine goblets.

How father ever found any book or note after he crammed them into every nook and cranny, I'd never know.

"It's here," Freya said, her bracelets jingling as she gestured. "We've traded spells quite a few times, and he always bragged about how he kept the most dangerous books in his study."

Freya rummaged through drawers, flinging parchments and knickknacks over her shoulders. Tasseled pillows thumped on the floor as she stripped them from leather chairs. Mr. Ragnar pounced on a discarded cushion, his tongue rasping across his paw, allowing a wave of fish-breath to choke the air.

Seriously?

I dodged a crate spilling with yellowed papers of weather predictions from four centuries ago. Father had a definite problem.

Mother walked to the heavy chest beneath the window, and grasped a small marble bust of Father. She gave a small smile and—the statue's face crunched against the brass lock once, twice, three times until metal shrieked and Father's nose clattered to the floor.

"Please be in here," she said.

The lid groaned open, and she tore through furs, old rings tinkling as she cast them aside. Leather bracers I hadn't seen since childhood surfaced and sank again. Oh. And of course, even more papers, these chronicling cabbage yields from Northern Asgard. Riveting information one should definitely never part with.

"I want to know how that trickster got to Midgard," she muttered, still churning through the chest's contents. "Though I suppose that's one step less for what I need." She laughed softly. "He's going to love my little surprise when he finds Sigyn doesn't know who he is."

"What?" My voice cracked. "You didn't tell me you took her memories."

"Balder, dear, that memory spell was quite necessary," she said, fingers trailing across the chest's brass fittings. "So much ancient knowledge locked away in that pretty head of hers...knowledge that certain parties would love to get their hands on." Her smile curved sharp as a blade. "But now? It's all beautifully blank."

Nausea roiled inside me, twisting tighter with each word.

"She did not deserve that," I said. "The curse was enough."

"Oh Balder," Mother stilled their searching. "I really can't have this whole 'who deserves what' discussion right now."

"You made an oath to me, Mother."

"And it is honored," she said. "Now, we must find this damn book. Your father's organization is atrocious."

But there was something about how she said those words that burrowed under my skin like splinters.

"And then what Frigg did to Sigyn in the forests of Vanaheim..."

My stomach hurt with the same sick dread I'd felt at five years old.

Mr. Ragnar's claws scraped wood as he launched himself onto the bookcase to my right. A potted plant toppled, ceramic exploding against the floor.

A lopsided clay raven rolled towards me.

I pulled the pieces from the dirt, brushing away earth to reveal the clumsy marks of a child's fingers pressed into clay. My thumb traced the crooked beak I'd shaped so carefully, trying to make it sharp like the ravens that perched on

Father's shoulders. A smile tugged at the corners of my mouth.

I was eight years old and Father had been away for a month to Vanaheim. But when Yule arrived, he burst through frost-covered doors, his laugh booming through halls, arms sweeping me up. Warmth radiated from his bear-fur cloak. Joy lit his face at the sight of me. That night, I made him the raven, my small fingers working the clay until they ached. Mother's voice cut through my pride: "Don't bother. He'll only throw it away."

But here it sat, kept all these years.

He cared.

I mean, the raven's head wobbled in my palm, slightly decapitated, but gods—he had *kept it.*

I smiled.

Freya screamed.

I whirled around, boots skidding on scattered papers, and scanned for blood. One of those infernal piles of books must have toppled over her head and broke her nose—

"What's wrong? Are you hurt?" My pulse hammered.

Freya twirled before the full-length mirror propped against the back wall, admiring herself with the satisfaction of a queen counting her jewels.

"The broth stage is working!" she said, delight filling each word. "I must have my artist capture this sensational glow I've achieved for the new coins to be minted. Imagine!" She traced her cheekbones. "Thousands of gold coins stamped with my face on them. This is a true dream come true."

Broth. The word curdled in my gut, reminding me of Mother's tactics to get Father to bend. The clay pieces pressed harder into my palm as my fingers clenched.

"Have you fed Father yet?" My throat tightened around the question.

Mother's eyes never left the tome on goat husbandry, pages crackling as she flipped them.

"I told you, hunger persuades."

Rage flared inside me as my jaw locked tight.

"Feed him," I growled through clenched teeth. "And I told you I wanted no more starvation."

She put down the book and reached for my cheeks. Her fingertips felt like spiders crawling across my skin.

"I know this is difficult, darling. Perhaps you should take a short break. What if you deliver a message to Hel for me?"

My heart slammed against my ribs at Hel's name, blood rushing in my ears.

"There's that scent again. Love." Freya's silver bangles clinked as she stalked closer, head tilted, nostrils flared.

"What message do you want delivered?" I asked.

Freya prowled around me, tracking the scent. Sweat beaded at my hairline.

"Inform her I am enacting sanctions," Mother said. "For conspiring in Loki's escape. There must be consequences."

Freya's shoulder brushed mine as she circled.

"Loki's escape isn't Hel's fault—"

"It smells stronger over here," she interrupted, her face inches from my hair, breath hot against my scalp.

I bolted to the open chest, camphor wood fumes burning my nose. Better than letting her catch whatever scent poured off me.

"And now it's gone again," Freya clenched her hands, rings glinting. "This is driving me mad."

"It's entirely Hel's fault," Mother said. "She is a traitor. She had one task, and instead she helped him escape. As punishment, she will receive no money, no support, not a single soul to help her. I'll strip her down to the bones." Her lips curved into a cold smile. "This is exactly why the curse must be sealed properly. No more of this family's endless scheming. And as for Hel...well, she'll learn her own special lesson about loyalty in the end."

My chest tightened at her words.

"No. There will be no lessons," I said. "You will leave Hel alone. None of this is what we discussed when I agreed to this curse—"

Mother yanked a heavy leather tome from a wardrobe shelf bowed under musty fur cloaks. The old binding gave a sharp crack as she spread it open.

She smiled as she traced runes burned into the yellowed pages, fragments of parchment crumbling beneath her touch.

"Of all the times to be stuck in Asgard," Mother said, pacing between towers of books, ignoring me. "What I would give to see Loki's face when he encounters what I have planned. Freya, I've witnessed your skill in this kind of magic. Look at this."

Freya turned the brittle pages, but the deeper she read down the spell, the faster her confident smirk faded, doubt creeping into her eyes.

"I can only summon one," she finally said, shoulders sagging. "For what you want...only he is capable."

Mother tapped the old leather, her gaze boring into the text.

"I always abhor needing him for these things. It's deeply humiliating. Thankfully we won't have to rely on him much longer."

"Oh?" Freya raised an eyebrow.

"I discovered the most fascinating potential in the Fall-rock Mountains last week," she said, excitement threading through her words. "Another element, if you can believe it. Hidden away all this time. Such raw power in that one. Very promising." A slight smile played at her lips. "Soon we won't have to deal with all this...nonsense."

My brow creased as unease prickled my neck. What was she talking about?

"Another element—?" I began.

"The spell," Mother sliced through the question, nail rapping against parchment. "Odin will manage it."

And I knew what she intended with Father. My gut twisted harder.

The clay raven's broken edges bit deeper into my palm.

"Balder, why don't you run along to the underworld—"

Run along.

As though I remained that little boy she could direct.

Something deep inside my bones shifted, something I didn't even know lived within me until now.

"Did Father ever want to take me on his travels with Thor?" The question erupted from my chest, shocking me. They tasted of metal and defiance.

Where had that come from? What dark corner of my heart pushed me to say the words? But I had said them, and they hung in the air, too late to retract.

I stared at Mother. Stared at the shock on her face as an uneasy silence hardened the room. Even Freya's breathing stilled.

"What is this?" Mother asked, a hint of forced laughter beneath the words. "Do you really think I'd keep you from him? How can you think that?"

Shock at my daring warred with the thunder of my pulse. But now that the question lived, it demanded answers.

"Answer the question," I said. "Did Father want me?"

"Did Thor say something to you?" Suspicion coiled through her tone.

"No, not at all."

She pinched the bridge of her nose.

"Well, had you come to me, and not gone behind my back by asking Thor, I could have told you the truth, and you wouldn't have all this stress he's put you under with his nonsense."

"And what is the truth?"

Her posture relaxed.

"I'm your Mother," she said. "I couldn't bear to be parted from you. I couldn't tolerate the possibility of you injured. What he wanted, where he wanted to take you, it was too dangerous. If I lost you..."

"So you were just concerned for me?"

"Your father was always thoughtless when it came to what was safe or unsafe," she said. "If he really wanted to spend time with you, he would have chosen to stay home, not traipse around the wilderness where any Jotnar or wolf could attack."

That truth landed like a stone in my chest. I had no defense against it.

He could have stayed.

I returned the clay raven to the shelf.

"I'm sorry how upsetting you're finding all this, but I've only ever done everything out of love for you. Out of safety for you."

She squeezed my upper arm, warmth seeping through my sleeve. For two seconds, I allowed myself to believe in that touch, in her love.

I sighed, dropping my thorns and sank into her embrace, breathing in roses and childhood memories.

"I know, Mother," I whispered against her shoulder.

"You were my greatest desire," she murmured. "My greatest blessing. He never loved you like I do."

Gods, the things she endured with that man.

But watching her break him now…

I was tired of all the suffering.

I stepped back, breaking her hold.

"I will return to Hel," I said. "But Mother, I insist that you feed Father. Promise me."

She looked at me, and for one terrible heartbeat, I thought she would refuse.

She nodded.

"If it brings you comfort," she said. "I will go to the kitchens first. Because I want you at peace."

Relief loosened the knot in my chest. I let out a shaking breath.

I had to trust her.

No.

I *did* trust her.

21

———

TAKE IT SLEAZY

LOKI

The Basel Historical Museum's limestone facade came into view ahead on Barfüsserplatz.

Our footsteps thundered across cobblestones as we weaved between businesspeople and tourists. Trams clanged and pigeons scattered around us, their wings beating against the autumn breeze. I gripped the box full of fresh pastries to replace the ones I had some *minor* responsibility in smashing. A peace offering. One I hoped worked...

Truth was, there were a million ways this plan could all turn into sour shark meat. One of them being my clothing, like the "Take it Sleazy" text blazing across my chest in mustard yellow, the letters crackling on worn black cotton. Or the infuriating holey foam clogs that squeaked with each step. Neither was exactly ideal for charming Sigyn.

However, I quite loved the charge of little old me being the hero. Of course, some extra time would have been nice. As it were, time ran thin, and on top of everything else, I had to rely on Balder keeping his mouth shut about my mortality to his mummy. I couldn't believe it came to trusting him. Disgusting.

"How are you actually making this look work?" Jorg's combat boots scuffed the pavement as he walked beside me, the strings of his black hoodie bobbing with every footfall.

"Because I'm me." I combed my fingers through the waves of my hair, arranging each strand to accentuate my sharp cheekbones and devastating jawline.

"I appreciate the faux leather jacket," Fenrir said, his green eyes tracking every detail of my horror show. "Don't be nervous."

"It's not nerves. It's me sweating because of this bloody awful plastic."

"But it's recycled," he said "You promised."

I took a long breath, trying to compose myself. The fabric rustled with the movement.

"Yes, yes," I conceded, tugging at my collar. "It's just that wooing Sigyn would be a whole lot easier if I didn't have to wear off the rack separates."

The museum's glass doors groaned open. Battle-scarred armor and centuries-old crests adorned the ceiling's stone ribs.

"We will wait here." Fenrir settled into a wooden chair at a table tucked in an alcove of the foyer. Coffee steam drifted from the museum cafe, turning the air bitter.

"I really rather you go back to the hotel," I said. "Frigg has eyes everywhere, and I don't want to make this even easier for her."

"I already explained," Fenrir said. "We don't want you out of our sight after you lost that coin the first time."

"And Fenrir has me if Frigg tries anything." Jorg rapped his knuckles against the tabletop as I scanned the displays and the ticket counter.

I tapped my shoe against the marble floor, arms crossed.

"It sounds as if you both don't trust me." I arched my eyebrow.

"I wonder why that would be," Jorg's words bit.

Fenrir grabbed his brother's sleeve, pulling him into the chair beside him. Jorg snapped open the menu, nostrils flaring as he read the choices of espresso or double espresso.

"I told you, we stick together," Fenrir said. "For many reasons. Now, go find her. I hope her position here isn't in the archives, because that may take more time to locate her if she's stuck in one of those basement type offices. Of course, this being originally a church, it could be a crypt. Gods. This could take ages."

I scanned the entrance hall, tuning out his rambling as I searched for Sigyn among the tourists and schoolchildren.

Woman photographing armor. No.

Mother yanking her toddler away from a rack of post-cards. No.

Employee yawning by the elevator. No.

Ah.

There!

A flash of honey ginger hair caught my eye, pulled back in a ponytail. Her head bent over the computer screen, shadows darkening beneath her eyes. The curse's drain showed in every line of her face, each day stealing more of her strength.

And the sign above her desk certainly didn't help.

I dug my nails into my palms as I read *Guest Services*.

Oh. That was mean. Even for Frigg.

My pulse thrummed as I marched towards her desk, rage building at the thought of her dealing with complaints about poorly lit manuscripts and 'historically inaccurate' tea service displays while Frigg's curse drained her strength. If any man started a conversation with 'actually' with Sigyn, I'd cut out his voice box."

The pastry box thumped on the counter as I slid it forward.

Sigyn's fingers paused over the keyboard. Her eyes flicked from monitor to box, lingering on the gold-leaf cafe logo embossed on the lid. A smile stretched her face, dimples appearing at the corners...until she lifted her gaze to mine, and recognition curdled her expression like spoiled milk.

Spectacular.

"You," she said, her tone laced with a thousand icicles aimed at my temples.

"Hello—"

"Are you stalking me now?" She pushed her rolling chair back, the wheels squeaking against the floor tiles.

I raised my hands, palms forward. The morning sunlight streaming through the lobby windows caught those flecks of gold in her narrowing eyes I loved so dearly.

"What? No, not at all," I said. "I thought I'd bring back your badge, and replace the cremeschnitte from last night, and apologize for the unfortunate misunderstanding between us."

I held out both the pastry box and her work badge, the lanyard dangling between my fingers. Her eyes flitted between my face, the box, and the badge. The scent of vanilla and butter wafted from the box's corners, and her nostrils flared slightly. She kept her arms firmly crossed over her burgundy blazer.

"Misunderstanding? You grabbed my wrists. There is nothing to misunderstand. You're a creep." Her chair bumped against the filing cabinet behind her.

"Yes, I did do that—"

"You kept calling me that strange name."

"I did, but—"

She lunged forward, snatching her work badge from my hand, the lanyard whipping through the air. Relief flooded her features as she pressed it to her chest, but her eyes lingered on the pastry box.

"You wouldn't get your clammy hands off me."

I bristled at that one.

"My hands are *not* clammy," I said.

Inhaling deeply, I loosened my shoulders.

"Thank you for admitting it. Your confession will make the police report much easier—" She reached for the phone on her desk.

Police? No. The memory of stale bologna sandwiches and fluorescent lights flashed through my mind. I would not let myself be imprisoned in a Midgardian jail again.

"Look, I admit I did those things because I mistakenly thought you were someone else in the poor lighting. It was an error in judgment, nothing more. I meant you no harm whatsoever. You have my word." I infused my voice with as much earnestness as I could, keeping my hands steady on the pastry box.

Her features softened as she considered my explanation, the icicles in her gaze melting. Perhaps a dozen of the original thousand at best. Her eyes flicked to the pastry box again.

She sighed, shoulders dropping.

"I suppose I can accept it being an honest mistake...but still. You terrified me. And you do have clammy hands, by the way."

I forced my grin to stay pleasant, arms beginning to tire from holding out the box.

"And for that I'm truly sorry. Again, please accept my

apologies," I said. "And these cremeschnitte as a peace offering."

The box's weight shifted as I held it out closer to her so she would smell more of that decadent vanilla cream.

She bit her lower lip, clearly torn between her desire for the pastries and her distinct hatred of me.

"If it makes you feel any better, I have already forgiven you," I said.

She tilted her head.

"Me? You've forgiven *me*? You have some balls—"

"Well, I'm glad you at least noticed when you kicked me in the groin, and rather hard I might add," I said. "I spent the night with ice down my trousers."

The corners of her mouth twitched upwards.

"Alright, that may have been *excessive*," she said. "But when someone says 'let me go,' you let them go. Now you have a second chance to respect my wishes. Leave. Prove you're actually the gentleman you're trying so hard to convince me you are."

"But I brought you replacement pastries—" I lifted the pastry box.

Her eyes locked onto it with naked longing before snapping back to glare at me.

"Oh, you absolute bastard."

Even Frigg's spell couldn't dim that familiar fire in her eyes. Gods, I loved her, even as she looked ready to murder me.

"Damn you for knowing my weakness," she growled, snatching the box from me. "Don't think this means anything. I've been trying to get my hands on these for weeks, and something always goes wrong."

"Wouldn't dream of it."

She pried open the lid, and for a breath, pure joy swept

across her face as she lifted a cream-filled pastry to her lips—

"Ida!" A gangly young man appeared around the corner, his name tag declaring him as Oliver. Sigyn shrank five inches in five seconds.

And there was the something wrong, right on schedule.

Oliver narrowed his eyes at the open pastry box.

"What do you think you're doing? You know you can't eat in public during your shift!" he said. "And where did you even get these?"

He snatched the box from her hands, his bony fingers crushing the cardboard.

"I'll be confiscating these. Consider this a warning."

Sigyn frowned as Oliver marched to the bin. The cremeschnitte hit the trash with a thud. Her fingers reached towards the bin, then dropped. The lid clanged shut. Her shoulders hunched.

Oh. I'd find a way to get him back for that. I fiddled with the pen on the desk, testing its weight and balance, deciding which of his eyes to jab it into.

"And why are you ignoring this guest? First, you show up here without your badge, and then eating on the job, and now..." Oliver adjusted his navy polyester tie. "You will help this guest immediately, unless you want me to report you to Margrit again for neglecting your duties."

A grin spread across his face, definitely on the smarmy side, his teeth too white against his dry skin.

Hold on...maybe I was too hasty with the stabbing part.

"Sorry for the trouble, but I—" His gaze fell to my chest, lingered there for a second or two, and slowly trailed back up to my eyes. A flush brightened his cheeks, spreading to the tips of his ears, and I knew exactly the thoughts racing through his head.

Every time. But could I really blame him when I was me?

The toddler's shrill scream over not getting the postcards filled the room, making Oliver jump and breaking him out of whatever heated fantasy he'd concocted.

"—I...hope she hasn't caused you any trouble."

"Not at all," I said. "Everything's fine."

"Well, then." He tugged at his collar. I smirked, loving how flustered I could still make humans. "How can Ida assist you today?"

"I'm Dr. Loki Laufeyjarson, a visiting scholar from the University of Reykjavik." There was no need for a *total* alias. I wanted Sigyn to know my real name, hoping it might stir the hazy memories buried beneath her altered consciousness. "I was hoping you could help me with my research paper I'm writing concerning...uh...concerning, ah yes... concerning the crockery of 16th century Swiss book printers. You see, I'm rather an expert on Icelandic 16th century crockery."

His gaze dropped again and raked over my shirt. I knew I was devilishly handsome, but this was getting a touch ridiculous.

"Icelandic crockery?" Sigyn repeated, confusion melting into outright suspicion across her features. "How does that in any way connect to Switzerland?"

I smiled.

"That's the connection my research hopes to find," I said. "I'm still in the theory stage."

I concentrated, feeling the familiar tingle of magic at my fingertips like static. It presented more of a struggle than it should have been. Everything was more difficult not being a god, but I managed to conjure an illusion of a university ID card. Maintaining it was like trying to hold water in cupped hands. One slip of concentration and the whole thing would dissolve.

"Here are my credentials," I said, the buzz of magic behind my eyes making my vision swim slightly. The photo on the ID wavered for one second before I steadied it.

Sigyn's eyes widened as she took the ID, her fingers brushing against mine. Every point of contact threatened to disrupt the illusion. Her suspicion seemed to waver, replaced by a hint of curiosity as she tilted the card under the fluorescent lights. I forced myself to breathe normally while keeping the holographic security features from flickering out of existence.

Oliver pushed her aside with his hip, smoothing his limp hair and licking his lips again like a nervous schoolboy.

"Loki, like the Norse god? How funny."

I smiled, though it felt more like a grimace. The effort of upholding the illusion while trying to be charming was giving me a headache.

He rubbed the back of his neck, no doubt imagining my mouth there trailing down. Well, if this is what it took to get what I wanted faster, so be it. At least my seduction was working on someone.

"Exactly like the Norse god," I said, my voice silken despite the pressure building behind my temples. I reached out and brushed the side of his hand on the desk. His cheeks flushed hotter with arousal, and I could sense his pulse quickening at my touch.

Out of the corner of my eye, Sigyn took a photo of my ID with her phone. Gods. Really? I suppressed both a wince and a smirk, amused by her caution even as I prayed to anyone listening we could hurry this all along.

"I-I'm a huge fan of the old Norse legends," Oliver stammered, leaning into my touch. His glazed eyes showed dilated pupils. Good. Keep looking at me, not the ID that's probably shimmering around the edges.

"Now, be a good boy and escort me to the proper resources," I purred, tracking my fingertips lazily along the back of his hand while simultaneously trying to keep the university seal from melting off the card.

He gulped in that delightful way that told me I was one move away from getting everything I wanted from him.

"What is happening?" Sigyn cut through my good work. "Oliver, this man just shows up claiming he is a doctor from Iceland and wants to know about Swiss crockery, and you're one look away from handing him the front keys. None of this makes any sense. And he speaks perfect Swiss German, which is quite convenient for an Icelandic researcher, isn't it?"

"I spent much of my youth in Basel," I said smoothly. "Academic family."

The ID flickered in her hands, but she was too busy glaring at me to notice.

Oliver gave a firm shiver, as if breaking out of a trance, which it kind of was. He reached over and took the ID from Sigyn's grip and handed it back to me. Thank gods.

"Ida, help Dr. Laufeyjarson." He handed her his skeleton keys. "With whatever he wants. I would, but I have a lunch meeting I cannot miss. Damn that Margrit."

As I slipped the ID back into my pocket, I felt the strain of maintaining the illusion dissipate like a released breath. Gods. I did not want to have to do that again if I could help it. My head pounded.

Sigyn clutched the keys.

"You can't be serious. I'm not yet sure that ID is even valid—"

"Ida! Stop, right now." He leaned in close to Sigyn, his

lips nearly grazing her ear, whispering urgent words that I strained to catch. "You know our museum is currently facing severe financial strain," he murmured, "especially after we lost funding from the Zurich-Bräuners. Expanding our reputation and securing additional funding sources is crucial if we want to open that new exhibit wing. This potential partnership with Dr. Laufeyjarson could be instrumental in impressing wealthy patrons and donors." His gaze flicked back to me, his voice growing louder, more insistent. "I trust you understand how vital it is that we accommodate his research needs without hesitation."

Sigyn's jaw clenched, but she nodded. The keys jingled in her grip.

"Good. I'll leave you to provide Dr. Laufeyjarson with whatever assistance he requires." He flashed me a grin. "We greatly appreciate you choosing our humble museum for your important work. And, if you'd like to discuss your findings with me afterward at dinner..." He glanced over me once more. "I'd be more than willing."

"I'm sure you would be," I said.

The toddler finally won against the mother, small hands yanking down the entire rack of postcards. It clattered to the ground, cards scattering across the floor.

Oliver hurried over to the commotion, dabbing at the sweat beading on his brow. He muttered a string of curses under his breath as he bent down to gather the postcards, his khakis pulling tight across his backside.

Insufferable little parasite. My fingers itched to conjure something particularly nasty in his next cup of coffee. But, I think that would truly do me in. Not being a god anymore was the worst. How was I supposed to enjoy myself now?

Sigyn's smile remained fixed in place, her lips stretched

taut, and doing little to hide the fury simmering beneath the surface. I recognized the emotion at once. Loathing.

And I found it absolutely thrilling, because the challenge always made it all the more fun. I gave her an hour before she'd be swooning in my arms, just like Oliver. Less, if I really applied myself.

"Shall we get started then?" I asked, leaning against the counter, my elbow sliding across its polished surface with practiced casualness.

She inhaled deeply.

"What can I help you with, *Doctor*?" she asked, the words clipped and terse and ready to bite my head off.

Grasping a glossy pamphlet from the stack by the register, I flipped through the pages, scanning for an exhibit. Any exhibit. The pages crackled under my fingers. I jabbed my finger at a random spot on the page.

"For starters, I'd like you to show me this."

"A stool?"

I glanced down, my finger pressed against the image of a simple wooden stool with a snail motif carved into its base. Not exactly the most inspired choice for wooing.

"How is a stool relevant for your alleged crockery research?" she asked, her eyebrow arched high enough to suggest she'd rather throw the stool at me than discuss it.

"Ah, yes, well...one can learn much from examining the craftsmanship of even humble objects," I said. "The...er... joinery techniques used can provide insight into the woodworking methods of the era."

Sigyn glared at me, her brow flattening.

"If I find this has all been some sick, twisted ruse to get to me..."

Perhaps I should have picked a more credible research topic. Like 19th century French pantomime.

"I swear to you it isn't," I said. "I want information. You would be surprised by the hidden insights found in over-looked objects."

Sigyn exhaled a sharp breath that may have bordered on a scoff.

"That's the first semi sensible thing you've said," she said. "Fine. But one wrong word, or any more handsy nonsense, and I kick you between the legs again. Understood?"

Alright. Maybe two hours until she'd be swooning in my arms.

22

A STOOL BY ANY OTHER NAME

"Thank you for this, I'm in real need of help," I said, stretching my lips into my most devastating smile. The smile that had once charmed keys from prison guards. I needed to speed this kiss thing up if I hoped to break this pesky spell before lunch. That would be a new personal best for me, beating that time in Alfheim with the hermit.

"No argument there."

She drummed across her phone screen.

Sigyn was as radiant as ever, especially when annoyed. That spark in her when she told me something particularly barbed sent a rush of heat down between my legs.

But while her wit remained sharp as those nails she obviously had eaten for breakfast, her usual confident posture had crumpled. Her shoulders curved inward as she walked. A storm cloud hovered over her, sagging her down, which didn't help my goal. It was hard to be horny when depressed.

I scrambled after her through the halls and exhibits, my shoes squeaking on the polished floors. Silver tea sets and jewel encrusted crucifixes gleamed beneath display lights. Medieval knights stared down from faded tapestries. Sigyn's face glowed blue from her phone as she swiped and typed, her gaze shifting between websites and documents.

We passed through exhibits, each glass cabinet brimming with echoes of lives once lived. And if I stared hard enough, our past whispered back from every gilt-framed portrait. Every tarnished silver spoon. So close I could reach through the shadows and touch it.

"This way," Sigyn said. Her eyes remained glued to her phone screen, thumb scrolling faster. "Let's keep this speedy. I have an appointment with archives at two."

I swallowed the lump in my throat, pushing the ghosts aside.

"I know we got off on the wrong foot, but I'd like for us to start over." I rubbed 'cucumber mint' lip balm all over my lips, wanting them to be as soft as possible for the best experience.

"Again?" Sigyn glanced up from her phone. Exhaustion crept into her voice. "Isn't this the third time trying?"

"Isn't it third time's the charm?"

She rolled her eyes and returned to her device. I'd never understand Midgardian's and their obsession with these glowing rectangles.

"Are you actually capable of normal conversation?" she asked.

We stood next to the display case housing a suit of armor. I believe had the glass not separated her from the broadsword, she would have used it to pin my foot to the floor.

I scratched the back of my head and tucked the lip balm into my pocket. This spell definitely was putting up a fight against my usually fatal allure.

"Alright, I'll give it a go. What about...how long have you worked here?" I asked. "Is this the type of conversation you want?"

"Yes, it's a start, mundane, nothing weird," she said.

"And are you going to answer the question? Usually, that's how normal, polite conversation works, I believe. I say something, and you say something back that isn't an insult."

Her lips pursed into a tight line that reminded me of Odin during council meetings.

"What was the question?"

"I asked how long you've worked here?"

How long has Frigg made you think you work here? What kind of altered memories am I dealing with?

She blinked, confusion flickering across her face.

"How long have I been here? I've been here...I...wait, that's not right. Actually, when did I start?" She chewed on her lower lip as she struggled to recall. "Now you've got me all flustered with your annoyances. I've been here a long time, alright?" Always those fuzzy spell induced edges. Typical so far.

A soft *ding* from her phone cut through the silence.

She stopped so abruptly I nearly collided with her back. Her eyes were fixed on her phone screen, flicking between the display and my face with growing dismay.

"You seem surprised by something," I said. "Or perhaps disappointed?"

Sigyn's knuckles went white around the phone case until plastic creaked under her grip.

"I...I have an old family friend who's a professor of Norse Studies at the University of Reykjavik. I emailed him about you, and they just replied." She swallowed hard. "I may have asked if you were actually their resident expert on 16th century Icelandic crockery, or if you were just some weird guy hanging around museums making up stories about dishware."

Her cheeks flushed. "Professor Bjornsson wrote back that not only does he know you, but that you're 'a brilliant scholar in multiple fields' and—" she squinted at her phone in disbelief "—particularly insightful about Norse trickster figures, despite your official focus on historical ceramics. And apparently, you're 'a great guy.'"

"How nice of him," I replied, a smirk tugging at my lips. "Dr. Bjornsson and I go way back."

Sigyn blinked, her grip on the phone loosening slightly.

Of course she had his email. Before Frigg's curse, we'd spent several months together at Reykjavik while I helped with translating some Nordic runes. I'd added a dragon or two to make the stories more interesting, especially the ones about me, and Sigyn had rolled her eyes at every embellishment. Now the spell had twisted those memories, making her believe she had some pre-existing family connection to Bjornsson, rather than knowing him as my colleague and her husband's collaborator. The magic was clever that way, warping real memories instead of creating new ones. Easier to maintain the illusion when you're working with what's already there.

"Were you hoping to find me a fraud?" I asked, genuinely amused by her detective work.

The fluorescent lights caught the tension in her shoulders.

"I...well, you have to admit, your story is rather far-fetched. I had to verify." She traced the edge of her phone case with her thumb.

I chuckled.

"Fair enough. I appreciate a healthy dose of skepticism.

Though I'm curious what else your contact might have shared about me."

I leaned against the wall.

"That you're...unconventional, but reliable."

"I'm full of surprises, I assure you."

She snorted, a hint of a smile tugging at her lips before she caught herself.

"I suppose if Professor Bjornsson says you're the type of scholar who would research what Swiss book printers ate from just to find some connection to 16th century Icelandic crockery, who am I to argue?" She looked me over, from my horrid sneakers to my magnificent hair. For a breath, I glimpsed a spark of interest. She cleared her throat before finishing, "Even if everything about you is so...aggravating."

"You'd be surprised how versatile Icelandic crockery enthusiasts can be," I quipped, pretending not to notice her watching my fingers trace the edge of the display case beside us. "Besides, you never know when you might find a teacup with a runic inscription."

"Is that common?" she asked, relaxing her death grip on her phone.

"Not at all," I grinned. "But that's what makes it exciting. Now, fair's fair. Since you've been prying into my background, I think I'm entitled to ask you a few more questions, don't you?"

She started walking again.

"Must you?"

"When did you move to Basel?"

Sigyn rubbed her temples, eyes distant, lost in Frigg's fog. Her shoulders slumped further, and in that breath, she seemed smaller, more fragile, as if her forgotten past was physically crushing her.

"I'm not sure...I can't seem to recall. I've always been here, I think."

"You *think*? You really can't remember anything at all before you arrived here?"

She shrugged, as if not remembering an entire chunk of her life wasn't something to concern oneself about. I suppose this shouldn't surprise me. Spells like this acted like a virus, even affecting those around her. Her colleagues accepted her as having always been there, their own memories bending around the spell like light around a black hole.

"You may notice the tapestries here—"

"Are you happy?" The words escaped before I could stop them.

"Don't you think that a little personal?"

"Where I'm from, it's only polite."

I gave a roguish grin. One that would usually have made her cheeks flush with heat.

Her expression remained annoyed.

"Alright, you are one word away from me walking," she said.

"What did I say?" I asked. "I only meant, are you happy in this field? I am curious about why you chose to work at this exact museum. We are both working in this field of history. It is only a colleague's curiosity. Nothing more."

She eyed me, gaze raking over my face like she was trying to peel back layers of skin to find the lie she knew lurked beneath.

"I actually got accepted to study under Professor Bjornsson at the University of Reykjavik for a semester," she said, fidgeting with her badge. "Initially it was about the printing connection. The paper used by Iceland's first presses came from Basel, you know. But what really drew me in were the stories those printers produced. The Norse mythology, the sagas..." She trailed off, her eyes distant. "The first Icelandic printed edition of the Prose Edda...there's something about those old tales that calls to me. But something came up at the last minute, and I had to give up my spot."

Of course she did. The spell had taken our months together at Reykjavik—her helping me with translations while I collaborated with Bjornsson—and warped them into a missed opportunity, an almost-was. Frigg had a cruel sense of irony, transforming happy memories into regrets.

She pressed against her sternum as she spoke, as if trying to touch something buried deep inside.

"I've been sad about that missed opportunity ever since. Our museum has this collection of early printed texts from Basel, and whenever I see the ones with Norse mythology, even just mentions in marginalia...I feel it in my bones, you know? Like the stories are trying to tell me something." She caught herself and blinked as if waking from a dream. "Sorry, I...I don't know why I told you any of that at all."

But I knew why. Beneath the spell stealing her memories, she felt a connection to me. To our shared past.

"I understand," I said. "Sometimes the paths we don't take haunt us the most. But your love of Icelandic history and mythology...it's palpable. Have you considered pursuing that interest further, even from here?"

The room tilted. First right, then left, the display cases blurring at the edges. Heat bloomed in my chest. I clutched my torso, as this something hot burned deep inside. I blinked, and the heat went away, as if it had never happened at all. Well, that was strange.

She stretched out and touched my shoulder.

"Are you alright?" Sigyn asked.

She looked at her hand on my shoulder, and yanked it

back like she'd touched fire, clearing her throat with a small cough.

"Yes," I said, drawing in slow breaths through my nose. "Quite alright. Lead on."

Damn heartburn. Yes. That's what it was. Probably from that applesauce I had at breakfast.

We entered an oak-paneled room meant to replicate a 16th century study. The recorded clap of horse hooves and rattle of carriages filled the space. Sigyn walked to a desk beside a leaded window, the artificial sunlight streaming through diamond panes.

The floorboards groaned beneath my feet, everything familiar. Real. And as we moved through the dimly lit space, those ghosts gripped my ankles again and pulled. We fell in love in rooms like this, surrounded by brass candlesticks and walls of mahogany. Aged wood and parchment filled my nostrils, and I lost myself in memories she didn't remember. Her bent over medical texts, candlelight in her hair, ink staining her fingers.

"Here is your stool."

"What? Oh, yes," I said, snapping back to the present. "I'm so overwhelmed seeing it in person."

She arched an eyebrow.

"I have to say, I've never seen anyone so moved by a 16th century stool before."

A hint of amusement danced across her features, and hope flickered deep in my insides that perhaps the ice was thawing.

"It's not every day one sees something with this crafts-manship. I love good woodwork. Look at that snail!" I pointed at the carved mollusk.

Her brow arched further. And then, the most marvelous thing happened. She laughed. A genuine laugh, not the polite kind she gave tourists, but the one that used to echo through our house in Malibu.

"Most don't notice the snail, I'll give you that," she said, her voice lighter, more playful.

Her gaze lingered on me as if reassessing. I believed I teetered on some edge with her. In a breath, something relaxed in her. Shifted. Her shoulders loosened, and the tension that had previously lined her face melted away.

And she smiled at me. The real smile. The one that crinkled the corners of her eyes.

"If this impresses you, I'll show you something better." She led me to a display case, keys jingling at her hip, eyes radiant with that familiar enthusiasm I loved about her. The look she got when discovering a new healing herb or mastering the intricacies of the spleen.

"This is my favorite piece in the museum. Most overlook it, as it's not outwardly impressive. But it's incredibly rare."

She hovered her fingers over the case. The blue and white glazed pottery gleamed under the display lights.

"An albarello?" I asked. "A medieval medicinal jar?"

Delight ignited her eyes, and she looked at me with a sort of respect that wasn't there before.

"Yes! You're the first to recognize it."

"Well, I am an expert on crockery, remember? Though I suppose Professor Bjornsson has already vouched for that." I couldn't resist the smirk that tugged at my lips.

She blushed and chuckled lightly.

The actual truth was I only knew what this was because she had dozens of these vessels in her study when I first met her, lined on oak shelves, each filled with herbs and elixirs. Their contents had stained her fingers different colors as she worked. Her attraction to this piece made sense. The remaining bits of her true self were pulling her to these things like a lodestone finding north.

"Tell me about this particular one," I said, relaxing against the wall. Finally enjoying her not wanting to kick me in the groin for the first time. "Maybe it holds the connection I'm looking for."

She looked at the albarello, her eyes soft and adoring. The way she used to gaze at me across candlelit tables.

"It's from the 15th century," she said, tracing the air above the glass. "What fascinates me is that it's from Johannes Kaufmann's print shop here in Basel. See the mark on the base? Apothecaries used jars like these to store their medicinal herbs and powders, but printers also used them for their pigments and inks. The designs painted onto the ceramic denoted the contents. This flowering pattern usually signified cardiac remedies in medical settings, but in print shops, similar vessels often held red vermillion ink." Her eyes lit up. "There's actually a whole collection of printer's pottery in storage from various Basel workshops. I've spent my lunch breaks cataloging them. Out of personal interest, of course."

Her voice swelled with excitement as she explained these vessels, and I glimpsed the woman I knew. That I loved. And I was determined to pull her out of this curse, fragment by precious fragment.

"Your knowledge is incredible," I said, meaning every word.

She fidgeted with her badge again.

"I may have a fixation. And I don't often get the chance to gush about these nerdy things I love. You wouldn't believe some of the pieces we have in storage," she said, momentarily forgetting her suspicion in her enthusiasm. "There's this whole set of vessels from the Froben printing house. I've been fascinated by how similar they are to medical vessels. Probably because printers often bought their containers from the same craftsmen who supplied apothecaries." She caught herself and added quickly, "Not that I should know all this. Just things you pick up working here."

I couldn't help but smile at how she downplayed her knowledge. Even cursed to believe she was a museum guide, she couldn't help but study everything around her.

"How about we now get a little naughty," I said.

Her brow flattened, and her expression hardened once more. She took a half-step back.

"You are determined to ruin everything, aren't you?"

"I notice you have a set of skeleton keys Oliver handed you. I'm only asking if you can unlock that glass case, and pop that off its shelf and let us get a closer look? Don't you want to examine it closer? No one is around."

She wavered, her eyes shifting between me and the albarello. She wanted to. Badly.

"I mean, yes, but, well, I really shouldn't...I'm not authorized to handle the artifacts."

I unleashed my most charming smile. Again.

"There are plenty of things in life we shouldn't do, but sometimes we have to think about the experience." I neared her, closing the distance between us, and her breath caught, just slightly. "Sometimes we need to see. To touch. And you have the key."

She fingered the key in her hand, thumb tracing its worn teeth, her gaze fixed on the vessel. Slowly, she reached out to the case, shoved the key in the lock, and twisted.

The hinges creaked as she lifted the lid. She hesitated for a heartbeat before reaching inside. She brushed the porcelain—she froze, spine going rigid, and her eyes grew distant, unfocused, as if seeing through time.

The albarello nearly slipped from her grasp before she caught it, hands trembling.

"Sorry, I had a strange flash. Like a fragment of a dream." She forced a feeble laugh that didn't reach her eyes. "Too many late nights reading history books, I suppose."

Now that was interesting.

"Do such episodes happen often?"

"No more than anyone else with a wild imagination." Her hold tightened around the vessel.

And this is what I wished for. Touching the albarello wouldn't break the spell, wouldn't suddenly make Sigyn burst through Ida's walls. But it might thin the spell just enough for the real Sigyn to stir beneath.

These were the threads I had to find and pull until I pulled her out of Frigg's magic. Until enough of her true self emerged for our kiss to reach her and work.

Maybe I was right about that one hour after all.

I dared inch nearer, pulse racing as I destroyed the remaining distance. The scent of her jasmine perfume mingled with old wood and glass polish.

"You still have such passion in you for these things." I reached out, grazing her fingers where they curved around the vessel's smooth surface.

Remember me. Please.

Confusion clouded her eyes. A crease formed between her brows as she searched my face, struggling to make sense of my words.

"Still? You know nothing about my passions. You've just met me."

And the shutter fell again with a bang.

"Nothing is familiar to you?" I asked.

Her knuckles whitened around the vessel as she gripped it tighter.

"Why should anything seem familiar?"

Her words gutted me.

"Why? Because—"

"Ida!" A severe woman walked towards us. Her name tag glinted under the lights—Margrit.

Sigyn returned the artifact to its case, the glass lid closing with a final click as she locked our memories away behind it.

"What are you doing handling the artifacts?" Margrit snapped.

"Sorry, I was only showing—"

"And why are you away from your post?" Margrit's lips pressed into a bloodless line.

"I'm doing as Oliver instructed me. I'm to assist Dr. Laufeyjarson—"

"I don't care what Oliver said. You're not authorized for tours, demonstrations, and especially not touching any of the collections. You're assigned to the help desk."

Fury ignited within me, scalding my veins. Rage cracked hot in my chest, spreading through my limbs. Actually, it was *quite* hot. Suspiciously hot, really. Sweat beaded at my temples and trickled down my neck. The room tilted again, but I couldn't bother with silly things like wondering *why*. Not when this stupid human dared speak to my wife like this.

I stepped forward, forcing myself not to reach for the dagger hidden in my coat pocket. Margrit should have been grateful I had been practicing my restraint. Usually, I would have already sliced through the jugular by now. I'd really come a long way.

"Now, look here Madam," I said. "She was only doing what I requested. I asked to see the vessel up close to inspect it better. She's done nothing wrong."

Margrit glared down her bony nose.

"Guest relations staff can't give tours or handle artifacts without the correct training. Oliver must have been ill to have allowed this overstep."

I mean, in a way he was...

"I want Ida as my guide."

"It's museum policy. No exceptions." She turned to Sigyn. "Go back to your desk now, or disciplinary action will be taken."

I opened my mouth to say a few choice words that would make her weep, but Margrit turned sharply, and walked away down the hall.

I curled my fist at my side, trying very hard to not race up behind her and rip her spine out through her throat. Searing heat lanced across my palm, almost like a cinder cracking. The sensation jolted through me. I glanced down at my palm, relaxing my stiff fingers. Nothing there but smooth skin. Yet for an instant, it had that same snap of heat like my chaos did. That familiar spark of power. What if...

No. Impossible.

That applesauce must have had something else laced in it. That was the only explanation. Nothing more than a phantom sensation fueled by my rage at Margrit's treatment of Sigyn. And some indigestion. Definitely indigestion.

"I should get back." Sigyn's voice scattered my thoughts.

She walked off.

I couldn't let her go. I needed as much time with her as I could get.

My mind raced, concocting a thousand schemes.

"Wait," I said.

I touched her shoulder as I had a hundred times before, stopping her. She turned and met my gaze. Her cheeks flushed again. Deeper this time.

Despite all that, she rolled me off her. I held out my hands, palms open. She was not mine to touch. Not anymore.

"You've been incredibly helpful to me, and you seem to know a great deal about this city and its history, dare I say, more than Margrit." I said. "I'd love if you could be my personal guide."

She crossed her arms.

"I appreciate the sentiment," she said. "But there's nothing you could do to tempt me to be your guide."

Damn her beautiful, beautiful stubbornness.

As she turned on her heel, I darted in front of her, desperation swelling within me.

I inhaled deeply, latching onto a plan. Was it the most noble? Hardly. But what choice did I have? This was about saving her. Saving all of us.

"You mentioned wanting to go to Iceland, to study at the University of Reykjavik," I said.

She stopped.

"I still don't know why I told you that."

"Well, anyway, considering my work with Professor Bjornsson and our ongoing research into Swiss printing houses, we could use someone with your expertise. I can arrange a fully funded year of study and research, with living expenses covered. And if the project yields results, there could be a permanent position."

Her eyes widened, a mix of shock and disbelief crossing her face.

"But...why would you do that for me?" Her voice wavered between hope and suspicion.

"This is a real offer. Professor Bjornsson and I have discussed bringing on someone who understands both the historical and practical aspects. You can verify with him, though you've already confirmed my credentials, haven't you?" I allowed myself a small smile. "Between his connections in Norse studies and my work in historical ceramics, we can make this happen."

And now I'd have to email Bjornsson immediately, before she could. *'Dear Professor, You know that email you received from Ida Wechsler? Well it turns out she would be a great asset to our team, so I've just offered her a job with us! Please go along with this as Ida is actually my wife Sigyn with her memories jumbled up by a curse placed on her by the very real goddess Frigg and I'm on a clock to get her to fall in love with me again and have a true love kiss to break the spell or Midgard will be taken over by Frost Giants who will wipe out all of humanity by devouring everyone so really this is in your own best interest and—'* Okay, maybe I should just stick with the first part...gods, what a lovely tangled web I was weaving.

Sigyn drummed against her arm as she considered.

"I don't understand. People just don't offer opportunities like this. What's your angle?" she asked, her eyes narrowing, searching my face for lies.

I took a deep breath, trying to find the right words that wouldn't send her running.

"No angle," I said, the half-truth bitter on my tongue.

"But why me?"

"Look," I said. "Someone who knows Basel's printing history this intimately, who's already documented local printers' vessels...I need that kind of expertise for my research. These specific vessels you've cataloged could be the key to understanding what Swiss printers were using before their influence reached Iceland. But it's more than that. Professor Bjornsson and I have discovered something fascinating. These same printers who were producing early editions of Norse mythology seemed to use distinct sets of vessels for different types of texts. The crockery, the mythology—they're connected in ways we're just beginning to understand." I paused, watching her carefully. "Someone who understands both the practical aspects of these printing houses and feels such a deep connection to the Norse tales...that's exactly what we need. And frankly, your passion shouldn't be wasted giving directions to tourists. This could be a win-win for both of us. You said yourself you regret losing your spot at Reykjavik. This is a second chance."

She twisted the edge of her shirt as she wrestled with the decision.

"I...I need time to think about this," she said. "It's a lot to process. A huge decision."

"I'm afraid time is not something I have much of," I replied, trying to keep the desperation out of my voice. "But, if I can be so bold, the trick about opportunities is not to miss them."

She nodded slowly, her eyes distant as if already imagining herself among the fjords and ruins of Iceland.

"What's your answer?" I asked, my heart racing.

23

FREE

BALDER

Hel

"Of course I gave Father magic to bypass his curse," Hel said over the harpsichord music twanging through her study. She hunched over the large oak table at one end of the room, her sleeves brushing against a stack of leather-bound journals. "And you can stop worrying about him trying to kill you again. Father knows that crossing me would be far worse than anything he could do to you."

She plucked a beetle from a jar with silver forceps. The beetle's green shell shimmered in the firelight from the massive stone hearth behind me.

I admired her defiance, envied her strength actually, opposing my mother's will. But dread gnawed at my stomach, matching the growing migraine hammering my skull in time with the harpsichord's metallic notes.

I twisted in my chair to glare at the corpse musician. His

skull sank into threadbare robes, eye sockets empty pits in his graying flesh as his skeletal fingers skittered across the keys inside the carved double doors. The notes ricocheted off the obsidian walls, where thousands of books crammed the shelves between the candles and glass cases of pinned insects.

"But why risk my mother's wrath?"

Hel's features hardened as she thrust the magnifying glass closer to the beetle. The pale blue skin of her right side gleamed almost luminous in the gloom.

"Your mother should know better than to call me a monster. I'm merely rising to the description."

Guilt lanced me at her words, because I never should have told her what Mother had said. But I was so angry at Mother...

"This was not my intention when I shared that with you," I said over the incessant trills. "And must you have a harpsichord playing right now? It's hard to concentrate with the music."

She lifted her withered hand. At her gesture, the player nodded, his powdered wig sliding forward on his skull. The fiery melody melted into something slow and morose.

I sighed. Not exactly what I meant, but I didn't dare say that right now.

"This is what the tension from both our parents is doing to us," she said. "Look, you know how my father is. I cannot stand to watch him pace my halls like a caged beast. I crave only the still, and that is impossible with him restless. Please stop worrying."

"But helping him escape..." I scrubbed my face. "Do you grasp the damage it may cause? Do you know the damage this means for you?"

Couldn't she understand? I feared for her.

Hel kept her attention fixed on her workstation, where brass pins gleamed beside glass vials. She dipped her forceps into a mahogany box and extracted a moth, its dusty wings trembling in her grip.

"I informed Frigg properly. I fulfilled my duty. Whatever mischief Father stirs now falls solely upon him. She has no proof for anything else."

Doubt continued to chew at me as she spread the moth's legs and pinned them.

"Yes, but Mother knows there's more. She knows you must have given Loki some type of powerful magic. She will punish you for it, regardless of proof."

The forceps froze between her fingers, but that inner fire in her eyes refused to yield.

The pin pierced the moth's wing with a sharp snap.

"I had to do what would give you and me our best chance." Her whisper barely reached me.

I stepped to her side and stroked her cheek, the blue skin withered and cool and absolutely perfect beneath my fingertips.

"She won't keep us apart. And you know the risks I'm already taking to ensure we remain together. Keeping your father's mortality secret from my mother is already one of them."

"Can you really promise me forever together? Can you really promise that your mother, the Salvation Weave, will not actually seek to separate us in the end? Because, I don't think you can. You are as much a prisoner as me."

My chest tightened at the fear embedded in her words, and at their truth.

Moving behind her, I wrapped my arms around her waist and drew her close as she continued to work on pinning the moth.

"Nothing will separate us." My lips brushed the nape of her neck as I pulled her closer, breathing in her scent of frost and rose. "You are my heart. My fate."

She turned in my arms, centuries of love swimming in her green eyes.

Hel relaxed against my chest, but tension still thrummed through her muscles. Her red lips grazed my cheek as the harpsichord's melody wove around us.

I wanted to dissolve all her doubts and fears in my embrace. But standing there, in the bowels of the underworld where ice crept through stone, my certainty frayed at the edges.

Her cold fingertips traced my cheekbone.

"You trust too easily," she whispered.

She turned back to her moth splayed on her worktable.

"Mother has implemented sanctions because of Loki's escape," I warned, unease creeping into my voice.

Hel unraveled the moth's antennae with surgical precision, pinning them in place.

She smiled.

"Let Frigg's decrees fall where they may. I have alliances with other realms."

Anxiety churned in my gut.

"Alliances she has now severed," I said. "We had a strategy. A plan. And now you blow it all up, trusting your father over me."

She scoffed.

"Your mother failed to execute a swift and tidy curse," Hel said, tone frosted. "Your mother lied about her intentions with Fenrir and Jorg told me everything. We are not safe. We never were."

"You are safe."

"How, when your mother controls everything I have,

even my armies?" She set her tools on the table, turning to face me fully. Her eyes held a dangerous glint. "But you, Balder...you're her son. You could command them. One word from you and they would—"

"Never speak of that again," I cut her off, my voice dropping to a whisper. The mere suggestion caused a shiver to run through me. "You're asking me to commit high treason."

"Is it treason to protect what she's out to gut?" She clenched her withered hand into a fist. "Father told me what she ultimately intends for me at the end."

"At the end? She intends nothing with you."

"Father says she will tear out my guts." Hel's voice hollowed. "To bind him permanently. This is how she truly plans to seal her curse."

Fragments of my mother's recent conversations flickered through my mind. Her cryptic mentions of "sealing" the curse, how her plans seemed to evolve into something grander, more final. The way she spoke of sacrifices needed for the greater good...

No. I shook the thoughts away.

"Your father is the God of Lies. You can't believe what he says. He wanted to scare you, so you'd let him escape, and it worked," I said. "Mother gave me her oath. There will be no bindings. She will not touch you. She will not harm you."

But even as I spoke, uncertainty burrowed deeper. How many times had my mother's promises sprouted thorns?

Hel snatched fresh pins from their velvet cushion, manipulating the insect with forceps that now trembled in her grip.

"Regardless," she said. "There's still that Jotnar wench Skadi begging for my spear in her stomach."

Bitterness flooded my throat as I wiggled my toes,

crammed in boots two sizes too small. I needed all the blisters and crooked toes I could manage.

"Other than my father's head, Skadi prizes you above all else," she said. "Even over skiing and killing."

True. I recalled her saying how she detested blood caked beneath her nails after a good battle or game of cards. I suggested less murder to better preserve her manicure, but she scoffed, saying she'd never consider it.

"Skadi has proven more...formidable than expected," I admitted. Carefully.

Hel stilled over her project, the tools hovering above the pinned moth.

"And this is another reason why I distrust your mother. Every action she makes threatens what we share. We cannot trust her."

Fear spiked through me as her fingers whitened around the slender pins. One wrong move and she'd pierce her own skin. I went to her side, eased the tools from her rigid grip.

"I'll speak with Mother on your behalf. I'll tell her you've shown remorse and emphasize that Loki manipulated the situation. She knows how cunning he can be. If I explain things carefully, she might understand. It could be enough to lift these sanctions, at least partially. But Hel, please. Don't do anymore acts of rebellion. Not while we are still in the thick of this."

Hel glanced up at me, eyes glinting in the strange gloom cast by the candelabras. Even the shadows seemed to watch us.

"And if I no longer wish to bend to her decrees?" Her words slipped out.

I froze.

"What do you mean?"

"I want guarantees, not good intensions," she said. "Your

mother drove me to help my father. After I swore I'd impale him to the roots of Yggdrasil. But I'd do anything, Balder, even that, to ensure we have eternity together. Because I love you."

Her words struck someplace deep in my heart only she could touch. Since being with Hel, I'd learned that love could be a shield rather than a cage.

She stood and walked to the opposite side of the table and grabbed a piece of parchment.

"Hel, I beg you. Please consider what you suggest…"

"I have, and it pains me to my core, because father was right. Frigg will never accept us. You know it's true, or you wouldn't hide our relationship in shadows."

She circled back and dipped her quill into a well of black ink. The quill scratched against parchment as she wrote a label for the moth specimen.

"I promise you," I said, moving closer. "I will guarantee we have our life together. I will keep you safe."

She smiled with centuries of sorrow and pinned the label above the moth. Her expression remained distant as a star, wounds of old betrayals visible in her eyes.

"You cannot even ensure grain for my bread," Hel said, each word bitter. "Did you forget that someone else once promised me I would be protected? All my father achieved was to end me up here."

Shame flooded through me at the raw truth of her words.

"I am not your father," I said, but the conviction in my voice wavered.

I walked to the hearth's warmth, studying her collection of pinned insects. Each one plucked from life, preserved behind glass. Caught. Trapped. Like her. Like me.

Something in me broke and I gripped the mantel, the

walls pressing closer. Why couldn't we be free? I loved her, and I couldn't say it to anyone beyond these walls.

"Balder..."

"I'm drowning," I said, centuries of suffocation pouring out. "Trapped by Asgard's expectations and hunger for me. And now Skadi is coming for me, and she won't let me go. And I'll be trapped deeper. I'll lose you. I can't lose you."

Hel dismissed the musician. The doors closed behind him with a soft thud and blessed quiet descended. Only the crack of embers remained, each pop like another breaking chain. Finally, I could breathe.

She joined me at the hearth, firelight coating her in copper and gold. She drew me into her embrace. In her arms, the monsters outside silenced. Here, I didn't have to be this shining thing, the perfect god. Here, I could simply be.

"No one will force your hand again." Her breath brushed my nape, cool against my skin. "This I swear to you." Her arms tightened, protective. "Skadi won't win. She won't take you."

"How can you know?" The whisper escaped me, fragile as moth wings. "You said yourself promises are not guarantees."

Hel turned me to face her, and in her eyes I saw something ancient, something powerful.

"Because this isn't a promise. You are mine." The fierceness in those three words sent heat coursing through me. Her words weren't a cage door slamming shut, but a promise of shelter.

I drew her closer, seeking her strength. Musk and rose clung to her chilled skin, as familiar to me now as breathing.

"I want us to be free," I said into the curve of her shoulder, the words both plea and prayer.

Hel drew back, laying her hands on my hammering heart.

"Here, in us, we have it," she said. "Here we are safe. You are safe."

Her words washed over me like a healing balm. This acceptance, this space to simply exist as myself. No manipulation veiled as protection, no demands masked as concern. Hel saw me. Not as Asgard's bright prince, but simply as myself...flawed, yearning, real.

And I was now home. Safe.

I am safe.

The realization settled in my bones like a truth I'd always known but never had words for.

"I can't stay long," I managed, though every heartbeat urged me to remain. To kiss her and have her. "I must return soon..."

My words dissolved as Hel traced an icy fingertip along my jaw, the contrast of cold touch and heated skin igniting sparks beneath my flesh.

"You can be spared twenty minutes," she said, her eyes dark with promise. "Do you trust me?"

"Yes." And I meant it.

She trailed her fingers down my throat in an exquisite caress that made me hunger more.

"Tell me then, beloved. What is it you want? You must be clear."

I burned under her touch, caught between the hearth's warmth and the delicious chill of her skin. Her question wasn't a test or a trap. It was an invitation to voice my deepest desires. Something I'd never been able to do until her.

I am safe.

"I want you to give me peace. To show me I'm yours." My

pulse raced beneath my skin as I offered her the words I knew she waited to hear. The words that would show her our shared purpose. "Let me worship you, *my queen*."

Hel's lips curved into that knowing smile that made my blood rush faster. She stepped closer, pressing her palms against my thundering heart, and everything faded into whispers.

"Very good. You remember."

This was power freely given and received. Hel wasn't about breaking me. She was about mending my broken bones. I trusted her.

Here, submission didn't mean erasure, it meant becoming more fully myself.

Hel moved to the far wall, where a bronze serpent coiled around a candlestick. She traced its scales, and something clicked deep within the wall. A section of the bookcase swung inward on silent hinges, revealing a hidden passage.

"Come." She extended her hand to me, and I followed her through the passage and into a private chamber. This wasn't our first time by any means, quite the opposite.

Firelight played across iron and silk. A massive bed commanded the far wall, its black iron frame rising towards the vaulted ceiling. Purple velvet curtains hung from the posts. The heat between my legs grew hotter.

"You can tell me if it becomes too much," Hel said, moving to a table. "I will stop immediately." Her fingers brushed over a length of crimson rope.

I nodded, understanding flowing between us. By giving me the power to stop her, Hel had given me something I never had before—real control. I chose every moment of submission, knowing it would be respected.

"I want your will," I breathed. "My queen."

And my will was the only thing that made her authority real.

Her smile deepened as she moved through shadows and firelight. Leathers and cuffs hung from the vaulted ceiling.

"I want your complete surrender," she said, eyes bright. "Think only of me, of this room. Let the outside world fade away. Do you understand?"

The tension left my muscles at her command. My thoughts stilled, focusing solely on her presence. On our breath and the crackle of flames. This was what I craved. Permission to exist only in this moment, with her. No manipulation. Just pure, honest desire and the safety to express it.

"Yes, my queen," I said.

She moved closer until our foreheads met, her breath mixing with mine. The air held the scent of beeswax and leather. She leaned in, brushing my lips against hers.

"You're so beautiful," she murmured. "And here, in this time and place, you're mine. You may kiss me."

I claimed her mouth, the living side of her warm, while the other burned with frost. She cupped my face, tracing my jaw with her thumb as her tongue met mine. Our breaths matched as I deepened the kiss, needing more of her. Each touch of bone against my lips sent another rush of heat through me. Gods. The taste of her was a benediction.

She pulled away, and the loss was almost unbearable.

"Remove my top," she said, her voice breath.

I slid my fingers beneath the lace, grazing her skin. Drawing the silk over her shoulders and head, I revealed her breasts to the firelight. The sight of her exposed flesh made the desire pooling low in my body threaten to drown me. Her nipples hardened in the cool air as I breathed in her scent.

"Kiss my breasts, Balder," she ordered. "Let me know how much you love them."

I cupped her right breast, loving the weight in my palm before pressing my mouth to her flesh. I closed my lips around her nipple, sucking gently. She shivered under my touch, a small sound of pleasure escaping her throat.

She arched as my teeth grazed skin. I moved to her other breast, my tongue circling, in slow, deliberate strokes. Her moans filled my ears.

Mine.

Pain blazed across my scalp as she yanked my hair back hard, forcing my head up. Her eyes fixed on mine, her chest rising fast.

"I said stop."

I stepped back, though everything in me ached to touch more. To feel more.

"Remove your clothes," she ordered. "Let me watch. And when you finish, walk to the bed."

The leather of the chaise creaked as she sat.

I undressed slowly as she reclined on the pillows. She gathered her skirts up around her waist and slid her hand between her thighs.

I removed each piece of clothing, and I burned watching her breathing quicken, her fingers move faster as I showed more, until I stood naked before her, hard and waiting. Her lips parted as her eyes held me. Her hand continued to move, and my pulse raced like a shot.

"What would you have me do now, my queen?" My voice was rough with hunger.

She stopped and rose, her skin flushed.

"Sit on the bed."

I walked to the iron bed, posts rising from floor to ceiling, with bars spaced for binding and rings worked into the frame. Crimson silk pillows and feather mattresses softened the metal.

She slid the remaining fabric from her body, letting her dress pool at her feet. I reached for her, desperate to touch any part of her, I could—

Her palm cracked against my skin, the sting of pain flaring into white-hot pleasure.

Her slap made me harder, and my pulse thundered in my ears as that exquisite pain sang through my veins.

"I didn't give you permission to touch me," she breathed, naked and flushed.

"No, my queen." I couldn't hide my eager anticipation, knowing what such disobedience might bring. My body thrummed hotter with desire at the thought of her punishment. I eyed the riding crop on the wall.

"That was the second command you disobeyed. For that, lie back and hold the bed posts. Let me see you all stretched out and open to me."

I clutched the iron posts, loving how exposed she made me as I stretched across the silk sheets.

She traced my chest, her fingers leaving trails of fire across my skin.

"Don't move until I command," she said, moving lower.

She wrapped her hand around me, and I gasped. Each stroke tested me, drove me to euphoria, drawing sounds from deep in me as I fought to obey.

"If you let go of the posts," she warned, "I will stop."

I gripped the bars harder, begging.

Her mouth claimed me. Cool lips, then deep warmth, and I nearly shattered. She drew back, her tongue tracing my length, and then took me deeper into the heat of her mouth.

I clenched the posts as pleasure pulled through every

nerve ending. My muscles strained as I fought not to thrust into that exquisite warmth. That pristine pleasure. She knew exactly how to undo me. When to slow, when to stop, when to devour. I pressed back into the pillows, gasping as waves of ecstasy threatened to drown me.

I fought to maintain my grip on the posts, fought against the overwhelming need to move. My breath came in ragged gasps as she continued to work me, each moment bringing me closer to surrender. And I obeyed, my hold on the posts turning painful as pleasure built to an almost unbearable peak. My entire body trembled on the knife's edge of release.

But I belonged to her. My pleasure was hers to give or deny.

She pulled away. Light kisses followed, each touch relief and torture.

She held my gaze as she lowered onto me with wonderful slowness, taking me into her. The sensation of filling her, of finally becoming one, nearly broke me.

"You're not allowed release until I say," she commanded, voice husky.

I gripped the posts harder, even though my hands ached to touch her breasts, her hips, her skin. But she had commanded, and I would obey.

Our eyes remained locked as she moved, setting a rhythm designed to destroy me. Her hips rolled, each thrust testing my control. She smiled as I struggled, watching me near the edge before slowing. In this beautiful torment, this perfect submission, I was hers, completely and utterly. Not because I was forced, but because I chose to surrender everything I was to her.

I am safe.

She shuddered, crying out as her pleasure took her over. Gods. I wanted to join her. I needed to join her.

Her skin gleamed with sweat.

"Now, let go of the posts and show me you worship me," she said, voice rough. "Let me know I'm yours."

The moment she released me, I seized her.

Took control.

I lifted her from the bed and carried her to the back wall. I pressed her against the velvet curtain that covered the stone, and her legs locked around me.

"Mine," I growled.

I claimed her mouth and thrust inside her. Her nails scored my back, and she moaned making a deep pleasure sear through me.

She rocked her hips against me, and that last thread of restraint snapped. I drove deeper, harder, pounding into her. Her cries echoed off the stone walls. Her nails carved fresh marks down my back, each sting fueling my need.

Nothing existed beyond this. Nothing mattered but her breathless cries, the perfect heat of her around me, the knowledge that in this moment, we belonged completely to each other.

When she finally shattered again, I followed. Her name tore from my throat as ecstasy ripped through me, and I held her like salvation itself.

She traced my shoulders as I buried my face in the crook of her neck. I wanted to stay suspended in this perfect moment forever, safe in her embrace where the worlds couldn't touch us.

But the shadows that kept us hidden would soon fade.

The worlds still waited. And they would feast.

"I love you," I whispered.

24

FOOL ME TWICE

Asgard

I walked down the hall towards my rooms, passing portrait after portrait of Freya, most of them her naked, limbs and hair sprawled across silk sheets. Three servants teetered on a ladder, backs straining as they hoisted another gilded frame while striped cats rubbed against the wooden rungs.

A servant's nostrils flared, lip curling as clumps of grave dirt fell from my hair and speckled the floor. I suppose that was better than the stench of rotting flesh clinging to my clothes. I fumbled with the wrinkles in my tunic, pressing the silk flat against my chest. Gods. If I had any hope of keeping up the pretense, I had to scrub the dirt from my skin before I gave my report to Mother, and more importantly, wash away Hel's lingering perfume.

Sweat beaded along my neck at the thought of Freya piecing it together...

Persian cats prowled the corridors, their paws padding

past Mother's chambers. I crept past her door, lungs burning from holding my breath—

"What more must I do to you to get you to comply?" Mother's voice shot through the inch of oak.

A crash exploded, and the clap of what sounded like books hitting the ground followed.

"I'm extremely familiar with all of your tactics, so maybe you need to find something new if you hope to sway me." Father's words rasped.

My skin prickled, gooseflesh racing up my arms.

"How about this, then?" Mother said. "Send the Draugr, or I'll bleed you out slowly."

I reached for the brass latch and cracked the door open and peered through the gap.

Mother pressed her splayed hand on Father's chest harder, pushing him further into the shelving of the bookcase. More leather-bound books tumbled to the ground, parchments and quills scattering across the plush rug.

He chuckled bitterly, blood trickling from the corner of his mouth.

"We both understand I'm too valuable for you to do that."

Mother's lip curled upward, teeth glinting. Veins pulsed at her temples.

"Don't be so sure. My patience has limits."

Father kept his gaze locked on her.

"You've yet to convince me of that."

She released him with a shove that sent him stumbling and walked to her desk of intricately carved oak. She snatched up a wooden box inlaid with mother-of-pearl. She cracked open the lid, revealing tidy rows of chocolates, each nestled in a basket of gold foil.

She plucked a chocolate out of its foil, rolling the dark

morsel between thumb and forefinger. Father's eye tracked every movement, his throat working as he swallowed. I'd only seen that look in wolves during midwinter, when food grew scarce.

"I want Loki dragged back to me," she said, fingernail tracing the chocolate's edge. "I want the wolf and the snake mine. If you keep refusing, well...I can match your stubbornness bite for bite."

She popped the chocolate in her mouth, eyes fluttering closed as she savored the sweetness. A muscle ticked in Father's jaw as his tongue darted across cracked lips.

"You'll need to tempt me with more than chocolate covered coconut," he said, shifting his feet. "Unless you have any caramels in that box, I'm afraid it's going to remain a firm no."

She snapped the box shut with a sharp crack and threw it on the table. Chocolates rattled inside.

"You dare—" She curved her fingers into fists.

I shut the door, but their curses still pierced through the oak, dredging up memories.

And in the hatred of a word, I was five years old and hiding beneath the table, hands clapped over my ears. *I wanted them to stop yelling.* But their screams continued. Glass crashed against walls. I sobbed silently into my knees.

Mother stormed off, not taking me with her.

Father called for her, his voice hoarse and breaking.

A door slammed. Muffled yelling pounded through the walls. The harsh crack of hand meeting flesh speared the air. Father grunted in pain. More screaming followed, raw and terrible.

And I remained frozen in my tiny sanctuary, pressing myself against the table legs, wishing I could disappear entirely.

Mother took in a sharp breath, tearing me out of the memory.

Gods. I wanted to walk away.

I wanted to run.

But I stayed. And I listened.

Something in me couldn't stomach leaving Father alone with her.

Why didn't I want to leave him alone with her?

"Raising the dead is out of my skillset," she said. "And I can't leave Asgard with Skadi breathing down my neck."

"I'm beginning to understand now why you've kept me alive, because I know it's not out of sentiment," he said. "Rule one. If you want to bargain for my help, since only I can give you what you want, give me something of benefit. You come to me with nothing but chocolates."

A guttural, choking sound took the rest of his words. I knew it was from Mother's hand at his throat.

"I have your life. What more could I offer?" she asked. "I know you, Odin. I know your greatest fear is death, and your greatest desire to beat death. This is my bargaining chip, since you want one so badly. I will let you have another day to live, as long as you keep doing what I want."

The roots keeping me planted grew stronger, burrowing through stone into earth below.

Father laughed, and it sounded like gravel being crushed.

"You seem very sure of that," he wheezed.

"I know how strong that pull to live is in you. You even gave up Loki to avoid your death when it came to having those king's sons." Her words carved the air like daggers. "The one you claimed to love above all others, cast aside like refuse. Tell me, when you watched Loki break, did you feel anything at all? When he begged you to explain, when he pleaded to understand why you'd demand the death of a child, did you enjoy keeping your silence?"

"Frigg, don't." His voice was barely a whisper.

"Or did you save your tears for later that night, when you came crawling to my chambers? Seeking comfort in my arms while Loki's world burned by your hand?" she asked, satisfaction filling each word. "You proved then that you're capable of destroying him. Now I want you to do it again. Send the draugr."

"This threat is nothing but a hollow bluff."

"A bluff, is it?" Steel hardened Mother's voice. "How about this, then? Either send the draugr after Loki, or I start executing those who defy me. Bragi seems a fitting first example to make." Her words fell like ice shards. "But we both know you'll choose Asgard, your life, over Loki. You always do."

Anger cracked in me at this threat, heat flooding my chest. I mean, we all grew tired of Bragi's rendition of "Ravens' Wings Over Valhalla," and how he made his voice climb to pitches no one should ever attempt. But you lived with it. Killing Bragi would be like killing a puppy, crushing something pure and defenseless. And that's why this was only a threat. It had to be. Just bluster. Saber rattling...she wouldn't actually kill the gods.

She wouldn't do that.

That's not what she meant.

I didn't like how I had to keep repeating this to myself.

"What do you want with all this bloodshed?" Father asked. "You risk everything on some twisted dream."

She gave a hollow laugh.

"Twisted? I'm only repairing what should never have been broken. Our family. Our legacy. The safety of our kingdom from Ragnarok." Her voice hitched before she steadied it. "I worked so hard to protect what you kept endangering. I dedicated everything to being your queen, to building Asgard alongside you. All I wanted was to preserve our realm."

"Preserve our realm? Don't you mean preserve your control? How could we ever rule as equals when you are who you are?" he asked.

"We had everything. We could have kept having everything. I loved you."

He scoffed.

"You speak of possession, not love," he said. "What I felt for Loki—still feel—" he paused. "The sacrifice I made that day you so happily bring up wasn't just him, but pieces of my soul. You could never comprehend such devotion. Your heart only knows how to own, not how to love. So please, stop pretending that you ever loved me."

The sharp crack of a slap pierced the air, rings splitting skin. A heavy silence followed, swollen with venom, broken only by their ragged breathing.

Enough.

I threw open the heavy oak door. Mother released Father hastily, silk skirts rustling as she stepped back, avoiding my gaze. He slumped to the ground.

"Stop this," I said, my words bursting out of me.

I stared at them. My parents. And the sight twisted my stomach. Mother standing straight-backed, Father crumpled on the floor. Hard to believe they'd ever been close enough to have me. Or was I made in hate?

Mother stepped back, shock on her face.

"How long have you been here?" she asked, fingers twisting in her skirts.

"Why, is there something you don't want me to see?"

"Of course not." She glided closer, but nervous energy

simmered below her surface. "You know I don't keep things from you."

Her gaze dropped to my hands, and she frowned, lips pressing into a thin line.

"Why are you covered in inches of grave dirt? And why is your tunic backwards? A simple trip to the underworld shouldn't have disheveled you this much." Her eyes narrowed.

Shit. I hadn't realized that...

"No, not at all." I tried to fix my crooked belt. "Got tangled up in a sarcophagus with an overly enthusiastic mummy. Apparently they get quite clingy after a few millennia of solitude."

I turned from her to Father as he stood, his joints popping. His eye patch had slipped sideways, revealing the scarred hollow beneath. Dark circles shadowed his remaining eye, and exhaustion bent his shoulders. I reached up, straightening the patch while he stood rigid. He flinched at first, then stilled as I adjusted the leather strap.

"Did Hel touch you? If Hel has done this—" A hard edge crept into her voice as she tried to fix my crooked belt.

"Has she fed you?" I asked Father, cutting her off. "She said she'd feed you."

Father's eye widened, blue iris sharp against bloodshot white. His empty stomach churned, the sound answering for him.

"She says a lot of things." His lips cracked as he spoke. "But feeding me would go against your mother's plans."

It felt like a slice across my chest. If she broke this promise, what about the other promise she made me...

No. I refused to accept that.

"I'm sorry, Balder," she said, brushing the dirt off my shoulders. Her bracelets chimed. "It wasn't intentional. I've been covered up with Skadi, and then all this Loki business. I'm sorry. I forgot."

I turned back to her. Was she telling me the truth?

"Forgot?" The word tasted bitter. "Mother, I am not you. And I refuse to be."

Her lips parted, shoulders dropping.

"How can you think that? How can you say that? Inferring I'm some cruel beast. It was an innocent mistake, I swear." She crossed to the chocolate box on the desk, heels clicking against stone. "I'll inform the kitchens immediately to send up food. Now, Odin, would you prefer chicken or beef?"

Father's gaze snapped up.

I watched her hands, her neck, her shoulders. Searching for any sliver of deceit. As I had that night when she mixed her blood with mine, swearing her oath to me.

Why was I doubting her? My chest tightened.

She seemed sincere...

No. She *was* sincere.

"Frigg never knew I saw her. If she had..."

Thor's words summoned a buried image—Sigyn's limp hand in mine as I kneeled over her body. The gore staining Mother's knuckles as she stood motionless above us both. I had to protect this woman.

"I shouldn't have said that. I swore to Father never to tell you about it." Thor's words hammered against my temples. I couldn't stop them.

Would she have done something more to Sigyn after her oath? Sweat beaded on my forehead.

Mother snatched up the box and strode to Father, silk skirts swishing. She jammed the chocolate into his mouth, fingernails scraping his lips.

"Here's that caramel you wanted so badly," she said, wiping her fingers on her dress.

I dropped my shoulders back, jaw unclenching tooth by tooth. My stomach roiled, but I pressed my palm against it, silencing Thor's words. Smothering the doubts blossoming inside me like poisonous weeds.

Thor knew nothing.

Mother had given her word. I had to trust in that vow. I had to trust in her.

I couldn't accept that everything I believed in was dust.

"Odin?" she asked again, tapping her foot. "Chicken, or beef."

He raised his head, fixing his good eye on mine.

"Beef," he mumbled. Chocolate stained his teeth.

Her smile twitched at the corners.

"Excellent. Right away," she said.

"Thank you, Mother," I said.

She reached up and patted my cheek, her palm soft against my skin.

I pivoted towards father, boots grinding dirt into the carpet.

"Now, the choice is yours," I said, stepping closer. "Send the draugr after Loki and his brood, otherwise beef can quickly turn into bread and water."

His split lips curved upward.

And his shoulders shook with laughter.

"Amazing," he said.

"What is?"

"For a second, you looked just like your mother saying that."

25

___

AN INCONVENIENT SUMMONS

LOKI

"*Tomorrow*?" Jorg asked for the third time as we walked through Petersplatz. "You really couldn't convince Sigyn to meet with you, oh, I don't know, TODAY?"

Leaves of crimson and gold splintered under our feet as we shouldered between carnival rides and children who darted past, fingers sticky with candy and grease from hot cheese pies. Branches creaked overhead, their leaves blazing with autumn fire in the afternoon sun.

"Sorry if I'm not meeting your timetable." Irritation hardened my tone as I sidestepped a running child. "At least my plan got her to agree to meet me at all. Of course, she made it perfectly clear it's all purely professional. Obviously, that will be temporary. I mean, look at me. I am irresistible."

We trailed behind Fenrir as he meandered between stalls. He smiled, examining bowls carved from olive wood and those ugly, naked angel sculptures that dangled from metal coils. The kind meant to decorate gardens with that perfect touch of kitsch.

Jorg's boot connected with a stone, sending it skittering across the plaza. His scowl deepened.

"Yes, offering her a fake opportunity under false pretenses is just the kind of solid foundation you need for her to fall in love with you. I shouldn't be surprised. This is exactly what I should have expected from you."

I knew it wasn't the most ethical, but I figured under the circumstances, Sigyn would understand.

Wind stirred the branches, and a cascade of leaves spiraled around us.

"Since we are doing this the old fashioned way, I need to ensure time with her," I said, dodging a group of tourists with cameras.

"If you can even break her spell before you lose that coin and fall back into the underworld," he grumbled under his breath. "I won't have Fenrir sent to Lyngvi because of your incompetence. I won't have my sister disemboweled for rope to tie your sorry ass to a rock."

"You are truly a beacon of positivity," I said.

Of course, I didn't dare tell him about the near miss I had almost dropping the coin in the toilet earlier that morning. I traced the outline of the coin through my jacket pocket.

Hunger gnawed at me as we wove between stalls brimming with cheese pies and Magenbrot.

But one bite of anything besides a rice cracker would destroy me. I knew, because I had daringly sampled Fenrir's hummus from the night before. It all seemed to be getting worse. Like my body kept shifting and changing, and not for the better.

I spent half the night in the bathroom, either perched on

or hunched over the toilet. My knees still ached from the cold tile floor. But the weirdest were the hot flashes, sweats, that now followed, like a heat burning in me.

"Let him be," Fenrir said, turning from the Raclette. "Romance takes time."

Fenrir stopped at a stall roasting almonds in large copper pots. Steam rose in spirals, carrying the aroma of caramelizing sugar and nuts. I inhaled deeply, my mouth watering. I could almost taste the crunch...

"You seem to forget that time isn't something we have much of," Jorg said, hands thrust deep into his jacket pockets.

"You really blow hot and cold, Jorg," I said, shoulder bumping against a passing tourist. "You were the one telling me I stood no chance because she hates me, and now you're wondering why I'm not faster. I know you delight in me always being in the wrong, but you are really starting to push my buttons."

He flashed me that smarmy grin, eyes glinting with the promise of more needling to come.

"Please stop being so torturous, you two," Fenrir scolded, reaching for the paper cone of candied almonds from the vendor. "It is what it is, and we have to make the best of it."

Fenrir's eyes closed as he tossed back a handful of the warm, candied almonds, sugar dusting his fingers. I didn't know I could be this envious.

"Wow," he said, licking his lips. "The one time I can't post on social media. My followers would love to know about these little treats. They are the best candied almonds I've ever had, even better than the one's at the World's Fair in 1873 in Vienna."

My mouth watered more as I watched him devour

another handful. Fenrir was doing a good enough job torturing me all on his own.

I looked away...and my gaze landed directly on the half wheels of Raclette cheese broiling beneath hot lamps. The vendor's scraper sent ribbons of melted cheese cascading over steaming potatoes. My stomach growled louder with hunger.

That final, thin thread of sanity inside of me snapped with an almost audible twang.

"Why are you laughing?" Fenrir asked, brow knit with concern.

"Am I laughing?" A muscle twitched beneath my right eye. "Oh, I suppose I am. I'm just on the verge of a breakdown, is all. Nothing to worry about. I'm *fine*." I stretched my grimace into a forced smile. "Enjoy your almonds."

Fenrir's eyes narrowed as he studied me, sugar crystals still clinging to his fingertips.

"Perhaps you should sit, take a breath," he said.

Sit? Take a breath?

Cold sweat plastered my shirt to my back. Hunger chewed at my insides like a rabid beast. My hands trembled with the effort of not grabbing everyone by their collars and making this all their problem.

The metallic click of Jorg's lighter cut through my spiral as he pulled out a cigarette. Orange flame danced at its tip.

Hallelujah.

"Give me one," I said, my voice cracking with a desperation I barely recognized as my own.

I needed something, anything, to dull reality trying to squeeze me until my eyes nearly popped out of my sockets. Jorg was right. We *were* running out of time, and the ways this plan could implode multiplied by the second. What if I couldn't break Sigyn's spell in time and get the incantation to Odin? What if my boys ended up cursed, and me bound with Hel's...*Hel*. She relied on me to save her life. Her safety rested entirely in my shaking hands and—dammit, I needed something to silence the storm of tragedy howling through my mind. And since alcohol was clearly off limits...

"There's a kiosk over there. Buy your own cigarettes," Jorg said, exhaling a long stream of smoke that curled around his smirk. "I think you have enough stollen money left to cover it."

"Jorg, for once, just, just..." I clenched my hands into fists as he grinned, smoke seeping from his nostrils.

Fenrir cleared his throat, loud enough to startle two pigeons away from their half eaten pretzel. Even they had more to eat than me.

"What?" I snapped, whirling towards him.

"Smoking harms your health. Let me find you something else to help you feel better," he said. "Something with turmeric, maybe? Yes. Turmeric is anti-inflammatory."

A laugh like breaking glass tore from my throat.

"You know what else harms your health? Me being stressed, hungry, and angry." My lips peeled back in a snarl as I leaned towards Fenrir, voice dropping to a dangerous whisper. "I'm warning you, Fenrir. I'm on the edge of completely losing it. And I will lose it if you give me anything with turmeric."

Fenrir's eyes widened. His throat bobbed as he nodded.

"Jorg, give him a cigarette."

Jorg's mouth twisted into that infuriating smirk.

"Are you really going to fall for this melodramatic nonsense?"

"Do it!" Fenrir said.

"Fine." Jorg slapped the crumpled pack and lighter into my trembling palm.

I wedged a cigarette between my lips and sparked the lighter. The flame exploded upward with an unnatural whoosh, illuminating my sharp features in a wash of firelight.

"Huh, that lighter never burst out like that before," Jorg said, staring at the flame with narrowed eyes.

I ignored his comment, as I ignored the odd sizzle sparking at my fingertips.

Snapping the lighter shut, I inhaled a long, desperate drag. Sweet relief flooded through me as the fingers of smoke filled my lungs. The nicotine swirled in my chest, its tendrils weaving through the chaos of my thoughts, softening their edges.

My exhale carried a cloud of tobacco.

"Better?" Jorg asked, hardly meaning it.

I grunted in reply as I collapsed onto a park bench. I inhaled more smoke before streaming out in lazy rivers while my stress dissolved into the autumn air. My shoulders unknotted. My eyelids drifted shut.

The silver band on my finger grew warm. No, actually, hot. Alright, now it seared the skin of my finger. Scorching heat radiated from the metal. My lids snapped open.

Dammit. Of course, Odin would choose now to want to chat.

I dragged myself up from the bench, smoke trailing from the cigarette between my fingers

"We need to find somewhere more secluded," I said.

"What is it, Papa?" Fenrir said.

"Are we needing ice cream now to help soothe our tantrum?" Jorg asked.

"I need someplace quiet. I need to concentrate."

Jorg and Fenrir's footsteps pounded behind me as I shouldered through the festival crowd, making for the

Botanical Gardens across the cobblestones. My boots crunched through scattered leaves as I wound through tree-lined paths, the din of the festival fading into a distant murmur.

The ring carved molten circles around my finger as I twisted it, its heat branding deeper with each rotation. Odin and his blasted impatience. The timing couldn't be worse.

"What's happening?" Fenrir's voice pitched higher. "Oh. Is it your stomach again? I told you cigarettes were bad for you. See Jorg, this is what I'm trying to explain—"

"No," I said, lengthening my stride. "I need to get to the seidr realm. Now."

Steam fogged the greenhouse windows ahead as I walked towards them, condensation beading on the glass panes. The faster I could get this over with, the better.

The door hinges creaked as I pushed inside, scanning gravel paths that snaked between islands of green life. Palms and banana trees stretched towards the glass ceiling while hibiscus flowers blazed crimson among ferns and orchids. Water trickled over stones in a corner pond where lotus blossoms floated like pink stars. Private enough.

They made to follow me. I raised my hand, stopping them.

"No. Wait here and watch the door. Make sure no one enters. I'll keep it quick."

"Why?" Jorg asked. "Wanting to keep it secret?"

Well, there was that, too.

Sometimes in the seidr realm you spoke like in your sleep. I couldn't risk them overhearing about that apple if it came up.

"No, I am more vulnerable in that state," I half lied. "Make sure no one finds me."

The ring seared deeper. *Dammit, Odin, I know.*

I slipped through the greenhouse doors before Jorg could press further.

Humidity wrapped around me like a blanket, thick with the scent of exotic flowers. Sunlight filtered through glass panes, painting dappled shadows across dense foliage and still water where lily pads drifted. The cigarette hissed as I ground it into the gravel.

I settled onto a bench beside potted Venus flytraps.

My jaw tightened as I closed my eyes, focusing every cell of my body on finding my way to the seidr realm. The greenhouse's sticky warmth dissolved into cool emptiness.

I deepened my concentration.

Sweat trickled down my temples.

The earthen scents of flowers and soil faded to nothing.

Cold water lapped at my feet.

I opened my eyes to Odin staring back at me. His short russet hair drifted as he stood in the void, his rugged build seeming to absorb the surrounding darkness. My heart lurched with an old ache recalling the thousand such meetings we'd made here before.

At least the journey had taken half the effort of my first attempt. Was it possible that something actually went right for a change?

"This had better be important," I said as mist kissed my bare skin, forcing ice into my tone. "I'm in the middle of—"

"Frigg knows you've escaped," he interrupted, passing his hand through my shoulder like smoke, leaving a tingle where our forms almost connected. "She is coming for you, and if she curses and binds Fenrir and Jorg...it's over. You need to run."

And this is what I gave up my cigarette for?

"As I thought. You've only come to give me boring news

of no consequence," I said. "Her knowing of my escape is nothing unexpected."

His jaw dropped as he stared at me.

"I'm glad to know my risking to inform you is boring and of *no consequence*," he said, voice rough with something more than anger.

"You always have incredible timing, is all," I said, mist curling between us. "You burst in and interrupt the one sliver of peace I've had since your wife cursed me—"

"Look, I'm trying to warn you. To help—"

"And then not even a 'so glad you made it out of the underworld despite your curse, Loki!' Or a 'You're incredible Loki, escaping what should have been inescapable!' Or a—"

"Frigg has forced me to send what will bring you all back to her," he snapped. "I kept refusing her demands, but...I'm sorry. You know how she persuades."

The words died in my mouth, and fury blazed through me as he moved closer. I fought the urge to step back, to put distance between us. Distance I resented needing.

"Did she hurt you?" I asked. "Are you alright?"

Once, I would have swept into Asgard to tear Frigg's hands from her wrists for touching him. Now? Now I should feel nothing but satisfaction at his suffering. Should savor the taste of his pain like fine wine. Should watch him break with a smile.

Instead, my heart twisted at the thought of her hands on him.

I was pathetic. Still caring for him. Yet I couldn't stop the protective instinct that rose in me like a tide, couldn't silence the voice that whispered *mine to hurt, mine to protect*. The familiarity of it made me want to scream.

I was really letting myself down.

"Don't worry about me." His form wavered. "It's you who

are vulnerable. She will drag you back into her hold, even if it is in pieces."

He sighed heavily, weariness etched on his features.

"Well, if you would get me that apple, I wouldn't be so vulnerable."

He rolled his eyes.

"I'm rather cursed and tied up at the moment, or have you forgotten?" he asked.

"I'm cursed too and relying on a coin to keep me from being pulled back to Hel," I said, gesturing at the surrounding nothingness. "If I can escape the underworld with a curse on my head, then you can get one measly apple. It would make all of this far simpler."

"Maybe if you focused on finding Sigyn faster, I could get you the apple."

"I did find Sigyn," I said. "We have a date tomorrow."

"Then where is the translation? Why hasn't the blood ritual been done? I need that incantation if I have any chance of breaking the Salvation Weave. Of course, I still need that newt heart, and wait—what do you mean by *date*?"

"Well." I shifted my weight, cool mist sliding over bare skin. "There's been a...a slight setback."

Odin's gaze sharpened like a blade aimed directly at my throat.

"What sort of setback?"

"Frigg took Sigyn's memories," I said. "She doesn't know who I am. She has an entirely new personality—Ida. Which is why I'm focusing on romancing her."

Odin dragged his hand down his face. Well, he tried, but his fingers passed through his forehead.

"Perfect. Just perfect," he growled.

"It's no problem for me," I said. "I'm confident about

breaking her spell. Shouldn't take but a tick more time, and then you'll have your bloody translation."

His chest expanded with a sharp breath.

"And how are you planning to break this memory spell of Sigyn's, hm? Oh. Don't tell me. You're considering true love's kiss, aren't you? You do realize you'll have to reach *Sigyn* for that to work, not just this...Ida persona Frigg created?"

Why was everyone doubting true love's kiss?

"What other choice do I have *but* true love's kiss?" I asked. "I'm taking her to places that matter to us. Places where she might remember. One kiss when the real Sigyn surfaces and boom—spell broken, a few drops of Surtr infused blood on *Laevateinn*, and you get your incantation."

"I can't believe what I'm hearing," he said. "You make it sound so simple."

"Yes, because newt hearts are so much better."

His brow flattened.

"And what if you run out of time? Or what if Ida falls for you but Sigyn remains buried too deep? You need a backup. Of course. It's always left up to me to clean up everything. I'll find another more straightforward way to break Sigyn's spell, too."

I bristled at his words. He sounded like Jorg. Whatever.

"Don't you dare underestimate me," I said. "I'll find the cracks where the real Sigyn shows through. I can handle a simple memory spell. Just as I can handle whatever Frigg is directing to ruin my day. Let me guess. She's having you send a dragon? That's a yawn."

He shook his head, and something in his expression made my heart stutter. Fear? For me?

The void trembled, mist swirling. Odin's expression

turned grim, and I saw in it the echo of countless battles fought side by side.

I tapped my foot faster against nothingness, fighting the instinct to move closer to him, to face whatever was coming together as we once had.

"Alright. Who has she sent to stop me?" I asked. "Valkyries? Trolls? Einherjar?"

I hated the Einherjar. Nothing but brutish thugs plucked from corpse-littered battlefields and stuffed into gaudy armor, like dolling up pigs for a feast.

"Worse than Einherjar," he said, and his voice held the same protective note it had carried millennia ago, when we'd still trusted each other with our lives

"Worse? What could possibly—"

More rumbles shook at me. Growls ricocheted around us.

"I'm so sorry, Loki. I didn't want to send them," Odin's voice echoed, thick with genuine anguish that cut deeper than I liked. "Run. Protect yourselves," he said. "They'll kill you, not expecting you to be mortal and weak."

Oh. He did not.

"I am not weak—"

The surrounding chaos obliterated my voice.

Fenrir and Jormungand's screams tore through the darkness.

26

GREENHOUSE OF HORRORS

enrir and Jorg hurled anything they could at the gift Frigg sent us. Clay pots exploded against rotting flesh. Trowels spun past. Broken chair legs and table posts flew. Sweat plastered Fenrir's shirt to his back as he vaulted over a worktable. Jorg's boots slipped on scattered soil while he grabbed more items from shelves.

My stomach dropped.

Draugr.

The dead. Actually, the extremely enraged dead.

The monsters crashed through the greenhouse walls, glass shards tinkling as the panels shattered. A dozen draugr stomped forward, boots crushing orchids and herbs. And then there was the stench. Waves of rotting flesh left to fester in the sun for days rolled through the air. Lovely.

Ok, I'd give Odin this one. This was worse.

Draugr weren't like Hel's mindless soldiers or Valhalla's warriors. No, draugr survived on a strict diet of warm blood and living flesh. They were nasty, violent, and always exceedingly hungry. I rubbed my neck, endeavoring not to think of their yellowed teeth chomping into my jugular and slurping me dry.

The draugr barely flinched as the hammers and garden gnomes Fenrir and Jorg threw at them bounced off their rotting bodies with soft thuds.

As satisfying as it would be to ram a garden gnome's pointed hat through their sinus cavities, only iron driven through their skulls could kill draugr.

My gaze darted around the greenhouse, mind racing for something, anything that could butcher these damned creatures.

Iron. We need iron. Now.

I spotted it. Garden tools scattered in the back of the greenhouse, a steel shovel and prongs gleaming under the light filtering through the glass. My lips tugged into a grin. Iron was in steel. I suppose it would have to be enough.

"Grab whatever tools you can," I shouted. "Drive iron into their heads. It's the only way to kill them! And if you don't hear a crunch and squish, do it again."

Jorg quickly took a pickaxe next to a large monstera and brought it down with a swing onto a draugr's shoulder. A good strike—had it been any other creature. The draugr didn't even scream or show any reaction, just kept marching forward as if a butterfly had landed on his shoulder. Jorg's eyes widened.

"Do you think I say 'ram iron into the heads' for fun?" I snapped as Jorg swung in wild arcs and spins at the advancing draugr.

"Ah, yes, because smashing undead skulls is so incredibly easy," Jorg said as he dodged a particularly vicious swipe from one of the monsters.

More draugr shoved through the greenhouse foliage,

trampling orchids and lilies. Even the Venus flytraps got squashed under gnarled feet.

A draugr bolted out of the large banana tree to my left, and flew their fist and jagged nails towards my nose.

I ducked, biting back a hiss as pain lanced through my bad shoulder. Probably not the wisest move, but all this heightened risk sent adrenaline surging through my veins. I smiled, loving the rush of a good maiming. Perhaps this day was turning around, after all.

Fenrir grabbed a two-pronged hoe, stopping a draugr seconds away from clawing through his chest. He swung, metal striking bone with a nauseating crunch. Draugr brains splattered his face. He shrieked.

"They're already dead, Fenrir." I grabbed a spading fork, testing its balance. "Don't get hung up on the ethics about all this right now."

It had been a long time since I used anything but my daggers for a fight, but I wanted as much distance between me and their teeth as possible. I refused to get gnawed on. One bite in my life was enough. Once they clamped down, they didn't let go. Like a snapping turtle, but more ill tempered.

I ran after a group of three.

"Papa, keep behind Jorg and me," Fenrir said, wiping green goo off his cheek. "You aren't at full strength."

"You sound like Odin," I grumbled. "I keep telling you, I'm not some weakly human. I can be useful. I'm still half Jotnar and half Aesir, just as strong as you—Gah!"

A kick to my stomach cut me short. Winded, I toppled back into the pond, murky water engulfing me. My shoulder erupted in fresh agony and I barely choked back a scream, thrashing for the surface.

I broke the surface and wiped duck weed and water out

of my eyes in time to see Jorg burst from behind a palm, chest heaving and brow damp with sweat. Flecks of draugr blood and gore speckled his clothes in greens and browns.

"Why don't we shift forms?" he panted, doubled over, catching his breath. "We can wipe them all out in five seconds that way."

I stood, flinging off a lily pad from the top of my head.

I blocked a swipe from a draugr charging me from my right, the beast's feet raking the gravel. My arm shook from the force. I may have forgotten how much stronger godly powers made me...

"No," I grunted, flinging the monster off the gravel and into the pond with me. "You'd level half the city because you both can't shift into anything smaller than a skyscraper." I drove my improvised weapon through its face with a crunch. "And second, and I really don't know how many times I have to say this, only iron to the head kills them!"

I jumped out of the water and onto gravel, barely deflecting the next draugr's attack. The force shot pain up my arms as I slammed my weapon down, shattering its skull. I snatched up a small trowel beside a birdbath and jammed the spade into an oncoming draugr's empty eye socket. Yellow fluids spurted out, splattering my face and clothes. I grimaced as the reek of spoiled fish covered me. Frigg had to send draugr.

"Good one," Jorg said, nodding approval.

I offered a tight smile, pushing back my wet hair out of my face with my forearm, already pivoting to confront the next monster. We fought back to back now, moving in unison. Jorg swung his pickaxe in a vicious arc, splitting a draugr's head open with a sickening crack. Goo exploded, the stench of rotten eggs following. No amount of shampoo would ever remove the stink from my hair.

"I don't understand," he panted, yanking his weapon out of a skull. "Why is Frigg unleashing these things if she is supposedly afraid of killing you?"

I smashed my elbow into a draugr's jaw and drove my trowel up through the back of its head until its jaws stopped snapping.

"Draugr are not lethal to a god." I twisted away from a new set of gnashing teeth that aimed for my arm. "Debilitating when they disembowel you and eat your liver? Sure, but at least our organs regrow and heal." I stabbed my weapon through a draugr's eye, fluids oozing and sputtering. "Sadly, I don't have that luxury now I'm not a god, but she doesn't know that. She thinks they'll only incapacitate me enough to drag me back to her. The pain of them lapping my blood the entire way to Asgard is a bonus to her."

Fenrir turned a shade of green.

Jorg slammed his pickaxe down with a sick crunch, splattering Fenrir with more putrid gunk and matter.

"Really?" Fenrir shouted. He turned greener.

"So she'll kill you by trying *not* to kill you?" Jorg asked.

I smiled, and a delightful shiver ran down my back. The thought heated between my legs.

"She's really invigorated me with this risk."

Jorg eyed me.

"Oh my gods, are you aroused right now?" he asked.

I shrugged.

"Facing imminent death is the best kind of aroused," I said.

"You're so gross," Jorg grumbled, shaking his head as he turned to fight another draugr.

A draugr grabbed me from behind, its long nails digging into my shoulders as drool soaked into my shirt. Gods. The smell. Rage replaced the heat growing in my loins.

"You ruined my least hideous shirt!" I twisted free of the monster's grasp, driving my makeshift spear through its eye and piercing its brain with one thrust.

Fenrir pushed over an iron bench onto a group of four draugr. They continued to claw and writhe beneath the heavy metal, still ravenous.

I tossed the trowel to Fenrir, but I sensed his reluctance as he eyed the tool in his grip, frowning.

"I'd do it myself, but…" I gestured at the gang of monsters approaching me. I had to deal with them first.

Fenrir grimaced harder, lips pressed together as he stared at the pinned draugr. The draugr roared and hissed and croaked beneath the bench.

"I hate this," he muttered, shoulders slumping. "I don't kill."

"As I've already told you, they're dead," I said. "Think of it as putting them down for a nice nap."

Revulsion twisted his features, the trowel hanging limply in his grasp.

"I don't know, I need to think about the moral implications—"

One tried to extend its neck to snap his ankle between its jaws.

"Fenrir, fucking stab them!" I snapped. "Or they'll eat you and not feel an ounce of guilt as they suck down your blood like one of your smoothies."

Shutting his eyes, Fenrir screamed and drove the trowel through the pinned draugrs' decaying skulls one by one. Dark blood splattered his clothes.

I opened my mouth to offer a few words of comfort, and perhaps a handkerchief. Glass walls shattered. New draugr poured through the palms and orchids towards us, stomping through the irises and shredding banana leaves.

Perhaps taunting Frigg had not been my wisest decision. But regret could come later. If we somehow survived this surprise.

Jorg's pickaxe lodged in a draugr's skull, felling the creature into a bed of crushed tropical flowers. He seized a square-headed shovel, beheading another with a clean swipe.

And he didn't notice the one approaching behind him.

No.

"Over here, you stupid bastard!" I shouted at the beast.

Drool slid down its chin, glistening in the light as it shambled towards me. The monster's tattered clothes flapped with each jerky step, the smell of decaying sardines growing stronger.

Three more draugr turned and followed him, their hollow eyes fixed on me with that same hungry look.

Shit.

I took off, sloshing through the knee-deep pond. My foot caught on a rock and I went down hard. Water closed over my head with a rush, pressing into my eardrums muffling everything into a dull roar.

And that familiar, cold, icy grip tugged on my ankles. And it wasn't from a draugr's hand.

Hel's coin.

I stuck my hand in my pocket, fingers scrabbling for the metal. It was gone.

Shit. Shit.

Panic surged, and my lungs burned for air. But I had to find the coin. The frozen tethers of the curse cinched tighter and pulled harder on my ankles, on my torso. Wrists. Everything spun as I opened my eyes in the murk, skating my hands over the slimy bottom of the pond, upturning stones and silt, desperation mounting.

The remaining air in my lungs smoldered to nothing. The world tilted and darkened, my body slipping further towards the underworld with each passing second.

I couldn't let it end this way. Not after coming so far, not after everything.

Something glinted beneath the mud.

There!

I dove my hand towards the silver, straining to reach. My disintegrating fingertips grazed the edge of the coin. A flash of heat surged through my body as I grasped it hard in my fist, my fingers whole and complete, that iced tether loosening and falling away in a snap. With a kick, I surfaced, gasping and retching and blinking through water and duckweed—and the gnashing teeth from a draugr aimed right for my neck.

Shit. Shit. Shit.

A hand fisted in my shirt, hoisting me from the water—Jorg. Our eyes locked for a split second, his gaze sharp with urgency, before he whirled and embedded his shovel in the attacking draugr's face with a satisfying pop and squish.

I caught my breath, coughing up pond water.

"I saw you slipping away," he said, his voice rough. "Are you alright?"

A flash of concern filled his eyes as he looked me over.

"Y-yes," I said, hating the nip of fear in me at having almost lost everything.

The concern cooled from his gaze, his features hardening once more.

"Good," he said. "Because if anyone is going to send you back to the underworld, it's going to be me."

Water rained off my shoulders in rivulets as Jorg and I fought our way back to Fenrir. Bones crunched and dead flesh tore as we barreled through the draugr. And still they kept coming, decaying feet crushing everything in their path.

Exhaustion seeped into my bones, but I tightened my grip on my weapon. To falter now meant death by having my kidneys eaten. I really hoped to avoid that, on top of everything else.

"We need to get out," I panted, sweat stinging my eyes. The greenhouse exit was distressingly far, and the writhing mass of draugr blocking any clear path didn't help.

"What do we do?" Fenrir asked, swinging his makeshift club at a draugr with only half a face. "They will follow us."

I flashed a sly grin, a fresh wave of adrenaline spiking.

"This way." I pulled them into the dense cover of the jungle of monstera and towering banana plants.

Ducking low beneath the broad leaves, we huddled together, crouching inside the tangled undergrowth as the draugr moved closer, their rotten stench flooding through the foliage.

I spread my fingers, palms out, and wove an illusion. Something to distract the gnarled horrors while we made our escape. The draugr shuffled closer, their clouded eyes drifting over our hiding spot.

I reached deep inside, calling up my magic, willing the illusion to take form. *Gods. That ID card was easy compared to this...*

But where my magic had once surged, only sparks sputtered from my fingertips now, weak and puny. Well, this was deeply embarrassing. The strain of projecting myself into the seidr realm had exhausted me more than I expected.

Ghostly, translucent figures flickered around the draugr, my illusions so pathetic and lacking in substance they were little more than faint distortions in the air. I grit my teeth, face flushing hot with shame and frustration.

"Gods. This is humiliating," I muttered through a clenched jaw, shoulders tensing. "Mortality has made my magic so temperamental."

"You're going to get us all killed," Jorg hissed, eyes blazing with a mixture of anger and fear as he watched the draugr approach.

"Just...give me a moment." More beads of sweat formed on my brow as I struggled to concentrate.

I had to do this. I had to find the power to save them, no matter how diminished I now was.

Focusing every cell of my weakened body, I willed my magic to answer my call once more, straining with the effort as the draugr closed in.

A hot surge flashed deep in my gut, surprising me. Where did that come from...it almost felt like...

A smoldering heat ignited within me, and my shoddy illusions cleared for two seconds, vivid and sharp. Clear. Well, that's interesting.

The draugr staggered closer, rustling and crushing the leaves and plants in their path, now only a dozen yards to our left and right.

I focused harder on that place inside of me...

All my feeble illusions evaporated in a breath as if snuffed out. But the heat pulsing in my palms lingered, almost as if it pulled at something deep from within me. It was just sweat from the exertion, surely...

"Get out of the way." Jorg stepped forward, jaw set, as he raised his hands.

Closing his eyes, Jorg wove a fresh, perfect illusion with an elegant wave of his fingers, conjuring flawless replicas of the three of us in the foliage. I watched, flooded with awe, as our spectral doubles burst into motion, racing away from the undergrowth. They could have been real flesh and blood. They sprinted for the exit, and the ravenous draugr mob turned to chase after them with a storm of inarticulate snarls.

It was masterful work, exquisitely detailed. Flawless. He even captured the perfect windswept wave of my hair.

Although, I noticed with a small frown that he made my brows a touch too arched and thin. Touché. I guess this is why Odin found it so infuriating when I did the same *embellishments* to his illusions.

Regardless, pride swelled within me. Jormungand's power had grown tremendously since I had seen it last. His illusory gift was breathtaking.

"Let's go." Jorg shattered the nearest pane of glass with a heavy swing of the shovel. Shards tinkled onto the ground, opening our path to freedom.

27

THE BLOOD OATH

"How long do you suspect until more draugr come?" Fenrir dabbed antiseptic on the gash above my eyebrow.

I stared at the faded floral wallpaper and beige carpet in our hotel room, trying not to curse louder. I'd experienced far less excruciating care on the battlefield.

"Well—Argh!" The antiseptic stung beneath my skin, sending needles of pain through my skull. "Are you sure you aren't dousing me with acid?"

A distant siren wailed through the cracked window, the sound of the city filtering in.

"Stop being a baby." He swiped ointment across the wound, his touch gentler now. "I realize you're still adjusting to your mortality, but it will get easier."

"I imagined mortality being more fun," I said. "Paper cuts. Near misses crossing the street. Mixing various substances together to snort. But this?" I jabbed a finger at the gauze and bloodied cotton scattered across the bedspread. "Lying next to a gassy troll's backside would be more delightful."

Every muscle in my body weighed a thousand pounds from exhaustion. And then the ache in my feet from all the walking made every step a delightful melange of stiff and sore. It never used to be this way.

Fenrir's throat rumbled with a chuckle.

"You'll adjust. You always do. If there's one thing you are good at, it's adapting," he said, a small smile stretching his mouth. "Now, let's see the rest of the damage. I'm not done playing doctor yet."

Oh goody.

I held out my arm to him, wincing slightly as he set to work cleaning the patchwork of scrapes and cuts. His brown hair fell across his eyes as he concentrated, brows pinching together as he gently wiped away the dried blood.

His smile faded as he swiped over the knotted scar...the scar that bound Odin and me together in blood. The reminder of a choice I once made lifetimes ago.

My gut squirmed at the hurt in his eyes.

And still, he helped me, after everything I did. After everything I caused. Why was he still helping me? He shouldn't help me. I didn't deserve it.

He dug his fingers into the tub of ointment and slathered the balm over my forearm.

I pulled away and slapped an ice pack on my arm, hiding the scar beneath the frost.

"Thank you," I croaked, throat constricting. "I think I'm well mended enough."

I stood and turned away from Fenrir's gaze, finding Jorg's reflection in the mirror across the room. He wrestled off his bloodstained shirt, tufts of his blonde hair sticking up wildly around his angular face as he inspected his own injuries.

The scar tingled deeper beneath the numbing ice pack.

Fenrir walked to the battered laminate desk next to his brother and began peeling ripe bananas into the second-hand blender he had purchased at the thrift store.

"Your fighting skills are quite impressive, Jormungand," I said.

Jorg tensed, as if my voice were an irritation all on its own. He dragged on a fresh black t-shirt and faded jeans.

"Mother felt it was important we know how to fight." Jorg squeezed out the words. "Especially considering who our father was, and his panache for inevitably bringing danger to our door even on a good day. Do you know how many Jotnar came looking for you to smash your skull into the flagstones? How many Dwarves made the journey to sever your head from your body? We almost couldn't get Brokkr to leave."

I grumbled about Brokkr beneath my breath. He really had tried his hardest to collect on our bet, the dear.

"Yes, well, anyway, your mother never mentioned your talent for magic. Your illusions today were remarkable. I never knew your gift was that powerful."

Jorg shrugged one shoulder, although a subtle spark of pride glinted in his eyes.

"At least one of us can still manage a decent illusion."

I let that barb slide.

"He's always been good with charms and illusions," Fenrir chimed in. "Like that time he made the meadow appear in the middle of winter, with poppies and bluebonnets and warm sunlight. It felt so real, I almost forgot the biting cold and snow around us."

Jormungand's lips twitched, the sharp angles of his face gentling.

"I just did what I had to back there," he muttered. "It wasn't that big of a deal, really."

Fenrir dumped a spoonful of hemp seeds over the bananas. He flicked the button, and the blender whirred with a dull roar.

"*Not that big of a deal*?" I asked. "Wielding both magic, especially illusory magic, and having shifting abilities, is an exceptionally rare combination of powers, Jorg. And the fact you have such control over them. I'm very proud of you, son."

My eyes met his in the mirror, and I hoped my words conveyed the true sincerity behind them. I was proud. Truly.

He regarded me as if I were the greatest fool north of the Ifingr.

"I don't want your praise," he said. "And I especially don't want your pride. Not anymore."

His scowl returned, creasing his features, his eyes hardening into green shards that wanted to cut me to the bone.

"Jorg..."

"Perhaps had you been around more than, oh, I don't know, an hour or two at mother's Yule feast, you'd have known about my abilities," he spat. "Do you know what it's like to always be told about your father's legendary skills with magic, but him never once taking even the faintest interest to actually ask about yours? Or to offer to teach you?"

"Jorg, I...I visited you as often as I could," I said over the roar of the blender. Over the roar of the guilt that consumed me. "There...There were duties I had to attend to in Asgard. There was always some kind of trouble or crisis I had to fix."

Even as I grasped for the same justifications, they rang hollow to me.

Jormungand barked out a harsh laugh.

"Fixing trouble you yourself caused, you mean. Or was it someone else who got Thiazi killed and made our lives that much more difficult in Jotunheim because we weren't just the sons of a traitor, but of a murderer of our own kin's blood as well?"

I narrowed my eyes, ignoring the bite of raw truth in his words.

Fenrir switched off the blender.

"It wasn't just your absence that was the problem," Fenrir said slowly. Cautiously. "It was..." He faltered, as if trying to find the right words. He cleared his throat. "I thought I had worked through and processed all of this with my therapist. Freud and Jung both told me...well...hmmm... You see, Papa, it's more like...hey, who wants a smoothie?"

Gods. No more smoothies.

"It was *what*, Fenrir?" I said. "Tell me."

He tapped the side of the blender, making the green sludge inside burp.

"Alright," he said, putting down the glass in his hand. "You made all three of us so many promises over the years. Wonderful promises. And you kept breaking them, again and again, until you finally broke us too."

Silence yawned between us, his words unbearable. Damning.

My shoulders tensed, and I swallowed hard.

"It was difficult to get out of my responsibilities in Asgard," I said, struggling for each word in my defense. "Often involving Thor acquainting my face with Mjolnir." I forced a laugh, trying to chase away the suffocating tension thickening around us.

Fenrir shook his head.

"I'm not talking about Asgard or Thor. I don't care about any of that," Fenrir said, voice hushed. "It's...You always promised me, repeatedly, that we'd go ice fishing. Just you and me. And every single time I believed you.

Every time I waited on you late into the bitter cold of the night. I trusted in you. And every time, you never once showed."

I shifted, grasping for more excuses. Justifications. Each crumbled to dust in my fingers.

"But," I said. "I always brought you your favorite Asgardian strawberries to try to make up for it."

Pain flittered behind his eyes. A deep pain that clenched my lungs.

"Everyone—Mummy, Jorg, our friends—told me not to trust you. Not to trust your empty words." His voice broke. "But I held on to that trust so tightly, for so long. I held on with everything I had. I believed that if I trusted enough, if I held on, when you came to me again, it would be different. We would finally go ice fishing together...I would have handed you the world if you'd asked, because I trusted you that completely. And I did, with that *last* promise you made me. I was so happy that night we camped beneath the stars, believing I had finally proven everyone wrong about you. You had come, as you said, and we were about to go ice fishing at last, except—"

His eyes glistened with tears as he swallowed hard.

A sinking horror that reached into the roots of my heart gripped my insides as I realized what last promise he spoke of now.

"It was a lie," Fenrir said. "You used the promise you knew I desired more than anything against me. To make sure I was right where the gods needed me to be, to take me from my home. From the Ironwood. From my mother. And I finally learned the lesson everyone tried to teach me about you."

His words struck my heart like a blade, white hot and unforgiving. I pictured him so clearly that day. I lied to him about going ice fishing. Because the lie was one I knew I could depend on.

Because I knew it would be easy.

And I hated myself for it, but I had to do it if I wanted Fenrir protected. If I wanted to save his life.

Odin promised me it would save his life.

His screams calling out to me to help him as the gods pulled him away rang in my ears. And I did nothing, because I had arranged it all.

Faded scars still wrapped around Fenrir's wrists, marks left by the gods' shackles where the links had bitten into his flesh.

"I didn't..." My voice cracked under the weight of a great and terrible shame. "You don't understand. There was a true reason."

"But we do understand the reason." Jorg pointed at the scar on my arm. "The reason was you chose to have Odin's cock in your mouth over protecting your own children."

The crude accusation hit like a strike in my guts. In that, he was wrong.

I met Jorg's eyes, anger and old hurt tangling in my chest.

"That's not true," I said. "And don't you dare debase my relationship with Odin to that. I loved him."

Fenrir's grip tightened on his glass, pain etching deeper lines across his face.

"We loved you, too," he whispered. "Why wasn't that enough?"

My heart clenched, regret drenching me in ice. I opened my mouth, then closed it, searching for the right words.

Memories of that first meeting pulled me under. The way Odin had looked at me not with disgust or fear at my nature, but with fascination. Wonder. He'd seen past my tricks and lies to something worth knowing. Worth loving. And I'd seen in him a chance to be more than just the chaos-bringer, the silver-tongued devil everyone feared. A chance at belonging. How could they understand?

"Going to Asgard was the path that offered a chance to improve things for all of you," I said. "Odin making me a god gave me a place in Asgard, a chance to be involved in their plans and to stop the bloodshed in Jotunheim. That's why I left. That's why I accepted Odin's offer to become a god."

Fenrir must have noticed something in my expression, because his face softened slightly.

"You're worried about him, aren't you? About what Frigg might do to him?"

"No, that's not—" I started, but faltered at his knowing look.

"He was your friend," Fenrir said gently. "It's okay to still care."

Friend. The word felt hollow compared to what we had been. What we'd seen in each other. But I wasn't ready to wade into those depths, not when my children's pain lay so raw before me.

"I believed I could make a difference in your lives," I said. "I believed I could protect you."

I searched Fenrir's gaze, finding only the reflection of my guilt.

Jormungand laughed. His smile never reached his eyes.

"Oh yes, we just loved the 'protection' of being bound and imprisoned," he said. "I adored rotting for centuries beneath the sea."

28

FLIRTING WITH DISASTER

Laughter, shouts, and music from the festival roared like dull, far away thunder as I waited for Sigyn. I stared at the tabloid newsstand beside yet another fountain with a basilisk spewing water into a trough. A blurry photo of a draugr made the front page. The article screamed in bold letters: CRYPTID SIGHTING.

Thankfully, humans would pay little attention and discount such sightings as nonsense. Fable. Myth. Lucky them. As for me, I had to keep a watchful eye as the draugr sniffed me out through the city. I already once had to dive behind a collection of trash bins when one sauntered past. But this game of hide and seek would only work for so long. They would find me, and when they did, they'd be even more pissed than before. Which would be quite unfortunate for my liver.

As I checked that Hel's coin remained safely in the pocket I'd stitched inside my shirt—I didn't want a repeat of what happened in the greenhouse, and Jorg's sarcastic remark about swallowing the damn thing was starting to sound reasonable. I wasn't about to tell them about nearly losing it down the bathtub drain. My mind kept drifting back to Fenrir and Jorg, their words echoing.

We loved you, too. Why wasn't that enough?

I pinched the bridge of my nose, trying to push the memory away. I wanted to be a good father to them. I tried. And I hoped that as long as I wasn't like my father, it would be enough. It wasn't. I was shit, just like him.

No, I was not like him. I loved my children, which was more than I could say for the great Jotnar Farbauti.

My pulse spiked at the sound of approaching steps, jolting me out of harsher memories of my father's fists.

Sigyn clicked across the cobblestones in heeled boots, her frame rigid, arms crossed across her black shirt. Today promised to be quite interesting.

I straightened my pleather jacket that luckily hid the bruise on my arm. I wished it also hid my shirt with some orange cartoon cat that hated Mondays.

No matter. I'd have Sigyn swooning in my arms before sundown. The itinerary I meticulously crafted was impeccable for tapping into those memories I knew still lived buried deep within her.

"Good afternoon, Dr. Laufeyjarson." Her gaze dropped two seconds to the cat and snapped back to my eyes.

"Please, call me Loki." I extended my hand.

Sigyn hesitated before clasping my hand, sending my pulse racing. It took everything in me to let her go.

"I think I prefer Dr. Laufeyjarson for now," she said. "To keep things clear that this is strictly professional."

The words were like a splash of cold water.

"Well, I was really hoping—" Irritation simmered behind her brown eyes, warning me I was one word away from her kneeing me in the groin again. "Shall we get started, then?"

"I think that's best. I'm still in shock that I even agreed to your offer at all. I'm half-convinced I'm having some sort of fever dream."

"You won't regret it."

"Oh, I'm already regretting it," she said. "I have a feeling this is going to be a long day that ends in a headache." She pulled out her phone, her fingers dancing across the screen in clicks and swipes. "I've made an itinerary—"

"What are the odds, so have I."

I dug into my pocket and removed a crumpled paper from the hotel notepad, covered in blotchy blue ballpoint pen. I smoothed the wrinkles out as best I could.

She pointed at the symbol I drew of Odin's incantation at the bottom of the page. The sharp Muspel runes nearly cut through the paper.

"What is that?"

I frowned.

Well, it was worth a shot to see if she'd recognize the runes despite her spell.

"It's just a sketch of a...well, how do I explain..."

"Is that a boar?" she asked.

"Are you sure it doesn't resemble anything else to you? Nothing running through your head looking at those runes? Like, oh, I don't know, an incantation perhaps?"

Sigyn wrinkled her nose in that adorably exasperated way I loved so much, though I fought not to show it.

"This entire page looks like the deranged work of a madman trapped in a room far too long."

Don't say the snarky retort. Don't say—

"And I suppose your clinical bullet points are so much better?"

Damn.

"Infinitely."

She showed me her list on her phone, perfectly formatted with crisp lines.

"How boring," I scoffed.

"Boring? Now look here Dr. Laufeyjarson—"

"How can I when your list has already put me half asleep?" I asked. "I appreciate you taking the time to make all of these very tidy rows of text. But that's not really what I had in mind."

Sigyn crossed her arms. Her irritation was always intensely arousing.

"And what exactly did you have in mind? More boar drawings?"

"Let's make a compromise?" I asked. "If you haven't noticed, there's a festival going on." I let the words linger, trying to echo our past first meeting during the carnival of Fasnacht. "Why don't we first enjoy the sights, enjoy some food, and then we can go through your extremely thorough plan?"

Sigyn's gaze drifted across the bustling Münsterplatz, people meandering around the crowded stalls. Above the laughter and chatter, a Ferris wheel slowly turned, its brightly lit carriages framed against the red stone cathedral.

"Is gawking at cotton candy and roasted chestnuts really the best use of your time?" she asked. "I don't see how cheese pies are helpful to your research on the crockery of 16 century Swiss book printers." She arched an eyebrow. "Or, is this where you finally admit this is all a sham to sleep with me?"

Cheeky.

"Living life is always time well spent for any project worth doing," I said. "The Herbst Messe has been serving food on locally made pottery since before those printers were setting type. Every traditional dish tells us something about the vessels that held them. Did you know some of those same pottery workshops supplied both the festival vendors and the printing houses? And there's a fascinating possible connection to Icelandic ceramic traditions through the trade routes." I smiled. "Besides, this Glühwein is served in replica sixteenth-century Basel drinking cups."

Sigyn blinked, as if surprised I actually made a valid point about the festival's significance.

"I suppose when you put it that way..." She tapped the side of her chin. She bit the inside of her lip. She sighed. "Alright. Fine. One hour at your festival. But after, I want to show you the locations of the mills and canals of the city. I have several pages of information on the most prominent book printers of the 16th century I'd like to go over. Maybe your Icelandic connection is here."

"Lovely," I said, unable to repress a satisfied smile. I'd specifically asked her to compile that list of printers, knowing she might stumble across traces of herself in the research. "I have no doubt my connection is there, waiting to be discovered."

* * *

WE WALKED through the bustling throng, every stone familiar, tormenting, and grinding me further into pulp as memories rushed me.

Wisps of her honied ginger hair pulled free from her ponytail with the breeze. I ached to reach out and tuck her stray hair behind her ear, to caress her cheek, flushed from the chilled air and kiss her deeply. I dug my nails into my palm instead.

She explained the history of the Platz. Its construction, the devastating earthquake in 1356, the ancient Roman artifacts archaeologists had discovered beneath the medieval layers.

And something miraculous happened. The more she spoke, the more I kept my mouth shut, the more her shoulders relaxed. She didn't roll her eyes quite so hard at my every breath. As she warmed to me, she shared more of her daily life, including her perpetual bad luck with public transit. Every attempt to leave the old city was thwarted by mysteriously broken trams or sudden work emergencies. She laughed it off as coincidence, never questioning the pattern. But I recognized the invisible bars of her cage. Frigg's magic held her within the old walls of the city, just as Odin's enchantments had kept Fenrir prowling Vienna's streets.

The sights and sounds of the festival swirled around us. Rides gleamed under the afternoon sun, their metallic surfaces glinting. Children's laughter mingled with the brassy carnival music piping from speakers. Roasting candied almonds and hot punsch saturated the air.

My stomach rumbled with hunger and then heaved at the thought of eating any of it. I told Fenrir putting those damned chia seeds in my smoothie was a terrible choice at breakfast. But he insisted the omega-3 fatty acids were essential to my getting better.

I popped a hard peppermint candy into my mouth, hoping to settle my nausea. If I knew anything about seduction, it was that vomiting on your conquest's shoes was hardly a good impression. Gry hardly appreciated when I had ruined their new leather boots after a night of heavy drinking at *The Black Raven*.

"Shouldn't you be writing this information down?" she asked. "Or would it be better if I wrote everything out in doodles on crumpled paper?"

She cracked the smallest bit of a smile.

I think she made a joke at my expense. Progress.

"I have an excellent memory," I said. "Actually, what if we go to that cafe and I finally buy you those pastries you're after? I'm determined you have them after the first set ended in the puddle because—"

"Because of you."

"Yes, and the replacements that were taken by Oliver. It's the least I can do, and then you can tell me all about the printers."

Sigyn brushed one of those loose strands of hair from her face I so longed to touch. Her expression softened slightly, considering my offer.

"You really know how to tempt."

"I'm glad you noticed."

"But, it's no use with the pastries," Sigyn sighed. "I'm doomed to never have even one bite, it seems. Same with my favorite coffee roast."

I lifted an eyebrow.

"What do you mean?"

"The coffee is always gone at the grocery store. It's like the cremeschnitte. I never catch a break to buy one, or if I do manage to snag one, I run into strange men and they fall into puddles." She gave me a teasing look. "I have never gotten even a single bite so far. It's like I'm cursed to only ever get 'medium' things in life," she said with a forced laugh. "Never the best, never the worst. Just...medium."

If she only could know her joke was fact. And it broke my heart to see her struggle against its strangle.

The candy turned bitter on my tongue. As the full weight of Frigg's magic crashed down on me. It wasn't just about a spell stealing her memories to safeguard the Salvation Weave from Sigyn's abilities, or about the curse imprisoning her to the boundaries of this city. No, it was far more insidious than that.

Frigg had also cursed Sigyn to a life of unfulfillment. She toiled away at a job that brought her no joy. Even a favorite pastry, a good cup of coffee, were always just out of reach.

White-hot anger raced through me at what Frigg had done. She hadn't only taken Sigyn's past. She'd stolen her hope. When I finally came face-to-face with that witch again, I'd make her hurt for every minute of joy she'd robbed from Sigyn.

A rush of heat flushed in my core, burning and hungry, like that hot prick of a needle I had felt once before, only this time, it dug deeper.

"What—what is your favorite thing of the platz?" I asked, forcing myself to calm. To focus. To cool. "Anything of crockery significance?"

Sigyn chuckled.

"Well, I'm afraid nothing to do with crockery, but, well, let me show you."

Her eyes lit as her gaze landed on the towers of the Münster Cathedral.

Sigyn grew more animated and excited, the lingering wariness seeming to fade further away with each step closer to the cathedral.

"The skill of the masons who built these walls is incredible," she said, hovering her hand near the red sandstone as if drawn to its warmth. "People spent lifetimes on this cathedral, making it the heart of their world. Generation after generation, praying, hoping..."

"You don't say," I murmured.

Her smile deepened as she gazed at the building, and for a breath, I saw Sigyn in the way she tilted her head, in the familiar reverence of her gesture.

We paused before St. George and his dragon.

"This statue..." Her voice softened to a whisper. "I love it most because—" She stopped, her eyes growing distant, unfocused.

My heart leaped. She was there, so close to the surface, as if remembering the day she'd told me why she loved this piece back in 1526.

"What do you see?" I urged, trying to hold that fragment of memory before it slipped away.

"Nothing," she said, but her hand trembled. "It's just..."

I held her gaze and stepped closer, as if I could somehow anchor her to this moment.

"Just what?"

"This all feels so oddly familiar," she said, her voice small and lost. "Do you ever get déjà vu?"

"All the time," I said.

I needed to get her inside before I lost her again. The Münster is where she had lit a prayer candle for me five hundred years ago. And where—

Joyful screams from a nearby ride jarred her out from wherever she had gone. She shivered, and I watched the spell drag her back down into darkness, like watching her drown all over again.

She swallowed hard.

"How about we..." she said. "...yes, how about we ride the Ferris wheel?"

She already turned and walked in the direction of the attraction. Her breathing seemed deeper than before.

"Ferris wheel?" I asked. "Wouldn't you rather explain all the stonework details inside the church instead? I'm sure there is loads of crockery inside."

She laughed.

"I saw on your list you wanted a view of the city," she

said, gesturing to the Ferris wheel. "The wheel offers the best opportunity to see the canals and other points of interest. One that doesn't require climbing over a hundred steps up to the church."

She had noticed that detail I had scribbled on my itinerary.

"I wouldn't mind the climb," I said.

"Come on." She reached out and grabbed my hand, tugging me towards the ride. The warmth of her fingers against mine made every rationalization and meticulous plan in my mind turn to mush. I'd always follow this woman anywhere.

We stepped into the swaying metal cabin, and I settled onto the bench, leaving an intentional space beside me. But Sigyn took the seat across from me instead, folding her hands in her lap. I swallowed my disappointment.

With a mechanical groan and lurch, the ride jolted upward, slowly lifting us higher. The festival shrank to a patchwork of color and sound. The Rhine glittered below as it wound towards the soft, rolling hills in the distance. Church steeples and clusters of tile rooftops peeked through trees blazing in shades of red, orange, and gold.

Sigyn stared out of the glass at the spires of the cathedral rising and falling behind her with each rotation.

She was so beautiful in those fluttering seconds. That ache to hold her, to touch, lanced through me again.

"There's the Middle Bridge over the Rhine, originally built in 1226," she said, each word filled with a brightness.

"And that tower?" I asked, transfixed by the strand of hair against her cheek.

"The Spalentor city gate," she said. "Fun fact—Basel used to have a double wall surrounding it, built in medieval times for added fortification and defense."

I smiled, recalling soaring over those walls in my falcon aspect, surveying the city below to find her.

"I remember," I said.

Sigyn raised an eyebrow.

"Remember? How could you remember that? The Victorians demolished the original wall during their idiotic remodeling craze."

Oops.

"Of course, I only meant I remembered seeing it... uhhh...seeing it depicted on an old map of the city."

Sigyn studied me for seconds that felt more like hours.

"You truly love this city, don't you?" I asked, eager to change the subject before her suspicions about me, already troublesome enough, grew any stronger.

"Basel is a hidden gem," Sigyn said, gazing out over the autumn-hued trees speckled throughout the city. "The Romans, the Habsburgs...so much history has happened here."

Like us. We happened here too.

"Your job at the historical museum must be perfect for you, then," I said.

Sigyn smirked, leaning back in her seat.

"Perfect..." Something melancholy settled in her eyes. "Well, actually..."

I shifted closer, hungry for any glimpse into the desires and dreams kept locked away. Anything to reconnect the fractured pieces Frigg blew up.

"Go on," I urged. "You're the one that wanted this Ferris wheel ride, so now you're quite stuck with me."

I leaned back and stretched out with a grin, trying to put her at ease.

She chuckled. Good. She was warming up to me. Finally,

we were getting somewhere. This was like chipping away at a boulder. A very grumpy boulder.

"I appreciate my job at the museum," she said. "I mean, I could do without the annoying patrons, like you." She cracked another smile. "But I don't think it's most people's childhood dream to spend their entire life sitting behind a help desk."

"Well, that will all be changing soon now you're coming to Iceland," I said.

Sigyn fidgeted with the cuff of her sleeve, like she always did when she was anxious.

"I...I have no idea why I brought any of this up," she said. "I'm grateful for my position—Oh, look at all those trees! Taylor will love seeing the autumn colors on our walk later."

Taylor? I suppressed a groan, remembering the difficulty it took to resolve things with Falael—not because I minded sharing, but because of Sigyn's iron-clad sense of honor. Her promises weren't easily undone, even when her heart wasn't in them.

"Who's Taylor?" I asked, keeping my voice carefully neutral despite the headache already forming at the thought of another Elf situation.

"An elderly neighbor of mine that I visit some evenings," Sigyn replied. "He's lonely after his wife passed, and his daughter lives in America."

I exhaled.

"I look forward to my evenings," she said. "It's the one time I can really dive into research. The museum's collection of Norse texts..." She trailed off, then seemed to catch herself. "I mean, I know it's not exactly relevant to my job here, but there's something about those old stories, espe-cially the ones about—" She hesitated, a slight flush creeping up her neck. "Well, the trickster figures. They're fascinating. When I first applied to the University of Reykjavik, that's what I wanted to study." Her eyes lit up with that familiar spark I knew so well. And as quickly, it dimmed again. "That's a silly dream though."

There you are. Even Frigg's spell couldn't completely bury your connection to me.

"Silly dream? More like a golden opportunity," I countered, unable to hide my enthusiasm. "Now that you've taken my offer at the university, you can pursue that dream. Professor Bjornsson's expertise in Norse mythology would be perfect for your interests."

Sigyn laughed, but it was a hollow sound.

"It's a bit late for me to become a scholar, don't you think? But...I do hope to make the most of my time there." She paused, her tone growing cautious. "Even if it's temporary. If it works out at all."

I frowned at her pessimism.

"Why wouldn't it work out?"

She shrugged.

"I'm well-suited for my current job," she said, the brightness drained from her voice.

"You're suited for so much more," I said. "I know you are. Believe that about yourself."

Sigyn smiled again, but the pain in her eyes gutted me.

"That's kind of you to say. But let's be realistic. Dreams are nice, but they don't pay the bills."

As we revolved overhead, I glimpsed familiar landmarks from our past dotting the streets below. The old apothecary where we bought elixirs for her father, the bustling open-air market where we'd walk, buying fresh bread, apples, and flowers.

If I could find the right words, the right memory...

anything to pierce the fog and wake her from this awful nightmare.

But Sigyn's gaze remained fixed on the people walking through the city below.

"See them all," she said. "Walking these streets. They don't even think of all the lives that have lived here before. Their joys. Their sorrows. Their loves. It's all forgotten. It's... it's so sad. And I can't stop thinking about it all. It's like I'm being haunted by ghosts in every crooked doorframe and cobblestone."

Her words trailed off as she fiddled with her engraved wedding band on her finger. The gold glinted in the slanting afternoon sunlight as she turned it round and round.

If only she could understand why she felt haunted. That the ghosts she sensed were real. And one sat across from her.

"Tell me about your ring," I said. "A family heirloom? Or...from a love, perhaps?"

Please remember me. Remember us.

"This?" She glanced down at the ring, brow pinched as if seeing it for the first time. "I...I don't remember where I got it from. I've always had it. I think."

I leaned forward, pulse kicking up as our knees brushed.

"May I?" I gestured to the ring.

Sigyn's eyes flicked up to meet mine, holding my gaze for a heavy moment before giving a slow nod. She extended her hand towards me.

I traced with my fingertips the intricate Asgardian knot designs circling the band in an unbroken loop.

"The craftsmanship is extraordinary," Sigyn said, voice hushed in the sliver of space between us. "But the patterns...they're strange. They seem Norse, but not quite. I've studied every known variation of Nordic knotwork, but these..." She frowned. "They're like nothing I've ever seen in the texts."

Because they're not in your texts. They're from Asgard.

I leaned even closer, my heart beating wildly inside me. Our breaths heated between us. Sigyn didn't retract her hand this time.

I brushed the pads of my fingers over her warm skin, mapping the contours of each knuckle of her hand. Home. And disappointment followed, because in a deep, perhaps foolish corner of my heart, I thought, wished, that a spark might ignite between us at our touch, like the first time we touched 500 years before. But why would there be? Especially now when I had no more chaos left in me.

"Yes, you're right about the origins," I said. "But these patterns...they remind me of something from those tales you mentioned earlier. The ones about trickster gods from the far north."

I flashed my gaze to hers.

Please. Remember our story.

"Like Loki?" She gave a small laugh. "I can't believe I'm discussing Norse mythology with someone named Loki while holding a mysterious ring. If this was one of those old stories..." She trailed off, shaking her head as if to clear it. "The patterns do have a similar style to artifacts associated with those myths, but..." She frowned, studying the ring again. "They're different somehow. More...real."

Because they are real.

"How so? Tell me."

"I don't know exactly. It's like..." She leaned closer. "Like they're trying to tell me something. Like I should know—"

Her phone rang with a shrill set of notes that sent a shock through me, shattering the fragile moment.

Sigyn flinched and pulled her hand away from mine as

the outside world came crashing back around us. I blinked, suddenly aware that we were no longer suspended high above the city. While I'd been lost in our conversation, in her eyes, the wheel had completed its rotation, bringing us back down to earth.

"It's the museum." Sigyn muttered, fumbling with her mobile as she swiped to answer. "I have to take this—Hello, wait...What? Now?" Her voice spiked in panic. "Alright, I'm on my way."

My heartbeat stuttered.

"What's going on?"

The Ferris wheel jerked to a halt, and of course, we had just reached the loading platform, our car first in line to be emptied. The attendant was already moving towards us, unlatching the door.

"I'm so sorry, but I have to leave. Immediately," she said in a breathless rush, words tumbling over each other as she gathered her things. "There's been some kind of emergency. Seriously. They seem to be getting more frequent lately."

Stupid curse.

"An emergency? What kind?" My heart plummeted.

"Oliver came down with something. He sprayed his lunch all over the reception area." She grimaced faintly at the description. "And they're severely short-staffed with a major school group tour arriving any minute. I need to go provide backup immediately."

Oh.

Dammit. I didn't think his system was that weak. Slipping that concoction I found in his coffee wasn't supposed to take effect for another hour at least. Why did these kinds of things always have to backfire?

Sincere regret signed in her eyes.

"I'm actually really, truly sorry about this. Hard as that is for me to understand."

"But...what about the canals? The list of the printers?" I asked, desperately grasping at straws to keep us together. "Our itinerary..."

"I'm sorry."

Sigyn slipped on her gloves and stepped out of the cabin, leaving me all by myself, and terribly, terribly depressed.

29

THE LAST DROP

BALDER

Mother sat rigid in her high-backed chair, jaw clenched, her rings catching the firelight as she gripped a silver goblet. Across from her, I stirred my watery fish stew, trying to avoid the bitter taste of overcooked potatoes.

"And then what Frigg did to Sigyn in the forests of Vanaheim...Frigg never knew I saw her."

A knot tightened in my abdomen as Thor's words replayed over and over in my mind, along with a thousand questions that wouldn't leave me alone.

What happened in Vanaheim between my mother and Sigyn?

"I swore to Father never to tell you."

Why would Father make Thor promise not to tell me?

Something almost like dread crept up my spine as it all gnawed at my edges.

Mother slammed down her fork, the harsh clang shattering the quiet. Several cats sprang from the table. Our servant, Brynjar, flinched standing to Mother's left. His weathered hands trembled slightly as he clasped them behind his back.

"I can't believe Loki and his spawn escaped the draugr." Her eyes pierced the empty chair beside me, no doubt picturing Loki's smug face. "That worm. That slippery weasel. What's the point of forcing Odin to have his former lover eaten if Loki still has his liver? I imagined this being completely more satisfying."

I set down my spoon, the grating scrape of silver against porcelain screeching through the empty feast hall, everything cold and dim and hollow and squirming with twenty cats. A tabby purred on the place setting beside me. A Himalayan rubbed between my calves.

"The draugr will find him." I nudged her already twice emptied goblet forward, the engraved vines and leaves stained dark from dried rivulets of wine. "Brynjar, a refill, please."

Brynjar's eyes widened, the worry lines around them deepening as he shifted in his well-worn tunic of rich blue linen.

"A thousand apologies, your Highness, but...we've no wine left after that last goblet. Only some spiced mead from Yule remains."

Mother's face froze in a smile, the kind you wear when you accept everything falling apart around you.

This wasn't good.

Shadows crept along the bare stone walls, broken only by the occasional flickering torch or candle stub burning low.

"Nothing left?" Mother asked. "Are we reduced to living in a wasteland?"

I followed her disgusted gesture at the gaps between the

silver platters that once overflowed with honeyed hams, pineapple spiced roasts, and berry tarts piled high. Now, half-eaten bread crusts and a wedge of hard cheese and a very flatulent Sphinx cat cluttered the empty spaces.

Brynjar bowed his head, his gray-streaked hair falling across his deeply lined forehead.

"Thor drank it all. This mead is the last in our cellars." He held up a bottle covered in cobwebs.

Mother sneered at the bottle.

"You expect me to drink cinnamon mead with fish stew? Where's the Vanaheim White?"

"Apologies, your Majesty." Brynjar's voice dropped to a whisper laced with fear. "Thor drank all the white wine as well. After this bottle, only the prisoners' beer swill remains."

Mother clenched the goblet so tight I thought the silver might crack.

She let out a breath that rolled with fury.

"Giving Thor every luxury was meant to earn his loyalty, yet he feasts while we starve. At this rate, that glutton will devour the entire hall, including the benches and candlesticks! Freya better keep count of her felines, or he'll eat those next."

I stared at the two chunks of fish and a single white cat hair floating in my bowl and suppressed a bitter sigh. There was truth to her words. The pigs in the pins ate heartier, and with far less cat smell. But the lack of decent food wasn't entirely Thor's fault. Freya insisted on a strict diet of finely diced beef and lamb for her cats on rotating days. And then Skadi's blockade tightened like a noose around our throats. Our food stores ran scarce.

"Alright. There is no more wine," she said, an edge to her

voice. "I can understand that. But where is the marzipan? I specially had it ordered tonight for Balder."

Brynjar paled, Adam's apple bobbing as he swallowed.

"Your Majesty, unfortunately, we had to prepare Thor's roasted boar first..."

"Now you tell me there is no marzipan." Mother drummed the tabletop with a sharp staccato. "You swore the kitchens could meet all demands, Brynjar."

"Yes, but that was b-before Lady Freya sent us the menu for her cats—Mr. Ragnar's diet is especially intricate—and then Thor, and..." Brynjar trailed off, sweat beading on his brow as Mother's gaze bored into him as if deciding which ear to cut off first.

"And?" Mother asked.

"And before we lost half our staff," he stammered, wringing the fraying hem of his tunic. "If we had more hands—"

I extended my arm.

"Half the staff is gone?" I asked. "What caused such losses?"

Mother waved my question away.

"There were grumblings in the kitchens," Mother said lightly, examining her nails.

"You mean you sacked them?" That knot in my stomach twisted tighter. "Grumbling is not a crime. Actually, I feel a little grumbling is more than earned after making one of Thor's meat cyclone sandwiches. Or Mr. Ragnar's dairy free mock tuna mousse."

Mother's smile was brittle and didn't reach her eyes.

"Even small complaints can spark rebellion."

"Why don't we discuss this—"

The doors burst open, the heavy oak cracking against the plaster walls.

"If you ever send me to that gross little prison again, Frigg, I will never forgive you. The mildew coating the walls has stunk up my hair!" Freya walked into the hall, candle-light catching on her dark hair and ivory gown. I sighed at the thick layer of green goo slathering her face. Every day was some other thousand ingredient beauty mask.

That was another funnel of where our food went, right into her edible facials and scrubs and three hour long nightly milk baths. I wasn't sure when I'd forgive her for snatching my last jar of apricot jam so she could mix it into her morning mask. She insisted the apricot brightened her complexion.

"Other than the mildew, how did your tea and threats go with Idunn?" Mother asked. "She should have appreciated the company."

"Excuse me?" I interrupted. "What tea? What threats—"

"Idunn refuses cooperation unless the curse is broken and all the gods' freed," Freya said, cutting me off. "She told me over a cup of chamomile that her apples will rot before submitting, even with our offer to tweak her curse. I mean, she'd still be miserable, but at least there would be less mold. She said she enjoyed studying the mold! Exhausting woman. I'll now have to double up the snail mucus beneath my eyes tonight to make sure I don't get any horrid bags because of her long-winded talks about fungal filaments."

A glob of the cream fell off her chin and plopped to the floor. A dozen cats leapt off the table and gobbled the fallen facial.

Mother's expression hardened.

"Bold words from a woman caged in a prison with mushrooms growing out of the walls and at my mercy."

But I caught the worried glance she exchanged with Freya. The servants' whispers hadn't escaped me either—

how Idunn's hands shook too badly now to tend her own garden, how her voice had weakened to a rasp. The curse was already taking its toll.

A shiver ran through me as the full weight of the situation we were sinking into hit me. Did they truly not see the problem? We depended on Idunn's golden apples to heal and sustain us. While Thor could defend us from external threats, the apples were our lifeline from within. If the rumors of her failing strength were true...

"Without her, we're the ones at Idunn's mercy," I said, forcing my voice level despite the growing unease churning in my gut.

"Only if she talks about botany," Freya said. Laughed.

I thought I was losing my mind. How could they laugh at this situation they put us in?

Freya wrung out a silk cloth from a silver bowl Brynjar presented her with and wiped the mask off her face. Small bits of green remained smeared in the creases around her nose.

"But you'll have no apples when the harvest comes in," I said, needing them to understand. "That means there will be no apples to heal our warriors when the war comes to our door. Or to heal us. These ramifications from the curse—"

Fire flashed in Mother's eyes.

"Are you blaming my curse, Balder? You know how I have everything under control. Or are you doubting me like everyone else?"

Sadness filled her eyes, and she stood from the table, the scrape of her chair harsh against the stone floor.

"Mother, please," I said. "That's not what I meant—"

Her heels rapped against the flagstones as she crossed to the windows. Raindrops snaked down the glass, casting wobbling shadows across her face. Beyond the panes, storm clouds swallowed the last threads of daylight. Freya stepped beside her and embraced her from behind, nudging her mouth next to her ear.

"Stop letting their rot get into your mind," Freya murmured, weaving her fingers through Mother's intricate braids. "You are the master of this house now, and your curse is iron clad. You've played this game before. We both have. This is a battle of wills, and yours is the strongest I've ever met. Be patient."

Mother leaned back into Freya's embrace, the purple silk of her high-collared gown rustling against Freya's chest. She seemed to draw strength from her words. Her touch. Freya's loose black hair fell forward as she held Mother tighter, their faces inches apart.

"Well then," Mother said. "If Thor and Idunn insist on being obstinate, they can both starve alongside us. Maybe the prospect of a long, cold, and hungry winter will finally motivate them to stand with us against Skadi."

I shivered despite the fire's warmth and curled my toes, trying to suffocate the sensation of Skadi licking them. None of this was going according to plan. Mother was supposed to have everything managed by now, the gods at her feet, Ragnarok a distant memory, and me not looking down the tunnel of a life in Jotunheim filled with cabbage and a wife who would make me traipse around her fortress barefoot.

I sucked in a sharp breath.

"Mother, please," I said. "Consider negotiating with Thor and Idunn. I'm sure you can reason with them."

"We have an ace in our hand with the Salvation Weave." She said. "They need more time to break. They will come around once they see how I can change their eternity to something more pleasant if they just bend to me."

I hesitated.

"Perhaps we should rethink our strategy—"

"Rethink?" Mother's eyes flashed with anger. "I would sooner see Asgard's towers burn before bowing to the demands of those two. I didn't cast this curse to be weak now."

My knuckles whitened around the handle of my knife, gripping it so tightly my hand trembled.

"Are you quite alright, Balder?"

I forced my fingers to uncurl, releasing the blade.

"Perfectly fine," I replied tightly.

Frigg never knew I saw her. If she had...

An urge punched me in the gut to confront her about what Thor had let slip. The questions burned at the tip of my tongue. If I confronted her, she would just evade the truth, or worse, break down in tears, asking how I could think her capable of such a terrible betrayal. She would insist our oath was sacred to her, that she would never break what we forged in blood. I could hear it all now.

I am a good Mother. Why do you always think of me so wicked?

Every word I wanted to say fizzled and extinguished.

"It will all be fine," Mother said, her voice steady. Sure. "Thor will change his mind. Where food goes, he follows. He will submit. As will Idunn."

"They will fall to you." Freya tightened her embrace. "And you will rule Asgard as it was meant to be ruled."

Freya pressed her lips to the crook of Mother's neck in a kiss, and Mother's eyes drifted closed. And a ghost rose.

I was six years old, and I walked into the library and saw Mother and Freya's reflection in a gilded mirror. Freya had her hand up Mother's skirt as they embraced. They made hushed cries I'd never heard before. Mother noticed me, her cheeks flushed. "Just two good friends playing," she had insisted with a reassuring smile. She gave me some honey sweets and told me to keep our secret. There was no need to tell Father.

Cold frosted my veins as Thor's damning words slammed back into me.

"Father was faithful to your mother. Always. Because she made sure he had no choice."

Time and time again, Mother told me how she had never taken another lover. Never would. She only wanted Father. And time and time again, I had believed her, because Father was the enemy.

He had to be.

He better be.

I turned my gaze away and picked up my bowl of leftover stew and the chunk of cheese next to a dozing tabby.

Mother stepped out of Freya's arms.

"Where are you taking that?" Mother asked.

"Am I not free to go when and where I please?" I asked, unable to keep the defiant edge from my voice.

Her eyebrow rose.

"Balder, that tone is out of character for you," she said. "I thought we were dining together?"

Guilt washed over me, but I pushed it aside. Forced it away. Back.

"I've lost my appetite," I said. "I figured I'd take it to Father. I rather he eat it than it go to waste, especially considering how slim things are now."

She tensed, a muscle twitching in her jaw.

"There's no need to take that to him. I already fed him, as you requested. Let Mr. Ragnar have it."

Freya shrieked, her voice echoing off the bare walls.

"Mr. Ragnar cannot have cheese!"

"See?" I asked. "Mr. Ragnar cannot have cheese, so it looks like Father is the winner tonight."

Mother's face hardened, not finding any humor in my joke.

"I forbid it."

"Forbid it?" I asked. "Are you serious right now? I'm not a child."

"I don't want you going to see him," she said, harder. "Or Thor. He's filling your head with doubts."

"Doubts? Or things you rather I not know?" The words slipped out before I could stop them, each tinged with bitterness.

Like you lying about never taking another lover. And never telling me about your visit to Vanaheim...

Mother stepped away from Freya and gently clasped my face in her hands, her fingers pressing into my skin.

"It is a mother's concern. I don't want your head filled with confusion and poison. I only want what's best for you. You look so tired, sweetheart. So stressed."

"Is this a command? Are you commanding me?"

She smiled softly at me, but the look in her eyes chilled me to the bone.

"Please put the bowl and cheese back on the table, darling."

Jaw clenched, I obeyed. She patted my cheek, and her smile deepened, like a feline full-fed.

She reached into the pouch at her side and pulled out three honey sweets wrapped in wax paper. She held them out to me, as she always did when I was a child trying to coax or reward me. Why did it feel like a mockery now?

"I've managed to stash a few away." She winked and smiled. "You seem so upset. I hope these make you feel better."

I took them, and I swear she exhaled the moment they left her hand.

"Don't forget," she said. "You know the truth, because you've seen the truth. Please don't stop believing in me. You are all I have, Balder."

I had seen much, that was true. The problem was, what had seemed so crystal clear to me was growing murky.

I grabbed the dusty bottle of mead from the table, right next to a snoring Mr. Ragnar.

"For me, then," I lied. "To drink alongside them."

I had no intention of drinking the mead.

But I knew someone who may.

"I swore to Father never to tell you."

30

INK

LOKI

Sigyn's lips traced fire down my throat, each kiss stoking my desire higher. Her weight pressed me into silk sheets as she moved above me, her skin glowing in candlelight. I roamed her body with my hands, memorizing every curve, every shiver as she gasped my name. Her hair fell around us, shutting out everything but the exquisite sensation of her.

She rocked against me with devastating slowness, each roll of her hips drawing me deeper into blissful surrender. Her skin tasted of honey and devotion.

"Loki," she breathed against my neck. "Loki..."

I reached for her, needing to pull her closer, to kiss her, to feel more of her heat—but my wrists wouldn't move. The silk sheets twisted, turned into rough rope, that bit deep into my flesh. Sigyn's warm weight transformed into crushing stone. Her sweet whispers became Frigg's laughter.

Yellow eyes blazed in the darkness. Through the shadows, I saw Frigg, light glinting off her blade as she stood over their tiny forms. Their last cries echoed in my ears as pain exploded across my body, venom dripping—

Fenrir shook me awake, jolting me from dark and pain and those yellow eyes that burned. My screams filled my ears. Cold sweat drenched my skin as I bolted upright, gasping for air.

"Papa, you're safe." Fenrir gripped harder into my shoulders, grounding me. Concern etched the deep lines across his brow as his eyes locked with mine "You're alright. You're safe."

The stone walls of the cave dissolved, replaced by the hotel room's muted floral wallpaper. Moonlight filtered through the window, but the shadows seemed to writhe and twist.

My heart slammed against my ribs.

I clung to Fenrir, my nails digging crescents into his arms. He didn't flinch, he only tightened his grip.

"I'm...I'm safe? I'm not there?" I rasped, my throat raw.

"It's a dream," Fenrir soothed, though his eyes reflected worry and a hint of fear. "Try to breathe."

I rubbed my wrists where my bonds had cut into my skin in the dream. I forced shuddering breaths through lungs tight with panic, willing my frantic pulse to slow. Tears pricked my eyes as flashes of the nightmare returned.

The snake. The screams.

Frigg standing over their small broken bodies...

The cotton sheets scratched my skin and suffocated me. I shoved them away.

"Are you dying, or what?" Jorg pulled off his covers and sat on the edge of the bed, rubbing the sleep from his eyes with a scowl. When he saw me, the scowl melted into worry. "Is he ok, Fen?"

I am safe. I am not in danger.

"I'm fine. It was just..." I rambled, raking trembling fingers through my sweat-damp hair. "This happens sometimes. One moment I'm here, then suddenly I'm back there, watching them die. All of them. Gone." My voice cracked on the last word.

Tears came, hot and vicious, spilling down my cheeks. Sometimes they did after the nightmares. Sometimes they didn't. My body shuddered with sobs.

I whispered, more to myself than him, "I lost them all..."

Fenrir caught me as I sagged, drawing me against the solid bulk of his chest. I leaned into him, taking comfort in his strength. In his steady presence. Fighting to regain control before I completely unraveled. I hoped I didn't frighten him.

I am safe. I am not in danger.

"Let me get you water," Jorg said.

Being back here in this city was wearing on me more than I realized it would. I was trying to awaken Sigyn's memories, and only succeeding in waking my own. Memories I didn't want to relive.

"It's all so close," I said.

"Try to focus on seeing Sigyn in the morning." Jorg handed me the glass. A fleeting bit of concern shone in his eyes.

Sigyn had called the hotel and said she could see me the next day. I needed her now more than ever. And she wasn't here. The ache for her felt like a knife in my gut.

I took the water and gulped down the icy liquid, loving how it calmed my dry throat.

"Try to rest," Jorg said. "I know it can be difficult after these kinds of...reminders."

He held my gaze for two more weighted seconds before returning to his bed, rolling onto his side.

"Yes, think of her," Fenrir said. "You'll need all your strength for the morning. You hate when you get dark circles beneath your eyes." He tried to make a small joke, the corners of his lips quirking upward, but the worry still festered in each word.

A hoarse chuckle rasped from my raw throat at his attempt to lighten the mood.

"You're right," I said, managing a wavering smile. "I can't greet my wife looking like death warmed over, can I? That's certainly not a good impression."

My legs trembled as I stood, and I stripped away the sweat-soaked sheets.

"What are you doing?" Fenrir asked, as I moved towards the bare cot.

"I can't sleep on the wet sheets."

I moved to lie on the thin mattress. Fenrir grasped my shoulder, stopping me.

"You can bunk with me tonight," he said, his eyes soft. Kind. "Please. You need real sleep, not another night of tossing and turning. Those creaky springs keep me awake, too." Another hint of humor lifted his mouth.

Why was he always so kind to me?

I didn't deserve such consideration.

Especially from him.

From either of them.

* * *

"Why do you keep looking behind your shoulder?" Sigyn asked, tilting her head slightly to one side. "Please don't tell me you're some conspiracy theorist."

We walked briskly down alleys, my gaze darting from fountain to corner shop to rattling tram, on high alert for any sign of draugrs. So far, all had been clear of those drooling beasts, but I knew they would eventually catch my scent. Of course, I couldn't reveal any of that to Sigyn.

"No, not at all," I said. "I'm making sure my hair looks good in the store windows. Ever since I switched to this Castille soap my son insisted I try, I've been fighting nothing but tangles."

A small smirk touched her mouth. Although, I didn't like the tiredness in her eyes from the curse feeding on her.

"You really are a peculiar one." Her gaze fell to my shirt, for the third time. Obviously she admired the definition of my chest through the cotton and—oh. That was the reason why. Not my incredible physique, but the three garish white stallions galloping across a frozen tundra on my shirt. Lovely.

"A peculiar one you like, I hope?" I asked, shifting my jacket to hide the horses.

She laughed, the sound warming me despite the chill in the air. A teasing glint sparkled in her eyes.

"Let's not go too far, Dr. Laufeyjarson," she said.

"When are you going to stop with this Dr. Laufeyjarson nonsense and call me Loki?"

She smiled, looking directly into my eyes. Heat built between my legs as she leaned in, ever so slightly, her body angling towards mine.

"When pigs fly," she said.

She turned on her heel and walked along the wooden planks that crossed over a narrow canal where water raced towards the Rhine river. As she moved, a gentle breeze carried her scent to me. A delicate mix of rosemary and something uniquely her.

Desire coiled tighter low in my body.

The water in the canal turned a waterwheel that was

connected to a tilted white plaster house. The Paper Museum, which better not let me down in stirring some of those memories in her.

I was determined to break her spell, just as I was determined to bypass Frigg's curse of horribleness one way or another to give Sigyn at least a single minute of joy.

"Before we go in, I have something for you."

As we approached the entrance, I pulled out a box from my bag.

Sigyn's eyes widened as she recognized the white box with the gold-embossed logo, its corners crisp and perfectly folded. The delicate twining 'S' of Schneider's Bakery gleamed in the light.

"Cremeschnitte?" she asked.

"I was there right at opening to make sure you got the freshest pastry I could."

Her face lit up as she carefully opened the box, lifting out the pastry, its layers of flaky puff pastry sandwiching thick vanilla custard dusted with a delicate snowfall of powdered sugar. As she was about to take a bite, a bird swooped down from nowhere, snatching the cremeschnitte right out of her hand, leaving only a trail of sugar dust drifting through the air.

Well, that's definitely not how I saw that going. Frigg's curse was formidable...

Sigyn let out a resigned sigh.

"I guess it was too good to be true. I told you I'm cursed," she said with a rueful smile.

"I'm so sorry," I said, already turning to chase the bird. "If you'll excuse me, I have a murder to commit—"

She caught my sleeve.

"It's fine. Really. I'm used to it. Let's just head into the museum."

The iron-bound door creaked open, and the rhythmic thump of hammers filled the room with thunder as they struck troughs full of a slurry of white linen, mashing rags into pulp. Dust motes danced in shafts of sunlight as the scent of wood and paper transported me to her printing shop centuries ago.

I studied her closely, desperate for even a spark of recollection in her as she moved through the sights and smells that should also have been achingly familiar to her.

She explained the exhibits and as delightful as all her *thoroughness* was, hearing about the differences in strength between wood-pulp, linen, and vellum, didn't much help keep my own memories from drifting to 1526. Sigyn's hair was neatly pinned as she inspected the apprentices' work. She laughed, and the pride in her eyes holding a freshly printed book stirred—

"You're staring at me again, Dr. Laufeyjarson," Sigyn said. "What is it you find so captivating? It better not be my breasts, or else we are going to have a very different conversation."

My gaze dropped from her neck where I had last kissed her in Fenrir's bathroom, the memory burning like coals against my skin.

"My apologies, it's only..."

I miss you.

"Only what?"

I wanted to grab her shoulders and shake the memories free. Instead, I bit my nails into my palms.

"It's only I'm curious if this next exhibit will hold that link I'm searching for."

The floorboards groaned as musty air hit our faces, thick with paper and dust and machine grease. Type cases lined the walls, their tiny metal letters gleaming dully in the dim light filtering through leaded windows. Everything looked lifted straight from Sigyn's old workshop, especially the printing press in the center, its handle worn smooth from use.

Her eyes finally lit as she walked beneath the strings of linen paper criss-crossing the ceiling. Old ink stung my nose, and I inhaled deeper, hoping the scent might reach some buried part of her.

"You like this room," I said, unable to keep the smile from my voice.

"I can't explain it," she said as she trailed her fingers across each display with reverence. "I've been here countless times. But, this time, with you in this space, it just feels..."

Her face scrunched, like someone trying to describe a dream.

"Familiar?" My heart hammered.

"Yes." She looked around until her gaze met mine and held—one heartbeat, two, three, four, five—longer than she'd ever allowed since the curse. Almost as if—

Color flooded her cheeks. She turned away, hiding whatever emotion I'd glimpsed.

"Tell me how it's familiar." I neared her. "How do I make it feel familiar?"

"I..."

"Yes?" I leaned in, holding my breath.

"I..." The mask slammed back into place, locking me out. "I don't think I want to share that with you."

"Oh," I said. "Is it that naughty? I'm exceedingly hard to rattle."

She turned away with an eyeroll.

"No, I think you'd find it silly."

Alright. On to the next attempt to jog that memory so we could hurry this kiss along. Gods. Love always took forever.

"I doubt that," I said. "But let's talk of something else if it makes you more comfortable. Explain these to me."

I pointed at the cases full of typeface on the other side of the room, fighting to keep my smile from betraying too much eagerness. I knew exactly what I was doing. I searched for any bridge back to her.

She laughed.

"The typeface?"

"And this is precisely why I have you to guide me."

She laughed.

The floorboards creaked as we crossed the room towards the cases.

"I confess the mechanics of old timey printing presses eludes me," I shrugged. "My expertise being more about crockery and all...But you seem to know your way around one. How did they manage it?"

Sigyn smiled.

"Well, first you'd need to arrange all your type pieces in reverse," she said, tracing the air as if setting invisible metal letters. "Then you'd use a leather-covered ball soaked in ink to carefully dab the raised letters. The paper goes on top, and the whole thing gets pressed—" She stopped and blinked. "Yes. Where was I? Oh, right. Did you know Basel was mostly known for its medical texts and—"

She spoke, and the past unspooled around me. Metal type clicked and clacked, the central press squeaked and thumped against fresh paper. Sharp ink burned my nose, so pungent Sigyn used to joke you could taste it.

The longer she talked, the harder I looked into the shadowed corners of the room, I could just make out the ghosts of the apprentices toiling away, calling out questions, or sharing a laugh in the haze.

"Why are you smiling like that?" she asked. "All wistful like?"

I cleared my throat.

"Why don't you show me how the printing press works?" I asked, not answering.

I moved closer to her, the drumming of the hammers echoing around us, drowning out the drumming of my heart.

"Show you?" she asked, her voice catching. "What do you mean?"

I dared another step closer, and smoothed my hand over the handle of the press, almost as if a caress. The tiniest flush of pink crept across her cheeks.

"The sign says it's a *hands on* experience." I held her gaze, our faces now inches apart, close enough that I could feel the warmth of her quickening breaths. "Show me. Please. I am a visual learner."

Sigyn's gaze dropped to my lips before darting back up, and *ah*.

I recognized that look flickering in her eyes.

Desire.

Finally, we were getting somewhere.

"I'll...I'll print you a short message," she said. "The two words I've been *dying* to tell you since I first met you."

Her laugh raised goosebumps along my flesh.

I drank her in as she set to work. She picked out typeface collecting the letters in her palm. She pulled out a piece of paper from a tray that said "take only one, please."

"You seem very familiar with this," I said, letting silk bleed into every hushed syllable.

"I've watched the demonstrations here during my lunch breaks," she said, then added quickly, "Out of curiosity, of course. The museum staff are very thorough in their explanations."

And I moved even nearer, closing the distance between us. Heat flared hotter in me as she licked that tempting curve of her lips.

For a suspended second, I thought she might lean in.

She walked to the iron machinery, and traced the letters and levers with her fingers. Agony feasted on me, remembering those same hands mapping my scars in candlelight, cupping my face during thunderstorms, threading through my hair as she whispered my name. The way she'd curl her fingers against my neck when she kissed me. The way she knew exactly how to unravel me with a single touch.

I swallowed hard. Watching her work the press with such familiar skill while she looked through me like a ghost cut deeper than any blade. Here she was, so near I could sense the rosemary in her hair, yet further than if she were in another realm. I'd give entire kingdoms to feel her fingers trace my jaw again. To have her remember even one of our nights together.

"Do you ever wonder about all the people that have touched these pieces before?" she asked, her words so soft I had to lean even closer to catch the words. "Their stories?"

Our pasts surrounded us now, echoing through every creak and groan of the old equipment. Thinking of all the lives woven through our story. Lives she had loved, lost, or forgotten...my throat tightened.

"I know of one," I said roughly. "It's the reason this research means so much to me."

"Tell me."

Sigyn's movements were fluid and confident, guided by muscle memory as she arranged the typeset. I recalled the countless times I'd seen her perform this very task at her shop in Heuberg, well, when I wasn't busy helping to rebuild the shop.

"There was a woman who worked in this very city in the 16th century," I said.

Sigyn's hands stilled over the type cases.

"She saved a print shop from burning, and taking half the city with it. She protected the press, which represented the livelihood of everyone under her employ, and nearly lost her life in the process."

The rich tang of ink scented the air as she rolled the fluid across the plate, the scent burning my sinuses. Black pigment smeared her fingertips.

"I like her," she said, a small smile playing at the corners of her lips as she inked the plate.

"Yes, I thought you might," I said.

"She must have faced incredible ridicule." She traced the type. "A woman running a print shop back then..."

"Nothing stopped her. Not the guild, not the church, not the whispers. She printed what she believed needed printing."

"And now you search to discover if she drank her tea out of Icelandic tea cups?" She laughed.

"Something like that."

"I wish I had that courage." Her voice softened. "To defy everyone like that."

"She is—" The word caught. "*Was*."

"You speak like you knew her. Like you were there."

My throat closed. Memories rushed in—her taking notes with ink-stained fingers by candlelight, sharing brown bread and cheese at midnight, that first kiss against the window during the storm that shook Basel's foundations...

I forced them down. Not now. Stay here, in this moment, with this version of her.

"Research for my work on printer's vessels," I said. "The guild records are remarkably detailed about her workshop's equipment. You remind me of her, though."

Sigyn stilled over the type cases.

"I know you mean this kindly, but I could never command apprentices and journeymen. I can barely manage my own schedule."

Frigg's magic crushed centuries of fire into dust.

"You seem to manage me just fine."

"Well, someone has to keep you from breaking the exhibits." Her lips curved.

I laughed, though my chest ached at that familiar teasing tone.

"Now," she laid the blank paper down, "shall we make this work?"

"Please."

She clutched the handle and something flickered behind her eyes. A shadow of memory pulling her elsewhere, somewhere through time. Somewhere I desperately hoped I still existed.

"What do you see?" My voice barely touched the air.

"See..." she said. "I don't even know. Sometimes I...I get these flashes. They aren't dreams. More like a memory, but —" She swallowed. "They make me wonder. It's what I stopped myself from telling you earlier."

"Tell me." I leaned closer, close enough to catch the tremor in her breath.

She turned, something stirring in her eyes.

"Do you believe in past lives?"

The drum of hammers filled the still, matching my heart.

"Without doubt," I said.

She pressed her lips together. I breathed in rosemary

and memories, willing her to linger in this now, just a heart-beat longer.

Then she blinked. The moment broke, and Sigyn vanished again behind Ida's eyes.

"I'm sorry, these strange daydreams sometimes..." She shook her head. "I don't want to talk about this anymore."

Her gaze cleared with each passing second, the fragile moment crumbling like sandcastles.

"Why not?" I asked. "Please, tell me more about these daydreams."

She looked back at the press, her expression hardening. She gripped the handle and pulled down the lever. The dull thud of the lever punctuated her request for me to shut up.

"Dr. Laufeyjarson, please. Let's drop this. I don't even know why I brought this up. You're always getting me to say the strangest things. Past lives are nonsense. Quite unscientific."

"But they aren't—"

She shoved the freshly printed paper into my hands.

"Here is your message. More fitting than ever."

Two words stared back, ink still wet, letters smudged:

Piss off.

31

AS THE WORLDS FALL DOWN

We ambled the cobblestone streets of Basel, fall leaves twirling through the winding alleys. Sigyn chatted brightly, the earlier tension forgotten as she pointed out the oldest coffee shop, the arched stone bridge spanning the Rhine, the cathedral spires in the distance. And the dear kept trying her hardest to connect each to some bit of found pottery or ceramic to help me.

The wind turned colder, autumn rain threatening on the horizon. But I didn't care if it rained buckets.

Because something marvelous happened.

Sigyn and I simply talked. About her favorite books. What she did during the evening when she wasn't helping old Herr Taylor. How she enjoyed a good croissant with black cherry jam. If she noticed how her voice grew more tired with each story, she didn't mention it.

I smiled, watching her honied ginger strands dance in the rising wind, tendrils escaping her braid that I longed to tuck back. A rosy flush bloomed on her cheeks from the growing chill. Or perhaps she was finally realizing how devilishly handsome I was.

Which meant we were tantalizingly close to me breaking her spell. One kiss, and I'd have Sigyn back. She would translate the incantation, do a quick blood ritual, Odin would end the curse, and I'd finally get my golden apple.

I couldn't stop grinning, fantasizing about that immortal vigor flowing through me again. Full nights of lovemaking, the strength to ram my dagger into Frigg's sternum, and most importantly, bowls and bowls of ice cream. Such lovely thoughts.

The sun sank lower, bleeding the sky from azure to flaming amber until storm clouds swallowed it completely.

We walked along the city wall at St. Albantor, quiet and removed from the streets. Gravel snapped beneath our feet.

"Today wasn't...completely horrible," she said, offering the smallest, almost imperceptible smile. Her eyes met mine with hesitation.

I arched a brow as my pulse quickened with the wind.

"Were you expecting horrible?"

She laughed, and my lips curved upward.

"Well, we got off to a rocky start when I kicked you in the...well. She glanced down, a flush spreading across her cheeks. "I hope everything has healed?"

"Never better, I assure you," I said. "You're welcome to check for yourself. I've been told they're quite marvelous."

She rolled her eyes, fighting a chuckle.

"Okay, I was going to apologize for that rude message I printed you, but I think it still stands."

"That's quite alright." I shrugged, delighting in her relaxed demeanor. "If I got offended every time someone told me to piss off, I'd have no friends left."

She laughed, the sound making my heart flutter.

"I can't believe I'm saying this, but I actually enjoyed today. With you. Even though you're seriously one of the most aggravating people I've ever met."

I beamed.

"That is the nicest thing you've said about me."

I drifted closer as cold rain speckled our cheeks. She didn't move away.

"You speak as if the day ends here," I said. "Let's get a drink at the *Goldenen Sternen*. You can lecture me about its history. I'm sure oodles of book printers drank out of crockery there."

Another frigid gust filled with icy droplets flecked my skin. Her hair whipped across her face, and I squeezed my fists against the desire to brush it back.

"I'm afraid I need to head back to the museum."

My heart sank into my stomach. Alright. Frigg giving her a job was really getting in the way of my progress with getting her lips on mine.

"Surely you can postpone for half an hour? I'm quite confident the building won't collapse without you..." The wind lashed around the corners of the wall and gate.

"Margrit almost fired me for breaking protocol when I opened that case. I can't risk any more mistakes," she said. "Even with the research position you and Professor Bjornsson are offering, I need a safety net. If the project doesn't work out, and I lose this position—"

"Then we'd find you another position," I cut in, impatience bleeding through. "You're capable of far more than Margrit allows, anyway. Your knowledge of Basel's printing history and Norse connections...the university would be lucky to have you. Professor Bjornsson and I could use someone who understands both the practical and mythological aspects of these early printing houses."

She put way too much care into this stupid museum job, and it aggravated me to no end. Not just because it was Frigg's doing, but because it crushed her, sank her entire body into the dirt.

"Find another one?" Her voice wavered. "This is the best job I will ever get. And realistically the highest paying."

Lightning crackled overhead. Rain splattered around us as thunder rolled through the hills.

"All you can do? All you're good for?" It took everything in me not to grasp her shoulders and give her a firm shake. Why couldn't she see her own self worth? "You can do whatever you like."

She stared at me like I was mad, twisting her wedding band. Not even a whisper of recollection from the gold.

"You seem to believe me far more capable than I am," she said, doubt clouding her eyes. "I can't jeopardize that because of an awful boss, even with the promise of studying in Iceland. What if it doesn't work—?"

Her words cut off as she stumbled. I caught her before she hit the cobblestones, my arms wrapping around her. Her body felt too light, too fragile against mine.

"I'm fine," she muttered, gripping my forearms. Her fingers burned through my shirt. "Been feeling a bit weak lately. Just tired from work."

My throat tightened. Not tired—cursed. The Salvation Weave was feeding on her, draining her strength like poison. Each day without breaking it...

Time was running out. We needed that incantation.

"Let me help you up," I said, voice rough. She swayed against me as I steadied her, her chest pressed to mine. I spread my hands across her back, remembering every curve.

"Thank you." Rain traced her cheekbones. So close. So

damn close. She stepped back, steadying herself. "I was trying to say what if it doesn't work out?"

I clenched my jaw, fighting the urge to pull her back. To tell her the truth about why she felt this fatigue. To kiss her until she remembered everything.

"You aren't obliged to stay in an unpleasant situation," I said, trying to keep my voice level despite the growing urgency. "Please stop thinking so small. And so small of yourself."

I thought she'd appreciate my encouragement, my belief in her abilities. That she would be grateful someone saw her potential.

Frustration simmered in her eyes instead, her back stiffening.

"What are you saying? That I should just quit?" Sarcasm saturated every word.

Actually...

"Now that's a marvelous idea."

And then we can speed up this whole spell breaking process with you spending more time with me...

"And abandon Margrit short-staffed?" The color rose in her too-pale cheeks. "I can't leave her in such a bad situation."

I couldn't believe what I was hearing. Even cursed and drained, she thought of others first. Even buried under Frigg's magic, Sigyn still bled through.

"Somehow, I suspect she'll endure the blow," I replied dryly. "Listen to yourself. You're more concerned about Margrit's staffing issues than your own future. What about the opportunity in Iceland? The chance to study, to grow?"

"I...I don't know if I should go at all. What if I'm not good enough? What if I can't handle the work? And being so far from home..."

My frustration boiled over.

"Not good enough? Can't handle it? Where's your spirit of adventure? Your curiosity?"

She flinched at my tone, and I forced a deep breath. I had to remind myself I was reasoning against magic. Not her.

"Look," I softened my voice, "I understand you're scared. Change is terrifying. But you're capable of significantly greater things than this. You're brilliant, creative, hardworking. You will be a true asset in Iceland."

Sigyn's shoulders slumped.

"You're wrong about me."

Rain pounded the cobblestones, drenching us in seconds. I shed my jacket, and held it above us. Droplets misted my face as I moved closer. Rivulets streamed down her cheeks as she hugged herself against the chill.

"Taking your offer was a mistake. I can't go," she said.

"Mistake? I'm offering you everything—tuition, expenses, a chance to break free," I said over the storm.

Her eyes flashed, body tense against mine.

"Well, I've changed my mind," she said. "Talking now, I see it all clearly. I can't abandon everything on a whim!"

"A whim? This is your future!"

She laughed bitterly, tucking herself further under the jacket as the rain intensified. She stared up at me, eyes blazing with anger and something else I couldn't quite name.

"My future is here. This job—"

"This job is crushing your spirit." The words exploded from me. "Where's the woman from the Ferris wheel? The one who knew every detail about Basel's printing houses, who was accepted to study under Bjornsson, who understood how these vessels connected to the Norse texts they printed?"

"She remembered to stop wasting time on dreams," Sigyn snapped, her breath hot on my face. "She remembered her place."

"Your place?" I asked. "Your place is wherever you damn well choose it to be."

She dug into my arms, body trembling with more than cold. Heat coiled between my legs. She was always most beautiful when she was angry.

"Stop it. Stop. You don't understand—"

"Then make me understand!" I roared, pulling her closer. Rain streamed down our faces, mingling like tears. "You shouldn't let fear hold you back."

"And what if this is all I deserve?" she shouted back, voice breaking. "What if Iceland is another place to fail? This life isn't what I wanted," she bit out, hair plastering against her forehead. "But it's what I'm good enough for. It's where I feel safe."

The pain in her eyes was unbearable. I cupped her face, forcing her to meet my gaze.

"Then you pick yourself up and try again. But at least you'll have tried. Sometimes you have to have faith."

For a moment, I saw a flicker of the old Sigyn—defiant, passionate, alive. Then doubt swallowed her whole.

Frustration and desire warred within me. I wanted to crush my mouth to hers, to remind her of everything she was. Instead, I leaned my forehead against hers, our ragged breaths mingling.

"Why are you fighting so hard for this?" she whispered, her lips so close I could almost taste them.

I had no answer she'd understand. The position wasn't

even real, yet I argued as if our lives depended on it. And in a way, they did.

I need more time.

Thunder rolled as our breath fogged between us. Raindrops traced her cheeks.

"You're so much more than you understand," I said, trying not to think how she shivered against me.

"Please stop saying these things." Frustration flashed across her features, but her voice lacked conviction. "Stop making me feel hope."

Rain soaked us. I'd give anything to pull her closer, to kiss her, and remind her she was mine, everything the magic strangling her told her she wasn't.

"Look at me," I said. Commanded.

Her gaze hardened. For a breath, she seemed ready to unleash her temper, to shove me away.

"Loki, I swear..."

She paused. Something shifted behind her eyes at my name.

"Loki." This time my name passed her lips like a prayer. The tight lines of anger softened. Her gaze deepened with something that made me hold my breath and hope harder than I ever had.

She searched my face as if seeing me clearly for the first time. Rolls of hot breath escaped between our parted lips.

And I dared.

I leaned forward. Just a little. Just enough that her heat warmed my rain-chilled skin.

One kiss and it would be over.

Her breathing matched my thundering heart. Raindrops clung to her flushed skin.

My lips burned to taste her. To feel her mouth on mine.

To break this gods-forsaken spell once and for all so we all could live.

"Loki..." my name sighed from her, nearly lost in the storm.

Our fates hung suspended on that endless moment.

Sigyn, kiss me.

She tilted her chin up, as if answering my unspoken plea. Rain drummed against my jacket overhead.

We will all be saved.

The bells of the Münster Cathedral tolled, deep and piercing through the howling storm.

Sigyn startled and tension coiled through her frame.

"I'm sorry, but I can't...I...I have to go..." She pulled back, shattering the thread between us.

I swallowed the rising fury in my throat.

So close. We had been so unbearably close.

Not trusting my voice, I pressed my soaked jacket into her hands. She managed a small, apologetic smile and disappeared into the rain.

I dragged in burning breaths. My mouth still ached with wanting. I slammed my fist against stone, welcoming the pain. This was wearing me thin. I wanted her happy again. Safe. Free of the darkness threatening to swallow us all forever if Frigg won.

And we are running out of time...

The Münster bells kept ringing. Five centuries ago, she had pulled me through those cathedral doors, past my protests and straight to a tray of sand studded with beeswax candles. Even then, watching her in that quiet place, my heart thundering in my chest, I knew I was hers. And yesterday, before this rain, I'd watched her pause before St. George's statue, her eyes going distant with almost-recognition...

And an idea struck me.

Places where love first takes root hold their own kind of magic. I'd seen it in the way she'd faltered before the statue, how her buried memories stirred stronger in spots where we'd made our story together. The Münster was where I'd first fallen in love with her, where that spark had caught and burned through centuries. If anywhere could thin Frigg's curse enough for Sigyn to feel what we once were, for her to want that kiss that would break this spell...it would be there.

I knew where I had to take her.

Inside those walls was our beginning. If I could make her remember that, make her feel it again...

Growls ripped through my plots. The stench of rotting meat filled my lungs.

Gods. You had to be kidding me.

Gravel crunched beneath my shoes as I turned to face them.

And my day got worse.

32

AN IMPROMPTU PARTY

I was so not in the mood for this.

Five draugr emerged from behind the trees and shrubs lining the end of the St. Albantor wall. Rain pounded their withered and rotting flesh, bones visible through ragged gaps.

Their clouded eyes fixed on me with a hunger that sent a cold spike of dread into my insides, which, quite frankly, infuriated me. When I was a god, this sort of ambush would have been absolutely delightful to perk me up. But now? Now had the slight inconvenience of me being able to actually die.

Painful as it was to admit, the thought of their teeth chomping through my ribcage wasn't very appealing right now.

"Hello again," I said, trying to keep things as pleasant as possible. Trying not to make eye contact with the one sporting a rusted shovel in his forehead, the one I had slightly lodged there in the greenhouse.

The draugr replied with guttural growls, their desire to rip my arms from my sockets and eat them abundantly clear. Shovel-face growled the loudest. Apparently, being dead didn't cure one of holding grudges. Fantastic.

I scanned for weapons. Tree branches? Too wet. Gravel? Unless they were afraid of pebbles. One sad, pointed stick lay nearby. Wonderful.

They slunk closer, tendons creaking like rusty door hinges. Thick drool dripped from yellowed teeth. One pulled out a sword, another a scythe. I couldn't help but smirk. Only draugr would bring weapons that could so easily be turned against them. If I could just get my hands on—

My back hit frigid stone. Damn.

And then a puddle splashed under my shoes, sending an unwelcome rush of cold water through the ventilation holes. Perfect.

So much pain was about to come my way. Well, it was nice having arms and legs while it lasted.

I drew my daggers at my hips, rain streaming off the blades. The nearest draugr's breath suggested a recent meal of week-old fish wrapped in Tyr's socks. This close range wasn't ideal, but what is life without a little risk of having your brain slurped out through your nostrils?

They surrounded me. I grounded my stance, my orange clogs squelching into the wet gravel as they closed in. I spun my daggers.

The draugr with the axe attacked with a shriek. He stomped through the shallow puddles, splattering mud across my trousers that made me shriek louder. A chunk of what might have been his cheek sloughed off with the movement, landing with a wet plop near my foot. Right. He was the first to kill. If I could only get a clean shot at his head.

I slashed my blade, locking his arm. Searing pain

erupted in my shoulder, the jarring movement shooting white spots to the edges of my vision. I gritted my teeth, and with a swift rotation, I sent his axe flying into the bushes. I aimed for his neck, but the bastard ducked.

Gods, aiming for their heads would be a lot easier if they stopped moving. And if bits of them would stop falling off and making the ground treacherously slick.

He tugged a machete from his belt and swiped at my stomach. A second draugr lunged with jagged yellow nails aimed at my back. Its rancid breath made my eyes water.

With a jerk and a yank that sent fresh waves of agony through my shoulder, I severed my left blade through the arm of the first, leaving the appendage dangling by a few strands of rotted sinew.

I tore through the wrist of the second, severing the hand completely in a beautifully clean cut. The hand struck the ground with a thud, fingers still twitching. Not their heads, but it would slow them down to some extent from pulling out any more surprise machetes.

I drove *Laevateinn* to the hilt in his left eye socket with a satisfying wet crunch, gagging as putrid fluid splattered across my face. Finally. I yanked out my blade, and fresh spasms ripped through my shoulder. The draugr collapsed.

"That's for dirtying my trousers." I wiped putrid goo from my face with my sleeve, which only made it worse.

I pointed my blade slick with gore and other yucky bits at the other three. My shoulder screamed, holding the position, but I refused to let them see me falter.

"Alright, who is next? How about you shovel-face? Let's see what's left of your brain, assuming you ever had one."

Shovel-face growled, and I didn't realize his already livid rotten face could look more livid and rotten. A maggot wriggled free from between his teeth.

He charged me, along with the final two draugr. They clawed and grasped and swiped with their swords and scythes. The scythe shredded my shirt, slicing a thin gash beneath. Gods, I missed being invulnerable.

I screamed and let a litany of unwholesome words fall from my mouth. Every time I aimed for their heads, they'd dodge or block or get in each other's way. It was like trying to swat three flies with one hand while swimming in sewage. Their rotting flesh made them unpredictable, limbs bending at impossible angles, joints moving in ways that would snap living tendons.

As I side stepped another swipe of the scythe, the shorter draugr nipped at my elbow, its teeth scraping my skin. The bastard. Ice spread from the bite, decay seeping into the wound.

"Stop nibbling on me!" I snarled.

I plunged my dagger into its eye socket, tearing through rotted tissue. I wrenched the blade free and skewered the scythe-wielder's temple. Two headshots in a row. Maybe my luck was turning.

The draugr straightened.

Alright, maybe not.

Shovel-face lunged from behind. His grip wrenched my arm as he slammed me against the medieval tower. My shoulder cracked against the red cornerstone blocks. He pinned me, his jaw unhinging as it rushed for my throat. A molar dropped from his rotting gums onto my cheek. Lovely.

I rammed my dagger into his torso. Ribs splintered beneath the blade. His grip loosened in a cloud of fetid air. I twisted free and staggered upright, muscles screaming. Even breathing stabbed pain through my chest, each inhale thick with the stench of decay.

The draugr stumbled back into the wall's covered arcade, its body smacking against the stone arch. I seized the shovel still embedded in its skull and drove it deeper. Bone crunched. The creature convulsed once and stilled.

Finally.

The last two kept charging. Seriously? Now this was getting absurd.

The last two draugr plowed through the rain. My shoulder blazed, pain shooting down to my fingertips. As a god, this would've been nothing. As a mortal, it threatened to drop me. I couldn't finish this fight, and that realization curdled in my gut. I never ran—but staying meant becoming draugr food.

Rain pelted my face as I scanned for escape. The St. Alban-Rheinweg stretched before me, old chestnuts thrashing in the storm winds. No cover except for stupid bollards that dotted along the asphalt. My gaze swept past the road to the Rhine. Perfect. Draugr couldn't swim. Their waterlogged flesh would tear apart in the current. If I could make it to the river...

I sprinted. Claws raked my back as the draugr pursued, their rotting feet slapping against wet stone. Pain lanced through my body with each stride. The squeaky squishes from my shoes really rather ruined the whole dignified escape thing. If Thor saw me running away like this, he'd never let me live it down. This was deeply embarrassing.

My feet pounded across the arcade's threshold onto St. Alban-Rheinweg. And beyond the road stood the river wall —a waist-high stone parapet running parallel to the street. The Rhine roared three stories below, its black waters churning against the embankment.

I raced across three lanes towards a bench and vaulted over the wood—and teeth clamped my calf mid-leap. The draugr had lunged low, its jaws locked like iron, its bite spreading liquid frost through my veins. The cold crept upward with each heartbeat.

I twisted in its grasp, using my momentum to slam both of us against the parapet. The impact drove my breath out, but I managed to plunge my dagger into its temple. Again. Seriously. How many times would I have to stab this thing in the head? Putrid brain matter oozed between my fingers. With each strike, the draugr's jaw loosened and released my calf.

Gods I hated these things.

I braced my good leg against the stone wall and heaved. Blood sprayed as the creature toppled backwards over the parapet. The Rhine's current shredded its rotting flesh into ribbons thirty feet below. One down.

The final draugr thundered towards me from the arcade. I pivoted away from the wall to dodge—my foot slipped on the slick pavement. Shit. Decaying fingers raked my shirt. *Laevateinn* slipped from my grasp.

The ground slammed into me. Stars burst behind my eyes as my shoulder hit the asphalt. *Laevateinn* skittered across the wet pavement and between the stone balusters guarding the river's edge. If it fell into the river, I'd never be able to retrieve it.

Dread plunged me in a lake of ice colder than any draugr's bite. Without *Laevateinn*, we couldn't do the ritual.

The draugr's mangled face loomed over me where I lay on the asphalt, jaw dangling by a tendon.

This day kept getting better and better.

I rolled right as the draugr's fists shattered asphalt where my head had been. Gravel sprayed. My shoes fought for grip on the wet surface as I lurched up between the creature and the wall.

The draugr lunged. I dove past it towards the parapet where *Laevateinn* teetered. Each step jolted fire through my wounded leg. Rotting hands clutched my shirt from behind. The river's roar drowned the draugr's snarls as I stretched toward *Laevateinn*, half-bent over the stone wall.

My fingers grasped the hilt as the baluster housing *Laevateinn* cracked. The dagger slipped in my rain and draugr-goo slicked grip.

With a desperate surge, I snatched *Laevateinn* free. The draugr's weight crashed into my back, shoving my hips against the parapet. We grappled at the wall's edge, shedding pieces of its corpse like grotesque confetti onto the footpath below.

I twisted in its grasp until we were face to face, my back to the street. Then I drove *Laevateinn* up into the draugr's skull. Bone crunched. Fluids burst. The creature spasmed and went limp, its full weight pinning me against the stone barrier.

I planted my feet and heaved the corpse sideways off me. It crumpled to the footpath between the road and parapet. I staggered over to its twitching form and stabbed it in the head. Again. And again. And one more for good measure.

"Why. Won't. You. Just. Die. Already?" These things were like cockroaches. You had to make absolutely sure.

Standing unsteady, I gathered my remaining strength and tipped the thoroughly ventilated draugr corpse over the stone wall. It tumbled through the air, breaking apart before it even hit the water.

Good riddance.

33

THE BROKEN

BALDER

I hesitated outside the heavy oak door, my heart pounding.

Did I really want to do this?

I started to turn and walk away down the hall.

"I swore to Father never to tell you."

With a deep breath, I forced my hand on the iron latch and stepped inside before I lost my nerve. The hinges creaked open, cutting through the silence.

Father sat hunched at his desk, surrounded by stacks of books and trinkets of brass and silver...a scene I had witnessed many times when I visited his study. But this time was different. He wasn't fixating on some dusty book, or scratching his quill across parchment. Instead, he held his head in his hands.

"I'll give your mother credit," he said. "This curse is incredibly intricate. I've read every book in my study twice over, just in case his efforts fail. That memory spell Frigg put on Sigyn is quite unfortunate. And I hate admitting I didn't anticipate it."

"His efforts? You mean Loki," I spat, familiar rage rising in my chest. "Why am I not shocked you make no secret of it? You two always plotted together against her."

Father laughed low in his throat.

"Did we?" he asked. "And why should I keep my plans secret? What do I have to fear from your mother now? What more can she take from me? Besides, I hope the thought of us breaking the Salvation Weave keeps her awake at night."

I didn't like how he underestimated her. Because there was plenty more she could do to him if she grew tired of his scheming.

"You really think you can defeat Mother's curse with whatever hair brained plot you have brewing?" I asked, fiddling with the package of honey candies. "She told me the Salvation Weave is unbreakable—"

"Every curse can be broken. If anyone tells you anything else, it's a lie."

Father reached for a book and tossed it to me. The leather binding cracked and flaked as I opened the book to a page adorned with intertwined hearts and blooming roses.

"I've identified the theoretical act of love that it would take to break the Salvation Weave." His gaze bore into me, searching for a reaction. "And therein lies your mother's genius. The act of love exists in concept, but it's practically impossible to execute. A Frost Giant has a better chance of surviving in Muspelheim. Which is why Loki better not fail attaining what I need."

"How so?" I asked, scanning the text detailing sacrifices and connections deep enough to rush blood.

He sat back in his leather chair.

"It would require a combination of circumstances. Imagine forging a magical chain from the sound of a cat's footfall, the roots of a mountain, and a fish's breath—all before breakfast. The components exist, but bringing them together..."

"The odds would be slim, if they exist at all," I said.

He nodded.

"But what troubles me most about the curse is how it feeds on us."

"Feeds on you?"

"Haven't you noticed how the gods grow weaker, trapped in her curse? How their strength is diminishing?" His eye fixed on me. "Think, Balder. What kind of magic could bind Fenrir? Even Gleipnir could barely hold him. Your mother's curse needs power, and we're the fuel she's burning to keep it strong. And everything that burns, becomes ash."

"You're lying," I said, but my voice wavered. Thor's words echoed in my mind.

"I feel drained. Like something's eating away at my strength day by day."

I clenched my hands at my sides, hating how everything felt darker. Colder.

I drew in a shaking breath. Each heartbeat seemed to whisper *truth, truth, truth,* a rhythm I couldn't escape.

"Mother worked exceptionally hard creating this curse. She wouldn't—" I swallowed, forcing myself to meet Father's gaze. "She said needing the gods' power was only temporary. I believe her."

"Temporary." Father's laugh was soft. "You always want to see the best in her, son. I understand. I did too, once."

Rain clicked the leaded windows, and the firelight showed a man weathered and beaten. Exhausted. The flecks of silver in his russet hair and beard seemed to have doubled. The fine lines around his eye etched deeper into his skin.

Part of me liked this look on him. But a larger part felt something else. I believe it was pity that twisted my gut.

I laid the book down on the table and walked closer, clutching the bottle of wine harder, hoping it would still my shaking hand.

"But maybe I don't need to worry about this act of love," he said, repairing himself, like a man who wanted to prove he still held power. "Because from what I'm seeing, your mother's plan doesn't seem to be going her way."

"And why do you say that?"

"Because I'm still alive. She'd kill me if things went well enough not to need me anymore." His voice kept that soft edge.

I hid my grimace, straightening my posture. I didn't want to admit my fears. The truth of the growing unrest. But I wouldn't give him the satisfaction of being right.

"It goes exactly as planned," I lied.

Father's eyebrow quirked, and he smiled in that always unassuming way of his. He could put you at ease in an instant, even now.

His gaze fell to the bottle of wine in my grip. A flash of need filled his face. He licked his lips.

"I see. That's why you have the spiced wine? Food must be plentiful."

I held in my annoyance at him always figuring everything out in two heartbeats and a breath. His skill at deduction was infuriating.

"I only brought it because I remember you liking it."

He snapped his gaze onto mine at that, his eye searching my face.

Rain pelted the windows harder as I extended the wine bottle to him.

He took the bottle, twisted out the cork, and guzzled the wine as if he hadn't had a drink in eons. Wine ran in small rivers into his beard.

Something about the desperation sent a tremor of unease rippling through me.

The empty bottle clattered to the table when he finished. He coughed and wiped the wine from his beard on his sleeve and—he stopped, laying his hand back politely at his side. He must have noticed the surprise on my face.

"Forgive my lack of manners," he said, his voice hoarse. "But I'm...Do you have anything else to drink? Or eat?"

"You will have a meal again at dinner," I said, wanting to stay firm. "I dare say you can wait three more hours."

Why was I here?

I shouldn't be here.

He shrunk in on himself.

"Please," he said. "I'm aware I haven't done much to deserve your goodwill, but I've had nothing to eat since she imprisoned me in here."

Mother said she fed him. She wouldn't lie to me.

I hated the doubt pricking me again.

"You've had ample food," I said. "Mother told me she went to the kitchens."

I noticed his awfully sunken cheeks, the hollows accentuating the angles of his face, a stark contrast to the sturdy man he'd always been. Doubt wormed its way deeper into my mind as I studied his gaunt appearance.

"Balder, please," he said. "I've had nothing. Your Mother stopped the servant right outside my door."

My stomach twisted. I felt his honesty, although every instinct urged me to call him a liar.

Mother was the liar. She lied to me.

Again.

Frigg never knew I saw her. If she had...

I should have made her swear an oath to me she'd feed Father, like I forced her to oath to me that night after the cave.

She wouldn't break an oath.

Are you sure about that?

I glanced at the bag of honey sweets in my palm, then pressed them into Father's hands. The familiar scent of honey and spice wafted up, a bitter reminder of simpler days when Mother's love seemed pure.

Father tore into the bag, and devoured them like a ravenous wolf who hadn't seen a scrap in weeks.

And I understood.

"She promised me she fed you," I said. Whispered. "She promised she'd feed you because she loved me."

I will honor our oath, Balder. Forever. Her words swam in my mind, along with the memory tingling in my palm where we had mixed our blood. *I will never—*

Father's eye softened with something like pity.

"Love doesn't demand constant proof of loyalty, son. It doesn't withhold basic kindness as punishment. That's control in the guise of love."

I wanted to argue, but his words hit too close to memories I'd rather forget. Mother's silent treatments when I showed too much affection to Father. Her subtle ways of making me prove my devotion again and again.

"And don't feel bad for believing her," he said. "She's rather good at making people believe her."

I crushed my nails into my palms, extinguishing the prickle burning my skin.

"Don't speak that way of her," I said.

He sucked the sticky honey from his thumbs and ringed fingers. Amusement glistened in his eye.

"Why have you come and risked her anger with this generosity?" he asked.

"I've risked nothing," I said. "She doesn't control me."

He laughed.

I wanted to punch that smirk off his face.

"Doesn't she?" He raised an eyebrow, his blue eye fixed on me.

Taking the chair in front of his desk, I sat and leaned back in the worn leather, gazing anywhere but at him. At the gloomy portrait of our once-proud family gathering dust above the hearth. At the maps curling on the oak desk. Anything to avoid his gaze.

I scoffed, even as my cheeks burned.

"She forbade me from seeing you or Thor, yet here I am," I said. "Defying her, because I do as I please."

He cracked a small grin.

"So you sneak around behind her back? Because she doesn't rule you? I see."

I bristled. My gaze snagged on the portrait of our family again, our painted smiles nothing but lies.

"I just don't want to deal with her temper," I muttered.

He nodded, the grin fading. He leaned back in his chair, the carved wood creaking with his movement. His eye softened as it settled on me, and I shifted, because I never had him look at me like that before.

Gods. Why did I come here?

No. I fully understood my purpose for being here.

This had been gnawing at me ever since Thor let it slip. I couldn't hold it in any longer.

"Why did you have Thor watch over Sigyn?"

His expression turned to surprise.

"What?"

"Thor told me you had him watch over Sigyn. And that one night he saw—"

I couldn't even say it.

"I didn't think you'd do well if you found out," he said, his tone gentle. "I know about the oath you had her make."

"Are you saying she broke it?"

He stiffened as he considered my words, fingertips tapping the worn leather arm of the chair.

"What I'm saying is what you want to know will mean more coming from her lips than mine."

I scoffed.

"So, you're giving me a non-answer. Figures. You always were useless as a father," I said.

He looked at me with a depth of sympathy that made my skin crawl. I hated that look. I didn't want his sympathy, his pity.

"I'm sorry I didn't do more to help you escape her control," he said.

Control. Why did that word cut me cold?

"I'm not under her control," I said. "I...I'm simply giving her the support she needs after you. Which is why I came to you with this question, instead of her. She has enough on her plate. I don't want to cause her more pain—"

"This sounds like an excuse."

"Excuse? You put her, *us*, through hell."

"I know I was a shit husband and father, but there is more than one side of this."

I forced a harsh laugh.

"Your side doesn't matter. Because you never loved her. Or me."

"I've always loved you." Emotion thickened his voice. "As for your Mother...I did love her. Once."

I laughed.

"I doubt that. You pulled her in and then used her and cast her aside when you grew bored."

He paced, his shadow passing over the ornate rugs covering the stone floor.

"I admired her more than anyone," he said. "I respected her. When we first met, no god or mortal could equal her brilliance, her spirit." He trailed his fingers along a shelf cluttered with peculiar relics and oddities he collected from across the Nine Worlds. "She taught me to defeat enemies not through force, but by finding their psychological weaknesses and turning them against each other. Her stubbornness in those early days led us to victory after victory."

"I can't imagine you respecting anyone," I said.

"She and I both wanted Asgard to thrive. She believed in our mission. Your mother saved my life countless times when I first took the throne. She could sense treachery like no other. She recognized our true allies and our enemies. Gods, she was everything I dreamed of—clever, fierce, passionate. And she wanted to build something lasting with me. I made her my queen because I loved her. More than the air in my lungs."

I didn't like how rough his voice grew with emotion.

"You have a funny way of showing your love, casting her aside, and all," I said, grasping for the safety of any familiar barbs I could.

I should leave. Walk away.

I wanted to walk away.

"After the wedding, with my throne secure, all I wanted was an heir. You." His eye darkened. "But your mother...The cunning that had won us kingdoms became my curse when she turned it against me. I saw how twisted she truly was, but I ignored it. Kept giving her whatever she wanted. Told myself if I just made her happy enough, our marriage would work." He laughed bitterly. "I was a fool."

"All I hear is how you broke her," I said. "How you pushed and pushed until she snapped."

He scoffed, bitter and sharp.

"Gods don't practice monogamy," he said. "But I swore myself to her alone because she demanded it. Another sacrifice to keep her happy."

Bile rose in my throat.

"Mother is a marriage goddess. Of course, fidelity is important to her. What did you expect?"

"It wasn't about fidelity," he said. "It was about control. Power."

"Explain." I leaned forward.

"She twisted my vow into a weapon, like everything else." The words came out raw. "By the time I realized what I'd agreed to, it was too late. She used my oath to bind me. And I paid dearly."

I chuckled.

"How terrible that you had to keep your vow to her."

He pulled in a deep breath. The sound was heavy with memories.

"She said if I wanted an heir, then I had to play by her rules. So I did. If my eye even wandered slightly, there was hell to pay. Another six months to wait for an heir. Then a year. Five years," he said. "I had no choice but to give into her demands, but my anger and resentment of her grew. What kind of marriage is this? What kind of partnership? She made me her dog."

Rain drummed hard against the windows. A fire crackled in the carved hearth.

Memories surfaced. Mother's crushing silences when I broke her rules. Her sharp words when I mis-stepped. Her cold distance lasting days if I exhibited too much joy at Father's return. He was the enemy, after all. Each memory clicked into place like pieces of a darker puzzle I'd refused to see.

"No matter how I complied, she would invent new accusations, new transgressions." His voice turned hollow. "Claimed I obviously cheated when I was away at war, or even at a feast. I never did. I kept my promise."

I studied his haggard face in the firelight.

"Why did you keep your word if you resented her so much?" I asked.

"Because I wanted you," he said. "She dangled you before my nose, the prize for absolute submission. We had hellacious fights over it. She hated me because I resisted her control. I hated her because she deceived me. Worse, she lied to me saying she loved me. But I would have endured any indignity for you."

His raw words pierced my bitterness, cracking the hardened shell around my heart. The truths emerging were like smoke. Impossible to grasp, impossible to escape, choking me with their implications. I shrank from them even as they demanded to be heard.

"What changed?" I asked, my voice barely a whisper. "How did you finally get me?"

Rain lashed the leaded windows.

"Somehow she sensed she had pushed me to the breaking point. That her grasp on me was slipping. She couldn't allow that." His mouth twisted. "So she finally gave me what I wanted most—you. That was the happiest day of my life. I thought things would improve. Instead, the control grew worse. Another chain added to my shackles."

I tensed. But I didn't want to release old hatreds yet. I was terrified of letting them go.

"What do you mean?"

"You became her perfect tool to control me," he said. "She used you to dictate where I went, what laws and policies I enacted in the kingdom. As long as I submitted completely to her wishes, remained a faithful, obedient husband in her eyes, she would permit me to see you." Disgust twisted his mouth. "I swallowed my pride. My dignity. I let her strip away my power. Became the perfect submissive spouse she demanded. But it was never enough to satisfy her."

The fire snapped in the hearth behind him, wavering shadows making the room quiver.

I choked out the question that frightened me most.

"And if you defied her, broke her rules?"

"She would withhold you as punishment. I had to do everything she asked in order to see my son. But even when I stayed faithful, followed every rule, she blocked us from being together anyway. All to control me, to keep power over Asgard. She knew I loved you too much to fight back."

He slammed a fist against the table. I jumped.

No. This wasn't possible. This isn't what happened.

"Loved me," I repeated. "You didn't even take me with you on trips. You didn't care."

I sank back into the worn leather armchair, blinking back stinging tears.

"I did care!" His voice cracked.

"You could have stayed. You could have stayed if you wanted to spend time with me."

"Stayed for your mother to only create another reason for me not to be with you, you mean?" he asked. "It gutted me whenever I had to leave you behind. I wanted you with me always on my travels, but she wouldn't allow it." He leaned forward. "All I could do was give you that puppy, so you wouldn't be alone when I was gone."

I was five years old, and I was sobbing and begging to join Father's latest quest. Mother told me he thought my skin too delicate for Jotunheim's cold. Later, she placed a squirming puppy in my arms.

"She told me she picked out Rune to keep me company."

He chuckled darkly.

"Of course she did."

Something fractured inside me, hearing his raw pain. I stiffened, clinging to familiar anger, desperate to hold on to any hatred I could.

"No. You chose him over us, over me, when you brought Loki here," I said. "That's what destroyed everything, not this..." My voice broke.

"The marriage had already been destroyed," he stated. "Only my heart was broken, because your mother had no heart to break."

"But why bring our enemy to Asgard? Why put us all in danger?" My hands shook. "What could possibly be worth that risk?"

I wanted to hurt him, to force him to take it all back. But the deep melancholy in his eye stopped me. I knew that look. I'd seen it in my reflection on countless nights, lying beside Nanna, my chosen wife, both of us drowning in isolation.

"It happened in Jotunheim," he said. "I went to kill the Destroyer—the one prophesied to bring Ragnarok. I found him, but..." He touched his ring. "I wasn't supposed to fall in love with the one destined to end me."

The room stilled except for the rain pattering the glass.

"So many years I tried," he said. "I was so unhappy, and I saw a future only of unhappiness. I had you, yes, but...

Whether or not I stayed faithful, Frigg used you as a pawn. Held you back from me. I was finished playing her game. You were old enough, and I barely saw you, anyway."

Father gazed out the rain-streaked window.

He sucked in a breath.

"Ten centuries is a long time to live without a kind word spoken. Without a touch. Loki mended what your mother killed," he said. "From the moment our eyes met, something shifted in me. Here was someone who saw me. Not as the Alfather, not as something to control, but simply as myself. When he smiled at me...It was like seeing the sun after a century of darkness."

I thought of Hel. How happy I was with her. The tenderness she showed me that Nanna never had. I felt whole with her. I never knew I could feel whole.

I cleared the emotion from my throat. I didn't want to understand him.

"The first night we..." Father hesitated, his eye distant with memory. "We were alone in the forest. My back against a tree. Loki shrieked in disbelief when I told him how long it had been since I'd shared anyone's bed. He asked me to close my eyes, then if he could kiss me. He then asked if he could kiss me elsewhere and..." Father's voice softened. "When he knelt before me, touched me...took me into his mouth...No one had ever touched me like he did. Like I was something precious rather than powerful. Something to be cherished rather than conquered. He was..." His voice broke. "I knew then Frigg never loved me. Not how he loved me."

His eye misted red, raw emotion threatening to spill over.

"Father..." I said, the word catching.

"He would leave little gifts in my study," Father continued softly. "Fragments of poems, rare books he thought I'd enjoy, trinkets from his travels. Not because he wanted anything, but simply to make me smile. Your Mother only knew bitterness and spite. But Loki...he'd wait hours in the stables to greet me when I returned from a journey.

The memory of them in the stables haunted me again, but this time because of what it meant. Father hadn't just found someone to warm his bed. He'd found someone real. Someone who waited in the cold just to see his face, who cherished him completely. Like what I had with Hel now. What I'd nearly lost forever because I'd let Mother arrange my marriage to Nanna. "Trust me," she'd said. "It's for the best."

It was always for the best.

Father withdrew a small wooden box from his desk drawer, and opened the lid.

"The worst part?" he asked. "Some mornings I'd wake up and for a breath, I'd forget the prophecy. Loki would be there, smiling at me like I was his entire world. And then I'd remember. Remember that every smile, every touch, every 'I love you' was leading us towards destruction. That my happiness was going to cost him everything."

He pulled out what looked like a letter, the parchment worn soft at the creases from countless readings.

"The night we made our blood oath," he said, "Loki wrote this. He was so full of hope, of all we could be..." His eye traced the words.

"'My love—I swear to you, by the blood we've shared tonight, that I will protect Asgard as my own. That I will stand beside you, not just as lover, but as guardian of your realm. Every dream you have for this kingdom is now my dream. Every hope you hold is my hope. Tonight, we've bound our souls together, and I swear I will never let anything tear us apart.'"

"Loki was so excited he could barely hold the knife steady that night. Made me swear to never keep secrets from him. To trust him with everything, always. And I looked him in the eyes, tasted his blood on my lips, and lied. Because I loved him too much to tell him the truth."

"You knew what he was destined to become," I said. "Yet you still bound yourself to him."

"Because I thought love could change destiny itself." Tears rimmed his eye in red. "When he would hold me at night, whispering plans for our future, I believed anything was possible. That if I loved him enough, if I kept that darkness from touching him, somehow..."

"But you destroyed it all," I said. "That day you returned and suddenly you were no longer together. No explanations."

"You know what haunts me most?" Father whispered, staring at the letter. "The day he gave me the ultimatum—him or the king's last son. The look in his eyes when I chose to kill him. When I betrayed everything we had built."

Something cold settled in my chest. Those deaths—I'd always known they powered Valhalla's protective spells. But I'd never connected them to Father and Loki's separation. Never understood the true cost of that magic.

"All Loki knew was that I chose violence over love. Power over him." His voice cracked completely. "He asked me why. Why I would throw away everything we had? He begged me to explain, to give him any reason that would make sense of my actions."

"Did you ever regret not telling him the truth?"

"Every single breath of my existence." Father's words were barely audible. "But not as much as I regret letting him believe he wasn't worth choosing. That he wasn't enough. That was the cruelest fate I could have given him. Worse than any prophecy. Because in trying to protect him from his destiny..." His eye swam with tears. "I may have ensured it. I killed those sons to save him, and in doing so, I might have killed the man I loved, too."

Rain clicked against the window.

Father stared at Loki's letter, his thumb tracing the ink.

"You asked my purpose for bringing Loki to Asgard, knowing the risks?" His eye met mine. "Because with him I could be just a man who loved and was loved in return. I wanted to believe that our love could change fate, and..." Ache filled his voice. "And I damned us all for a chance."

The rain and our breathing filled the heavy silence between us, as I thought of Hel and how I would risk anything to keep that love.

And I finally accepted understanding.

"You better leave," Father said. "Your Mother will not like you having been to see me."

I rose, but then he moved to his desk, pulling open a drawer I'd never noticed before.

"Wait. There's something else you should see."

From the drawer, he withdrew a second small wooden box, worn smooth with age. His hands trembled slightly as he opened it.

Inside lay a collection of folded papers. Dozens of them. Yellowed and creased from repeated handling. He selected one and held it out to me.

"What is this?" I asked, taking the fragile parchment.

"Letters I wrote to you. One for every time your mother kept you from me." His voice roughened. "Loki would sit with me those nights, while I wrote them. He knew I'd never be able to send them, but he said..." Father's voice caught.

"He said someday you'd understand. That someday you'd know I loved you."

I unfolded the letter with unsteady fingers:

'My dearest son,

Today you turned seven. I watched from my window as you played in the courtyard. You've grown so tall, and your laugh— gods, your laugh is my world. I wanted so badly to come down, to scoop you up and spin you around. To tell you how proud I am of you, how much I miss you. But your mother saw me watching and hustled you inside.

Loki found me later, drinking alone in my study. He promised me that someday, somehow, we'd find a way to be a family. All of us. He spent hours helping me carve that wooden sword I'll never be able to give you...'

The words blurred as tears filled my eyes. I looked up to find Father watching me, his own eye glistening.

"There are hundreds more," he said softly. "Every birthday. Every achievement I witnessed from afar. Every time I ached to hold my son."

My hands shook as I folded the letter.

"Why show me this now?"

He gave a small smile.

"Before now, this moment, would you have listened when you want to hate me? When you want to blame me for everything?"

No. I wouldn't have listened to any of it.

"But you need to understand. Loki never took me away from you. He was the only one who truly understood how much I loved you, who helped me hold on to hope through all those years of separation," he said.

I traced the worn edges of the letters, each crease telling a different story than the one I'd believed.

"Mother said..." I started, then stopped, the familiar

excuses turning to ash in my mouth.

"I know what she said." Father's voice was gentle. "But now you know the truth."

I stared at the box of letters. At everything I thought I knew. At everything that now shifted, leaving me unsteady, unmoored.

"Take them," he said. "They've always been meant for you."

34

IN TEA IS TRUTH

LOKI

The rain stopped, but the evening chill didn't. The bitter cold of the evening air pierced my damp clothes as I limped towards Cafe Schiesser. I winced with every movement, cursing Odin. I knew Frigg had made him send those draugr, but it was still his fault for learning necromancy in the first place.

I shoved open the heavy wooden door of the cafe, the warmth and aroma of coffee and apple tarts washing over me. I trudged up the creaking stairs, water dripping off my shirt and trousers, leaving a trail of damp footprints on the worn wooden steps. I scanned the cozy interior, with its dark wood panels and low-beamed ceilings. Fenrir and Jorg sat in the corner by the window, overlooking the red Rathaus across Marktplatz.

Jorg didn't even lift his eyes off his sketchbook as I approached, his pencil scratching across the page. Fenrir's eyebrows shot up as his eyes found the blood staining my calf. At least someone seemed to care.

"You look like you lost a fight with a troll," Fenrir said. "And why are you all wet?"

I pulled up my trouser leg, showing him the jagged bite mark. Fenrir hissed at the grisly puncture wounds, his eyes widening.

At least that cold burn of the bite had dissipated.

"Draugr, actually," I said. "An ambush. Nearly ate my leg."

I sank into the empty chair with a grunt, the carved wood rough against my sore back.

Jorg twisted his wrist, and I felt the tingle of magic coat us. A shimmering veil of illusion settled over our little corner.

"What's all this for?" I asked, glancing around the dimly lit space.

"I made you appear normal," he said. "So the server doesn't ask us to leave because of the sight of you. You're leeching water into the cushion and soaking it through. Not to mention humans don't much enjoy blood around their coffee and cakes. Why am I always having to explain this to you? Oh, that's right. It's because you always have to cause a scene."

Obviously, he was making up for the kindness he showed me last night.

"I'm terribly sorry my flesh wound is inconveniencing you," I snapped. "And how dare I possibly disturb the coffee and cakes of the old man across the room."

"Here, take this," Fenrir said, draping his coat over my shoulders. "You must be freezing."

The coat's warmth enveloped me as I sagged back into the chair. My whole body throbbed and ached.

Fenrir nudged a steaming mug of chamomile tea towards me.

"Drink. It will help."

I grimaced at the chamomile. I never drank tea if I could help it. But today looked like it would be an exception. I took a tentative sip, and the hot liquid soothed my throat. I hated relying on anything that might roil my guts, but the warmth was too glorious to resist. Gods. I hated what was happening to me. I was actually enjoying tea.

We sat in silence for a few seconds, only the clink of cutlery on porcelain and the dull roar of conversations echoing through the coffered ceilings.

Fenrir leaned forward.

"What about Sigyn?" he asked, his voice low so as not to carry over the murmurs of the other patrons. "You're back far earlier than we expected. Oh. What did you say to her? Please don't tell me she kicked you in the balls again?"

I raked my hand through my tangled hair, wincing as my fingers caught on knots and globs of draugr guts.

"Please, I'm not that much of an idiot," I said. "Although, she did get mad at me when I tried to push her to—"

"Push her to what?" Jorg asked, his tone sharp.

I grinned to lower the terribleness.

"To quit her job. To go to Iceland and accept the position I am providing her." I exhaled heavily. "She didn't appreciate the pressure."

Jorg's scowl deepened.

"She's cursed. She can't even leave if she tried. And furthermore, because you seem to have totally forgotten... THE ICELAND POSITION ISN'T EVEN REAL!" he bellowed. "The only thing that you should focus on is getting her lips on yours."

"You think I don't know that?" I asked. "I'm struggling to stay patient. The museum job Frigg gave her cuts into our time together. And watching her suffer...seeing the curse drain her strength with each passing day...it's destroying me."

Jorg gripped his pencil tighter, the skin pulling taut over his knuckles.

Fenrir cleared his throat.

"Besides you most definitely insulting her, is she falling in love with you?" he asked.

"I suspect she was close to kissing me," I said. "Or slapping me. It's fifty-fifty."

Fenrir rubbed his temples, a sigh escaping his lips.

"I need more time alone with her," I continued. "I feel like I'm close. Then we can perform the steps to break the curse, and I can get—" I stopped myself from saying the secret part out loud about Odin's apple...

"Can get what?" Jorg asked, his ears missing nothing.

I tapped the table.

"For all we know, Skadi has breached the border by now..." I said, changing the subject. "We will soon have more problems than draugr, if that's the case. Those Frost Giants haven't tasted Midgardians in eons."

He tossed his pen down with a clatter.

"As you keep reminding us every day. *Frigg grows stronger. Skadi could be at Asgard's gates as we speak.*" He mocked my voice. "Then maybe pull yourself together, stop insulting her, and move this romance along."

"I'm doing my best under the conditions," I said, wincing as a sharp pain lanced my shoulder. I took four pills, chasing them with a sip of tea. Although, my shoulder wasn't nearly as bad as it usually would have been after such a battle. Actually, it was almost miraculously better. Odd, but best not to think too deeply about it.

"Perhaps try harder," Jorg said. "I realize that's a hard concept for you."

The snot. I think he was trying to make me pay for the kindness shown to me last night.

"Today, when she touched the printing press, there was a flash of clarity," I said. "I saw Sigyn fighting through a fog to get out. I thought...A heartbeat more and she dissolved from my grasp and back into Ida."

Tears stung, and I wiped them away from the corners.

Fenrir squeezed my shoulder while Jorg's scowl deepened into shadow.

"I know it's difficult seeing her like this," Fenrir said.

We plunged back into silence, sipping our drinks. Patrons chatted and laughed, lamplight slanting through the windows. If only these Midgardians knew they teetered on the brink of a full out Jotnar invasion...followed by inevitably being ground into bread. Poor dears.

"I'll call her and explain. Apologize. Yes. That's what I'll do to fix this," I said. "And then, I will take her to the one place guaranteed to stir her memories. Gods. We need that stupid incantation translated, and I'm worried we've already run out of time."

Jorg's face contorted with an emotion that ran deeper than mere annoyance.

"I think apologizing is an excellent first step," Fenrir said, lips curving into a smile that reached his green eyes. "And there is still time as long as we keep breathing."

Steam curled from my mug as I tapped a restless rhythm against the ceramic.

"I didn't expect true love's kiss to be this difficult," I said.

Jorg leaned back, his posture coiled like a snake ready to strike.

"Of course you didn't," Jorg spat. "When has anything been hard for Asgard's favorite pet? Everything served on silver, garnished with lies."

"Brother, please," Fenrir said. "This solves nothing."

"No!" Jorg's fist hit the table. "I'm done protecting his feelings while he plays victim. He hasn't changed. He'll never change."

"You don't see—" Fenrir started.

"I see perfectly." Jorg's eyes burned cold. "He's throwing a tantrum because, for once, his silver tongue can't conjure what he wants. He stumbles through this like a drunk because he can't think past his own desires. When has he ever worked for anything beyond emptying a mead barrel?"

"Oh, emptying a mead barrel is all I'm good for?" Blood trickled from my fingers where they crushed the mug.

"Your life was a feast in Asgard," he snarled. "Time you tasted the bitter dregs we drank."

Something ancient and raw erupted in my chest.

"A feast?" I asked. "You think I feasted in Asgard? I *survived* Asgard."

"Poor father," Jorg's voice dripped mock sympathy. "How you suffered on silk cushions, drowning in wine. Every whim granted because Odin so loved that mouth of yours."

"You know nothing," I ground out.

"Don't I?" His sneer carved deep. "You lived free of care, especially care for us."

"I've always cared," my voice broke on the words, decades of guilt choking me.

Jorg's eyes narrowed.

"You're being unfair to Papa, Jorg," Fenrir said.

Jorg laughed.

"What's unfair is watching our father choose godhood over his own children. What's unfair is seeing him still crawling after Odin, even after everything. Tell me, *Father*. Was a seat in Asgard's halls worth our suffering?"

I had chosen godhood, chosen Odin. But not for the reasons they believed.

"I told you why I left Jotunheim for Asgard. I thought becoming one of them would protect you," I said. "I believed having Odin's ear would give me the power to keep you safe. That being among them would let me control their fear of you."

My voice faltered slightly at the mention of protection, a flash of the builder's leering face crossing my mind—those yellowed teeth, the calloused hands. I swallowed reflexively, the bitter taste of that particular failure coating my tongue with onion.

Jorg laughed. Cold. Brittle. Like I told him a capital joke.

"Answer me one thing. Did you ever truly love us?"

"If I have to answer that—"

"Stop. That's all I needed to hear," he said. "Because all you had to say was 'yes'."

The break in his voice shattered something in me.

I reached for his hand across the table. He tried to jerk away, but I locked my fingers around his.

"I do love you." My voice splintered. "I do. Never doubt that. Had I known their true plans..." Tears threatened to choke me. "I only ever wanted to give you your best chance."

Jorg ripped his hand from mine, trembling with fury as tears carved paths down his cheeks.

"Best chance?" He exploded from his chair, striking the table. "How could you ever think giving us away would give us our best chance? I still remember that day..."

That day.

His gaze turned hollow, and I knew he was drowning in the same memory I'd tried to drown in mead for centuries.

The lies were meant to keep the gods from harming

them, to make them submit without a fight. The lies were all for their safety.

And it cost me everything.

I squeezed my eyes shut, but their cries echoed through centuries of nightmares. My children pleading for me to save them.

"Papa! Help us, please!

"We will be good!"

"Father, please help."

The only way I survived standing there and watching it happen was by clinging to the belief that this was their only chance of survival.

"You came the night before," Fenrir said softly, his voice barely audible over the roar of my heartbeat in my ears.

Time collapsed.

And the past swallowed me whole.

The campfire's crackles and pops cast a warm glow across our Ironwood campsite. I burrowed deeper into furs. It was so damn cold that night.

"You promised me," Fenrir's voice cracked. "You promised that we'd go ice fishing on the frozen lake nearby in the morning. Just the two of us. It was all I wanted."

I nodded, muscles rigid as I fought back tears. But the memories kept flooding in.

"Fenrir, I—"

"I woke that night," he cut in, eyes glazed with pain. Haunted. "The fire had died to embers. Your furs lay empty beside me. I was terrified. I searched the darkness. Something felt wrong, but I ignored it, because I feared for you. I called out."

From my hiding place behind the large oak, I watched him stumble through the forest, his breath clouding the air.

Calling for me.

"Papa! Papa! Where are you? Papa!"

I followed him, careful he wouldn't sense me.

Distant voices carried on the wind. The gods were here.

My heart pounded as I crept through the trees after my son. Doing what I promised Odin I'd do. Ensuring the gods found him where we agreed.

"I reached the lake," Fenrir whispered. "And my blood froze. There, beneath the moonlight, stood a group of gods. And you beside them. And you know what? Relief flooded me at first, because you were safe."

Shame burned like acid.

"You wouldn't look at me," he said. "But the gods met my eyes. Their golden ropes gleamed in their hands."

The bottom dropped out of my stomach.

"Papa, what's happening? Help me!"

"Restrain him," Tyr said.

The gods lunged forward with their ropes. The cords strangled my son while I just stood there.

"Papa! Do something! Please, don't let them take me! I'll be good!"

"And you just walked away. Without a word. Without a look back. Without an explanation." Tears etched lines down Fenrir's face. "You left me. You left me terrified and alone."

He ripped out my guts.

Fenrir wiped the tears away with the back of his hand.

"And I was thrown into the abyss like refuse," Jorg snarled, yanking us back to now. "When Odin led me onto that boat and sailed into the Bermuda Triangle, a part of me kept waiting for you to stop it. But of course, you never came."

My jaw clenched until my teeth creaked, old guilt threatening to choke me.

"I swear on everything I am. If your mother and I had known Odin's intentions..." My voice cracked. "We never would have let him take you from the Ironwood." I searched their faces, needing them to see the truth burning in me. "Never."

Fenrir's eyes glistened with another rush of tears.

"You still saw us as monsters needing containment." He wiped his cheeks. "Why else would you agree—"

"No." The word erupted from my chest. "Not for a second." I reached across the table, not quite touching them. "You were our children. Perfect. Beautiful. When I held you as babes, when I watched you grow..." My own tears threatened. "Others saw monsters, but I saw my sons and daughter. My brilliant, wonderful children. Every scheme, every plan was to safeguard you from their fear. Their ignorance. Never because we feared you. We loved you."

"I rotted for centuries in that frigid ocean prison." Jorg's words shook. "And now I'm freed from one cage only to be banished to Hel, even when Ragnarok was never my fault."

"And I remain exiled in Midgard," Fenrir said. "I want to go home. To the Ironwood. To see it once more. To see my Mother again."

"You can go home," I said. "When this ends, we'll all be free. No banishments. No exile. We can put all this pain behind us and it will fade like a nightmare."

Fenrir leaned forward.

"No more cages," he breathed.

I nodded.

"No more cages. No more fear. This freedom is within our reach now," I said. "Odin promised me once we break this bloody curse and restore him as Alfather, he'll clear your names across the realms—"

The words died on my tongue. I hadn't meant to say that...

"What did you say?" Jorg asked.

"Odin...*promised you*...to clear our names if we reinstate him?" Fenrir's voice wavered. "*Odin?*"

I rubbed the back of my neck, cursing myself for the slip.

"Yes," I said. "He'll use this to prove our loyalty. As Alfather, he can convince the realms to accept our family. Don't you see? This is good. This shows Odin wants to make amends. We finally have a real chance here."

The wolf flashed gold in Fenrir's eyes, and sweat collected at the small of my back.

"He could have done that before as Alfather."

"No, he couldn't, because the other realms would never agree. They required proof, but now he has the proof they need to actually do it—"

"You said helping alone would free us," Fenrir said. "So this whole time it was another lie? Another deception?"

Jorg's laughter rang hollow through his tears.

"I told you, Fenrir," he said. "He hasn't changed. He's still spinning his webs of lies. I believe that means you owe me that bet."

"I didn't lie," I said. "I just...left out Odin's involvement, as I knew you'd react this way. But the result remains the same—our freedom."

"This is how it all started. With Odin's promises," Fenrir said, his voice harsher than I ever heard. "And you've tangled us in his web again." His breath hitched. "I thought you had changed, Papa. I wanted to believe...I did believe... Again. And again—" his voice crumbled, breaking me into pieces.

"Wait," Jorg cut in. "You only make deals if there's something in it for you. This isn't just about wiping our ledger clean. What else did he offer you?"

"Nothing," I said.

"Tell us what he offered." Fenrir's quiet words struck harder than any shout. He knew.

My hands grew cold as sweat beaded on my neck. I shifted in my chair, buying seconds, mind racing for a way to soften what they'd already guessed.

"I know Odin has fooled me before," I said carefully. "Trust me, I've paid dearly over and over. But this time is different. This time it's real. Please, if you'll listen—"

"Stop stalling," Jorg said. "What else did he promise you?"

I drummed against the table. The truth sat heavy on my tongue.

I met their eyes, desperate for understanding.

"He promised me one of Idunn's golden apples."

Jorg went still, color draining from his face before rage flooded back. His knuckles whitened on the table's edge. Next to him, Fenrir flinched as if I'd struck him, something dying in his eyes. I believe it was his trust in me.

"And why would he do that?" Jorg's voice shook.

"To restore some of my immortality because—"

"I don't need your reasons," Fenrir choked out, his face twisting with fresh betrayal. "I'm tired of reasons and intentions and justifications. I..." he faltered. "Gods. I remember you and Sigyn whispering about this apple back in Colorado. How did I miss that *this* was your true motivation, and not our freedom? I truly believed we were helping people by restoring Odin, but it was only ever about helping you." He wiped his face. "Why can I never see through your lies? The worst part is, had you been honest, I still would have helped, anyway. We could have avoided all this suffering."

Tears tracked down Fenrir's cheeks as his faith in me shattered. I wanted to take it all back.

Couldn't I take it all back?

This isn't what I meant to happen. This isn't what I wanted.

Jorg wrapped his arms around Fenrir.

"Thanks for helping me win my bet, Father. Proving me right is the one decent thing you've ever done for me."

Jorg's lips quirked in triumph.

"You never learn," he said. "You'll always stumble into the same traps. Into the same nets you weave."

"What you are saying?"

"Your true tragedy."

"And what's that?"

Malice glinted in his eyes.

"Isn't it obvious?" he asked. "You have your clever words and jests, but the joke is always on you in the end."

He undid me in those words.

"And now," Jorg snarled, standing and stepping towards me. The illusion around us wavered, his fury bleeding through the magic, drawing quick glances from nearby patrons before solidifying again. "Now you've made us the punchline too. Again. Nothing's changed. Without this apple to make you immortal for precious Sigyn, we wouldn't be here defending our enemy."

I saw the strike coming but didn't move. Maybe I deserved this. His fist connected with a sickening crunch, stars exploding behind my eyes. The force threw me backwards, chair clattering as I hit the floor. Hot blood gushed from my nose, each heartbeat sending fresh crimson spatters onto the wooden boards. The metallic taste filled my mouth as the cafe spun around me.

"Stop this!" Fenrir yanked Jorg back, tears streaming down his face. "Hasn't there been enough pain already between us all?"

"I want him to feel it," Jorg's voice trembled with centuries of rage. "He abandoned us!" He jabbed his finger at me, blood pooling beneath my head. "Left us to rot, and now he'll do it again! No more excuses. He needs to face what he did to us!"

Jorg thrashed in his brother's grip like a wild thing. His chest heaved with ragged breaths.

"I want him to bleed!" The words tore from him like a wounded animal. "Let me make him pay for every lie!"

Fenrir locked his arms around Jorg, holding him back.

"Brother, I know this rage. I drowned in it too. But it's a prison. You must break free to find peace."

I pushed myself to my elbows, watching my son shake with generations of agony. Without Fenrir between us, I think he would have beaten me to death on this cafe floor.

"He has to pay."

"He suffered enough in that cave."

"Don't defend him," Jorg spat, tears mixing with fury. "His *noble sacrifice* for his other family. His other children."

Jorg tore free, his eyes burning into mine with raw hatred.

"If only Father had fought that hard to protect us," he hissed.

No. That accusation I would not accept. Rage erupted like magma through my veins, burning away the pain. I surged to my feet, blood streaming down my chin, fists clenched at my sides.

35

HORSEPLAY

"You think I didn't fight to protect you?" The words tore out of me, copper-tinged and raw.

The clatter and conversation of the cafe faded into a distant hum. My heart hammered against my ribs as I faced my sons, tasting blood on my lips.

Jorg sneered.

"Oh yes, we understand your significant effort. That's why we are all having such a fantastic time together right now."

I curled my fingers into fists, not from rage but from the desperate need to hold on to something, anything. Blood kept dripping from my nostrils.

There was one story I'd never told, one truth I'd buried so deep even Sigyn didn't know. Perhaps...perhaps if they learned what I'd truly done, what lengths I'd gone to...

"You want to know if I fought for you?" My voice came rough, thick with blood and memory. "Then let me tell you about the deal for Asgard's wall."

A bitter smile pulled at my split lip as confusion flickered across their faces. A terrible vulnerability settled over me finally letting this poison out.

Jorg lounged back, overhead lights catching his hair. He thought he knew this story. They all thought they knew.

"What is there to tell? It was to keep the Jotnar out," he said. "I've heard this story a million times. Your stupid deal almost lost us Freya and the sun and moon to that builder. Typical you, never thinking of the consequences. Serves you right—"

The words hit harder than his fist had. My ribs constricted around my thundering heart as ages of guilt and rage threatened to choke me.

"Jormungand, for once, listen—" My voice came thick through the blood still trickling from my nose.

"What twisted logic runs in that mind of yours?" he asked. "What possible reason did you have for suggesting such an insane bargain?"

"YOU!" The shout ripped from my chest. "Everything was for you three!"

I raked trembling fingers through my copper hair, heart stampeding against my ribs. The metallic taste of blood filled my mouth as I collapsed back into my chair, eyes fixed on the floor's worn patterns.

"Why?" Fenrir asked, his voice breaking through the clink of porcelain and indistinct voices thrumming through the cafe.

"Whispers were spreading about you three, rumors of the danger you posed to the Nine Worlds." I lifted my gaze to meet his, my split lip throbbing. "Fear overtook me. It wasn't a sensation I was used to, but it pounded in every beat of my heart the louder the whispers grew. The more threats and plans fell out of the mouths of the gods. When the builder came, I saw my chance. If the gods had their wall—"

"They'd feel safe from us," Fenrir breathed.

"Yes." I dabbed blood from my chin. "The gods would feel protected behind their wall. Safe from their imagined threats. But truly, you'd be safe from them. I didn't care about Asgard, only you. So I sold them on the bargain—one winter to build the wall."

Jorg scoffed, rolling his eyes as he shook his head.

"As if anyone could build a wall in one winter."

I stared into my cooling tea, watching dark swirls mirror my thoughts.

"That was the point," I said. "Get as much of the wall built as we could for free, then finish the rest ourselves. The trick seemed perfect until...until everything went to shit."

Memories circled like wolves.

"How was I supposed to know about his magic? And that fucking horse..." My voice gave way. "The builder cheated, but the oath bound us. He built and built, and...That wall grew higher each day while the gods' fury mounted. We couldn't lose Freya, couldn't plunge the worlds into darkness. My desperate plan to keep you safe in the Ironwood had backfired. I had to fix it, no matter what it cost me."

Jorg sneered over his coffee, blood staining his knuckles from striking me.

"Oh yes, the heroic tale of how you seduced a horse. At least someone enjoyed your performance."

He raised an eyebrow, as if he got me.

That little brat. He tried to needle beneath my skin, and it was working. I clenched my jaw, fighting the urge to reach across the table and throttle him.

"Yes, that's the story they tell," I said. "Braggi's drunken poem turned legend. The gods spun their tales, added their jests. Yes, I gave Sleipnir to Odin, but—" I choked on the words.

"What really happened?" Fenrir asked softly.

Gods. This was going to get real uncomfortable in five seconds.

"The builder...he looked like a horse mated with a troll in a nightmare. I mean his teeth. He could have demolished a bucket of carrots in five seconds. But he had appetites. Specific ones. That last winter night, I shifted form into a woman and trudged to him through the snow. It only took a few words to convince him."

Jorg's eyebrows shot up while Fenrir squirmed.

"His hands..." I said. "Callused fingers tracing my shifted curves. His onion-sour breath hot against my neck as he took what I offered. Hour after hour in that frozen barn, straw scratching my back, his weight pressing down. By dawn my thighs were bruised, my lips swollen from his rough kisses. Even now, on bitter winter nights, I wake tasting onions."

Fenrir looked ill. Jorg's smirk had vanished.

"I chose it all. I would have done anything to save you. Even that. Especially that."

The silence stretched like a wound between us.

Jorg leaned forward, and for a heartbeat, I thought he was going to thank me. To tell me he finally understood.

A crack of laughter burst out of him from deep in his gut.

"And that's it?" he wheezed, wiping tears. "That's your big, emotional confession? You willingly went and had sex with someone you found hideous? How incredibly decent of you."

Heat rushed to my cheeks, my fingers aching for his neck.

"You try finding a turnip and that much honey in the dead of night. It took weeks to wash out of my hair!"

Jorg's laughter grew louder, booming through the cafe. Fenrir shot me a look that said I should have stopped talking the moment I first walked through the door.

"You once told me that sex work was the highest art form," Jorg said. "Now this sob story is meant to sway me? That another excuse will satisfy? Because that's all I hear. An excuse."

Pain and frustration coiled inside me. How could I make him see? The truth wasn't an excuse.

"Everything was for your sake—"

His palm crashed onto the table, rattling dishes.

"Stop," Jorg said. "Stop saying that. I'm so damn sick of hearing it."

"Hearing what?" I asked.

"That you tried to save us," he said. "That you wanted the best for us. That you meant to protect us." He pulled in a shaky breath, steadying the tremble that had crept into his words. "You never once considered the ramifications your choices and actions had on us. I just wanted a father who stayed."

My throat closed as tears mixed with blood. I looked between them, really seeing them, not as the children I'd tried to save, but as the men I'd broken. Every scar, every hardened line in their faces, was carved by my hands. By my choices. By my arrogance in thinking I knew best.

"I did what I thought—" Words died as centuries of self-deception dissolved. "You know, I kept that repulsive Jotnar busy until morning, ensuring he failed. Ensuring we kept the sun and the moon. The gods swore it was all enough to let you stay in the Ironwood." Old anger rushed over me.

"Odin promised me it would be enough—" Dark laughter bubbled up, tasting of blood and tears.

It was never going to be enough.

I was never going to be enough.

Every scheme, every sacrifice, every clever plan had only driven the knife deeper into my own heart.

I stood, chair shrieking against the floor.

Meeting Jorg's eyes through my tears, I saw my failure reflected in their depths.

"You were right about me," I said. "The joke was always on me in the end."

36

BONES

*J*ust another excuse.

That cut deep.

My mind kept replaying Jorg's words. The barbed truth in them. And when his voice faded, Fenrir's face surfaced. The realization hardening his features that perhaps he was wrong to have forgiven me for what I did.

I loved them. I loved my children so much that I bargained away the sun and moon themselves to protect them. I thought I acted in their best interest. First by leaving Jotunheim and following Odin to Asgard, and then later by surrendering them to the gods when worries festered about their abilities.

I was wrong.

In trying to keep them safe, I only caused them more harm.

I felt cold.

Alone.

And it was deserved.

Because excuses were all I had to give them.

Then there was Odin and his always excellent timing.

Odin summoned me to the seidr realm again to deliver the delightful news. He had theorized the act of love it would take to break the Salvation Weave, and more importantly, what that meant for our efforts. If I failed to restore Sigyn's memories through true love's kiss, if she couldn't translate the incantation, all hope was lost, because this act of love was, as he put it, *unattainable*.

Our only chance at breaking the curse was staying the course.

Which, rather, put me in a bad mood. And the fact Odin's image kept flickering, as if his energy was waning, didn't help. That was very unusual for him. Perhaps he had just had a restless night. Or eaten some bad shellfish. Either way, the message was clear. I had to succeed, or else we were all completely fucked.

* * *

THE FERRY BOBBED as we drifted across the Rhine, the wind snapping and biting. Strands of Sigyn's hair whipped around her face as we neared the shore. Wonder lit her soft, rounded features as she craned her neck to study the Gothic spires of the Münster piercing the pewter sky.

I shifted my borrowed joggers to better hide the jagged bite mark from yesterday's draugr encounter. The undead creature had shredded my jeans when it clamped onto my calf, forcing me to borrow these from Fenrir. The small nibble on my elbow had been hard enough to explain away to Sigyn. She barely accepted my flimsy story blaming an ill-tempered cat. I definitely couldn't let her see this one.

"You seem quiet today," Sigyn said, her warm brown eyes lingering on the purple bruise blooming around my eye where Jorg's fist had pounded into my face—also unhelpful.

"Just admiring the tile work of the roofs," I lied, plastering on a smile. "And thinking about all the historical sights we've seen so far today."

Our boat lurched as it bumped against the dock. Wind gusted off the slate-gray river, carrying the scent of wet wood and diesel.

Sigyn smiled, her eyes crinkling at the corners.

"Don't apologize. I'm quite enjoying the silence for once," she said. "But please try to avoid any more tussles with cats. I'd hate to hear your explanation for a missing ear next."

Still that sharp sense of humor.

"I am also deeply embarrassed by my behavior yesterday," I said as we stepped onto the weathered planks of the pier. "In more than one way. I'm sorry, again, for overstepping. I truly only meant to help—"

"I already told you, it's fine," Sigyn said. "Let's just enjoy today before you find some way to ruin it, shall we?"

I chuckled, and her eyes gentled as they settled on mine, those flecks of gold near her pupils I so loved vibrant in the light. Heat flushed my body despite the cold shooting needles into my cheeks and fingers.

Could being back at this cathedral already be working?

"Your color looks off." Her face pinched with concern. "Are you feeling well?"

I sighed. Of course, she'd notice my clenched jaw and the sweat beading at my temples as I did my best to ignore my sour stomach. Why would anything ever go easily?

"I haven't eaten anything today, is all," I said.

I chose not to mention spending the morning with my head in the toilet after accidentally eating Jormungand's yogurt instead of my non-dairy vanilla. I really hoped that golden apple would stop whatever was happening to my insides. As well as stop these strange fever-like spells that always followed. They were getting worse. Heat would surge through my bones, leaving me drenched in sweat, my temperature spiking to match that of the sun. It was all extremely vexing.

Worry clouded her face and my heart tumbled, recognizing that look—concern. Care. Something more. I knew all her expressions. She wouldn't look at me like that if she hated me, which only meant...

Hope fluttered in my chest again.

Sigyn rummaged in her bag and pulled out a small package. A lump lodged in my throat as she tore open the foil.

"Lackerli." She extended a ginger biscuit towards me, the spices filling the air. She took the other for herself. "You need to eat. Ginger will help if you are peaked."

"Thank you," I said.

The scent of honey, orange, and clove shot me back centuries to that first taste in her study in Heuberg. Before all the horror.

My stomach growled, but I stopped myself from taking a bite.

"Are these dairy-free?" I asked.

"Yes."

"What about cumin? Anis? Hazelnuts?"

"None," she said.

She took a bite, crumbs dusting her lips as she pressed the biscuit further into my hands.

Should I dare?

And then she smiled at me. Gods, I loved her smile.

I bit into the biscuit, the sweet spices coating my mouth,

at once familiar and agonizing. Eating these hard spiced rectangles had been our ritual those evenings after working side-by-side to rebuild her shop. And now...now, we shared them like strangers.

"Oh, before I forget—" I pulled out the carefully wrapped package of coffee beans. "I found that dark roast you mentioned loving. The one from that little shop on the corner. I thought maybe you'd have better luck with getting this instead of the pastry. Perhaps we can share a cup later?"

"You found it? How? It's always sold out, and I check daily."

"I have my ways," I said. The dagger at the shopkeeper's throat had been incredibly effective.

Sigyn's eyes lit up, a flicker of pure joy crossing her features. She reached out, and in that fragile moment, I saw echoes of who she'd been.

The package hadn't even left my hands when the bottom split open. Dark beans scattered across the cobblestones like marbles, their hollow bouncing echoing in the sudden silence. Sigyn's smile crumpled, first into sadness, then into something worse.

Acceptance.

"I'm so sorry," I said, dropping to my knees, trying to scoop up what I could.

"Don't bother picking them up," she said, watching the beans roll away with a defeated sort of look. "I told you, it's a curse. There's no point."

* * *

WE CLIMBED the worn stone steps from the riverbank towards the Münster. Festival music drifted over from the square, then dissolved into hushed reverence as the heavy cathedral door thudded shut behind us.

Our footsteps echoed into the buttresses as we walked down the nave, and memories feasted on me. Emotion saturated every cell of my body as I walked beside her, now this shadow of who she had been. In this very spot, centuries ago, I had realized what it meant to be truly safe, truly loved. The memory carved into me...Sigyn lighting a candle for me, the God of Chaos, believing its fragile flame could somehow light my way home through the darkness. Even then, she had more faith in me than I'd ever had in myself.

Now, I wasn't a god anymore. I was just a broken thing, hoping beyond hope that my desperate prayer would somehow be answered, that she would remember me, remember us.

"You..." a man's voice rang across the nave. Multi-colored light spilled through the rose window, painting the stone floor where tourists lowered their cameras to stare. I turned to see the same gray-haired gift shop clerk I'd slightly terrified during my Ragnarok era. Books lay scattered at his feet on the stone floor, their pages fluttering in the draft from the heavy wooden door.

Ah. Well. This was awkward.

"Hello, been awhile," I said, trying to put decent cheer into my tone. The man's violent trembling definitely didn't help my efforts in convincing Sigyn that I was a decent and delightful person.

A young couple hurried past us, whispering in Swiss-German, their footsteps echoing off the vaulted ceiling.

The poor dear backed up several steps until he hit a display of postcards, the fine wrinkles around his eyes creasing with fear, and a dash of awe. I couldn't blame him. I had been rather intense—and quite naked—during our first encounter. But if he ruined things for me now...

The man jabbed a shaking finger at my face.

"W-W-World Breaker," he stammered. "The Destroyer."

Sigyn's gaze darted between us, confusion pinching her brow. The last remaining tourists scurried towards the exit, leaving us alone.

"What did he call you?" she asked.

"Don't kill me!" he whimpered, dropping to his knees.

I forced a laugh that came out more like a squeak.

"And why is he asking you not to kill him?" Sigyn's eyebrows climbed higher.

My laughter rose in pitch.

"Oh, ignore all that. He's just an old friend," I said, gripping his arms and yanking him to his feet. "We joke like this all the time." I locked eyes with his, attempting to communicate that he better play along or else. "He pretends I'm going to hurt him very, very, *very* badly, and I always joke back that I definitely will if he keeps whining."

I hardened my stare. He shook more intensely.

Another manic burst of laughter escaped me as I clamped my arm around his shoulders and squeezed—definitely a tad bit too tightly.

"Isn't that right, my dear friend?" I leaned into his ear, gripping his shoulders tighter. "Play along," I whispered. "Or I really will kill you."

He started to cry.

I ruffled his thin, gray hair roughly.

"This guy, always the prankster," I said, grinding my knuckles into his scalp.

What little color remained in his face vanished. His eyes rolled back, and he crumpled to the floor.

Sigyn rushed to kneel beside him, patting his cheek.

"Sir? Can you hear me?"

"Don't worry about him. It's all part of the game," I said, tugging Sigyn's arm. "Actually, let's go somewhere more private before this guy starts more fun and games. He never knows when to stop."

I steered her in the opposite direction, wanting to put as much distance between us and the clerk as possible. I knew he'd wake screaming about me having tried to end the worlds. That would definitely spoil the mood I was trying to set with Sigyn.

"I really think he needs our help—" she said.

I clasped her hand, my pulse leaping at the tiny gasp that escaped her lips as I squeezed her fingertips. Her skin was warm against mine.

"Trust me."

Her lips parted slightly, and heat rushed through my chest when she didn't pull away.

I gave her my most devastating smile, tracing her fingers with my thumb.

A faint blush stained her cheeks.

"Where do you have in mind to go?" she asked.

I nodded towards the shadowed archway across the nave.

"Let's explore the crypt," I said.

Sigyn raised her eyebrows, but laughter danced in her eyes, telling me she rather liked the idea. Thank gods.

"Isn't that rather morbid?"

I gave another roguish grin, savoring how her eyes lingered on my face.

"The sarcophaguses will be atmospheric. Unless, of course, you're frightened..." I let the gentle taunt hang between us.

Sigyn's eyes flashed at the challenge.

"I've never turned down the chance to see a good crypt."

We descended worn stone steps, the hush deepening. I reluctantly released her hand, the narrow staircase forcing space between us. I ignored the slight itch tingling my palms. Obviously, thanks to all the crypt dust flying about.

Arched ceilings stretched into the flickering gloom, faded frescoes barely visible in wavering candlelight. I remembered when bright reds, blues, and golds had blazed across that ceiling before the reformation stripped it bare.

Sigyn drifted to a crumbling wall filled with images of saints and angels. And she belonged among them. Divine and eternal. Her fidelity still burned brightly within her, even though I could no longer sense its familiar warmth.

"Why are you staring at me like that?" she asked.

"What? Oh. No, I am staring at that fresco behind you. Tell me about it," I said, my voice echoing softly off the arched ceilings in the heavy silence.

Sigyn brightened, and her mouth I so longed to kiss again, curved into a smile. My lips burned hotter remembering our almost-kiss at the wall yesterday.

I drew closer.

"This is the oldest part of the church," she said. "We get such a rare glimpse into the past down here."

"The old legends depicted here are quite fascinating," I said, positioning myself beside her so our shoulders nearly touched.

"Yes, like this one here." She traced the air over a faded fresco, her arm brushing mine. "I love this story of Helga. Officially, she was known as a pious noblewoman who funded the church's construction. But there are whispers of a far more interesting story."

She pointed at Helga's tomb below, and I caught the

fragrance of her perfume, vanilla and amber. My heart thundered as she leaned closer to show me the carved sarcophagus, a woman peaceful in repose.

"By day, she was the perfect Christian patron. But in secret, she collected and preserved the old Norse sagas that were being destroyed during the Reformation. She believed all wisdom was worth saving, even from faiths different than her own."

Her hair tickled my shoulder as she turned to me.

"Legend says she fell in love with Erik, a Norse merchant who shared her passion for these stories. He would bring her manuscripts from his travels, and together they created a hidden library of tales that would have been lost otherwise. The church officials never suspected that one of their greatest benefactors was secretly preserving 'pagan' stories."

The candlelight danced across her face as she gestured to the carved knight standing vigil. We were close enough now that I could sense the heat radiating from her body.

"They say some of those manuscripts are still hidden somewhere in Basel. Erik continued their work after her death, and she was honored with burial here because of her public works, while secretly being remembered by scholars for her true legacy. That's why this story resonates with me. It's about finding ways to protect what you believe in, even when the world tells you it's wrong."

She glanced up at me, her eyes dark and wide. A blush crept up her neck as she quickly looked away. My pulse raced at how her breath hitched.

"Or, at least, that's what the myth says."

I moved even closer until the fabric of our coats whispered together.

"And do you think myths are real?" I asked, my voice rough with wanting.

"You tell me, you're the one named after a Norse god...
Loki."

Her eyes met mine before dropping to my mouth, then
quickly to the floor. She cleared her throat, deliciously flustered. Heat sparked hotter between us in the still.

I walked to a small alcove lit with votive candles. Their
warm glow summoned a thousand ghosts—her fingers
laced with mine, her lips against my throat, whispered devo-
tions in the dark.

Sigyn joined me and the rosemary in her hair made my
head swim.

"I read they used to keep hundreds of prayer candles
upstairs," I said. "The old records mention the vessels they
used to hold them were quite similar to those used in
printing houses. It's a shame they tucked these away down
here."

I made a mental note to have another firm "discussion"
with the gift shop clerk about this. I thought I made myself
perfectly clear the first time...

"They're beautiful, aren't they?" she asked.

I ached to touch her as a hush of absolute safety
enveloped me. But it had always been that way with Sigyn.
With her, I found a peace I'd never known before. With her,
I was seen. I was wanted.

I was loved.

"Yes," I rasped, my throat tightening. Tightening quite a
bit, actually. Obviously, from all this emotion storming my
insides.

I held her gaze, and Sigyn swayed closer, until I could
feel the heat of her body through our clothes. Her breaths
quickened. Deepened.

I said another prayer.

Please, Sigyn. Love me. Remember me. I am yours.

She studied the flames, her profile achingly beautiful in the wobbling light.

"I always wonder what prayer each candle represents," she said.

"I always wonder which prayers get answered."

Our breaths mingled in the shrinking space between us. Her gaze met mine, dark and deep with something that made my heart stutter.

"Why does this all seem so familiar?" she murmured. "Like I know you. Truly know you."

Candlelight traced the sweep of her cheekbones, the curve of her lips.

"Maybe I'm from one of those past lives you spoke about," I whispered.

She searched my gaze and I burned for her. Every cell in my body screamed to pull her close, to crush my mouth to hers. But, this had to be her choice.

She grazed my chest, lingering over my racing pulse.

Please. Love me. Remember me. And this will all have been a bad dream.

"Are you a ghost?" Sigyn whispered, her breath warm against my skin.

"I'm the truth your soul already knows."

I lifted her chin, drowning in the depths of her eyes.

"Am I really about to kiss you?" She tilted her head back further, curling her fingers into my coat. "I must be mad. You're infuriating."

I smiled, struggling to control myself.

"I don't know about the infuriating part, but as for the other...that's entirely up to you."

With a sharp tug, Sigyn pulled me into her embrace. Her lips met mine, and my heart nearly burst. She tasted of honey and spice from the lackerli, and something deeper—something eternal.

I felt her love in that kiss. The brush of her soul against mine. Her peace and steadiness flowed into me like a river and I drank her down. I gorged on her fidelity, on that burning light that had always been uniquely hers. Joy coursed through me, and for those racing heartbeats, I was whole again.

I could have died in that kiss, her body pressed against mine, her fingers tangled in my hair.

She remembers. She's come back to me.

I wanted to cry and laugh all at once. But most of all, I never wanted this kiss to end, never wanted to stop feeling her warmth against me, her heart pounding against my chest.

The spell is broken. Thank gods. I have Sigyn back. And now we can all be saved.

Her mouth claimed mine again, hungry and desperate. I backed against the cool stone wall of the crypt as she pressed closer, trailing down to the band of my joggers. I hardened more than I thought possible as her fingers brushed against me. Candlelight shimmered across her face as I traced the curves of her waist.

She kissed a burning trail down my neck, and I groaned, the sound echoing in the sacred silence. My blood thundered in my ears as her hands roamed across my chest. The scent of candle wax and stone mingled with her perfume.

"I need you," she whispered in my ear. "Now."

My control shattered. I spun us so she was against the frescoed wall and took her mouth, skating my tongue against hers. Sigyn dug into my shoulders as I pressed closer, her body arching into mine. Wanting poured into each desperate kiss. She pushed my trousers further down with her thumbs. I gripped her leg, lifting her skirt, and hooked her knee around my hip, pulling her tighter against me.

"Loki..." Her voice was a ragged whisper against my hot skin.

I breathed her in, losing myself in her warmth, in her touch, in her taste. I traced the line of her neck with burning kisses as her head leaned against the stone. The crypt filled with our ragged breaths. Her hands blazed a path down my stomach, igniting every nerve ending as she traced even lower.

"I've missed you," I breathed against her lips. "Gods, how I've missed you."

Sigyn stiffened in my arms.

"Miss me? How could you miss me?"

She pulled away, and the loss of her warmth nearly killed me. No. Of course. She was right. This was all too soon. She just had a memory spell broken, after all. That probably left her a little lightheaded. Maybe that useless clerk upstairs had some water for her...

"Oh, right. You wouldn't know what's all happened since you got cursed," I said, tidying my clothes and putting myself back together. "Well, Frigg also took your memories, but they're all back now, thanks to me. You are not easy. But now, if you could just do a quick translation and a little, very minor blood ritual, seriously, it's no big deal, the Salvation Weave will break—"

"I can't believe what we almost did..." Her voice sharpened as she stepped back, straightening her skit, and righting her coat. "I should have known better, but I somehow lose all sense around you."

What? No.

No, no, no, no...it can't...

My blood rushed in my ears, the sensation of her kiss still burning on my lips. The floor seemed to drop away beneath me as joy crumbled into ash. I clutched her shoulders, desperately searching her face for any trace of the woman who had just melted against me, who had kissed me like she remembered every touch we'd ever shared.

"Sigyn. It's me. Don't you remember?"

"And now you're using that name again," she said. "My name is Ida."

Cold dread crept through me. This couldn't be real. Not after feeling her so completely in that kiss.

I clutched her arms harder, searching her eyes. In their depths, I saw something that terrified me more than emptiness. A flicker of fear. Of me.

"The kiss should have worked." I whispered, hating how my voice broke. "True love's kiss breaks any spell, that's how it works, that's—"

"You really are a psycho! I should have stuck to my gut—"

And then I understood, the truth hitting me like a blade between the ribs. The kiss had failed not because there wasn't passion—gods, there had been passion—but because I wasn't kissing Sigyn at all. I was kissing the shell Frigg had created, a woman who might desire me but couldn't possibly love me. Not with centuries of memories locked away behind Frigg's walls. Everyone had tried to warn me. Jorg. Odin. They'd known what I'd refused to see. That true love's kiss needed to reach the real Sigyn to work. And I had no idea how to find her.

"Then it failed," I said, my voice hollow. "The kiss failed. And there won't be another chance, will there? Not when half of you is buried so deep..."

I released her and turned away, scrubbing a hand down my face. My one solution, my certainty that love would be enough—it shattered like glass.

"What are you talking about?" she asked.

I took her hand, desperation clawing through my chest. If the kiss couldn't break through Frigg's spell, maybe there was still a way to reach into her memories, to find some crack where my wife still lived, still loved me.

I had to pull her out. Pull her free.

"Don't you remember me?" The words rasped out. "Can you really not remember any of it?"

"Remember what?" she asked, tension stiffening her words.

I pressed my fingers into her knuckles, into the bones of her hands, as if I could push our shared past back into her body through touch alone. As if I could make her remember how these same hands had once healed my wounds, had held me through darkness.

"Search your memories," I pleaded. "Your dreams, your heart—can't you find even a fragment of us?"

Sigyn tried pulling away, eyes wide with fear. Fear of me. After everything, we'd survived together.

"There has never been an 'us'," she said.

Her words were a knife to my heart.

"We love each other," I said. My throat itched. I spoke through the emotion. "The real you knows me."

"I've only known you a week," she said.

"You've known me a lot longer than a week," I said. "I love you. And you love me. We fell in love in this city five hundred years ago."

"Why are you doing this?"

I grasped her hand, turning the engraved ring to catch the candlelight.

"All of it was supposed to thin the spell, to help you break through. The research about printer's vessels, dragging you to these places in Basel...each held importance to you—"

"No..."

She shook her head, her face a mask of disbelief and growing horror. But she touched the ring. She glanced into the shadowed corners of the crypt, as if some buried part of her recognized this place.

"Please stop."

"You feel it too," I pressed on. "Those strange flashes you mentioned, that sense of déjà vu—remember what you asked me at the Paper Museum about past lives? That's not just Ida wondering. That's Sigyn trying to reach through."

Her eyes widened at that, and I seized the thread.

"You say you feel like past lives are real. Your fascination with Norse mythology, your deep connection to those trickster tales you told me about on the Ferris wheel...that's because I am your past," I said. "Our love is your past, your present, and your future. Those aren't just random feelings. They're your real memories trying to surface through Frigg's spell. I'm your husband."

Sigyn froze, gazing between the ring, and my face as understanding flickered in her eyes. For a moment, hope blazed in my chest.

Then her cheeks flushed, tears gathering at the corners of her eyes. Not from recognition, but from fury.

She wrenched her hand away from my touch like my skin burned her.

"All of this talk of past lives. Of memories...You're mocking me."

She took slow, tiny steps away from me.

She yanked the ring from her finger and tossed it into the shadows. The clink of metal echoed.

"No," I said. "That's not true."

"Playing me the fool," she said, still inching towards the stairs. "You're deranged, and you can leave me alone."

She turned and bolted.

I planted myself in her path, blocking her way out.

"Stop this."

She tried to shove past me, but I had to stop her. Not when I was so close to reaching her. I grasped her shoulders, forcing her to face me.

"I'm not mocking you. You've had your memories taken from you, and I'm trying to get them back. We need them back because only you have the knowledge that can break the curse."

I withdrew *Laevateinn* from my coat. She stumbled backwards, heel catching on stone, but I clamped my hand around her arm.

"Oh God. You're a serial killer, aren't you?" she gasped, gaze locked on the blade. "It would be my luck I fall for the murderer. And I almost had sex with you—"

"Look," I said, juggling the dagger to my other hand so I could pull the crumpled paper from my pocket. The parchment shook as I held it out between us. "These symbols, these runes...you know what they mean. Deep down, you understand this language."

Her eyes darted between the dagger in my grip and the intricate patterns on the page, her face draining of color.

"You actually expect me to believe in magic?"

"You're always joking about being cursed when things break around you. The pastry, the coffee beans. But it's not clumsiness. It's an actual curse."

She laughed, but it was sharp, brittle.

"You're using my figure of speech as proof of some real curse? You're more deranged than I thought!"

She tugged back. I gripped her sleeve tighter with my dagger hand, the paper clutched in my other. I had to break through. Had to make her see.

"If you can't remember, then believe. I'm asking you to have faith. Trust what you feel when you touch these things, what stirs inside you in these places. The real you is in there, and it's the only way to save all of us." I lifted *Laevateinn* closer to her, its edge flashing in the candlelight. "Your goddess powers are still there, just locked away with everything else. Once you translate this incantation, all we need is one drop of blood on this blade. Only one drop, and Odin will finally have the final piece—"

"Let go of me!" She fixated on the gleaming blade. "You're completely mad!"

"Please," I pushed the parchment closer to her face, my hands shaking. "Look at the runes. Really look at them. Focus. The knowledge is inside you—you need to concentrate. That's all I'm asking."

She yanked her hand free and snatched the paper. For a moment, my heart leaped as her eyes fixed on the symbols.

"These mean nothing to me." She gripped both edges of the parchment and tore it straight down the middle.

"No!" Horror crashed through me as she ripped it again and again. "Do you have any idea what you've done?"

I dropped to my knees, and I gathered the fragments. I could try to recreate the symbol. Odin had made me memorize every curve, every line. But one wrong stroke, one misplaced rune, and the whole translation would be meaningless. Or worse.

"You seriously need help and a lot of some kind of medication."

I cleared my throat, but it kept tightening. I sheathed *Laevateinn* back at my hip, the cold stone of the crypt floor biting through my knees as I reached for her. I caught the hem of her wool coat, clutching the fabric like a lifeline.

"That woman I told you about, the one that saved the print shop?" I pushed the words out, one by one. "That was you. I was there. That's how I know that story—"

My face itched more. It took everything in me not to scratch my flesh off my skull. I gripped her coat tighter, the wool bunching between my desperate fingers.

"And you're expecting me to believe your story even more with that?" She squirmed harder, trying to twist her coat from my grasp. "That was over five hundred years ago. That is impossible."

"It is possible, because you're a goddess and I'm a..." I faltered. Once, I could have shown her the truth in flames and chaos. Now I was just a man on his knees.

"A what?" She wrenched one side of her coat free.

"Nothing anymore that would convince you like it once did."

My fingers slipped from the wool as Sigyn broke the rest of the way free. She stepped back, out of my reach, leaving me kneeling on the unforgiving stone.

"I was right. You really are mocking me with this now. You are vile and—and your face."

"Your face," she said.

"What about my face?"

"It's swelling."

I touched my puffy lips and tongue. The lackerli...the damn almonds must have triggered this allergic reaction.

My throat constricted. I stumbled, vision swimming, and Sigyn caught me before I hit the ground, lowering me to the cold stone floor. Each breath came as a thin wheeze through my narrowing airway. Panic flashed in her eyes as I struggled to draw air into my lungs.

Fumbling for her phone, Sigyn called for an ambulance, her voice shaking as she relayed our location in the crypt. Time blurred as I fought for each breath, the candlelight smearing into halos. My chest heaved uselessly as my throat closed further.

My pulse pounded in my temples.

Sigyn tore through her bag with trembling hands. She pulled out a small bottle, nearly dropping it as she wrestled with the cap. She pressed it to my lips.

"Drink," she commanded. "I take this for my hayfever, but it's an antihistamine. It will help you."

I tried to swallow the bitter liquid, but my throat spasmed. I choked and sputtered, managing to get some down.

"You...must...believe me," I wheezed, the words barely audible.

"Try to breathe." She brushed my hair back from my clammy forehead, her touch achingly gentle.

She pressed two fingers to my wrist, counting my racing heartbeats. A strange crackling sensation sparked where her skin met mine, like static electricity jumping between us.

Something flickered across her face—recognition, confusion, fear.

I couldn't let her go. Not yet. I clutched her hand, squeezing weakly.

Dark spots danced at the edges of my vision as she monitored my pulse.

"The...ring..." I choked out, words gurgling. "The words...forever..."

"Save your breath," Sigyn said. "The ambulance will be here any minute."

I pushed on in a ragged whisper, desperate to make her understand.

"Forever...and a day...like our vow..."

Sigyn's lips parted.

"How do you know that?"

No more words would come.

37

FORKED TONGUES

BALDER

Mother's sharp nails clicked over the map, each tap marking another village fallen to Skadi. The carved pieces spread like a plague across our lands as she advanced. The most ruthless warlord in the Nine Worlds had breached Asgard's defenses, and she was coming. For us.

For me.

The scouts' reports confirmed my worst fears. The Frost Giants had joined her forces. Without Thor's lightning, without Father's power, we stood no chance against their combined might. My thoughts kept straying to darker options...

Jormungand and Fenrir's strength could match these monsters. Hel's army of dead warriors waited in the under-world. And she'd offered me command, being Mother's son.

I'd called it treason then.

Now, watching another marker fall on the map, my

hands shook. The pieces crept closer, a noose tightening around Asgard's throat. But it wasn't just our realm's defeat I feared. It was what came after. Skadi would claim me as her prize. I'd become her trophy, paraded through her fortress while she cooed over my "delicate arches."

A cat sprang into my lap, claws pricking through my trousers. Mother hunched over the map, jaw clenched tight enough to crack teeth. For all her schemes, for all her careful plots, I could see the strain fracturing her composure.

"You said our troops could hold Skadi off for another week," Mother snapped at Freya. "Instead, one Frost Giant treated an entire unit like a box of chocolates. One! And there are hundreds more of them marching with Skadi."

Freya tossed her hair, rings flashing as she gripped her brush.

"That tricky vixen." She dragged the boar bristles through dark waves. "I must give Skadi credit. Her siege craft has always been flawless. She may not know how to wear shoulder pads properly, but she knows how to make a war deliciously exhilarating." A flush stained her cheeks, as if aroused. "However, if she stops Dagfinn from finishing my portrait for the new coins, I will be thoroughly enraged. I won't have all that seaweed broth I've been drinking for my complexion go to waste."

"The storms I made Odin conjure should have bought us more time." Mother swatted a cat off the map of Asgard's eastern border. The feline hissed and slithered under a nearby chaise.

The doors burst open. A messenger stumbled in, face ashen, chest heaving.

"My queen..." He swallowed hard. "The Jotnar have breached Midgard. Odin's protective barriers are failing—

his enchantments weaken by the day. Few remain intact, and soon all the realms will be exposed. Without these defenses, the Midgardians will perish."

My blood ran cold. Father's protections were disintegrating completely. Mother's curse worked far more rapidly than she'd intended.

Even Freya's smirk faltered, genuine fear flashing across her features before she masked it with another stroke of her brush. But Mother merely studied the map, utterly unperturbed by the news of our realm's defenses falling.

"Mother, how can you be so calm?" I asked. "The Jotnar are in Midgard!"

"Because this threat will all be over soon enough," she replied coolly, not even looking up. The certainty in her voice chilled me more than the news of the breach.

I couldn't help a bitter scoff.

"Father's storms were bound to fail. Even Skadi knows Thor lacks patience for weeks-long tantrums. She smells our weakness." I twisted the ring on my finger. "I will not be Skadi's."

Freya's nostrils flared as she prowled closer, sniffing.

"There's that scent again. Love mixed with..." She leaned in and smelled my hair. "Mushroom. Or is that mildew? Oh, I know. *The grave.* How intriguing! Balder, what are you up to?"

"Balder," Mother's voice cut through. "If a marriage alliance is what it takes to satisfy Skadi and bring peace, then you will perform your duty."

I stared at her, hoping I'd misheard. She swore she'd always protect me. She swore I'd never be a political pawn. But then, what had my marriage to Nanna been but that of a pawn?

"No," I said.

"No?" Her eyebrows arched. "She's only gaining more alliances by the day. They're already dividing Asgard like a pie." She jabbed her finger at the map. "And you would say no to what could stop this? I thought you wanted to do what was best for your people? For the worlds?"

Each word felt like another weight pressing down on my chest. I couldn't breathe.

Lounging on her settee, Freya brushed her hair with long strokes.

"Psh," Freya said, though her voice wavered slightly. "They will start betraying each other before it ever comes to that, anyway. Stabbing each other in the back is what Jotnar do best."

"Asgard will fall by then, with me locked away in her fortress," I said under my breath.

How much time did we truly have left before the last of Father's defenses fell?

Mother's gaze snapped to me, something flickering behind her eyes as she searched me.

"I shouldn't have said that about marrying Skadi. I'm sorry," she said, voice softer. Kinder. "I would never force that on you. I swear you will not become hers."

Her rings clinked against the table as she reached for me.

I stepped back.

"And how will you do that?" I asked. "The troops that don't still side with Father have lost all motivation. All this death is beating down their morale. I need assurance, Mother."

"Then I will motivate them," she said, and I couldn't tell if the steel in her voice was meant to reassure me or warn me. "Anything to protect my dearest boy."

But her earlier words lingered in my mind. *If a marriage alliance is what it takes...*

"How?" I asked.

Mother smiled. I didn't like that smile. It was the same one she'd worn when ordering the executions.

"With the best persuasion there is. Those that continue to show any resistance can dangle from the gallows." She snapped her fingers at a soldier. "Ivar, make it so. The prince has requested more assurance."

"Yes, my queen." The soldier bowed his grey head and took his leave.

"Mother, no," I said. "Not like that. Please. I don't want anyone killed on my account. You misunderstand me."

"Balder, you say you want assurance I will protect you, and now I give it, and still it isn't good enough? I'm only trying to be a good mother."

Bile rose in my throat.

"The soldiers need food and care now, not more blood. Please, show them compassion."

"You think love and comfort win wars?" she asked. "Only a firm hand works. I don't lose wars. I haven't yet, and I won't lose this one." A soft smile curved her lips that didn't reach her eyes. "Because, unlike your father, I do what is necessary."

A chill writhed in my body. How many more would die for her version of "necessary"?

"How long until her armies reach us?" Mother asked Freya.

"Twelve hours. A day if the mountains slow her up," Freya said. "I am looking forward to the war. I must get my armor shined. I refuse to go into battle without it absolutely gleaming, and—"

Her words faded into background noise as she unfolded

maps, plotting which route would let the sun shine on her armor brightest and bring out the highlights in her hair.

Hours. We had only hours left.

My heart ripped at the thought of Hel. Her fierce smile, her green eyes, the way her fingers traced my jaw. All of her gone.

Mother cleared her throat, dragging me back.

"I will admit, the report that Dyrdal was burnt and pillaged sickened me." Her voice dropped. "Skadi showed no mercy to the villagers. Myrfel will be next."

Dyrdal was nothing more than a humble farming village. Barley and cabbage. The image of villagers put to the sword, homes torched...

Mother took a slow sip of steaming bergamot tea.

I will martyr Asgard first.

Rage scorched my veins.

And something in me shifted. I couldn't explain it, but I had to end this. Now.

"Stop this madness," I said. "End this curse before Skadi bathes Asgard in blood. If we stop the curse, we stop the war—"

Mother's cup rattled on its saucer as she set it down with an abrupt clatter.

"Stop the curse? What poison has addled your mind?"

I curled my hands into fists, nails biting into my palms as I struggled to keep my composure. She had to understand, had to see reason.

Freya remained silent, her attention focused on a stack of letters she sifted through.

"This is all over your slights with Father and Freya's burnt palace," I said. "That is not enough reason to over-throw a people and feed them to the wolves."

"You know there is more to this than just that," she

snapped. "This is for the betterment of the Nine Worlds! You agreed—"

"Yes, I agreed for the betterment of the Nine Worlds, but this isn't making them better. It's only putting them all at risk." My voice rose. "Only fire, ruin, and corpses will come of it."

She looked at me as if I had wounded her.

"So you take your traitor father's side after everything? After all I've done for you?" She shook her head, her lips twisting into a bitter sneer. "I thought you cared."

The brutal accusation hit like a jagged blade, but I lifted my chin. I refused to back down. Not with Asgard burning.

"I take the side of the people, not either of you. With Skadi threatening Asgard, we need all warriors, all gods. We must free Thor. And Father—"

Freya scoffed, finally looking up from her letters.

"Free them? Imagine Odin's wrath on us for usurping him. No thank you."

I locked eyes with her.

"Yes. We would face justice for what we've done. We'd get what we deserve."

Freya laughed.

"Always so dramatic, Balder. You made your choice in this war. Now you must own it."

Choice.

Loki's voice echoed in my head, sharp and condemning. *"One day, you'll face a similar fork in the road, and you'll have to pick between doing what's right and doing what's selfish."*

My hands felt cold, clammy.

"All I see standing before me is a coward."

I glanced at the map, at all those fallen markers. At what my silence, my compliance, had wrought. How many had died?

"We've stopped your father's madness," Mother said. "Asgard is already better off now without him."

The image of smoke rising over the charred ruins of Dyrdal hardened my resolve. No more running. No more hiding.

I shook my head.

"No, Mother. It isn't."

"How can you say such things to me? Especially now?" Her voice climbed in agitation.

"Because this is all so cruel. You're being cruel. To everyone."

She sighed as if I were a five-year-old boy again.

"Sometimes love must be cruel," she said. "Not because it wants to be, but because it must. The things we cherish most need protection, and protection demands sacrifice. The deeper the love, the greater the price we pay to keep it safe. Only those willing to stain their souls truly understand what it means to love completely."

I searched her eyes and found something worse than malice—absolute conviction.

"*And then what Frigg did to Sigyn in the forests of Vanaheim.*"

"Love cannot be cruel," I said. "It protects, heals. Not destroys. Love is gentle."

Her laugh was soft, almost tender.

"Is it?" she asked. "Love gave me strength when my hands shook. Love steadied the knife when I carved what I hated to kill."

Her words dredged up the screams and copper-scented air.

"What horrifies me most isn't that you believe love justifies cruelty. It's that you're capable of such butchery and dare to call it love."

The slap rang out, snapping my head aside. I tasted iron, lifting my hand to my throbbing cheek.

"So like your father. I expected more."

I straightened.

"And is that what you told yourself about Sigyn in Vanaheim? That it was love?"

She kept holding my gaze, looking like a fragile, wounded thing.

"You turn against me. Like all the others. I trusted you."

"Mother, I'm not turning against you. I'm trying to save you. There's still time to find peace, to choose a different path." I reached for her hand. "Let me show you that love doesn't have to wound."

She pulled away, eyes hardening.

"I should have known better than to think you could understand." Mother smoothed her skirts with sharp, rigid movements. "Loki will come and ruin everything, like he always does. I can't let him win. I cannot. And once he learns about your father, he will only seek greater revenge."

"Learns about what?"

Freya's brow creased.

"Why haven't those damned draugr ripped that trickster apart by now?" she said. "Missing one attack is understandable, but two?"

"It's almost as if Loki knew to expect the draugr," Mother said. "As though someone gave him inside information...Oh. I have been a fool."

The way Mother's eyes narrowed made a knot of dread form in my stomach.

"I stripped Odin of every scrap of power," she continued. "I kept watch over him constantly. But still, he found a way to warn Loki of the draugr."

"You know how equally slippery Odin is," Freya said,

opening another letter, this one very official looking. "I'm not surprised."

I kept my mouth shut. I should reveal that gaudy awful ring I noticed on Father's finger immediately. I should remain loyal to Mother.

I clamped my mouth tighter.

Freya burst out laughing, reading the letter.

"What is it?" Mother asked.

"Well, at least you can find some solace in knowing that Loki is puking his guts out right now in a Midgardian hospital. He has hives, too." Freya's eyes gleamed with malicious delight. "Oh. This sounds dreadful. I cannot wait to read everything."

"Hospital?" Mother asked. "A mortal hospital?"

"Apparently, Loki can't keep anything down. Wish I could see it."

"That's impossible for a god to be ill enough to end up needing a mortal hospital unless he is—oh, now that's interesting."

I stiffened, fresh terror rushing through me as I finished the thought.

Unless he is mortal.

Mother went still, and a slow, terrible smile spread across her face. It made the hair on my arms stand up. This wasn't her usual calculated smile. This was something hungrier, more predatory. The smile of a woman who'd found salvation in someone else's destruction.

"I've wanted to do this for a long time," she said. "I hope Odin is still of use."

She swept towards the doors, skirts swirling.

"Are you sure? Wouldn't the binding be worse?" Freya called after her. "Are you sure you want to give that up? The screaming would be delicious."

"Binding? What is she talking about?"

Mother paused on the threshold.

"This has never been about doing what's worse to Loki," Mother said. "It's about doing what's safest for all of us. And, this might be the very thing I need to stop Ragnarok *and* Skadi."

38

ANTI-HERO

LOKI

The nurse's fingers clicked on the keyboard, the plastic clacking echoing off the sterile hospital walls. Harsh fluorescent lights bleached the color from his face as he reviewed my chart. A touch of confusion pinched his brow.

"I'm here to confirm some of the information in your chart," he said, glancing over at me briefly before returning his gaze to the computer screen. "For example, you put your birth year as zero. Obviously that is a system glitch—"

"No, that's about right," I said. The mattress crackled as I burrowed deeper into the pillows, their stuffing long since beaten flat by countless heads. "Zero would be the closest approximation in your Midgardian years."

His expression soured further, new lines etching his forehead as he sighed. He clicked and clacked on the keyboard again, muttering about always getting the *special* patients. Humans just never got it.

"And gender?" he asked, not looking up from his screen.

"Ever changing." I shrugged.

His chin moved in a mechanical nod, his attention anchored to the monitor as his wrists hovered over the keyboard.

"Any known allergies?"

"Apparently everything in this wretched realm."

I grimaced as I looked down at the welts covering my skin, each one stinging with the fire of a million hornets. All this because I had to eat one pathetic biscuit.

The nurse rolled his eyes at that one.

"Right..." He made a few more clicks. "Well, I'll leave the rest to the doctor to deal with."

The nurse's orthopedic shoes squeaked on the linoleum as he walked out the door.

I glanced around the cramped space, the speckled drop ceiling and white curtains making this entire *delightful* experience all the more cozy. I grumbled beneath my breath. I'd been in dungeons with sheets that had higher thread counts than these white cotton rags. Anything below 600 was a war crime.

My hand instinctively moved to my waist, feeling for the coin through the thin hospital gown. Panic flashed through me until I remembered—Jorg's sarcastic suggestion about sewing it into my underwear had turned out to be the best idea after all. Thank the gods that hospitals were more likely to leave patients' underwear on than anything else. The small bulge against my hip reassured me it was still there, safe.

The door squealed opened.

Fenrir pulled back the divider, and concern creased his face. Behind him stood Jorg, his sharp features arranged in careful neutrality. But I recognized that look. The same forced calm he'd worn as a child, standing at the lake's edge, trying to convince everyone, including himself, that the deep water didn't frighten him.

I guess he did have some concern for me. Somewhere.

"We waited outside the church for you and saw the ambulance take you away," Fenrir said.

"Leave it to you to land yourself in the hospital," Jorg said. "What stupidity did you commit this time?"

Or perhaps not.

Fenrir shot him a glacial look before turning back to me, brushing back a dark lock that had escaped his bun.

"Papa, are you alright?" Fenrir studied the red marks coating my arms and running down my neck and over my chest.

"Oh yes. I'm having the best day of my life." I winced as I shifted positions on the thin mattress.

"Your lip hasn't been this swollen since our final Yule feast together, when Hrungnir punched you for that comment about his mother," he said.

A brief smile flickered across my mouth at the memory. Hrungnir had made the mistake of kicking me out of his feast. So naturally, I gave the hall a detailed review of his mother's bedroom prowess. Or the tragic lack thereof. Worth every crack of broken bone when his fist connected with my jaw. The humiliation on his face had been *exquisite*.

"Tell me something I don't know," I grumbled, shifting again and bracing for that fiery pain to stab me in the shoulder with the movement. It had been several hours with no medication, and the breakthrough pain was always a bitch.

However, oddly, none came this time. Whatever. I couldn't handle anymore weirdness today.

"How did this happen?" Jorg asked. "I hate to even ask, but I'm sure it's entertainingly pathetic."

I scratched behind my neck. This was awkward. I would have preferred to tell him I had simply insulted someone else's mother again.

"Well, I..."

"You *what*?" Jorg asked, arms crossed over his chest. He looked too eager.

"I ate a damn biscuit, that's what. Are you happy?"

Fenrir tilted his head.

"A cookie did this to you?" The disbelief was clear in his tone.

I scrubbed a hand down my face, wincing as my fingers grazed the swollen skin around my lip.

"Trust me, I'm equally embarrassed."

"You should be." Jorg smirked.

"Sigyn offered me one," I said. "How was I supposed to say no to her?"

"All you had to do was kiss her," Jorg said. "How could you bungle something so simple?"

"I did kiss her," I snapped. Another nurse glanced up from their desk in the main room, but I barely noticed. All I could see was Sigyn's face. The way she'd looked at me like I was a stranger. My wife. Now just...gone.

"I don't understand—" Fenrir said.

"It didn't work." I lowered my voice to a whisper, though I wanted to scream. Failure pressed against my chest like a mountain of ice. We were all going to die because I couldn't even manage this one simple thing. Because I couldn't save her. "That's what there is to understand, and we are more screwed now than ever." Desperation clawed up my throat. "Maybe I need to have sex with her...Do you think that would do it? We almost—"

Jorg scrubbed his hand over his face with a groan, shoulders slumping.

"No," he said. "I doubt that would solve this."

Fenrir shook his head, clearly baffled, while I sat there drowning in memories she no longer shared. Every smile, every fight, every reconciliation, locked away where I couldn't reach them. Where I couldn't reach her.

"But true love's kiss was supposed to break the spell and get her memories back," Fenrir said.

That awful feeling of dread slithered through my body.

"The spell is too strong," I said. "I should have listened. I should have known better. I thought taking her someplace that mattered to us had thinned the spell enough for the real Sigyn to surface. Instead, I just...I kissed Ida. It's like trying to unlock a door when someone's built a wall in front of it. The key is right, but I can't even reach the lock." I wiped away the beads of sweat forming on my brow. "I guess I overestimated. Miscalculated. Again. As I always seem to do. And I had to eat that lackerli. I was so stupid—"

My stomach heaved violently, a wave of nausea crashing over me. That strange heat bloomed in my chest again, like molten metal spreading beneath my sternum, followed by a thousand needles pricking from the inside out.

I clamped a hand over my mouth just in time. Fenrir snapped out of his daze long enough to lunge for the trashcan, thrusting it into my hands before I spilled my guts.

Jorg shifted in his leather combat boots, looking anywhere but at my pathetic, miserable state. But the tension in his jawline and the worry lines creasing his brow betrayed the concern he couldn't quite conceal this time.

I managed to suck in a ragged breath as my stomach finally calmed. I swiped bile from my lips with the back of one shaking hand.

"Damn almonds," I muttered weakly against the lingering nausea. "What, Jorg? No scathing remark?"

He didn't meet my gaze.

"You need to focus on getting better," he said, his words not wrapped in their usual razors.

The doctor walked in, her gaze fixed on the tablet screen she held in front of her, stylus poised as she read over the data through her tortoiseshell glasses. Her white lab coat hung crisply over her narrow shoulders.

"Well, remarkably, you're cleared for discharge," she sad, thinning lips pursed in a puzzled frown as she glanced up at me. "Though this reaction was unlike any allergy I've ever seen before. Actually, none of the doctors on the floor have experienced this."

"In what way was this reaction different?" Fenrir asked.

The doctor tapped her stylus on the screen.

"The initial symptoms were catastrophic," she said, scrolling through her tablet with a deepening frown. "Anaphylaxis, severe angioedema, respiratory distress. By all medical standards, you should be in intensive care. Your tryptase levels were off the charts."

She peered at me over her glasses.

"Yet your latest blood work shows no trace of the reaction. Your vitals are perfect. The hives have completely resolved, which is..." she trailed off, shaking her head.

Resolved. No, I still was covered in those horrid—I glanced down at my arms, expecting to see the constellation of angry welts. My fingers traced bare, unblemished flesh. When had that happened?

"Impossible?" I offered, still staring at my mysteriously healed skin.

"Medically unprecedented," she corrected, setting down her tablet. "The human body doesn't simply bounce back from systemic shock like this. Even with epinephrine and aggressive treatment, recovery takes days, sometimes weeks.

You went from critical to normal in hours, with minimal intervention." Her eyes narrowed slightly. "Have you experienced anything like this before?"

That burning sensation flared in my core again, as if in answer. I ignored it.

"First time for everything," I said with a weak smile.

"Well," she said, clearly unsatisfied but professional enough not to push, "as irregular as this case is, I see no medical reason to keep you admitted. Your tests are clear, your breathing is normal, and your cardiovascular function is actually exceptional. I'll have the nurse bring your discharge papers."

I exhaled in relief.

"Great! I'm all better." I ripped the IV line from my arm. "Now, I must get to Sigyn—"

"Sir!" The doctor lunged forward, alarm flashing across her face. "You can't just—" She grabbed a gauze pad from a nearby tray and pressed it against the blood beading from my arm where the catheter had been. "That's not how we remove IVs. You could have caused an air embolism or—" She shook her head, clearly calculating whether to call for backup. After a moment, she seemed to decide it wasn't worth the battle, given my miraculous recovery.

Humans and their silly worries over things like *air embolisms.*

She secured the gauze with medical tape, then turned to Fenrir and Jorg. Her thin brow creased as she made a note on her tablet.

"Your father is lucky that woman was there when this happened. Her quick thinking and giving him that antihistamine saved his life."

The doctor's words shattered something inside me. Even now, even with her memories locked away behind Frigg's spell, Sigyn was still saving me. As she had for centuries. But this time, she'd walked away thinking I was just another creep.

The doctor's footsteps faded down the hallway, her muttering about protocols and flight risks barely registering. The thin thread holding me together, the one I'd been clinging to since watching Sigyn get cursed, finally snapped. I slumped forward on the edge of the bed, head dropping into my hands as it all crashed down.

Something shifted in me, deep and violent. Hot tears sprang to my eyes and ran down my cheeks, and for the first time, I didn't have the strength to stop them.

"Papa?" Fenrir's deep voice was gentle as he gripped my shoulder firmly.

A ragged, gasping sob tore from my chest as I crumpled further.

"I've lost her for good this time," I choked out between breaths. "This damned curse is worse than I realized, and I can't save her. I can't save any of us. Odin was clear. Sigyn translating that incantation was our only chance to break Frigg's curse before the Salvation Weave is sealed. Now, the bindings will come, and there's nothing we can do to stop it. And you will suffer because of my failure. Again."

"We will find another way," Fenrir said.

"There is no other way," I said, voice cracking. "This was it. I was supposed to save you." My hands trembled as visions of what awaited my children crashed through my mind. "And Sigyn...gods, she doesn't deserve any of this. She's the only true thing I've ever known. Do you know why I fell in love with her? Because she's real."

"I know." Fenrir squeezed my shoulder.

"We shouldn't work together, chaos and fidelity, but we do. In some significant way that I've never understood. And when I'm with her, I know everything will be alright. She believes in me when I don't believe in myself, and I..." My voice broke. "I trust her. I fully, unequivocally, trust her."

The tears came harder. Fenrir pulled me against him in a tight embrace, enveloping me, and warmth spread into my core. My son. Soon to be bound in chains because his father couldn't save him. Again.

Jorg cleared his throat from where he lingered against the wall. My other boy, trying so hard to be strong even as the memory of the ocean haunted his eyes.

I swiped at my raw cheeks, struggling to regain control. Trying not to think of the cave waiting for me...

"I can't let Sigyn get eaten by the Frost Giants," I rasped out. "That's what will happen to her after we are all..." I couldn't finish. Couldn't voice the horror of what was coming because I couldn't break one simple spell.

"We will figure this out," Fenrir said.

His unwavering optimism only further fueled my self loathing. It stirred those dark parts of myself I hated admitting existed. Those parts that said I was poison to everyone I dared to love. A father who brought nothing but pain to his children.

"How?" I asked. "It's over. I won't blame you if you leave me here. In fact, I recommend it. You need to go and hide in the farthest corners of the worlds while you still can. Don't let Frigg find you. We failed, and when the bindings come..." I swallowed hard. "At least you might still escape. I've already destroyed enough of your lives."

"No," Jorg interrupted, an unfamiliar resolve steeling his tone. "This defeat is what Frigg wants, and our family has endured enough defeat through the millennia. I will not get bound and thrown into the ocean again without a fight."

"I will also fight until the end," Fenrir said.

I forced out a hollow laugh, shaking my head.

"Your optimism is to your credit, but sometimes you must recognize when you've lost. This is a curse we are talking about, one I can feel strangle me harder every day, even with Hel's coin—Hel." I touched my chest, my arms, my wrists, trying hard to erase the feeling of cold rope binding them tight. "I've condemned her to die."

Fenrir's boots skidded against linoleum as he leaned forward. The fluorescent lights carved deeper shadows in the crease between his eyes as he studied me.

"Stop speaking like this," he said. "It's not over yet."

"I'm starting to be realistic." A bitter chuckle clawed its way up my throat. "I always fail when it truly counts."

The words tasted like ash on my tongue.

"What do you mean?" Fenrir asked.

Each of my spectacular failures over the long centuries swam through my mind. Tragedy followed by tragedy, with a heaping side of humiliation, for that extra spice.

"Your brother said it best." I glanced at Jorg. "The joke is always on me in the end. And it is again, now, right on schedule, right when it truly counts, because it is my destiny."

Jorg stiffened, my words seeming to strike deeper than I intended.

"And if your failures have taught us anything, it's that you don't stop trying," Fenrir said. His lips stretched into a big, reassuring grin.

"Fenrir. Please stop trying to make me feel better. Really."

"We won't let you stop fighting," Fenrir said. "Because we won't stop fighting."

He turned to Jorg. His brother met his gaze across the

cramped hospital room, and something unspoken passed between them.

I swear. His unwavering optimism would be my death. The mattress creaked as I slumped deeper into its thin comfort.

Jorg pushed away from the wall, boots striking tile as he moved closer. Those green eyes, so like my own, locked onto mine with an intensity that pinned me in place.

"We won't," he said. "Besides, this time will be different."

I arched an eyebrow.

"How so?" I asked.

"Because this time, you have us," Jorg said. "This time, you aren't alone."

39

A FROSTY APOLOGY

As long as I still drew breath, I refused to surrender.

True love's kiss may have failed to restore Sigyn's memories, but we weren't completely without options. Just stuck with a far more treacherous one. Even with Frigg's spell burying her memories, Sigyn's divine blood still flowed beneath Ida's skin. I'd seen how she responded to things from our past—those moments when something deeper stirred. But asking her to believe, to have faith in something she couldn't remember? That was harder than love could ever be.

If I could somehow get her calm enough, get her to focus on the runes...maybe, just maybe, her goddess nature would surface enough to translate the incantation. It would be like trying to read through mud. Laborious, uncertain, requiring perfect concentration. And even then, we'd need her to trust us enough to offer one drop of blood to *Laevateinn's* blade, all while believing in powers she thought impossible.

But if it worked...if we could guide her through each precarious step...that drop of divine blood might transmit the translation to Odin. The curse would break, and we'd all be saved.

Simple. Except nothing was simple anymore, and every hour we delayed made success less likely. With Frigg's power growing, the gods' power draining away, the realms became more unstable by the hour. I could feel the walls weakening. I could feel the ice rushing through the breaks in the barriers, just as I had in Dr. Thorne's office back in Colorado.

I didn't like what accompanied the ice.

Gods. Convincing Sigyn to participate in a blood ritual was already nearly impossible. Trying to do it while wearing this ridiculous shirt of kittens in space riding slices of pizza? That added insult to injury. At least my lip had returned to normal. More than I could say for my black eye from Jorg's fist at the cafe.

My stupid clogs squeaked against the museum's tiled floor as I walked through the glass doors. The vaulted ceiling soared overhead, its Gothic arches throwing long shadows over the display cases filled with medieval trinkets. Tourists clustered around a suit of armor, their phones raised to capture its dull gleam through the glass. The scent of coffee and pastries wafted from the cafe in the foyer, where visitors hunched over laptops and paperbacks at tiny round tables.

Sigyn stood at the welcome desk, her fingers flying over stacks of brochures as she arranged them. Beyond her, swords and axes hung on the walls. Thankfully, out of her reach.

I caught her eye and gave a small wave.

Her shoulders tensed beneath her navy cardigan. Even with her honey-ginger hair pulled back in that severe ponytail, and a glare that said she wished me to die by a thousand cuts, she was beautiful. Radiant.

I ran my hand through my copper waves, letting them fall around my sharp features. The perfect bounce in my hair had never let me down yet in wooing—

"You need to go," she snapped, her hands moving faster over the brochures, as if organizing paper could make me disappear.

A family of tourists approached the desk. Big mistake.

I fixed them with my best "I've ended civilizations for less than this interruption" glare. Something flickered hot behind my eyes, and they fled so fast the father tripped over the velvet rope barrier. Strange. I hadn't inspired that level of terror since losing my powers. That warmth in my face had felt almost like the old days, as if...no. Not important right now.

"I know I'm probably the last person you want to see."

"I guess you being a *god*," sarcasm drenched the word, "gifted you with all kinds of perception."

I approached carefully, hands open at my sides. This time, I wouldn't make the mistake of showing Sigyn the dagger too soon. First, I needed her trust.

A tour group shuffled past, their guide's voice droning on about medieval burial practices.

"But I had to come to thank you for saving my life. I hope you don't regret it too much."

I tried for a reassuring smile, hoping my little joke would break the tension.

Rage flashed in her eyes as if she calculated the force and velocity needed for her knee to meet my groin.

"Don't read too much into it," she said. "It was the right thing to do. Of course, had you been in a room with a slug that was also experiencing anaphylaxis, I would have attended the slug first."

So vicious. So perfectly Sigyn, even if she didn't know it. She continued straightening the brochures with more force than needed. This was going swimmingly. Gods. Why did the blood have to be given willingly? I could have this all done in a matter of seconds if I could prick her elbow...

The espresso machine in the cafe hissed and steamed, the barista calling out orders over the murmur of visitors.

"Now," she said. "Consider me thanked and leave. I'm tired of your fussy attitude about the weather, pretentious opinions on food, and awful fashion."

Her eyes traveled from my kitten shirt down to my orange reptilian-branded foam footwear.

"Awful? I'll have you know—" I stopped, my reflection in the closest display case catching my eye. The kittens riding pizza slices through space were bad enough, but the shoes? I'd gut Frigg for this.

I pulled in a calming breath, running my hands through my hair again.

"Look, you have every right to be angry," I said. Gently. "But I didn't only come to thank you. There is an incantation only you can understand, translations only you can make."

She pressed her lips together in a thin, unhappy line, the muscles in her jaw tightening.

"Not this again..."

"I know you don't believe me about...well, everything," I continued. "But please, I swear on my life I meant you no harm. I need you to look at something. To read it."

I pulled out the carefully taped-together paper from my pocket. A school group rushed past, their excited chatter about legends and dragons and giants echoing off the vaulted ceiling. If they only knew actual giants were on the way, and about to eat all of them real soon...

"I don't know how you knew about the inscription in my ring. Probably some trick. You asked my coworkers or... somehow slipped it off my finger without me knowing."

I took a tentative step closer, hating the wariness in her eyes. The aroma of coffee and warm pastries from the cafe mingled with the musty scent of ancient tapestries and polished wood.

"You know that's not true," I said, taking another step towards her. "Deep down, you sense it. This connection to me. Why else would you be so drawn to those Norse myths? To the stories of trickster gods?"

Tears collected in the corners of her eyes. She shook her head, arranging and rearranging the same stack of medieval history pamphlets.

"You actually made me care for you."

"Please understand—"

"For once, stop talking," she said. "You lied to me. I believed you about the research position with Professor Bjornsson. That I could actually study what I've always dreamed of." She let out a harsh laugh. "How fitting that you're named after the god of lies. I fell for every single one."

Once she had defended me against that title. Now she wielded it as a weapon, not knowing how true her aim was.

"I should have trusted my gut that you were a fraud from the beginning," she continued. "I should have remembered there is never more for me than this."

"But that's just it," I said. "There is so much more inside you than you realize. More than you give yourself credit for. You can read things others can't. Understand things they never could. And now, so many are relying on that knowledge only you posses to save them."

Her eyes softened slightly at my words, clouded with a swirl of emotions. Doubt, curiosity, a flicker of hope she couldn't fully extinguish.

"Why do you keep making me feel like there is actually hope?" she whispered, almost to herself. "Every time I'm around you it flares."

Without thought, or perhaps from a need, I reached over and touched the back of her hand that held the brochures. They crinkled under the pressure of her anxiety, just as her soul crinkled under Frigg's curse.

"Because that's what you are. Hope. And we are connected."

A spark of warmth shocked where my hand met her skin. And for a flutter of a heartbeat, I felt a surge of her fidelity enter my skin in a dizzying rush.

Sigyn yelped, the brochures falling to the floor as she jerked her hand back from my touch.

"What...what was that?" Sigyn breathed.

I reached back over and took her hands in mine, pressing my thumbs into the tops of her wrists. Each point of contact sent tiny sparks through my skin, like striking matches in the dark. And running beneath the echo of her warmth, her hope, something smoldered in my core...

"It means this is real." I tightened my grasp on her fingers, pressing into her knuckles, willing her to feel the truth in our touch. "You have to open yourself to the impossibility."

The conflict played across her face as she teetered on the edge of belief...

Screams shattered the cold air, echoing through the arched ceilings of the museum. The explosion of breaking glass followed.

If those damned draugr found me and ruined this moment...

I turned, adrenaline surging as I braced for their attack and—

Frost crystallized on the display cases.

A wave of dread washed over me as a gang of rough Jotnar stalked through the foyer, gripping clubs and swords. The temperature plummeted further with each thundering step. Behind them ducked a Frost Giant, his blue-ridged skull scraping the vaulted ceiling. The massive war axe in his hands could have cleaved a longship in two.

Their clubs smashed into glass cases, launching bronze daggers and silver chalices against stone walls. Medieval swords and iron shields pinwheeled through the air as more glass shattered. The cafe erupted in chaos, laptops abandoned, coffee splashing across tiles as patrons fled.

The school group that had been chattering about giants moments ago huddled behind an overturned display. Their teacher's face turned ashen as he herded them towards the emergency exit, all while watching the Frost Giant using a medieval tapestry as a handkerchief.

The Jotnar's laughter boomed through the destruction as they watched humans scatter like mice. One Jotnar snatched a knight's helmet and jammed it backwards onto a fleeing security guard's head. The guard staggered into a wall while the Jotnar's laughter rattled the stained glass windows.

This was exactly the type of thing we gods worked so hard to prevent. Midgardians weren't cut out for dealing with giants. And now Frigg decimated all of that protection, which meant—

Shit.

If the Jotnar had reached Midgard, time ran thinner than I thought until everything blew up in our faces. Literally, once the Jotnar discovered Midgardian gunpowder.

"What's happening?" Sigyn asked, her eyes wide with shock.

She stared up at the Frost Giant, who muttered "ouchie" after knocking his head on the chandelier. Plaster rained down as he tore the fixture free, stomping after his companions, who were now gleefully discovering the drinking fountain. One Jotnar pressed the button, yelping in delight as water sprayed his face. Within seconds, they'd turned it into a weapon, taking turns aiming the stream at fleeing tourists.

I leapt over the counter, grabbed Sigyn's arm, and yanked her down below the desk just as a club whistled overhead. It smashed into the wall, showering us with debris in a choking cloud.

We had to get out of here.

I peered around the edge of the desk, scanning for an escape route. Beside me, Sigyn retrieved her purse from beneath the counter, slinging it across her body with one smooth motion.

The Jotnar's rampage echoed through every hall. More crashes, more splintering wood as they discovered the 18th century china collection.

Most guests had fled or hidden, though the braver ones filmed with their phones from behind overturned benches. The teenage barista showed better sense, vaulting his counter and sprinting for the back door, leaving his espresso machine hissing steam.

Keeping a firm grip on Sigyn's wrist, I tugged her along the wall towards the back of the museum. We stuck to the shadows, ducking behind a toppled statue of some forgotten lord.

"Emergency exit?" I whispered.

Sigyn nodded, and pulled me left, breaking into a stumbling run down a corridor lined with medieval weapons.

Every thundering footstep behind us rattled the remaining display cases, a reminder that discovery meant death. Or worse, ending up as the Frost Giant's lunch.

I smashed my elbow through the nearest display case, ignoring the bite of glass against skin. I grabbed the hilt of a medieval broad sword.

"What are you doing?" Sigyn tried to force the sword out of my hands and back into the case. "This is museum property!"

"What I'm doing is saving our lives," I said, yanking the broadsword free. The weight felt good in my hands, familiar. I thrust it towards her. "Take it. You'll need it."

Sigyn stared at the weapon like I'd suggested she juggle baby seals.

"I won't allow museum pieces to be—"

Five Jotnar rounded the corner, their snarling faces twisted with bloodlust. Their heavy boots cracked the marble floor with each step.

"Maybe just this once," she muttered, fingers closing around the hilt.

We took off running through the museum's halls. My heart slammed against my ribs as I clutched Sigyn's hand, pulling her deeper into the building's maze.

An alcove appeared ahead, a heavy metal door set into its shadows.

"Stairwell," she gasped between breaths.

I shoved the door open and pushed Sigyn through. But as I turned to follow, a hand like gnarled ice clamped down on my aching shoulder. Pain lanced white-hot through the joint as I was yanked backwards.

"Look at this pathetic human," rumbled a voice I knew all too well.

Damn.

The rough hands spun me around and I found myself face to face with Hivor. His horribly untrimmed eyebrows shot up in surprise. Seriously, had grooming standards completely collapsed in Jotunheim?

The other Jotnar crowding behind him froze, those beady eyes narrowing with unease. Even the Frost Giant stopped using the Renaissance processional crucifix as a backscratcher to stare at me, his jaw slackening. Christ's golden face looked appropriately pained as it scraped against Frost Giant hide.

"Loki?" Hivor released me like I'd burned him. Again. "What are you doing here?"

Just perfect.

"Hey guys. Oh, a little of this and that." I straightened my posture, ignoring my screaming shoulder. Keep it light, keep it friendly. "Lovely weather for destroying a museum, isn't it? Though I have to ask. How exactly did you find your way to Midgard? The barriers between worlds are usually so...particular about visitors."

"Here on business, I'm afraid," Hivor said, subtly positioning himself between me and the exits. "When Skadi mentioned the barriers were weakening, well, we had to investigate for ourselves." His grin showed too many teeth. "Turns out they're more than weakened. The others are following soon."

My stomach dropped at 'others.'

"Others? Do tell." I forced a pleasant sort of smile.

"You know, the usual crowd. Hrungnir, Fjallbjorn, Stonefist, Skafnir—"

"I want to see what a 'beach' is!" One piped up behind him as he kept listing off clan after clan. This was incredibly bad.

"I want to ride on a merry-go-round!"

Oh. This was worse than bad. This was catastrophic.

"And you?" I pointed at the Frost Giant, whose head brushed the ceiling like an overgrown toddler at a dollhouse party.

"Just checking how plump the Midgardians are," he rumbled, licking his lips. "They all lived in caves the last time I was here—"

Hivor cut him off with a nervous laugh.

"He's only joking," he said quickly. "Look. We only want to have a little fun. We want no trouble from you."

"Good. Then I suggest you get out of my way and skip on back to Jotunheim—"

"Leave now?"

"Yes, unless you'd like a repeat demonstration of why Frost Giants melt. I'd hate to ruin this lovely floor. The cleanup staff already has enough to deal with."

Hivor drifted his hand to the scar on his arm where I'd seared his flesh long ago. At least he remembered what I was capable of. Or what I used to be capable of.

"Alright, maybe it would be best if we...hey—" His gaze narrowed on my face. "Is that a black eye? Since when do gods bruise?"

My heart skipped. The punch from Jorg's fist should have healed by now. Though, oddly, it didn't throb as badly as it had this morning.

"It's nothing, just trying out a new look," I lied, forcing casual indifference into my voice. "Mortals call it makeup. Really adds mystery to my aesthetic, don't you think?"

I flashed him a sharp grin, ignoring how the movement pulled at tender flesh.

Don't notice how my hands are shaking. Don't notice the sweat beading on my forehead.

Gods. This was so embarrassing.

"Though I suppose you wouldn't know anything about improving one's appearance." I eyed his unkempt eyebrows pointedly.

Hivor bared his yellowing teeth with a snarl. His gaze caught on something else—the scar visible at my collar where Surtr's blade had nearly taken my arm. The wound that should have healed months ago. Though, now that I thought about it, the angry red had faded to pink...

The Frost Giant leaned closer, sniffing.

"You smell different, too." His nose wrinkled. "Almost like a..a..." He sniffed again. "Like a mortal."

My stomach dropped. I'd forgotten about their damned sense of smell.

"And why do I smell a rat?" Hivor asked, his nostrils flaring. "The Loki I know would have already turned me into something unpleasant for getting this close."

"And here I thought you'd appreciate my politeness," I said. "I just never can make you happy. Furthermore—"

He lunged forward and grabbed my shoulder, his fingers digging into the exact spot where divine steel had carved through muscle and bone.

I couldn't stop the spasm of pain forcing a strangled grunt out of my lungs. No, no, no.

Hivor's beady eyes lit with realization.

"You aren't a god anymore!" Hivor said, laughter and disbelief and delight running beneath his words. "Gods don't stay wounded. Well, this changes everything."

The hall erupted with thunderous laughter as they closed in. Their massive forms cast shadows over me, no longer afraid of the god I used to be.

"Look how the mighty have fallen!" one bellowed, clutching his belly. "The Trickster needs mortal medicine!"

"Remember when he used to turn us into toads? Guess

chaos can't fix a broken nose anymore!" Another flicked my face with a finger like an iron bar.

The Frost Giant wiped tears from his eyes, accidentally crushing the knight's helmet he'd been playing with.

"Look! His bones don't even heal fast anymore!" He squinted at me. "Does that mean if I eat him now, he won't grow back?" He seemed genuinely puzzled by this new development.

Shit.

Hivor grinned, baring crooked teeth.

"Just like old times, isn't it, runt?" he sneered, squeezing my injured shoulder harder. "Back to being the weakest Jotnar in the Nine Worlds. Though I must say, you're even more pathetic than when you left us. At least then you could take a punch."

The others circled closer, their eyes shining with cruel delight.

I drew both my daggers from my hips.

"Don't think I can't still kick your ass, god or not," I warned, finding the familiar grip of the daggers as I took a half-step to the side. "Or have you forgotten the time I broke your jaw and three ribs without a drop of godhood? As I recall, you cried for your mother. Though given how ugly she is, that probably made you cry harder."

His grip tightened, but I caught the flicker of remembered pain in his eyes. The Jotnar and Frost Giant stepped back half a pace at the sight of my blades. Even without my power, they knew better than to underestimate Dwarven steel that had tasted Jotnar blood before. Good.

"Do you know what Skadi promised the one who brings her your head? The crown of Midgard itself." His eyes gleamed, though he kept a wary distance from my daggers.

"King of all these pathetic mortals. And here you are, powerless, dropped right in my lap."

Hivor was probably right about the kingship. Skadi always did have a flair for dramatic rewards.

"Bold of you to assume she'll keep her word," I shot back, though I knew she would. Skadi might be cruel, but she always paid her debts. "I'm sure she's too busy with packing all those shoes of hers."

They laughed harder, spittle flying out of their mouths. The Frost Giant smacked his knee, his heel cracking into the tile floor.

"She broke through the borders of Asgard days ago," Hivor said, his lips curling beneath his black beard. "Soon all the Nine Worlds will be ours. And now I'll rule this one, thanks to your head." His massive fingers flexed. "I've waited centuries to be more than just another Jotnar warrior. And you, Trickster, are my ticket to a crown."

Fear speared my gut and stirred. And now I had an ambitious would-be king to deal with.

"You won't win," I said.

I slashed upward. My blade caught Urs across his chest, opening a deep line that welled blood. He howled, stumbling back. My second dagger found the meat of Hivor's thigh, and his roar of pain shook dust from the rafters.

Three more lunged at once. I ducked under a swing and drove *Laevateinn* into a forearm. But there were too many. A ham-hock of a hand caught my wrist mid-strike, crushing until bones ground together. My daggers clattered to the floor as another Jotnar wrenched my arms behind my back.

Massive fists pounded into my body from all sides as I struggled to break free. My death would buy Hivor his crown. Each blow landed as if they could already touch the power that would come with ruling Midgard.

A brutal strike cracked against my temple in an explosive burst of light and agony. My nose crushed with a crunch of cartilage and bone. Warm blood gushed down my throat, choking me.

I twisted and strained to deflect and dodge. Agony blossomed from a thousand points. Too many hands, too many Jotnar hungering to tell stories of how they helped bring down the trickster Loki.

A particularly vicious punch hit into my jaw and I reeled backwards, legs betraying me as I crumpled to the floor. Rage burned hotter than the pain.

I pried my eyes open, squinting through swollen lids. Blood dribbled from my lips. Looking up at Hivor, I spat crimson onto his boots.

"Bad manners," growled Urs. He crashed his fist into my ribs and bone snapped. White-hot pain seared through my entire left side.

Still worth it.

"You used to know your place before mixing your blood with that Aesir trash," Hivor said, eyes gleaming with malice.

I glared up at him through the blood and swelling and pain. "At least I don't have cabbage breath," I wheezed.

Anger raged in his eyes.

He drew himself up to his full height, lip curling back.

"It's time you faced Jotnar judgement," Hivor growled. "Skadi will mount your head above the public privy."

Rough hands forced me to my knees, fingers like iron bars digging into my shoulders. The tile floor swam beneath me as black spots danced at the edges of my vision. This couldn't be how it ended. Not on my knees in a museum, about to be beheaded by a Jotnar who couldn't even groom his eyebrows properly.

The rasp of steel against leather forced my eyes up. The ice axe that emerged from Hivor's back seemed to drink in the fluorescent light, its blade telling stories of clean cuts through bone and sinew. I'd watched him take three heads with that weapon during the last giant war. My throat suddenly felt very exposed.

Gods Brokkr would have loved to see this.

"Could we possibly reschedule the execution?" I asked, unable to quite keep the tremor from my voice as the edge found the hollow beneath my jaw. "This really isn't a good time."

Hivor grinned down at me, as if savoring this moment. He pressed the blade harder, drawing a thin line of blood.

"Skadi said to bring just the head," he mused. "She didn't specify how cleanly it needed to be removed."

My eyes fixed on him, refusing to show the terror turning my bones to water. Refusing to give him the satisfaction of seeing me break. But inside, a voice screamed that I couldn't die.

Hivor swung the axe down in a whistling arc towards my neck—

A scream pierced the air.

What the—

The medieval broadsword erupted from one of the Jotnar's chest. He went rigid, then slid backwards, legs buckling as dark blood fountained from the wound. Sigyn staggered under his weight as he slipped off the blade and hit the floor. She stood over him, chest heaving, crimson droplets pattering from the sword's edge.

"Let him go," she shouted, voice shaking but grip steady on the blade.

The Jotnar's roars of fury and laughter drowned my words begging her to flee.

"I don't know who in Ymir's eyelashes you are," Hivor snarled, spittle flying, "but you're interfering with my coronation! Kill her."

Two Jotnar lunged for her. Sigyn dove aside as one grabbed at empty air. The other forced her towards the wall. Behind them, the Frost Giant lumbered forward, still trying to figure out why the small thing wasn't running away.

She raised the sword higher, its bloodied edge gleaming.

"Your fight is with me, not her!" I shouted. "Leave her alone."

"She made it her fight when she killed one of us," Hivor growled. "We won't let her ruin our chance at the throne."

Sigyn's sword found another Jotnar gut. Blood sprayed her cheeks. Her eyes widened as if in shock at her own violence.

The Jotnar pinning me shifted his grip and I took my chance.

I slammed my fist into my captor's face with every ounce of strength left. His grip loosened just enough. I wrenched free, surprising myself with a burst of speed. Perhaps Fenrir's green juice regime wasn't completely useless.

I lunged towards Sigyn, but Urs clamped around my ankle. The floor rushed up to meet me. Air exploded from my lungs as I crashed down.

"Careful with the merchandise," I wheezed as he dragged me backwards. "Skadi won't make anyone king if you damage her trophy beyond recognition."

Sigyn managed one more swing of the broadsword before a Jotnar clamped around her sword arm. The weapon fell from her fingers, the steel ringing against tile. She fought in their grip, but they pinned her arms to her sides. Her face flushed with fury and fear as she met my eyes across the hall, where Urs dragged me back to Hivor and his waiting axe.

Hivor stood over me, blade glinting at my throat.

"Time to claim my crown," he said, drawing back for the killing blow—

"I told you to let him go!" she screamed.

Azure light erupted from Sigyn like a newborn star. The shockwave hit with physical force, slamming the Jotnar holding her through display cases. The Frost Giant took the blast full in the chest, his massive form cartwheeling through the air before crashing into a suit of armor. The impact shook the entire hall. He didn't get up.

Urs released me, fleeing as the light grew impossibly brighter. Power pulsed outward in waves from Sigyn's outstretched hands, azure flames dancing around her. Her eyes blazed with divinity as hope and fidelity poured from her.

I leapt up, every muscle humming with the energy cascading through the museum. Beautiful. Terrible. Because I knew the price she would pay thanks to this fucking curse. Wait—I could leap? After that beating, I shouldn't even be standing, let alone moving this easily. The broken ribs that had been stabbing into my lungs moments ago now just...ached.

Blue light rushed back into her body and the hall fell silent.

Well, except for Hivor, who groaned from where he'd landed, trying to push himself up. I walked over and slammed my shoe into his face. The foam squeaked as it connected, but the crack of his nose breaking was deeply satisfying.

"That's for the attempted beheading," I said. "And the eyebrow situation."

Sigyn's knees buckled.

"What...what did I just do?" she breathed, catching herself against a broken display case. Her face had gone pale, dark circles suddenly prominent under her eyes. The azure flames in her irises flickered and dimmed like dying embers. Frigg's curse, feeding off her power, drinking it down like Thor at a feast.

"What I've been telling you." I stepped towards her, ready to catch her if she fell. My movements were surprisingly fluid for someone who'd just had every bone in his body rearranged by Jotnar fists. "You are a goddess. You are hope. And that draining sensation you're feeling right now is the curse we must break."

Sigyn shook her head, swaying slightly. She took a stumbling step backwards and wrapped her arms around herself, as if trying to hold herself together.

I snatched up my fallen daggers from where they'd scattered during the fight, sliding them back into their sheaths at my hips.

"No, I'm not the kind of person who does these things." Her gaze flicked around the demolished hall, to the dead Jotnar tossed across the floor. Her words came out breathless, drained. "I'm not the kind of person who *can* do these things."

"But you are. And every time you use your power, it will exhaust you more. The curse feeds on it." I took out the incantation from my pocket. "Just translate these runes. One small blood ritual to break the curse, and you'll—"

"Blood?" Fresh fear gripped her as I reached for the dagger. "You want my blood?" She stumbled back another step.

"Sigyn, please, if you'd just—"

She turned and ran towards the stairwell door, though

her footing was unsteady. She threw it open and disappeared down the steps, the door slamming shut behind her. A click of a lock followed.

Dammit! Wrong move, wrong timing. I should have waited, should have...

I tried to yank the door open, but it wouldn't budge. I pounded my fist against the steel. Footsteps rumbled on the other side.

The lock clicked open. The door burst open.

"Sigyn?"

"What happened? We heard screams and crashing glass," Fenrir said as he and Jorg stepped through the doorway. "Sigyn ran past us in a panic."

I touched my nose, which had most definitely been broken. Not a crunch. Not even a wince of pain. It was perfect. Odd...

"I'll explain on the way," I said, already moving towards the stairs. "Skadi has breached Asgard's borders, and the Jotnar are here. Wait, why are *you* here?"

"Got coffee across the street while keeping an eye on you," Jorg said, falling into step beside me. "Because knowing you, these things always happen. And as we said, you aren't alone in this."

I rolled my eyes but muttered a 'thank you' as we descended the stairwell, Fenrir close behind. Between flights, I quickly told them about Sigyn's power eruption saving me from a near beheading.

"And next time you're keeping an 'eye on me,'" I added, "maybe step in before I'm seconds away from losing my head to a Jotnar with an axe."

I touched my side where Urs' fist had certainly cracked a rib earlier. I winced, expecting sharp pain, but found only a dull throb.

But I had bigger problems than mysteriously healing injuries. Like Jotnar using humans as fun toys. And Frost Giants treating them as snacks. And that's only if Frigg's draugr didn't eat them all first.

We emerged into dim evening light, the street eerily empty and silent. A scattered trail of fleeing museum visitors pointed towards the park, but no sign of Sigyn.

"She came this way," Fenrir said, his nose twitching as he scanned the cobblestone path. Lamplight glowed in the growing dusk. "Though these roasting chestnuts from the cart make it hard to—wait." He stopped beneath an oak tree and pointed at something beneath a weathered park bench. "There."

Sigyn's purse lay abandoned on the damp ground, its leather strap twisted as if dropped mid-run.

"Her bag," I said, stepping forward to retrieve it.

Fenrir shot his hand out to stop me.

"Papa, no! You can't go through her purse. It's her personal property."

"Son, how do you suggest we find her if we don't know where she lives?"

"I don't know! But there are rules about these things!"

Jorg rolled his eyes and shouldered past us both, his combat boots scuffing against stone as he snatched the bag from my hands.

"Oh, for Ymir's sake—" He reached in and tossed the wallet to Fenrir, who caught it like it might bite him, holding it at arm's length with two fingers.

I plucked the wallet from Fenrir's outstretched hand while Jorg continued rummaging.

"Nothing interesting in here anyway," Jorg muttered, searching through the contents. "Just normal stuff. She does have good taste in pens…"

"Fenrir, calm down. And so you know, I own more purses than Sigyn," I said, flipping through her wallet. "And I'm far pickier about them than she is. Trust me, she'd understand the circumstances. This is hardly the worst violation of privacy she's endured from me."

Fenrir shot me a pained look, clearly wrestling with his principles.

"Fine. But we're only looking for her address."

"Got it," I said, holding up her driver's license and committing the numbers to memory. "1242 Hammer-straase—"

"Good," Fenrir cut me off, swooping in like an avenging angel to snatch both wallet and purse from our hands. "That's all we need. And I'm making sure this gets back to her exactly as we found it."

40

THE CHOICE

BALDER

"At first, I found your father's attempt to break my curse amusing. So much effort, all for nothing."

I kept pace with Mother as we swept through the central study. The cats scattered from the desk and leather-bound volumes.

"But his constant meddling became irritating, especially how he's been poisoning your mind against me, Balder. And now that I've discovered a new element in the east, I no longer need to keep him alive as a thorn in my side."

She pushed through the heavy oak doors into the feast hall.

Our footsteps echoed off the high vaulted ceiling, the massive space empty save for the remnants of the morning meal. Discarded cups, bread crumbs, and the lingering scent of stale beer.

"Your father should have known better than to keep interfering. Still, he serves one final purpose. He can confirm whether Loki is truly mortal. I must be certain before I act. There is too much at stake to make a mistake now."

"What are you planning?" I asked as we passed beneath the wall of shields. The truth about Loki's mortality felt like poison in my chest.

"There might be a simpler solution to my Loki problem. A permanent one." She got that smile that made my stomach lurch. "Skadi wants nothing more than Loki's head. Even more than she wants to conquer Asgard or possess you. And now, for the first time, taking his head is actually possible. I need your father to confirm what I suspect about Loki. With one death, I can save Asgard twice over—give Skadi the prize she truly wants, and eliminate the prophesied destroyer. All the threats would be gone forever." She pushed open the kitchen doors. "You asked for my protection from marrying Skadi. This is how I'm providing it. I thought you'd be pleased."

"Pleased?" I spat. "How would this please me?"

We threaded our way through the clatter of pots and pans of the kitchen, servants pressing themselves against hot stone ovens to let us pass. Steam rose from bubbling cauldrons, and the aroma of baking bread.

"Don't you see? Even the need for the tree's commands would be gone. Two birds, one stone. No, wait...actually it would be *three* birds. Oh! This is simply a marvelous turn of events."

We emerged into the western corridor and the salt-thick air.

I needed to keep her here, to stop her from hunting him down. To prevent her from killing him. From taking his head...

"Your curse still infects Loki," I said, forcing conviction into my voice. Praying she couldn't hear the desperation beneath my words. "Whatever magic allowed his temporary freedom, he will return to the underworld. The curse guarantees that. Isn't that enough?"

She stepped to one of the arched windows that lined the corridor to Father's chambers. The dark sea pressed against the rocky shoreline far below, white foam exploding against black rock.

"Nothing about Loki is ever guaranteed," she said. Our shadows stretched long against the wall as a torch guttered in the sea breeze. "If it's not his own slithery talents, it's his friends helping him. I've already thwarted one escape attempt before from Sigyn while he wasted away in that cave."

And in those words I knew.

"That's why you went to Vanaheim," I said. "You threatened her."

She sighed, the sound swallowed by the crashing waves outside the open archways.

"I suspected some ludicrous rescue attempt for Loki from her. She was trying to get back to Midgard. All I had to do was wait for her to cross from Alfheim's protection and into Freya's territory. I told Sigyn she was on a failed mission when I found her in Vanaheim trying to get to Loki."

"But Sigyn could never reach him there. And if she somehow did, it would be impossible to break him free."

"That was hardly enough assurance," she said.

The waves seemed to pound in time with my pulse now.

"No. There's more," I said. "What would make her stop? What did you do to her?"

"Nothing violent if that's your concern," she said. "I only provided some extra motivation to turn back. I gave her a choice: return to Alfheim and stay there, or, if she ever attempted to go to Loki's cave again, I would burn Falael's orphanage to the ground. Sigyn simply had to decide whether she wanted more blood staining her conscience."

Thor's words filled my mind, cold and damning. And I hadn't listened to him. Didn't want to. Because what it meant terrified me.

"I swore to Father never to tell you about it."

My stomach pitted and fell to my feet. Because I knew she would do it, and Sigyn did too. She knew because she had killed her children, so what would stop her from harming other children in the same guise of protection?

And I had let it happen. All of it. I'd been so proud of myself for getting Mother to agree to the curse instead of the binding, thinking I'd found a better way. Believing I'd stopped the horror. But I'd only given her time to plan something worse. Every scream in that cave, every drop of children's blood, every moment of Loki's agony...

I shared in that guilt.

I was on the wrong side. Had been all along. And now, I had to do all I could to stop her. She had to be stopped.

"You would kill more," I whispered. The torches sputtered in their brackets as another gust swept through the archways, bringing with it the taste of salt and storm.

She turned from the window, giving me that smile that made me feel like a five-year-old child again that couldn't possibly understand.

"Would you really have wanted all of that mess in the cave to have been for nothing if Sigyn set Loki free? That would have been crueler."

She lied to me. Everything was a lie.

"You told me draining the gods' powers would be temporary." My voice shook. "But that was another lie, wasn't it? You're stealing their power, all of it, and you never planned to stop. You aren't giving it back."

The waves crashed harder against the cliffs below, drowning out my ragged breathing.

"We need to hurry," she said. "Soon he won't have enough strength left to be useful to us at all."

Horror spread through my veins in seconds. The corridor felt colder, darker.

"So your plans for Hel are true," I said. "You're intending to murder her. To use her guts to bind Loki in the earth—"

She sighed, turning back to face me.

"She is of his blood, Balder. You saw enough to understand how he must be bound. The magic necessary. Hel is the only way."

My world tilted on its axis. Everything I thought I knew about her shattered like glass. The torchlight fractured in my vision as I struggled to stay upright.

"You're going to hurt everyone. My friends. My family. Thor..."

"Of course, that's all changed now if Loki is mortal—"

I held her wrist, the pieces finally clicking into place. Her unreadable smiles. The way she'd dodged my questions about the binding. Her talk of permanent solutions...

Our shadows merged and twisted on the wall as we struggled.

"You broke the oath you made me." The words tore from my throat like the wind had ripped them free. "You swore to me after that night in the cave. You vowed you would find another way to bind Loki, one that didn't require children's entrails or a parent's suffering. The curse was supposed to be clean. Simple. Just magic and intention, not blood and screams."

"An oath about children, dear one. And Hel is not a child." She tried to pull away, but I held firm. Lightning flickered in the distance over the sea, illuminating her face in harsh sheets of white.

"Stop twisting the words," I said. "You swore two things to me that night. You swore you would never do the horror again. Never use entrails for binding, never cause that kind of suffering. And you swore you would never threaten another child for the sake of 'the greater good.'" I clenched her wrist harder. "But you broke both the moment you cast this curse. Because this was always your plan, wasn't it? To bind Loki and his family beneath the earth. To use Hel's guts for your binding. The curse was the first step."

"And then you threatened those orphans," I continued, bile rising in my throat. "You used innocent children to control Sigyn. You broke everything you promised me."

"I told you earlier, sometimes to love truly, you must be cruel. But it remains love all the same." Lightning flashed again, closer now. "I love the Nine Worlds, and I will not let one god destroy them if I can stop it."

"I can't accept this anymore," I said, my words nearly lost in the growing thunder. "All this time, I believed in you. I thought you'd changed after the cave. That you understood there had to be limits, even in the name of protection."

"Balder, I'm doing this for you, for all of us. To secure our future." She grasped my hands, her grip almost painful. "Please, you must see that. I protected us, and sometimes, you must do what no one else is willing to do for the safety of many, over the safety of a few."

I held her stare and saw her, truly saw her, for the first time. The sea spray from the windows misted around us like tears.

She wrenched her hands from mine.

"I see that you're a monster to anyone who stands in your way."

Sadness flickered across her face as she let my hands slide from hers.

"Monster? I am tired, Balder. That prophecy has kept me up more nights than I can count. He has robbed me of peace. I want safety for once. And I can only have it when Loki is truly gone. When anything connected to Ragnarok is gone."

She reached for Father's chamber door, but I caught her wrist again, desperation clawing at my chest. The corridor had grown dark now, the torches struggling against the storm winds.

"Stop this. Haven't enough people suffered?"

She yanked free of my grasp, but her eyes held that same pitying look she'd worn watching Loki's children in Sigyn's arms, knowing what she would do to them.

"Time grows short for your father."

She tugged on the latch of the door, and the hinges creaked open.

Father slumped over his desk when we entered, face buried in scattered papers and ancient texts. Maps of the nine worlds spilled across the wooden surface, their edges curling.

He lifted his head, and a sheen of sweat glistened on his forehead despite the room's chill. Something was wrong, beyond the curse's drain. He fixed her with his one eye, trying to maintain his usual steel, but his hands trembled holding the chair's arms.

She marched up to him, footsteps muffled by the patchwork of rugs. Thunder growled.

"First things first. Where is it?" Her eyes blazed, scanning his chest, his arms, his hands.

"What nonsense are you on about now?" he asked, shuffling papers into messy stacks.

She smiled, finding her target. She leaned across the desk, scattering papers as she grasped his wrist. Her nails dug crescents into his skin. The contact made him flinch.

"This." She yanked his hand closer, the ring glinting in the light. "I know." She tore off the ring with enough force to break skin. Father hissed through his teeth. She straightened, triumphant, dropping the ring into her leather pouch while he massaged his raw knuckle.

He tilted his head, forcing an amused smile that cost him visibly. Fresh beads of sweat trickled down his temples.

"Took you long enough to figure out," he said. "You really thought I would let you take Asgard easily?"

He leaned away from her, pressing one hand against his stomach before gripping the armrest.

"I expected some idiotic attempt." She planted her palms on his desk. "But what's happened to Loki changes everything. His condition has raised questions I need answered."

Fear flashed across his face before he could hide it.

"What's happened to Loki?"

Her smile widened at that slip, that glimpse of his heart.

She shoved away from the desk and stalked around it.

"The mighty Alfather, so afraid of death you'll betray anyone to avoid it," she purred, stopping behind him. "Let's test where your breaking point for Loki is these days. I am curious."

He let out a dry, mocking laugh that dissolved into a wet cough.

"You never understood love, did you? Only power. That was always our difference."

She circled back around the desk.

"Tell me what I want to know, and I'll let you keep your life."

No. No more of this.

I took a step towards them. Crackling energy sparked around her like a shield, pushing me back.

"Tell me what's happened to his chaos," she said. "Tell me if I'm right."

My heart hammered against my ribs.

"Stop, Mother. Don't do this—"

Father's eye flicked to me, a warning in its depths. His fingers whitened where he gripped the chair arms.

"Your desperation is showing, Frigg." His voice came rough, but still carried that edge of mockery. "What's wrong? Your perfect plan not working out as you hoped?"

She struck like a viper, digging her fingers into his jaw.

"I can feel your power draining away." She pressed her thumb into his throat as she forced his head back. "Soon you won't even have enough left to maintain this facade of strength."

"No. This is where we remain, Frigg." Each word was steady but lined with pain. "Watching each other suffer, as we always have."

"Stop this now—" She silenced me with a look that froze the words in my mouth.

Father wheezed as she loosened her grip. Another bead of perspiration ran down his temple. "Always so certain you know everything. So certain you can control it all." He coughed. "But you've already lost, haven't you? That's why you're here, demanding answers like a child throwing a tantrum."

She tightened her hand on his jaw. A second longer and slowly, deliberately, she pulled her hand away. She stepped back, leaning against the desk as she watched him with the patient intensity of a cat at a mouse hole.

"Lost? I've won. I've cursed your precious Loki. Your

power is mine. Asgard will be mine. All I need now is confirmation of what I suspect, and then—" She pushed off the
desk and bent close to his ear. "Then I can finally end this
game we've been playing."

"If you were so sure you've won," Father said, each word
labored, "you wouldn't need my confirmation at all."

Something dangerous flashed in Mother's eyes, but she
remained perched on the desk edge, unnaturally still. Just
watching. Waiting.

"Is his chaos gone? Has he done what I think he has?"

I couldn't breathe. Couldn't move from my place by the
door. As much as I hated admitting it, Father and Loki were
our best hope at stopping this curse.

A spasm of pain doubled him forward. Father gripped
the desk edge, as he fought to keep his face straight.

She slid off the desk and prowled closer.

"You're a coward, Odin." She settled her hand on his
shoulder, deceptively gentle. "And I know when it comes to
your life, you'll always choose yourself. You'll give me the
answer I need." She bent to his ear, voice softening. "Is Loki
mortal?"

His head snapped up. "What have you given me?" His
skin had turned waxen, sickly in the firelight.

She pushed away from him with a scoff.

"Loki is puking his guts out over a biscuit and needing
mortal medicine," she said, pacing behind his chair. "Something has changed, and if something has changed...there are
options that weren't there before."

Father clutched the desk again, a cry tearing from his
throat as blood streamed from his right nostril.

My heart pounded.

Mother circled back to face him.

"Feeling it now, aren't you?" She braced her hands on

the desk, leaning over him. "I knew you'd figure it out. Heil-jagift. It's going to get worse from here. Looks like you're in the stomach pain phase. Next will be bleeding out, and then you'll feel your insides boil."

"What's happening to him?" I said.

"I've had the poison in you for days now." She traced his jawline. "I don't envy you all the fluids about to seep out of you."

"Poison?" The word tasted like bile. "You poisoned him?"

She straightened, turning to me with that terrible smile.

"Actually, *you* poisoned him. The dose was in the honey sweets."

The room spun. My knees threatened to buckle.

"You used me to murder my father?" Raw horror gutted me. "I trusted you! I—" The words cracked. "Those sweets...I could have eaten them myself. Your own son—"

"Beautiful, isn't it? How the curse weakened him just enough for the poison to take hold. For anyone else, even you, my dear, it would have been nothing more than an upset stomach. A mother always protects her child." She watched the blood drip from his nose with almost scientific interest. "And a mother also always knows her child...you're so good. So predictable in your kindness. I knew you'd never let him go hungry. Not even when I warned you not to. You should have listened to me."

The calculation of it all froze my blood. She had thought of everything, counted on our habits, our weaknesses. Used my goodness against Father.

She reached into her skirts and drew out a small vial. The dark liquid gleamed in the light as she held it up between us.

"The antidote. Tell me, and it's yours."

Her fingers curled around the vial. Even with her power

crackling through the room, sparking against my skin, I might have tried pushing through her magic and attacking her, but not while she held Father's only chance at survival. One wrong move and she could drop it, destroy it. I couldn't risk being the cause of Father's death twice in one day.

An agonized grunt pushed out of Father. He hunched over the desk, jaw clenched. His nails gouged the wood, splintering the finish.

She swirled the vial between thumb and forefinger, light glowing through the dark liquid.

"Is Loki mortal?" Lightning flickered outside. "Better hurry. When your organs start liquefying, speech becomes quite difficult."

"Don't do this, Mother!" I said. "I beg you."

She didn't even glance my way. Her free hand brushed a loose strand of Father's hair back, fingertips lingering on his cheek. Her tears glistened in the firelight.

"I hate how you always make me hurt you," she whispered, tracing the lines of his face. "Stop making me wait you out. Stop making me watch you die. Just tell me so I can stop. You betrayed Loki before for less."

Father pushed himself upright, spine straightening despite the obvious agony. His eye met hers, unflinching.

"You think I'll break again?" he asked softly, blood staining his lips. "You think my fear of death will betray him twice?" A smile ghosted across his face, full of a terrible gentleness. "I learned something when I lost Loki. There are worse things than dying. I've already lived through the worst thing. Watching him realize I was too much of a coward to love him properly. So kill me. Let my last act be choosing him. Let him know that this time, when death came for me again..." Blood ran from his eye, scarlet threads down his face. "I chose him. I finally chose him."

She stepped back, blinking tears. Thunder cracked. Lightning threw their shadows sharp against the walls.

"Tell me..." Her voice turned gentle. Too gentle.

I watched my father's face and saw something I'd never seen before—peace. Not resignation, not defeat, but the quiet certainty of a man who had finally found the courage to face his greatest fear. And in that moment, I understood with devastating clarity. He would not break. This wasn't a test or a negotiation. This was a man choosing to die rather than betray Loki a second time.

The truth crushed the air from my lungs. He would let the poison take him. He would die here, on his knees, with Loki's name unsaid on his bloodied lips. And in his eye I saw that this, somehow, was his redemption.

But I couldn't let him die, not when I knew what could save him. He was my father.

And without him, what little remained of Asgard's protections would die with him. Skadi would destroy everything. And Loki, mortal or not, couldn't break Mother's curse alone. He needed Father.

But telling her Loki's secret, breaking my oath to Hel, could destroy everything we had left to save.

And what choice did I have but the gamble?

Hel, please forgive me.

"Give him the antidote," my voice shook. "And I will tell you, because I know."

Her eyes snapped to mine, bright with hunger.

"How?" She tightened her fingers on the vial.

"Loki lost his godhood. I don't know how, but he did," I said. "He no longer has his chaos. It's completely gone. That's why he is sick. He is mortal now."

Her smile stretched wide, almost feral. Thunder rumbled as she set the vial on the desk.

She prowled closer.

"Why didn't you tell me this before?"

The magic holding me relented, and my body sighed. I rubbed my wrists, trying to move towards the door.

"You know the truth about Loki now, that's what matters. Please, we need to help Father."

She closed the distance between us in two swift steps, pulling me into an embrace that felt like a trap.

"Because of you, we are saved. We have won. Thank you."

"Yes, yes, now, the antidote." I tried to pull away, reaching for the vial. "Quickly. You promised—"

Her arms fell away. She stepped back, leaving me cold. She unstoppered the vial and tilted it. Dark liquid splashed onto the floor, the familiar sweetness of port wine rising between us.

"Oh, my sweet, sweet boy," she said. "Always so good. There is no antidote. Were you really expecting me to allow your father to live after all he's done?"

The wine soaked into the rug, spreading like blood. I'd been playing her game while she'd already decided the ending. And I'd given her exactly what she wanted.

"Why do this?" My voice cracked.

She drifted back to Father, trailing her fingers along his cheek almost lovingly.

"Because I will always do what it takes to protect," she said. "And do you really think I'd keep allowing him to try to break the Salvation Weave? No. I had to stop that nonsense. Now, where is that—"

She turned to rummage through drawers, and I stumbled to Father's side. His skin was hot against my palm as I helped him sit straighter. Another spasm doubled him over.

"Water," he rasped, clutching at my sleeve.

My hands shook as I grabbed the goblet from his desk, sloshing water over maps and papers as I filled it. Most spilled down his chin when he tried to drink, his throat working weakly. I dabbed his face with my sleeve.

"Here we are." Mother stood at his cabinet, holding a slender dart of wood, its tip honed deadly sharp. Mistletoe. The same mistletoe Loki had used to kill me.

My fingers found the spot on my neck where it had pierced me. The phantom sting made me shudder.

"What are you going to do with that?" My voice wavered.

She cradled the dart like a precious thing.

"I'm going to kill Loki Laufeyjarson with my own hands." She tested the point with her thumb. "I've tried casting him out. I've tried sending draugr. It's as it always is in the end...if you want something done right, you have to do it yourself. Skadi will be please with my gift of the trickster's head."

Father pitched forward and I caught him as his legs gave out. We hit the floor hard. Foam bubbled from his mouth. I tried to cradle his head, keep him from hurting himself.

Her eyes barely flickered to Father's writhing form as she admired the dart, turning it in the light.

"Mother, please—" I pressed my sleeve to Father's mouth, trying to wipe away the foam. His skin burned against mine.

"Please what? 'Don't do this?' I need him dead, Balder." She stalked towards the door. "If you continue fighting me on this, I'll have to confine you to your rooms—"

And I saw what I had to do.

She wasn't the only one who could play games.

"I was trying to say, please be safe."

I rose from Father's side, keeping my movements measured. Careful.

"I apologize for my behavior earlier. As you said, I wasn't ready for all this...excitement." The lie flowed easier than expected. "But I'm beginning to understand now. The necessity of it all. The love behind your actions. I see what must be done."

And I did understand, with terrible clarity. Everything I'd believed about her, about the curse, about Loki—I'd been wrong about all of it.

She paused at the threshold. "Really?"

I nodded, though the motion felt like betrayal. But I needed her to believe in my loyalty if any of us were to survive.

"You were right. I should have told you sooner about Loki's mortality. But an oath bound me to silence. Yet Asgard must come first—that's why I broke it." I forced warmth into my voice. "Thank you for protecting us. For protecting me."

Her smile warmed as she gripped the door handle.

"No, thank you. Now, I suggest you leave him before he starts to smell. Trust me, it will be horrifying."

The door slammed behind her.

My shoulders sagged. I turned back to Father, slumped against the wall where I'd propped him. Each breath rattled in his chest.

"She'll kill him now." His voice shattered on the words. "After everything he sacrificed to save us, I couldn't even protect him. Not when it mattered most."

He turned his bloodshot eye to me, and I saw what was truly haunting him. Knowing Loki would die believing Father had betrayed him one final time.

Blood and tears streamed down his cheeks.

"I had to choose. It was either your life or his secret. And without you, without Asgard's protections..." I swallowed hard. "But that doesn't mean we've lost. I have a plan."

I gripped his arm, trying to lever him up. His legs buckled and he nearly collapsed again, his weight heavy against my shoulder.

"What do you mean?"

"Because," I shifted to better support him, "I'm finally making the choice I should have made from the beginning. When I saw how far she'd go...Even if it means standing with Loki instead." The words felt strange in my mouth, but right. Like a truth I'd been avoiding too, long.

"What choice?"

"I'm going to Hel." I tightened my grip on his arm. "I'm taking her army, and we're breaking this curse before the poison destroys what's left of you. You just have to hold on." Thunder cracked outside. "And then you'll live. Then we will all truly be saved."

The foundations shuddered. Something massive slammed against the gates.

"Skadi," he said. "She's here."

41

TRAUMA TRAM

LOKI

The tram jerked and swayed around each bend, tracks clacking beneath us as we hurtled towards Sigyn's apartment on the west side of the city. I hoped this was where she had fled. That she was safe.

I scrubbed the cold sweat away from my brow, the thousand possibilities gnawing my insides into ground meat. My leg bounced with nervous energy until Fenrir shot me a concerned look from where he sat clutching her purse, his fingers white-knuckled around the strap. At least her address from the ID inside gave us somewhere to start, and the tram was the fastest route.

The carriage rattled past neon-lit windows and street lamps glowing through the drizzle, their light fragmenting across the wet glass. An old woman kept stealing worried glances our way, clutching her grocery tote closer with each passing stop.

Across from us, Jorg shifted restlessly, unable to fully extend his lanky frame. He pushed his hand through his cropped blond hair, brow creased. Frigg's curse hung over us like a sword, and here were my sons, walking straight into danger with me.

If this was the end...if this was my last chance..

"All these centuries," I said, watching the city blur past. "All these eons of lies and hurts and secrets..."

"What are you talking about?" Fenrir asked. "Papa?"

Our seats creaked, and the tram groaned around another tight corner as we snaked through the city. I gripped the metal pole beside me.

"I've been so wrong. About all of it..." I said. "I can't let us go forward without—" The words caught.

Fenrir released the purse with one hand and grasped my fingers. Firm. Assured.

"You better not be trying to send us away again. It's been decided. We are with you until the end of this, whatever that end may be."

Warmth coated me at his words, but shame quickly followed. I studied the worn floor of the tram.

"What are you jabbering on about now?" Jorg asked, shifting forward in his seat until the metal creaked.

Needles bit the back of my throat. I swallowed hard, the sway of the tram matching the roil of emotions within me.

"I should have told you both the truth about accepting Odin's bargain from the beginning. I should have told you about the apple." My chest constricted with each word, guilt breaking free. "I believed the gods when they told me taking you away would to keep you safe. But I was wrong. *It was wrong.* I should have found another way. I should have fought harder for you. We could have stayed in the Iron-wood, kept our lives there. I should never have left."

We swayed as the tram squealed around another turn. The city lights blurred in stripes on the rain-streaked windows, matching the blur in my vision. Every memory of my failures, every moment I'd chosen deceit over truth, threatened to pull me under.

"Gods," Jorg said, slumping back against his seat with an exaggerated eye roll. "Please, stop speaking all mushy-like. It's stomach churning."

"You're being too hard on yourself, Papa," Fenrir said, giving my hand another supportive squeeze. He leaned closer, trying to catch my downturned gaze.

I smirked sadly, the expression feeling brittle on my face. The gentleness in his voice made it worse. How could he still show me kindness? I pulled my hand free.

"I've hurt you," I said. "I've hurt you, and I'm...I'm..." Each word felt like it was being torn from deep within me.

"There's no need for this..." Fenrir said, reaching for me again.

But there was every need. I had to say it.

"I tried to be a good father," I said. "I made a decision never to strike you like my father struck me. Never to call you wicked, or lock you outdoors all night in the cold for spilling a bowl of stew. But I failed you in every other way that mattered. I let them take you from your home. I let them tear our family apart. I abandoned you. I hurt you." My voice broke. "Not with fists, but with my choices, my actions, my absence—I hurt you far deeper than my father ever hurt me. I became exactly what I swore I wouldn't be— worse than him."

"You didn't become worse," Fenrir said.

Jorg kept staring at his shoes. Red misted his eyes as he dug his fingers into his knees.

"Fenrir, please," I said. Every defense, every mask I'd worn for centuries lay shattered at my feet. "I'm done making excuses. Let me own my actions. I've harmed my children. I've hurt you. And...I'm so sorry. Please know that. I'm sorry. For all of it. For everything."

Jorg nodded slowly, his breath hitching. He cleared his throat and muttered something that sounded like a curse, turning his face towards the window.

Fenrir wiped a tear away.

"I will do better," I said, my voice steadier now. "I will be better."

"Thank you, Papa," Fenrir said. "That means more than you can know."

He pushed himself up from his seat and hugged me. He squeezed hard, nearly lifting me off the seat, and I was transported back to when he was small enough to lift, when a hug could solve any hurt. Now my son held me as if he could keep all my broken pieces together. I buried my face in his shoulder.

Rain clicked at the window as we passed under a streetlamp.

He let go and sat next to Jorg, who scrubbed roughly at his eyes with his sleeve.

"Oh, this is just perfect," Jorg said, his voice rough. "Here I am, trying to maintain a perfectly reasonable millennia-old grudge, and you have to go and..." He sighed. "I know I said that I didn't get the same treatment as Fenrir and Hel. That Odin sought to keep me to my cold fate, but..." He laughed bitterly. "Gods damn it all, it isn't exactly true."

"What are you saying?" Fenrir shifted closer to his brother, the seat creaking beneath them.

"I'm saying..." Jorg pulled in a breath, his shoulders rising with the effort. He drummed his fingers rapidly against his knee. "I'm saying that it's far easier to be angry. To paint everything in nice, simple black and white. Villain and victim." His laugh was hollow as he slumped back.

"Much harder to admit there might be...shades of gray in there."

Jorg met my eyes.

"I want to hate you," he said. "For so long, that hate was my one constancy, the fuel that drove me. The image of you standing there, letting them take me away...that kept me warm in the cold depths. I found a kind of peace in the black. But my imprisonment in the sea is not entirely your fault. Well, at least not one percent." His mouth twisted in a sardonic smile as he picked at a loose thread on his sleeve. "And believe me, I've done the math."

"Jorg, I appreciate you trying to make me feel better—and I say 'better' in the broadest sense of the word...but—"

"No." Jorg shook his head. "That day Odin took me out to the Triangle...it was only for show. Odin told me we had to put on some sort of ridiculous performance to appease Frigg, or something like that. I gave up trying to keep up with Aesir drama, but the point is..." His voice had taken on an edge of desperation, as if the words were being pulled from him against his will. "My rage and centuries of anger at Odin, at you for handing me over to him, at every god that took in breath, wouldn't allow me to see the lifeline he was handing me."

"What did you do, brother?" Fenrir placed a steadying hand on Jorg's shoulder.

Jorg stared through the rain-streaked window.

"All I heard in Odin's pleading was my fate being controlled by gods again. I decided to make my own fate." He clenched his hands into fists. "My temper flared. I was so angry. We fought. Struggled. I slipped and fell into the waves. Odin grabbed my hand and tried to pull me back into the boat. He tried to save me. But I..." His voice cracked. "I told him to go to Hel and let go of him. I sank into the sea, because I rather choose my fate, even if that meant being the ocean's than Odin's hidden monster."

"Jorg..." I whispered.

I understood all too well the comfort of feeding that rage, of holding tight to blame. And now I had to accept that in this, at least, Odin was actually, irritatingly, innocent. The bastard.

"I thought in that moment I was taking control... choosing my terms rather than submission to the hidden captivity Odin had planned. Of course, as I lost myself deeper into the cold and darkness, I regretted my decision immediately. But it was easier to make you the villain, Father, to blame you for giving me away, than face my own rage. My pride. My stubborn need to destroy myself rather than bend."

Jorg lifted his head, fresh tears in his eyes.

"I created my tragedy. I suppose the joke was on me in the end. It's like they say. Like father, like son."

My heart shattered for my son. I wanted to embrace him, to somehow heal his wounds. In his pain, I saw my reflection. The same stubborn pride, the same self-destructive defiance that had shaped both our fates. The same need to choose destruction over submission, even when it meant our own undoing.

I reached out to him. He didn't move away. I laid my hand on his shoulder. I squeezed.

The tram shrieked to a stop with a jerk. Through the fogged windows, I could make out Sigyn's building. The main door hung askew, ripped clean off its hinges.

Shit.

42

SEIDR AND SEEK

We thundered up three flights of stairs, my lungs burning with each step. The scent of curry and mothballs grew stronger as we reached Sigyn's floor.

No.

Her door hung askew, its mangled hinges barely clinging to the frame, splinters of wood scattered across the threshold.

My heart pounded as we entered the flat. I scanned the tidy living room. A faded blue sofa with neat embroidered pillows, a maple table with an unlit candle, a desk stacked with books in perfect rows. The normalcy was jarring. No signs of a struggle, no overturned furniture, nothing to match the violence done to her door.

"Sigyn?" My voice echoed through the flat.

I held my breath, praying to hear the clink of dishes, the shuffle of feet, even a distant cough. Anything to indicate Sigyn was safely home.

Only silence answered.

I marched through to the kitchen, my footsteps muffled

on bright rugs. Dishes were neatly stacked in the drying rack, counters wiped clean. The kitchen timer still ticked softly, marking minutes that suddenly seemed important.

"I'll check the bedrooms," Jorg said, voice tight. "I don't like this."

Nor did I. The normalcy seemed staged. Wrong. Like a theater set awaiting its actors.

Jorg gave me a grim nod before disappearing to search the bedrooms. His hand didn't leave the concealed blade at his hip.

Cold sweat slicked the small of my back as I returned to the living room and spotted her work badge left on the coffee table. The lanyard was twisted, as if dropped hastily. Something was very wrong.

Fenrir closed his eyes, nostrils flaring as he inhaled deeply. His shoulders tensed. I'd seen that look before, never for anything good.

"What is it?" I asked, pulse racing.

"Sigyn was here approximately half an hour ago. But there was someone else here too. I don't recognize the other scent..." His jaw clenched. "Pine, and something more primal. Not of Midgard." Fenrir's eyes flashed with concern, gold bleeding back into his usual green.

I dug my nails into my palms, the sharp sting helping focus my anger into something useful, something I could wield.

I would kill whoever touched her. Slowly.

A tingling sensation spread through my finger, followed by a burning flare that made me hiss. The ring. Odin was summoning me, the metal band growing hotter by the second until it was like molten steel against my skin. His timing was as impeccable as ever.

"Both bedrooms are empty," Jorg said, returning from

searching the back room, brow creased in concern. "Bed's still made, nothing disturbed. Why are you gripping your hand like that?"

"Odin," I said, the ring now searing enough to make my eyes water. "He better be bothering me because he has information on Sigyn. If it's anything else, I swear…"

I needed somewhere to sit before I made the journey. The last time I'd tried this standing, I'd cracked my head on a table. The lumpy couch would have to do. I sank into the cushions, ignoring my sons' concerned looks as I closed my eyes and steadied my breathing. The familiar steps came easier now. Slow inhale, hold, slower exhale. Let the body grow heavy. Let the mind grow light.

A chill coursed through me as I felt the shift begin. I was surprised by how quickly I entered the seidr realm this time, slipping into the mist as easily as I had in my pre-mortality days. My consciousness threaded through reality like a needle through silk.

I drifted through the shadowy realm, limbs swallowed by the ice. The familiar ethereal cold settled into my bones, turning my breath to frost.

A figure stood in the gloom, a dark silhouette against the swirling gray.

I marched towards Odin, each step leaving ripples in the mist, preparing an absolutely devastating set of grievances.

"You better have a good reason for—"

My voice choked off as the temperature plunged further, sharp enough to steal my breath.

Frigg materialized from the darkness, her form solidifying like ink bleeding through paper. Dread coiled in my gut as her smirk spread wider.

"Did you and Odin really think you could keep this

communication secret from me?" Frigg asked. "You are stupider than I thought."

The first flicker of fear sparked through me as implications crashed home. If she was here instead of Odin...

Gods, Odin. My stomach lurched at the thought of him at her mercy.

"What have you done to him?" My voice came out rough, raw with a panic I couldn't hide. That old, familiar ache bloomed in my chest. The need to protect him, even after everything between us.

Frigg tilted her head, though her smile held all the warmth of a serpent's.

"And I thought your first thought should be about what I've done with Sigyn."

The fear exploded into something worse. Bile rose.

"You have her."

Sweat beaded my forehead as anger replaced the fear, curling through my chest like smoke. The initial shock crystallized into something fierce and raw. Each heartbeat pumped fury through my system.

"Oh yes," she said. "I have her. She really does scream quite a lot."

Something snapped inside me. A dam broke, flooding me with a rage so pure it burned. I lunged forward with a roar, but my hands passed through nothing but mist as Frigg's laughter resonated through the void. The fury built higher, hotter, consuming everything else.

"You'll pay for whatever you've done." My pulse drowned out everything but my growing fury.

Frigg's laughter rippled through the mist again. "No, I *can't* pay," Frigg purred. "Only you can, especially in your current state."

What did that mean?

I forced a laugh, though my heart hammered against my ribs.

"What's wrong, Frigg? Still can't stand that he chose chaos over your perfect little order?"

"Are you accusing me of jealousy? Oh, you stupid boy. You think this was ever about love?" She circled me, each word dripping with disdain. "Do you really believe I cared who warmed Odin's bed? This has only ever been about protecting the realms from you. From that chaos that would burn everything to ash."

"How noble of you," I said. "Such a selfless protector."

"But now that chaos in you is gone. The great harbinger of Ragnarok, the Destroyer, reduced to nothing but meat." She leaned closer, voice soft. "Do you know how long I've waited for this? For you to finally be...temporary? For me to finally slit your throat?"

"I think you're trying to threaten me, but you're going to have to speak more plainly."

"You see, I know." Her voice held a new edge that made my skin crawl.

"Know what?"

"That you're mortal. And that changes everything."

Fucking Balder.

Because it *had* to be Balder who told her. Shit. I knew he'd break. That cowardly worm. Although, Odin also didn't have the best of track records with me and betrayal...

Regardless, if I did anything before Frigg gutted me, which she absolutely would, I wanted to murder Balder one last time, and finally wipe that sanctimonious smile off his face.

The bitter pleasure of that fantasy lasted exactly two seconds before the reality of my situation hit like a kick to the chest. Terror clawed up my throat, threatening to choke me. Without my godhood, I was just flesh and bone. Breakable. Killable. Each obstacle she'd inevitably set wasn't an inconvenience anymore. It was a death sentence. No coming back, no healing, no second chances. Just oblivion.

But she had Sigyn.

"Nothing clever to say now?" she asked. "No sharp retort?"

My hands trembled, but not from fear anymore. Something else was building in my core, something that burned darker, deadlier.

"If you want your precious Sigyn back," she continued, drinking in my reaction, "Come and get her. I have her at the Münster."

The words crystallized something inside me. Let Frigg think my mortality made me weak. Let her set her traps. Death sentence or not, I'd tear through her whole fucking army to get to Sigyn.

My fury returned like a tide, consuming every fiber I contained until it burned away the last traces of fear. I refused to give Frigg the satisfaction of seeing my terror. Sigyn was all that mattered now.

A violent, wrenching sensation seized me as she expelled me from the realm, like a boot to the sternum. All breath left my lungs in a rush of icy air.

I gasped, my eyes opening to the dim apartment. The transition back was like being dragged through broken glass, but I barely noticed through the haze of fury.

The last time I had felt this depth of wrath was when the gods had tied me to that rock, when I had sworn vengeance against them all. When I had meant it.

I clenched my fists tight enough for nails to bite my palm, anger burning my insides like molten metal. The rage was different now. Hotter, more alive.

"She has Sigyn," I spat through gritted teeth.

"Who has her?" Fenrir and Jorg exchanged an uneasy glance.

"Frigg." I ran my hands through my hair, startled by their scorching heat. "And Odin..." The words stuck. Gods, not like this. Not by her hand. "If she's killed him..." I couldn't finish the sentence, rage and grief churning within me. And the fact we needed him if we still stood any chance at breaking the curse.

My throat constricted with emotion. My wrath surged through me, sparking and spiraling like a storm. Even my eyes burnt with an old heat, pressure building behind them until my vision blurred red. My skin flushed hot enough to steam in the cool air. And suddenly, I had purpose again. A purpose as sharp and clear as a blade.

I would make Frigg regret every breath she had ever drawn.

My guts rolled and one of those odd sparks split through me, stronger than any I had experienced before. Stronger even than that jolt when I touched Sigyn in the museum. It felt like lightning shooting through my arteries.

A burst of light made me look up.

"What the—" Jorg said, taking a step back.

The candle on the table had ignited in a blaze, filling the air with vanilla and brown sugar. The flame danced unnaturally high, throwing wild shadows that seemed to writhe with my anger.

"How did that happen?" Fenrir asked, his eyes tracking between me and the flame.

My mind raced too fast to care.

"Frigg knows about my mortality."

"Then we need a different plan," Jorg said. "Every guard, every trap she's set, can kill you now. Permanently."

"Going in with just daggers against a goddess is suicide," Fenrir said.

"We don't have time for a different plan," I snapped, but softened at their concerned faces. "I know what this means. But every minute we wait..."

I found a worn satchel and flung it open, the musty scent wafting up as I stormed through the kitchen.

"Papa—"

"No. If we have any chance of saving either of them, of breaking this curse, we fight. Now," I said. "Grab the knives. *All* the knives. We are going after Frigg."

I grabbed every blade I could find—steak knives, bread knives, paring knives. My lips stretched into a vicious smile as I imagined slicing through Frigg with their serrated edges.

"This feels like a trap," Fenrir said, shifting his weight as he rummaged through other drawers for anything else that could be a weapon.

I dumped the knives into the bag, the steel clattering together. They may not kill a god, but they could do enough damage to whatever guards she'd stationed there. And right now, dealing damage was all I could think about.

"Oh, it's definitely a trap—Fenrir, no spatulas. We want to stab them, not smack them."

I slung the heavy satchel over my shoulder, the weight solid and reassuring against my back.

43

———

THE CHURCH

We walked into the Münster Cathedral, our footsteps cracking against the stone—well, most of our footsteps. The ridiculous squeak of my clogs echoed through the vaulted chamber with each step, rather ruining the ominous aesthetic I was going for.

Meandering through a gothic cathedral in near darkness was not exactly how I'd planned to spend my evening. I brushed the hilts of my daggers, their cool metal a small comfort against what I knew was a monumentally terrible decision. But what choice did we have?

"Why does she want us here?" Jorg's voice was barely a breath.

I had a suspicion.

The air hung heavy with centuries of whispered prayers, my own joining them as I scanned the forest of massive sandstone pillars.

"Gods. This is definitely a trap," Fenrir muttered, eyes darting from shadow to shadow, muscles tense beneath his flannel shirt.

"Of course it's a trap." I gripped my daggers harder,

reminding myself of the blades strapped around my calves, tucked in my sleeves, in my jacket, and the one slipped beneath my belt. Just in case this all went exceedingly sour.

Stained glass windows cast muted patterns across the worn flagstones the further we ventured into the church. Candle wax and incense blended with the stone, growing heavier with each squeaking step.

Noises erupted. Metal scraped stone. Fabric rustled. Boots thudded on flagstones.

Aesir and Vanir guards slunk out of the shadowed alcoves and from behind the sandstone columns. Their armor glinted in the weak moonlight filtering through the stained glass. Hands clenched sword hilts.

Finally.

"About time," I said, scanning the wall of drawn weapons. "I was beginning to worry you'd never show. But then, you lot always were a bit slow."

The rasp of nearly twenty swords being drawn echoed through the cathedral. One guard stepped forward, his eyes traveling slowly from my face down to my feet. His lip curled.

"Nice shoes," he smirked.

My smile sharpened to a knife's edge.

"I'll take your fashion critique more seriously when you're not dressed like a reject from a Renaissance faire." I shifted my weight, letting the clogs squeak against the stone. "Though I suppose your blood will wash out of these more easily than those inferior leather boots of yours."

A low growl came from the Vanir guard beside him, revealing a wad of spinach stuck between his front teeth. Lovely. And here I thought Freya had good taste when it came to choosing her guards. He yanked the bag of knives from Jormungand's hands, tossing it aside with a dull clank.

"Alright, now that's rather rude—"

"Don't even think about shifting," he barked, eyes darting between Fenrir and Jormungand. "You do and this entire church comes down, burying us all. But then again, we know the wolf won't risk harming innocents. And you, Loki? Well, we hear you're not exactly feeling yourself these days."

Laughter bounced off stone walls, multiplying until it seemed to come from everywhere at once. And there was at least one answer as to why Frigg chose this location instead of some remote battlefield. The church, the city, was her sanctuary from Fenrir and Jormungand. She knew we wouldn't risk killing civilians, and ourselves, for that matter. I'd give her this one.

"Please, if you want your threat to be, well, *threatening*," I said, "at least remove that entire garden of spinach lodged between your teeth. Otherwise, I'm going to have to remain underwhelmed by this whole menacing tête-à-tête."

The guard's face flushed red, his jaw clenching as he fought the urge to check his teeth. Behind me, Jorg barely suppressed a snort of laughter.

"Ever the comedian." Frigg's words cut through the tension like ice. "Though I suppose we should savor these little jests while we can. Death tends to dampen one's sense of humor."

She stepped to the edge of the balcony overlooking the nave, the glow from recessed LED spotlights casting shadows across her face, accentuating the cruel curve of her smile.

"This is where I originally planned to seal the Salvation Weave," she said, watching me with calculating eyes. "Basel...where magic and memory intertwine so perfectly.

The city holds power in its very foundations, built on centuries of your sacrifice and devotion."

"Where is Sigyn?"

"You almost understood, didn't you? Taking her to your special places, hoping to reach her through *true love's kiss.*" She traced the symbols on the stone. "But you missed the larger design. While true love might break a simple spell, where true love first ignited? That kind of place creates bindings that last eternities. I needed a nexus. Somewhere your love ran so deep it could strengthen my curse to be powerful enough to trap you."

She confirmed my every suspicion in those words. Cursing Sigyn to Basel hadn't been chance. It was choreographed. Basel was always her endgame, and she'd placed Sigyn exactly where the binding would be strongest.

"You didn't just twist our love into a weapon," I said. "You're using it to lock the curse permanently in place."

"Picture it. After the wolf and the snake were cursed, I would have dragged you and Hel from the underworld to join Sigyn here. All my pieces in place. The binding would have been exquisite. You writhing against the stone, bound by a curse powered by the gods and strengthened by your sons. Every memory of love in this city would become a permanent anchor." Her voice took on a dreamy quality. "Bound in your daughter's entrails while your faithful wife hovered above with her bowl, each drop of poison she caught corrupting her devotion further, until the curse crystallized into its true form. I've crafted the Salvation Weave so meticulously that no single act of love could break it. Not even the gods have enough power to undo my work." She clasped her hands together, almost giddy. "The perfect symmetry of it all—using your own love to seal the Salvation Weave forever."

The memory struck without warning, searing venom eating through flesh, my screams echoing off cave walls. My hands trembled before I clenched them into fists, letting rage burn away the phantom pain. Rage was safer. Rage I could use.

I stepped forward, only stopping when a guard pressed his sword against my throat. The cold steel bit into my skin, an unfortunate reminder of my mortality. This really was an inconvenient time to be corporal.

"Are you done monologuing, yet?" I strained against the blade at my throat. "Where is Sigyn? If you've hurt her—"

Frigg's smile widened.

"Oh, you mean *Ida*?"

Out of the darkness, Frigg yanked Sigyn forward. She ripped the gag from Sigyn's mouth, and oxygen rushed into her lungs with a pained gasp as Frigg dragged her near the pipe organ. Cuffs bound her wrists, the same cuffs that Frigg used to suppress Odin's magic. My heart didn't just stutter, it shattered, each beat a fresh wound.

"Unhand me, you witch!" Sigyn cried, her voice hoarse and raw. "I am not this Sigyn person! How many times do I have to tell you?"

Sigyn's hair fell wild around her face, mud caking the cable knit of her sweater. Even now, even without her memories, she fought like herself. All fury and defiance. The sight of her struggling gutted me. Five centuries of protecting her, and here she was, bound and afraid, not even knowing why I'd tear the world apart to reach her.

"You survived five hundred years of venom for her," Frigg's voice hardened. "Burned realms. Started Ragnarok. All that pain, all that chaos—" Her smile turned razor sharp. "And now she doesn't even remember who you are."

Sigyn slammed her heel down hard on Frigg's foot and

wrenched herself away. Frigg's grip loosened with a yelp of pain, and for one heartbeat, Sigyn was free. But before she could take another step, Frigg shot out her hand, seizing her wrists. Frigg jerked her backwards and forced her to her knees. Sigyn's scream tore through the vaults and ripped through my guts.

Something hot and molten crackled in my core, primordial and violent. I lurched forward—the guard's sword bit deeper. I froze, shocked by the sting and warm trickle of my blood.

Oh. Right. Mortal.

Shit.

My eyes locked with Sigyn's and terror stared back at me, not a trace of recognition in her.

"Don't worry," I called out over the growing knot in my stomach. "I'm coming for you. You'll be alright."

"Oh God, please don't make this worse," Sigyn shouted through her tears.

Well. That was certainly a knife to the gut I hadn't been expecting.

Frigg's laugh filled the buttresses.

"Even through her memory loss, she knows you're a menace. This is truly a delight for me to witness."

The guards tightened their formation until I could smell the leather of their armor. Behind me, a low growl rumbled in Fenrir's chest. Jorg shifted his weight.

"Haven't you taken enough?" I asked.

"Me?" Frigg's eyes flashed with an old hatred.

She pulled out a slender object, its pale surface gleaming in the cathedral lights. My blood ran cold staring at the mistletoe dart I had used to kill Balder.

The guards circled closer, their boots scraping against stone.

"Now, now," I said, straining to keep my voice light with the sword hard at my throat. "There's no need to be so dramatic. Why don't we talk this out in a more refined way? Like over the mutilated body of your corpse, perhaps?"

She pressed the dart against Sigyn's pulse. Sigyn's breath hitched, but that familiar strength in her eyes didn't waver.

Leather creaked as hands tightened on sword hilts. Sweat beaded at my temples.

The old god in me would've charred them to metal hunks by now.

But that god was dead.

"You killed Balder," Frigg said. "You killed him without a thought other than to annihilate the Nine Worlds. How can I allow a being who does that to live? You would see worlds burned if they slight you. Realms slaughtered like lambs to satisfy your rage. One moment of anger and you took. And it wasn't enough. It's never enough for you. You'd do it all again if someone dared to wrong you." She dug her fingers into Sigyn's arm.

The worst part was she wasn't entirely incorrect. I'd started to tear reality apart when they bound me in that cave. And when she murdered my children, I'd set the wheels of destruction turning to let it all burn. Even now, seeing Sigyn in Frigg's grasp, something dark and ancient stirred in my chest, whispering of devastation.

Kill them. Burn them. Destroy them.

"And why did I do that, Frigg?" I spat. "You made me the Destroyer you feared. You killed my sons, bound me in their entrails, and acted shocked when I became the monster in your nightmares. You want to talk about slaughtering innocents? About taking everything?" My laugh came out bitter and sharp. "You taught me that lesson first."

"But, now that you're mortal—"

"Must you keep rubbing that in?"

"We are playing a very different game now that everything has changed. Now that what I can *do* has changed."

The guards had us surrounded, their armor forming a cage of steel and leather. Behind me, Fenrir's growl vibrated through the stone floor. Jorg's fingers twitched towards weapons we no longer had.

The dart bit into Sigyn's neck. Blood welled up and traced a crimson line down her throat, soaking into her sweater. She glared up at Frigg with that familiar steel in her eyes. That defiance that was so painfully *her* it made my chest ache.

And I saw Frigg's game then, saw through all the theatrics, clear as the blood on Sigyn's neck.

Well, if that's what Frigg wanted, I'd give it to her.

I struck the guard's wrist, sending the sword at my throat clattering across the red sandstone floor. Before they could react, I rammed my shoulder into the nearest guard, a lanky Vanir whose armor rattled like it was two sizes too big. He stumbled into his companion, a stocky warrior with a face that suggested his mother might've been intimate with a troll. Their armor clanked as they lurched apart. The gap was barely wide enough, but I seized my chance and bolted for the spiral stairs leading to the organ loft.

Three steps in, pain exploded in my side. A Vanir guard's sword pommel—wielded by what appeared to be a walking mountain with braided, red hair—slammed into me. Air whooshed from my lungs. I staggered, gasping for air, gulping for breath, ribs screaming. My legs wobbled as I fought to stay upright.

Frigg dragged Sigyn upright by her hair and yanked her through a heavy wooden door. Sigyn's shrieks bounced off the high ceilings, growing fainter as they disappeared into the bowels of the cathedral.

I clenched my daggers, sweat slicking my palms.

A blade whistled past my right ear. I dropped, stone scraping my knees raw through my trousers. With a forward thrust, I jammed my blade into a Vanir's thigh. I loved how his cry choked on agony as he crumpled, clutching his spurting wound.

I vaulted over his writhing and, frankly, whining form. Gods. It was just a leg. He had another one.

Ten Vanir guards rushed towards us between a grove of enormous pillars, a delightful mix of veterans with scars and fresh-faced recruits who looked like they'd rather be anywhere else. I weaved between them, their armor scraping against the stone as I slashed and stabbed.

A roar tore out of Fenrir's throat as he barreled into two Aesir guards. They flew like rag dolls, crashing into the medieval oak pews with a crunch of wood and metal.

A sword sliced across my shoulder, parting flesh, splattering the red sandstone with blood. Hot pain flared. Crimson soaked into my shirt, really bringing out the rainbow laser beams shooting from the kitten's tiny paws.

"Congratulations. Now you've ruined my least favorite shirt." I spun, slashing deep into the Vanir guard's arm. She shrieked as her sword clattered down. The stench of spilled blood mingled with the incense and candle wax.

How I missed this! Nothing quite like a little desecration to get the blood pumping.

Three Aesir guards surrounded Jorg—all built like oxen and about as clever—as he struggled against a wall of stained glass.

"Jorg!" I leapt towards him, my daggers blurring as I deflected a flurry of strikes. I was actually a little proud of how well I could manage without my element, as if a strength I'd forgotten I possessed punched its way through my muscles and sinew.

He raced to a pillar. Sparks flew as steel met steel, but still they kept coming out of every nook and cranny.

I sank my dagger into a guard's hamstring, turned, and wedged the blade between the weak point in his armor and thrust up into his armpit.

Sigyn's screams echoed through corridors. The guards' blood on my blade wasn't enough anymore. Not while she was suffering somewhere in this maze of stone and shadow.

Jorg slammed his shoulder against one of the red sandstone pillars supporting the Gothic vaults. Grime shook loose as the column trembled, medieval carvings spiderwebbing with cracks. Above, the pointed arches creaked. Chunks of masonry broke free where pillar met vault, raining down as the centuries-old joints separated.

"Jorg, what are you doing?" Fenrir asked, kicking a Vanir guard into the baptismal fount with a splash. "The whole thing will collapse."

"It's not a load bearing pillar, just there to hold up the decorative arches," he shouted back, his voice strained as he struck the pillar again. "Figured I'd let gravity do the work and take out the entire group."

The pillar groaned, leaning further with each blow from Jorg's shoulder. The arches spanning to the adjacent pillars buckled and cracked, sending more debris clattering to the floor. The handful of remaining guards looked up, their eyes widening with an endearing look of horror as they took steps backwards. As if that would save them.

"I think this is a bad idea," Fenrir said.

The stone column swayed.

"I believe I agree with Fenrir, disappointingly," I said.

"Don't worry about it."

The pillar tipped past its fulcrum. A rumble followed. The ground shook. The multi-ton pillar toppled like a felled giant, sending rows of wooden chairs flying like scattered matchsticks. Several guards disappeared under the avalanche of stone and splintering wood, their screams cut short as chairs and masonry crushed them. So much for sanctuary.

Shockwaves rippled across the cathedral floor, the vibrations rattling my teeth.

The stained glass windows shattered, exploding multi-colored shards over our shoulders. I squeezed my eyes shut and ducked. Tiny slivers pelted my back and arms.

Clouds of plaster dust and pulverized rock choked the air, clogging my lungs. Through the haze, I could make out chairs skidding across the flagstones, some still spinning from the impact. One had caught a guard in the chest, pinning him against another pillar. That was definitely a wrong place, wrong time kind of situation.

"That stopped them," Jorg panted, a hint of pride in his voice. "You're welcome."

Dismay filled Fenrir's features as he stared through the dust at the contorted limbs jutting out from beneath the fallen pillar and scattered chairs. The flagstones darkened as pools of blood crept across their surface.

"You could have just blocked their path with the pillar." Dust clung to Fenrir's eyelashes and hair. "Not crush them."

Jorg and I shared a look. Poor Fenrir wasn't cut out for this sort of work.

Before I could comfort Fenrir, movement caught my eye. Through the settling dust, the surviving guards emerged from the rubble. Three pulled themselves up, shaking off debris and drawing weapons while two more slipped from the alcoves, their armor coated in plaster dust. The temporary reprieve was over, and we were running out of pillars to drop on them.

"We need to move," I said. "Now."

Sigyn's muffled cries pierced through the haze, the sound cutting through me like a knife. A guard shouted commands. We picked our way over the broken masonry, careful not to slip on the blood-slicked stone.

"Up there!" Fenrir pointed towards a narrow spiral staircase that vanished into shadows. "That's where her cries are coming from."

"Where does that lead?" Jorg asked.

Cold dread settled in my stomach, followed by annoyance. She chose the western tower to exhaust me even further from climbing a thousand steps up the staircase before what she had planned next.

I bolted up the narrow sandstone stairwell, taking the worn steps two at a time. I grazed rough walls for balance, centuries of grit coating my palms. Fenrir's labored breaths and Jorg's clanking sword echoed in the tight spiral, the sound amplified by stone all around us.

The spiral staircase opened onto a solid door. Light leaked through cracks in the thick timber. Sigyn's cry jolted my heart. I slammed my good shoulder into the weathered wood of the door, biting back a grunt as pain shot through me.

The iron hinges groaned but held.

"Together!" I backed against the curved wall. Fenrir and Jorg joined, faces set. We braced, muscles tensing.

"On three," I said. "One...two...three!"

We charged, slamming into the door. Wood splintered, hinges shrieking. I burst into the tower chamber, stumbling on the uneven surface. The massive bell loomed above, the bronze surface catching what little light passed through the tower's openings.

An invisible force slammed the shattered door back.

No.

"Father!" Jorg's voice rumbled through the barrier, followed by the thud of fists against an inch of oak.

I attacked the door's edges, searching desperately for any weakness in the magic. A crimson aura pulsed around the frame, crackling with energy. Frigg's magic, unmistakable and infuriating. My fingers burned where they touched the barrier.

"Dammit!" I slammed my fists against the magic.

Of course she'd separate us. This was her game all along. Sigyn as bait. My children locked away, leaving me alone and mortal to face what came next. I'd known it walking in, hadn't I? Some part of me had always known exactly what she wanted.

"Took you long enough," Frigg said. "You certainly are slower in your mortal state."

I turned, forcing steel into my spine.

Frigg stood near one of the massive bells, its shadow falling across her face. The silver cord in her hands writhed with magic as she bound Sigyn against a heavy wooden beam. Two guards emerged from the shadows behind her, hands on their weapons.

I recognized that type of cord she wrapped around Sigyn's wrists. The same kind of unbreakable binding the Dwarves had forged to chain Fenrir.

"Sigyn, it will all be—"

"Alright?" Frigg finished, laughter beneath the words. The mistletoe dart glinted in her grip. "I suppose you aren't completely wrong about that, because I'm taking no more chances with you, Liesmith."

At her nod, the guards moved. The burly one with the braided beard seized my arms, pinning them behind my back while his wiry companion moved his nimble fingers over my waist and legs.

"Looking for something specific?" I asked as daggers clattered to the floor, followed by knives from my sleeves and blades from the straps around my calves.

His fingers burrowed into my coat pockets, skimmed across my arms, but when he pulled *Laevateinn* from the sheath at my hip, Frigg's sharp intake of breath made my heart stop.

Her eyes locked onto the blade, a knowing smile curving her lips as she took it from the guard.

Fuck.

44

———

MISTLETOE AND STEEL

"Oh, you always were full of tricks, but this?" Frigg held *Laevateinn* up to catch the light. "What a delightful surprise. You brought me something better than I could have ever hoped for. How thoughtful."

Shit. Fuck. Damn. Shit.

"What, that old thing?" I asked, trying to ignore the guard's hands roughly patting down my legs. Again. "Please. I only keep it around to spread butter. If you're really in the market, may I recommend one with rubies? Something gaudy is more your style."

She pressed the mistletoe dart's tip against my blade.

"I see Odin's plan now. How you two intended to break the Salvation Weave. Cute." She dragged the dart's point across *Laevateinn's* surface, metal screaming against mistletoe as she etched runes. Each stroke burned new runes into the steel, leaving trails of light that pulsed.

Huh. Interesting. I didn't realize that was possible with *Laevateinn...*

My stomach twisted into knots as she worked, transforming my dagger into her own conduit with a few simple scratches. The fresh runes blazed brighter, carving paths for her magic to flow.

I shoved away the memory of Odin yelling at me to learn all of *Laevateinn's* powers once we discovered it was more *wand* than dagger.

Frigg flicked the blade towards a wooden beam. The runes flared, and the timber exploded in a shower of splinters. Fragments peppered the floor around us as dust rained down from the rafters. Scorched wood filled the air, minging with the metallic tang of magic.

Yeah. Definitely could never tell him about this.

"Wonderful," she said, examining the smoking remains with bright eyes. "A wand gives me real power, not like those cumbersome rune tiles always spilling from my pouch. Now I can wield magic freely, without being bound to those stones. This is a true gift."

The dagger's light pulsed with each word, like a heartbeat.

"Dwarven steel can kill anything that bleeds. But fused with my magic? It can do so much more," she said. "You've slipped every curse, broken every binding, cheated every death. But now?" Her smile widened. "Tonight, you'll draw your last breath. Then I'll hunt down your monstrous offspring. And I won't just kill them." She twisted the blade, its runes flaring white-hot. "I'll erase them. No afterlife. No rebirth. Gone, as if they never existed."

The guard's calloused fingers made another pass over my torso as Frigg's gaze slid to Sigyn. Terror seized me.

"Starting with her." She pointed the glowing blade at Sigyn. "You'll watch as I strip away her soul, leaving nothing but an empty shell. Then it's your turn, Loki. Once I've erased your essence, I'll take your lifeless head to Skadi."

The runes pulsed faster, hungrier. Each beat matched my racing heart, my terrifyingly mortal heart. One wrong move, one slip, and it would all end. No coming back. No tricks. Just oblivion for me and for everyone I loved.

But the rage...gods, the rage still burned as hot as it had when I was immortal.

"You will not touch my wife," I said. "You will not touch my family."

A smile slithered across her face.

"*You will not touch my family*," she mocked, feigning my voice. "Your command carries as much punch as a dying mouse's squeaks from a trap." She looked at the guards, eyes sharp with distrust. "Check him again. Thoroughly. Our Liesmith always has a trick or two hidden away."

The guards raked their hands down my arms and torso. The burly one's grip tightened while his wiry partner continued his search with renewed determination.

I swept my gaze over Sigyn's trembling form, my heart clenching as she met my eyes for a breath. The cord bit into her flesh, red marks forming where she strained against the wooden beam.

"This is between you and me, Frigg," I said, acutely aware of the guards' boots crunching dirt behind me. Every step bringing them closer to finding that last knife. "Leave Sigyn out of this. Leave my children out of this. Take me. I'm all you really want."

Frigg's smile deepened, hollowing her cheeks. The night air whispered through arched windows, carrying with it frost and diesel and the promise of a long, *long* fall.

"Leave her out of it?" Frigg stroked Sigyn's cheek, her long nails leaving faint red lines on her skin. "Poor Loki. Even Odin made that mistake, imagining he was able to hide her in Alfheim. As if one could outrun prophecy." Her smile turned cruel. "Though I must admit, Falael was a clever choice for her protector. Such noble deeds. Dull as dishwater, of course, but I suppose that was the point."

I fought back a grimace because, damn her, she wasn't wrong. The Elf had been as exciting as a glass of lukewarm milk, even with sharp cheekbones.

"She was always going to end up here. Tonight. With me. No matter how many tried to change her fate."

The guard scrabbled his hands along my trousers again. My heart slammed as his fingers grazed my waist.

"I would usually have to pay several gold coins for such intimate service," I said, fighting to keep my voice light despite the steak knife burning against my skin beneath my belt.

He reached for my belt, creeping closer towards the only blade that mattered now. Sweat trickled down my temple and I absolutely loathed the sensation. My jaw tightened, mind racing through a dozen scenarios, each ending with me dead.

I could break his neck...and then Frigg rams the blade in Sigyn's neck...not an option.

The guard brushed the worn leather of my belt—
BONG!

The bell's sound crashed over us. The floor shuddered beneath our feet, tremors racing through the red sandstone walls. Centuries-old oak beams creaked overhead. Frigg's face contorted in pain as she refused to release her grasp on my dagger or the mistletoe. The guards covered their ears, letting me go.

And I seized the moment.

I found the slender blade in the sheath sewn into the back of my belt. I slid it into my sleeve, its sharp tip pressing my forearm.

BONG! BONG! BONG!

The bell continued to clang as the guards regained their composure. His hands returned to my belt, probing the leather. Finding nothing, he grunted and stepped back.

"Finished, my queen," the guard said as the ninth toll faded.

I exhaled.

Frigg shook her head slightly, as if to clear it, then straightened.

"Good." She held up *Laevateinn*, its runes pulsing and hungry. "Go deal with the wolf and the serpent, but do not kill them. Their ending must come from this blade, just like their father's. I want no interruptions for what comes next."

The guards nodded, scooping up my pile of confiscated weapons.

The pounding at the door intensified, Fenrir and Jorg's muffled shouts growing frantic. Wood groaned under their fists and shoulders.

The guards wrenched the heavy door open. Fenrir charged—and bounced off the invisible barrier like a stone from steel. The air shimmered where he struck, magic rippling like heat waves. Jorg clawed at the barrier, unable to breach the threshold.

The guards pushed through, and screams erupted from the stairwell.

I started to run to help them—

"Move towards that door, and I'll ram this steel into Sigyn's neck."

I stopped, hatred burning in me until my breath was nearly gone. All these centuries, and still she knew exactly how to trap me. Frigg slipped the mistletoe dart into the leather holder at her hip, and twirled *Laevateinn*, its newly etched runes glowing with purpose.

And a cold dread settled in my stomach.

I saw where this led. Where it had always been leading. Another choice. Another sacrifice. Another way to break me.

"So," I choked out, throat constricting around words I didn't want to say. "I take it you're only going through all these theatrics because you want to make a deal with me now I'm mortal? A sacrifice—my life for Sigyn's? For my children's? That seems like a fair deal. I can make it easy for you."

Sigyn's breath hitched, a soft "No" escaping her lips.

Frigg chuckled as she approached.

"Sacrifice." She twirled *Laevateinn* faster between her fingers, the blade singing as it cut through the air. "And I thought I made my intentions clear when I said I am ending you all."

She rammed the dagger into my armpit with a crunch.

White-hot pain exploded. I bit back a scream, tasting copper as my teeth tore into my cheek. Each pulse of those runes felt like they were eating me from the inside out. She wanted me to suffer first. Wanted me to feel every second of my erasure before she ended it.

"Just let it be me," I pushed out.

"Tell me how. How can it only be you? How can it only be you when you leap off every gallows I put you on?" she snarled, twisting the steel. Fire lanced through me. "That's the problem with sacrifice. You always find a way to survive it, to turn it to your advantage. But this time, there will be no escape, no clever bargain. This isn't sacrifice—it's extinction."

She yanked the blade out with a squelch. Blood gushed out of the wound, running down my arm and dripping from my fingertips.

My legs buckled. I fell to my knees, floorboards digging into my kneecaps. The hidden knife pressed against my arm. I reached for it—

She grabbed my hair, wrenching my head back, drawing a strangled gasp from my lips. Frigg forced me to look at her, her eyes burning with hatred.

"I am going to kill you slowly, agonizingly," she hissed, her face inches from mine. "And right at the end, when there is still enough breath in your lungs, I will destroy Sigyn."

She let me go and drove the dagger into my left thigh. She yanked it out of my muscle and a howl ripped from my throat, mingling with Sigyn's scream. The pain blazed, stealing my vision for shuddering seconds.

"How I've waited for this." She dragged the blade along my collarbone, leaving a thin line of fire.

I forced myself to focus on her through the haze of pain. I crept my fingers towards my sleeve, where my last blade waited, inching forward.

"How I've starved," she said. The steel bit my cheek. Blood trickled down. "And now it's finally over."

She carved down my other arm, cold edge slicing flesh. I clenched my jaw, teeth grinding against a groan. I stretched for the steak knife hidden in my cuff, every movement pulling at the fresh wounds.

Cool metal brushed my fingertips, and Frigg's grip clamped my shoulder. She yanked me forward, throwing me off balance, her fingers digging into the gash she'd carved.

She raised the dagger, aiming at my chest.

And in that heartbeat, I saw my one chance.

I twisted, agony ripping through the torn muscle of my arm, and let the knife slide from my sleeve into my palm. Each movement sent fire through the fresh cuts, but I closed around the hilt. I drove it upward through the wall of pain. Metal crunched into Frigg's shoulder bone as I plunged it deeper.

"You little shit!" Frigg snarled, face twisting with rage and disbelief.

She staggered back, clutching her wounded shoulder. Blood seeped between her fingers, soaking her tunic. Seeing her immortal blood spilling sent a thrill through me, even if the wound wouldn't last.

I struggled to my feet, using the massive bell frame for support.

I smiled.

"One of those tricks you were oh so concerned about," I rasped, tasting copper with each word.

She lunged, steel flashing. I pivoted, wounds screaming, and dodged. *Laevateinn* grazed my neck, air rushing past my ear.

Frigg's momentum carried her forward. As she spun to face me again, I raised my blade. Our weapons clanged, my steel knife clashing against *Laevateinn* in her grip. The impact reverberated up my arm, nearly numbing my fingers. Each blow shook my body, her weapon unnaturally strong and sharp thanks to her new runes.

Sweat stung my eyes as I ducked and weaved, the musty tower air filling each gasp. Soles thudded against wood. Blades whistled. I parried Frigg's strikes, muscles screaming, bones jarring.

My blade found flesh again. I grinned, loving how she cried in pain.

But before I could take a slice through her larynx, the wound on her collarbone sealed itself, leaving only a faint line.

Damn her immortality. That was the problem of not

having a decent Dwarven steel blade. My knife was no more threatening to her than a pointed stick. I was capable of only maiming her, and therefore, only pissing her off further. Wonderful. Excellent.

Her dagger sliced my forearm. Cold burned. Blood steamed.

Frigg's next strike sent me stumbling backwards towards the door leading to the roof. Wood splintered as she slammed my back into it. Hinges shrieked, giving way. We tumbled onto the cathedral's steep roof, sliding down the slick diamond-patterned tiles before I caught myself on a raised ridge where two sections met.

The Rhine churned past the Münsterplatz, and moonlight flooded my vision as I fought to keep my footing on the sharply angled surface. My shoes skidded for grip on the glazed tiles as I scrambled up the slope. If I slipped I'd slide straight off the edge and end up a lovely splat on the cobblestones below.

"You cursed Sigyn," I snarled between ragged breaths, blocking her strike. My blade grated against the cross. "You've orchestrated every tragedy in my life. In the lives of those I love."

"And I'd do it all again," she said. "Because you are a mistake."

Her blade slashed. I dodged backwards, shoes sliding on the cathedral's steep pitch. Below me, diamond-patterned tiles in red and green created a maze of angles and valleys, each section a deadly slope towards the edge. Wonderful.

"It was you. Every threat, every attack on my children in the Ironwood. When they were just trying to live in peace. When they never hurt anyone. It was all you."

We fought along the edge, wind howling around the

Gothic spire. My foot struck a loose tile, and it fell away, my heart lurching as I caught myself inches from the drop.

"It was impossible for them to simply 'live in peace,' Loki. Yggdrasil showed what they would become." Her blade kissed my ear, severing hair. "But Odin kept searching for alternatives. For loopholes. As if prophecy were negotiable. He thought hiding them would be enough. Someone had to do what he wouldn't. What he kept refusing to see—they were never children. They were always monsters waiting to feast on us."

Her blade flashed. "And now his weakness, his constant choosing of you over what must be done...it's finally cost him everything. His life included."

A void opened in my chest, endless and cold. The world tilted sideways as my mind refused to process her words.

"Odin's dead?"

She smiled.

"The poison works slowly. He might have a few breaths left in him." She leaned closer, her words honeyed. "I gave him the chance, you know. Tell me if you're mortal, or choose death. He surprised me, I'll admit." Her smile widened. "The man who once betrayed you out of fear of death? This time he didn't even hesitate before choosing the poison."

The words shattered through the fortress I'd built around my heart. For years I'd nurtured my hatred, telling myself it had killed the love. That his betrayal had burned everything between us to ash. But now panic seized me, wild and primal, and I knew...I knew with sickening clarity that I'd been lying to myself all along. Without him, we couldn't break the curse, but that thought felt hollow, distant, compared to the raw agony of knowing he was dying alone, having finally become the man I'd always believed he could be.

Please don't die...

"You're lying," I said. "This is another trick."

Don't die believing I hated you. Not when I never managed to, not really.

The prayer rose unbidden from that secret place where I'd buried everything soft, everything vulnerable, everything that still ached for him. I hated myself for it. Hated that after everything—after all the years of practiced indifference—losing him would still tear me open like this.

The raw honesty of my reaction terrified me.

Don't leave me...

"Oh, Loki." She brushed the dagger's tip along my jaw. "Always looking for the lie, the scheme, the trap. But sometimes the truth is so much more satisfying. Odin is drowning in his own fluids because of you."

Anger and sorrow tangled in my depths. At her, at myself. I slammed into her, sending us skidding across the tiles. She kicked me loose, and I rolled, catching myself on a ridge, my heart as raw as my scratched palms.

"You sick fuck," I snarled, voice thick with tears I refused to acknowledge. The wind gusted, and I couldn't tell which hurt more—losing our last hope of breaking the curse, or finally admitting to myself that I'd never stopped loving him.

Focus. Calculate. Move.

I forced the grief down deep where it wouldn't suffocate me. Later. I would break later. Right now I needed distance between us, needed to think past the agony in my heart. I tracked her movement across the roof, measuring the space between us with each step.

"I should have killed him eons ago to protect Asgard

from your chaos," Frigg said, advancing along the narrow ridge. I retreated along the sharp decline, mind racing through escape routes even as I fell back on old habits.

Deflect. Distract. Survive.

"While you flitted around Asgard wreaking havoc. That feast where you turned all the mead into snakes was just spite."

"The cups needed more excitement." I grinned at the memory. "And everyone learned valuable lessons about checking their drinks."

"Almost starting multiple wars with Jotunheim." She gained the better position, forcing me to scramble down to a lower section, gripping an ornate cross.

"They were asking for it with those ice sculptures. Absolutely tasteless." I ducked as her blade whistled overhead. "And technically, we got excellent trade relations out of that whole mess—"

She charged down the incline, cutting off my diplomatic assessment. I dove aside, rolling across the tiles. My shoulder struck the raised edge between sections, sending loose tiles clattering off the roof.

"Making bad deals with the Dwarves—"

"You got Mjolnir out of that!" I called up, genuinely offended. "Thor hasn't stopped swooning over it for centuries. Really, you should be thanking me—"

"Almost losing us Freya and the sun and moon over a wall—"

"As I recall, you did agree to that one—" I dodged another swing.

She lunged, forcing me down the slick tiles until I found a stone ridge, shoes scraping.

"All I recall is how each of your choices brought us closer to ruin," she said. "Every step you took, every bond you formed, weakened the barriers I fought to maintain. Each time I had to step in, had to sacrifice more to keep the realms from burning."

I laughed, ignoring the spike of pain in my chest. Although my cracked rib didn't hurt as much as it had minutes earlier.

"Your sacrifices? Is that what you call murdering my children in that cave?" Bile scorched my throat, memories searing behind my eyes.

Something cracked in Frigg's face, grief or madness, I couldn't tell.

"You think I wanted that?" she asked. "They were innocents. Babies. Do you know what it cost me? I am a goddess of family, of motherhood—" Her breath hitched. "But I saw what was coming. I saw what your love would unleash. Two souls or millions, Loki. That was the choice. That was always the choice." Her eyes burned with tears she wouldn't let fall. "But you couldn't stay away from her, could you? Even when the prophecy was clear. Even when they warned you. And so I had to become the monster, had to stain my hands with infant blood, because someone had to pay the price of your defiance. This is why I hate you."

Her blade flashed. I parried, the force sending me sliding until I seized a stone spire, its edges biting into my palm as I pulled myself up.

Rage and grief tore through me, blurring my vision with tears and fury.

"Don't you dare." I gained the high ground where the diamond patterns met. "Don't you dare try to justify murdering Narfi and Narvi. I was there. I saw you. They were hours old. Still wrapped in their birthing blankets." My voice cracked. "They had barely opened their eyes."

The memory of their lifeless bodies, so small and

perfect, flashed before me. How their tiny fingers had still been curled into fists. The way they'd looked as if they were only sleeping, nestled together like they'd been in the womb. My hands trembled, knuckles white around the hilt of my blade, as I stared down at her across the slope.

"You talk of prophecies and millions saved, but all I see is a coward who couldn't bear to challenge fate itself," I said. "You had a choice, Frigg. You could have fought alongside us, helped us find another way. Instead, you chose the blade in the dark. The knife in the cradle." The pain in my body had nothing to do with my physical wounds. It was an old agony, as fresh now as the day I'd lost them. "Some goddess of family you are. How many prayers for safe births have you answered? How many mothers called your name in their labor pains? Did you think of them when you murdered my sons? Did you bless their tiny heads before you—" My words bled with five centuries of grief.

"I held them first," Frigg whispered, and something in her voice made my tears rush harder. "I blessed them, yes. Kissed their foreheads. And then I did what had to be done, because your chaos had already damned them." Her eyes hardened even as tears finally spilled down her cheeks. "The price had to be paid, Loki. If not by them, then by all the worlds." Her voice turned to ice. "And now I'll finish what I started that night. The tree demands all of you."

Magic, cold and merciless, coiled around my body and squeezed. The pressure forced air from my lungs, making me gasp and my ribs creak.

Her power hurled me across the sharp incline. I slammed against a gargoyle jutting from where two slanted sections met. Stone raked fire across my back, tearing fabric and flesh.

Another surge sent me tumbling down the incline. I

scrabbled across glazed tiles as I picked up speed until I grasped the gargoyle's mouth at the edge. Stone fangs bit deep as I jerked to a stop, legs swinging over the square. My knife slipped free, vanishing into darkness.

Shit.

I clung to the weathered stone, each gust threatening to tear me loose.

Frigg approached along the narrow ridge, holding the dagger, my blood glistening on its tip. My stomach churned at the scent of my mortality.

"No! Please, don't hurt him!" Sigyn screamed. She huddled in the tower, and the sight of her there, terrified and lost, knowing I would die a stranger to her...It was a special kind of hell I hadn't known existed.

My grip slipped again. Fresh panic surged as I scrambled to regain my hold, muscles burning against rough stone.

I locked my eyes onto Sigyn's across the rooftop.

"I know you don't remember me," I called to her, voice raw with everything I needed her to understand. "She's taken your memories, but she can't take your heart. You are Sigyn, Goddess of Fidelity." My fingers slipped further, but I had to finish. Had to make her understand. "You found me in my darkness five hundred years ago and you loved me until I remembered how to love myself." Tears burned in my eyes. "You are everything that's good in this world, everything I never deserved. And knowing you, loving you, has been worth every moment of pain."

Tears carved trails down Sigyn's dirt-smudged cheeks.

"I will always love you," I whispered hoarsely, the words swallowed by the wind.

At least our last words would be ones of love.

"How disgusting," Frigg sneered.

Frigg's boots crunched on loose tiles as she reached me.

She yanked me from the gargoyle, dangling me over the precipice.

Basel spun below, street lamps blurring into a nauseating swirl.

I stared into her eyes, letting her see every ounce of hatred I'd cultivated over centuries. Let her see the father whose children she murdered, the husband whose wife she'd stolen, the god whose family she'd torn apart piece by bloody piece. Let her see what she'd become. The woman who would poison the man she once loved, who would choose prophecy over mercy until there was nothing left of either of us but this moment. I wanted her to remember this. To remember that even at the end, she hadn't broken me.

"If only I could have done this earlier," she said, dangling me further over the edge. "I would have saved everyone the pain caused by your wretched existence. I could have saved myself."

She pressed the dagger to my chest, its cold energy seeping into my core as wind howled around the spires.

"You could have chosen mercy. This suffering was not inevitable."

"It was always inevitable."

The dagger pressed harder. My heartbeat thundered, each pulse potentially the last. But I wouldn't give her the satisfaction of fear, even though inside I was screaming.

A growl shattered the night air.

"NO!"

Jorg erupted from the tower, charging across the steep pitch. His eyes blazed as he launched from the higher ground.

The impact sent us sprawling. As Frigg's grip loosened, I slammed onto the slick tiles and slid down the sharp incline. For one terrifying moment, I skidded towards the edge where green tiles met empty air.

Fenrir shot out his hand, catching my sleeve before I slid over. With a grunt, he hauled me back onto the ridge where roof sections met.

Frigg leapt up and charged us, *Laevateinn's* runes blazing in her grip as magic crackled down the blade.

45

WRATH

"How did you get through that damn door?" Frigg snarled, charging us along the ridge. Sweat gleamed on her face as wind whipped her hair.

Jorg's laugh cut sharp and mocking from near the tower wall. My heart pounded at the sound, and relief trickled down my spine.

"Next time, make your magic better. That was a joke of a spell."

A scream ripped from Frigg's throat. She pivoted as Jorg pounced. He caught her wrist, but she seized his arm and wrenched. Bone snapped. My stomach churned as Jorg howled, his limb twisted nearly from its socket.

Magic sparked along her fingers.

"You want a better spell? How about this?"

Energy burst from the dagger, slamming Jorg into a gargoyle. He crumpled, clutching his mangled arm, and my world narrowed to the sight of my son's blood on stone.

Horror surged through me as I staggered towards him. Frigg spun back, murder in her eyes. She raised *Laevateinn*, runes blazing.

"ENOUGH!" Fenrir's roar shook the air as he leapt from above, crashing into her. The dagger spun from her grip, skittering down the pitch. Her pouch spilled, scattering her runes across the tiles. I was especially glad to see that blood-marked hex stone tumble between the roof's gaps.

She kicked Fenrir away and lunged for the dagger, but froze when his eyes flashed molten gold—a warning from the wolf within. His sturdy frame blocked the path to her weapon, and fear flickered across her face at the reminder of what he could become. With *Laevateinn* now beyond reach and the threat of the great wolf looming, she scrambled for her runes instead. She slid on the steep pitch, desperately grabbing at the skittering tiles. Without either the dagger or her runes, she'd be powerless. At least she had a chance of snatching some stones before they all fell through the gaps.

And this bought us extra seconds.

I lurched towards Jorg's crumpled form by the gargoyle. Behind me, Fenrir ran to Sigyn with the dagger, fumbling with her chains. The bonds held.

Fear stabbed through me at Jorg's broken state. His arm twisted past his shoulder, skin purpling. Blood trickled from where he'd struck the stone.

I cradled his head, examining the gash above his eye.

"Stay with me." Fear choked my words as I checked for other wounds.

Jorg's eyes fluttered open, a weak smile forming.

"You do realize I'm not dying?" he grunted.

"A hit like you took from a goddess..."

"You're always so dramatic," he cut me off, though pain threaded his voice. "It's just a broken arm. And the headache will clear in time. Give me a second..."

He inhaled deeply, steadying himself against the stone. Then he traced intricate patterns with his good hand. Soft blue light wove around his injury like pale threads, pulsing in time with his heartbeat.

Magic crackled across my skin. The hairs on my neck rose as a sharp crack echoed as bone snapped back into place. Jorg flinched, a curse hissing through clenched teeth, but relief washed over him as the bone aligned. Sweat beaded on his forehead, but his eyes gleamed with satisfaction.

"Incredible," I breathed, as the last wisps of healing magic faded. "I can't even heal a scraped knee."

He flexed his arm, testing the repair. "Not bad, eh?" Pain still shadowed his grin, but there was pride there too.

I pulled him up, steadying him. "Can you run?" I watched Frigg racing towards us, clutching two rune tiles she somehow managed to salvage, and the mistletoe dart I did not wish to experience. Fury twisted her face, and magic crackled around her like lightning.

Gods. Would she ever give up?

"Let's go," he said.

We bolted across the slick tiles. My heart pounded with each step, waiting for the whistle of Frigg's magic at our backs.

Inside the tower, Fenrir guarded Sigyn, muscles tensed as he gripped *Laevateinn*. The weapon hummed in his grip.

"I have no idea how to use this thing," he said. "But I know enough that this should do the trick with the magic she carved into it."

"Thank you," Sigyn said softly, her eyes finding mine. "For not dying up there. What you said..." She swallowed hard, something flickering behind her eyes. "About light in the darkness. It felt true."

My heart twisted. Even as Ida, she still saw right through

me. "Well, I've always had a flair for dramatic speeches while dangling from heights," I said.

Jorg studied the glowing runes on Sigyn's chains, his eyes narrowing at the complex patterns of binding magic. Symbols pulsed with a green light against the iron.

"Give me *Laevateinn*," I said, reaching for the dagger. "I can break the chains—"

"Please, we'd be here all night." Jorg took the blade from Fenrir before I could grab it.

"I've been using that dagger longer than you've been alive," I said, more than slightly offended.

"Yes, and you still don't know half of what it can do, obviously." Jorg traced the blade through the air, speaking words that made the runes on *Laevateinn* flash. The chains shattered like glass.

Thin cuffs still bound Sigyn's wrists, their runes blocking her magic, but she was free. Her eyes met mine again, still clouded with confusion but bright with determination.

"Here," Jorg said, flipping *Laevateinn* back to me. "Try studying its capabilities next time instead of just stabbing things."

"Show-off," I muttered, grasping both the dagger and Sigyn's hand as we ran. Her fingers intertwined with mine instinctively, as if some part of her remembered.

We ran through the tower door.

A blast of magic sizzled the air, missing our heads. Ozone and burning hair filled my nostrils.

At least one rune down, one more to go.

We ran down the winding stone steps, centuries of worn grooves trying to trip our feet. Frigg's enraged screams echoed behind us while we spiraled downwards, the sound seeming to come from everywhere at once. Another surge of magic seared past, scorching my skin before exploding against the wall in a shower of sparks and stone.

Thank gods. The last rune gone. Now she was without magic.

We hit the cathedral's main floor, racing past the toppled over chairs and the few remaining guards who tried to snatch us. Jorg wrenched open the massive doors. The frigid night air slammed into us when we burst out of the cathedral into a maze of narrow medieval streets. White-washed buildings with deep red trim and green shutters pressed close on either side, our feet hammering pavement.

We bolted towards the Rhine, twisting through streets barely wide enough for two people. Shop windows glowed amber in the night. We had no thought other than to run. To get away as far as we could.

Cars roared past as we emerged onto wider streets, headlights slicing the darkness. We swerved around them, tires screeching and horns blaring. The stench of burning rubber choked the air.

"Did we lose her?" Fenrir gasped as we veered onto an avenue.

Rubber squealed against asphalt to our left, too close. Then again, closer.

"Keep running," I huffed. "Keep running until we lose her."

As we hit The Middle Bridge, traffic thickened. Swiss flags and Basel's cantonal banners snapped in the wind above us as we weaved between cars, their engines growling and exhausts spewing fumes that made our eyes water. Tram lines glinted in the pavement as drivers shouted curses in three languages. The Rhine surged beneath the massive stone arches, its dark waters glinting.

A piercing screech of brakes shattered the air. Ahead of

us, a sedan swerved violently as its driver's face contorted in terror, eyes fixed on something behind us. Tires smoked against the wet pavement as more drivers saw it, too. Their expressions morphed from confusion to fear. Metal screamed against metal as cars collided in a chain reaction. One vehicle spun sideways, its hood crumpling against the stone railings. Another flipped onto its roof, glass tinkling across the pavement like scattered diamonds.

More vehicles skidded to avoid the wreckage, sealing off both ends of the bridge. Car doors flew open as people abandoned their vehicles in panic. A mother yanked her children from a minivan, an elderly couple stumbled away from their crushed sedan, a group of tourists scrambled from their rental car. They weren't just fleeing the crashes. They were fleeing something worse.

My heart stopped.

Frigg was here.

Shit.

And we were trapped.

Sigyn's fingers slipped against mine. Her nails raked across my palm as something yanked her backwards. I spun towards her, arm outstretched to grab her again—

Iron fingers dug into my shoulder and forced me around. The world blurred into shadows and streetlights until my vision focused on Frigg's eyes boring into mine.

Pain exploded in my chest as she plunged the mistletoe dart into my heart. The impact drove the air from my lungs, and for one suspended moment, I could only stare at where it protruded from me.

Agony followed, blazing through me, white-hot and absolute. Each heartbeat felt like being torn apart from the inside, muscle and flesh fighting against the mistletoe embedded in my heart. My throat constricted, allowing only a choked gasp. Blood filled my mouth, and the taste was terribly real. She'd done it. After everything. She'd actually won.

Frigg's smile widened, her eyes gleaming with sadistic pleasure, taking in her death blow.

Fenrir, Jorg, and Sigyn watched in horror, pinned by Frigg's guards. Fenrir thrashed against two men, Jorg faced a knife, and Sigyn strained against her captor. Even without her memories, the fear in her eyes was for me. Always for me. Black spots danced at the edges of my vision as I tried to memorize their faces. My last sight would be of those I failed to protect.

"Did you really think you could escape me?" Frigg asked over the river's rush. "I may not have *Laevateinn*, but you are still mortal, and this mistletoe can still kill you. And now I have my wish...you dying by the same blade you used to take Balder's life. That you used to start Ragnarok."

I lifted my chin, jaw clenched, and met her gaze without flinching. Even as my heart struggled against the mistletoe piercing it. Even as each breath felt like glass in my lungs. My knees shook from the strain of standing.

"I'm going to enjoy watching the light fade from your eyes." She twisted the mistletoe, tearing flesh. "Farewell, Loki Laufeyjarson."

She pushed the mistletoe in deeper.

46

BURN THROUGH THE WITCHES

She twisted the mistletoe against my ribs.

My heart thundered, waiting for the end. My lungs heaved, pulling in air tinged with the metallic tang of blood.

But I still lived.

Frigg's eyes widened, her grip on the mistletoe hardening. Confusion flickered across her face.

"Why isn't this working?" She drove the mistletoe in further, scraping my ribs, cutting through my sinew.

But I still lived.

And my insides burned. Not with death, but with something ancient and familiar. A smoldering heat spread through my veins like liquid fire, awakening every nerve ending, every cell. Something primal, powerful, that I thought I'd lost forever. It sparked in my core, then exploded outward, racing through my body like lightning through storm clouds.

I gasped, overwhelmed by the intensity of the sensation. My skin prickled, as if a thousand tiny embers danced across it. The surrounding air crackled with an energy I knew better than my heartbeat.

Chaos.

My chaos.

Frigg's eyes fixed on the wound that should have killed me.

"Why aren't you dying?"

She was right. Why wasn't I dying?

I should be dying.

I should be dead.

I looked down at my hands. Faint wisps of smoke curled from my fingertips like old friends coming home. A laugh bubbled up from deep within me—part relief, part exhilaration, part wild disbelief.

My chaos, my element burned in my core again. Back and hot and ravenous.

But how? I sacrificed my chaos to seal Surtr into the amulet. I had been mortal. Yet my element smoldered in my chest, despite having given it away. *How was my chaos back?* It was supposed to be impossible.

Impossible. The word echoed in my mind.

And I laughed louder. Because I was Loki. The God of Chaos. The God of Mischief.

The Trickster.

Everything about me was impossible.

Rage erupted in my chest, rabid and scalding and yearning for blood. My nails bit into my palms as the air shimmered with heat, distorting Frigg's shocked expression.

And then fire.

My fire.

I gasped as it surged through me, molten and crackling. After months of emptiness inside of me, the sensation was intoxicating. It sparked wildly in my marrow, set my veins ablaze with pure, untamed power.

"Oh, Frigg," I said, loving the terror dawn in her eyes. "You have no idea what you've awakened."

The maelstrom writhing in my bones threatened to consume everything. My eyes blazed, coating the world in crimsons and golds. And in that moment, I understood.

I wasn't dying because I was a god again.

Or was it I was *still* a god?

The particulars didn't matter.

The air sizzled, thick with scorched earth. Power raced through my arteries, an inferno building beneath my skin, begging to be unleashed. The old Loki was back, and Frigg was about to understand the true meaning of pain.

The mistletoe dart still protruded from my chest. Cute. Mistletoe was Balder's weakness, but not mine.

I gripped it, the plant sizzling against my palm as I wrenched it free. It crumbled to ash in my fist, scattering across the bridge. My flesh knit together, erasing the wound as if it had never been. Gods. How I missed that.

"No." Her face twisted with terror and disbelief. "You are mortal. Your chaos was stripped—"

My laugh roared through me like wildfire, scorching my chambers from within.

"Looks like I'm not so mortal after all. I'm as surprised as you are about this unexpected—what shall we call it? Rebirth? Is that the right word?" My face split in a wicked grin, embers cracking at the corners of my mouth. "But now isn't the time for all those boring questions as to *why* and *how* and *what does it mean*, when all that matters is how very, *very* pissed off you've made me." I raised my hand, letting flames dance between my fingers.

Fear flooded Frigg's eyes as I stepped towards her, each

footfall leaving smoking craters in the pavement. She stumbled backwards, the flags above us snapping violently in the heat-whipped wind.

"I'm going to savor your scalding flesh melting from your bones," I purred.

Her guards moved to stop me, weapons raised. In their haste, they released their grip on Sigyn, Fenrir, and Jorg. Poor dears. I didn't hesitate. Flames roared from my hands, wrapping around the guards like hungry serpents. Their screams pierced the night as fire consumed them. The stench of burning hair and cloth and the river's damp filled my nostrils.

"Father!" Jorg's shout cut through the crackling flames.

His feet pounded the ground as he raced towards us. He vaulted over a crushed Mercedes, its alarm still wailing. Sigyn and Fenrir followed, weaving between the wrecked vehicles. Steam hissed from an overturned taxi nearby, the acrid smell of burnt rubber and leaking fuel blending with the stench of burning guards as they flung themselves into the river below.

Magic crackled at Jorg's fingertips as he neared us, making my heart lurch. I had lived this nightmare before.

And I refused to again.

"No!" The word tore from my throat. "Stay away!"

"Don't shut us out," Fenrir pleaded. "You need our help—"

Energy pulsed in me, a tidal wave of power tingling from core to fingertips. My jaw was set, muscles straining as I extended my arms. The air around my hands shimmered and crackled with terrible purpose.

The ground split. Flames erupted, devouring the air and stretching towards the stars. A wall of fire cleaved the night, its reflection dancing on the river below and painting the bridge's stone arches in hellish light.

Fenrir, Jorg, and Sigyn skidded to a halt as heat blasted outward. The inferno's roar drowned their protests.

Through the flames, Sigyn's eyes found mine, begging me to let them through. To let them help.

But I had to keep them safe.

I surged the wall higher until their forms vanished behind the curtain of fire. The heat dried the tears I refused to acknowledge.

I turned back to Frigg, heart thundering against my ribs. Now, we were trapped together. Fitting, really. I'd spent so many years playing the villain in her story. Might as well make this performance count.

My family would survive this time.

The inferno raged against autumn's chill, creating wild gusts that whipped at our clothes. My copper hair lashed across my face.

"Do you really think that fire can protect them from me?" Frigg spat, her cloak flapping against her calves as she stalked between two mangled cars, their paint bubbling and peeling in the heat. "As soon as I kill you, that fire goes out, and then they will be mine."

I laughed, the sound harsh and bitter. I laughed to hide the shudder racing down my spine.

"If only you learnt magic without needing to rely on those little squares." I pointed at her bag of runes, flames flickering at my fingertips. "If only you hadn't lost Laevatein. Maybe I'd be afraid."

I took two more steps towards her, almost drunk on the raw power thrumming through my body. The prospect of finally ending her, of ensuring my family's safety, sang in my blood like wine. Killing Frigg was going to be insanely more satisfying now.

I dropped my hand to my hip, reaching for Laevateinn—and found nothing. I patted the empty sheath again, then checked my other hip. Then both hips again. Alright, this wasn't funny...

"Looking for this?"

My heart stopped as *Laevateinn* emerged from her sheath.

"I imagine it was rather hard to stay focused with that mistletoe wedged in your heart," she said, a smile playing at her lips. "But distracting enough for me to relieve you of this lovely blade."

Heat surged through my veins, anger burning away the last traces of confusion. Of all the underhanded, conniving. She'd played me perfectly. And now she had the one weapon that could truly destroy me. Perfect.

Her fingers whitened on the blade's hilt. The runes flickered in sync with the nearby flames, hungry for my blood.

"Hey, let's talk about this," I said, holding up my hands. "I thought you were afraid of unleashing my big, bad chaos? What happened to binding me beneath the earth for eternity?"

Snowflakes drifted down, vaporizing with a soft hiss as they touched my shoulders and arms. I sensed Jorg's magic in the snow, trying, exceedingly badly, to put out my fire.

"Oh, I'm done with careful plans." Her laugh held an edge of hysteria. "Done with strategy. Done with your smug little face and your endless tricks. I want you gone. And if your chaos escapes? Fine. Let it. I'll hunt down every spark, every fragment that tries to be reborn. Should be much easier to bind when it's fresh and new, don't you think?

Rather than dealing with..." she gestured at me with the blade, "whatever this insufferable thing is that it's become."

"Insufferable? I prefer charming."

"I prefer dead."

Well. She'd officially lost it. All that careful planning and strategy, thrown away for the simple pleasure of destroying me. I had to admire her dedication to spite.

I circled her, the ground beneath my feet smoldering. Steam curled from my skin.

"Throwing away your grand finale with the curse just for the satisfaction of killing me?" I rolled fire between my knuckles like a coin.

"I always knew I was your favorite obsession, but this is getting embarrassing."

Frigg's eyes narrowed, tracking the flame. Her patience snapped. The blade slashed through the air. I stumbled back, my feet scraping against the icy asphalt and tram tracks. *Laevateinn* whistled past my chest, missing by a hair. She shrieked, the rage in her voice mixing with the rushing water below.

I reached for my power, ready to blast her into the Rhine —and felt only embers where an inferno should rage. The wall of fire protecting my family had drained more than I'd realized. I gritted my teeth, forcing heat through my depleted core. Come on...

With agonizing slowness, warmth seeped through my veins like molten lead rather than the usual liquid fire.

I managed to blast her back. The force sent her skidding across the frost-covered bridge, past ornate lampposts. But the effort left me panting, hands braced on my knees.

I smiled through the fatigue, trying to savor what little rush remained. Straightening, I raised my hands for another attack. My insides ground raw as I scraped at my power, reaching deeper, desperately trying to fan those weakening flames. I grunted with effort, sweat beading on my forehead despite the cold.

Only a few pathetic sparks flickered from my fingers, dying before they reached Frigg.

Well. That was mildly embarrassing.

But why...Oh. Right. Still cursed. I'd almost forgotten about that particular problem in all the excitement of having my chaos back. I could feel the Salvation Weave now, wrapped around my power like a parasitic vine, steadily drinking.

My jaw clenched as Frigg's smile widened, her exhale misting in the frigid air. She knew exactly what was happening.

"The Salvation Weave won't let you win," she said.

Ice crackled under her boots as she stalked me through the maze of crushed steel. I ducked between abandoned vehicles, using their mangled frames as cover, but each step felt heavier than the last. A delivery van lay on its roof to my left, its cargo scattered across the frosted pavement. Ahead, a compact car had spun sideways, its hood crumpled against the stone railings like an accordion. The bridge had become a graveyard of steel and glass, and I was quickly running out of places to hide.

My legs wobbled, chest heaving. Sweat trickled down my face as I focused inward, desperately willing the dying embers in my core to ignite. Just a little more. Just enough to end this. To keep them safe.

They remained cold.

Fucking curse. Right when I was getting back into it...

I stumbled, gasping as my limbs turned to lead. My core felt empty, scoured raw, like someone had reached inside and scooped out everything that made me me.

Frigg pounced, and I barely managed to grasp her arm, stopping the blade inches from my throat. Gritting my teeth, I forced what little heat remained through my palm. Wool sizzled and Frigg shrieked, jerking away as smoke drifted from her coat.

But even that small effort drained me further. My grip loosened as my power faded to nothing. I massaged my chest, scowling as my chaos already flickered inside me like a guttering flame, the curse lapping it up like one of Freya's cats at a bowl of milk.

The air crackled.

I looked up, and my heart stopped. A ring of twisted vehicles hovered in the air, suspended by Frigg's outstretched hands. Their headlights cut through the snow like metal frames creaking as they hung in the sky. Oh, this was going to hurt.

"Surprised?" she asked. The word curled from her lips like frost.

I raised an eyebrow.

"I have to admit, I am a little..." I forced a smirk to hide my rising dread. I had to get *Laevateinn* away from her. This was getting ridiculous, and I was running out of both options and time.

The first car hurtled towards me with crushing force. I dove, feeling the wind of its passage as it crashed where I'd stood. Glass exploded across the stonework. I rolled to my feet, breathing hard, only to see a second vehicle already arcing down.

I leapt aside as a Mercedes slammed into the bridge's balustrade. Stone cracked. The impact sent tremors through the whole structure. Before I could recover, a BMW followed, then the delivery van. Each near-miss left me more drained, my movements growing slower, more desperate.

Snow fell heavier now, blanketing the bridge in white. The surrounding wreckage looked almost peaceful, half-buried in fresh powder. Crushed metal jutted from snow-drifts like broken bones, abandoned vehicles casting long shadows in the dim light.

I walked towards Frigg, each step melting the ice beneath my feet, leaving a trail of steaming footprints. But my usual confidence felt as hollow as my power. She was stronger than ever, and I was barely managing on fumes.

Frigg lunged through the snow, *Laevateinn* a deadly silver arc. I twisted away, the blade whistling past my ear close enough that the runes' dark energy made my skin crawl. I shot out my arm, knocking hers wide, but she snarled and she raked her free hand across my face.

I stumbled forward. She seized the opening, crashing into me. We grappled for control, slamming against a nearby sedan hard enough to dent its door. Our breaths came in desperate gasps, clouding the frigid air between us as we struggled against the frozen metal.

Frigg gripped my shoulder, using it as an anchor while hooking her foot behind my knee. I felt her weight shift, muscles tensing—

The world tilted.

My feet left the ground.

Frigg's face contorted as she heaved.

I was airborne.

I was falling.

The Rhine rushed up to meet me, wind roaring in my ears as the bridge's massive arches blurred past. I hit the water like concrete, the impact driving what little air remained from my lungs in a burst of bubbles. Numbing cold engulfed me, snuffing out my newly returned chaos as completely as a candle in a storm. Water flooded my mouth and nose while I thrashed, disoriented in the murky green depths.

Water...No. She had to drench me in water...

I could feel it immediately—the connection to my flames severed. The fire wall I'd created would be extinguished now, nothing but smoke and steam where it once raged. My family would be rushing forward, no longer held back by my barrier.

Through the murk, a massive shape formed above. Water hardened into layers of ice, growing and sharpening into a spear aimed at my heart. The icicle plunged, racing closer with each fading heartbeat. I fought to swim back from Frigg's magic, but the cold seeped into my bones, turning my limbs to lead.

Frost crept across my skin. Icy tendrils snaked along my limbs, hardening like chains. Panic surged as my mobility faded. I thrashed, but my movements grew sluggish, useless against the penetrating cold.

I looked up through the water. Frigg's distorted figure stood on the bridge, her form a dark blur. Through the rushing current, I heard her voice, muffled but unmistakable.

"Your little fire show is out," she yelled, her words barely reaching me through the water. "Let me help you with that. They can wait their turn to die."

Even submerged, I felt the surge of power above—that distinctive cold pressure that accompanied her frost magic. She was using *Laevateinn*, sealing off the battlefield. No interruptions. Just her and me. She wanted this kill all to herself, wanted to savor it without my family's interference.

But I refused to die here. Not when my family still

needed me. Not when that witch still threatened everything I loved.

I reached deeper than I ever had, past the dying embers of my fire, beyond even the curse sucking me dry. My lungs screamed for air, but I focused not on my fading power, but on my sons' faces, on Sigyn's smile. On Fenrir's laughter when he was small. On Jorg's quiet strength. On the way Sigyn looked at me like I was worth saving. On Hel having me tell her about constellations. Fists clenched. Muscles strained against the ice.

A warmth bloomed in my chest—not fire, but something deeper. Something the curse couldn't touch. Love, fierce and protective, spread through me like molten steel, melting the ice from within. My inner flame roared back to life, fueled by an unbreakable will to protect my family. To be the father, the husband, the god they believed I could be.

The cold pressed in, relentless, trying to snuff out this newfound strength.

But that flicker of warmth grew hotter, fed by memories of every moment I'd failed them before. Every time I'd run instead of fought. Every promise broken. Not this time. This time, I would stand. This time, I would protect them or die trying. I latched onto that resolve, pouring everything I had into nurturing that tiny ember of hope.

Slowly, agonizingly, the water heated. Bubbles formed, creating a small pocket of warmth. The effort was excruciating, every second a battle against the overwhelming cold. My muscles screamed. My chest felt ready to burst. But still I pushed. Cracks appeared in the ice, thin fissures glowing orange from within.

I pushed harder, thinking of Sigyn's faith in me, of the future we could have if I survived this moment.

And Odin...he couldn't die for nothing.

Fire burst from my skin. The ice shattered. Water boiled. A shock wave spread through the river.

I kicked upward, my hands slicing through water and leaving trails of fire in their wake. And I kept going.

Fire erupted from my palms, plunging into the river. Water boiled and churned until a vortex formed, lifting me skyward. I shot up, riding a column of steam and flame as the bridge rushed closer.

I must protect them.

I landed hard on the bridge, concrete cracking under my feet. Steam billowed around me as I crouched between a jackknifed truck and the mangled remains of what had been an expensive sports car. Paint blistered and peeled in waves from the heat radiating off my skin.

Frigg stumbled back. I lunged, closing around her arm. She hissed as my touch seared through her sleeve, smoke curling from the fabric. Metal clattered on stone as the dagger fell. I roared, channeling every spark of my renewed power outward.

She yanked free, eyes darting to the fallen blade glinting on the frost-covered stone.

My jaw clenched. I thrust my hands forward, and fire blazed from my palms. Frigg dove and rolled towards *Laevateinn* as flames struck the car behind her. The heat was intense enough to make the metal hiss and warp.

Rubber smoke choked the air as the surrounding vehicles buckled. Side mirrors melted like candle wax, dripping onto the pavement. Tires sagged and bubbled. Metal groaned. The maze of wreckage that had trapped us was becoming a molten barrier between us and the rest of the world.

If Fenrir also thought I'd be responsible for repaying these melted cars...

I lunged for the dagger as Frigg closed around the hilt. We collided hard enough to drive the air from my lungs. We rolled across the icy bridge, wrestling for control of the blade, the frozen surface biting into our skin.

Fingers clawed. Fists struck. The dagger skittered away across the ice. My hand found it first—cold metal against my burning palm. I gripped tight as Frigg fought to pry it loose.

Behind us, her ice barrier shuddered, long cracks splitting its surface as my family's assault intensified. A section near the top shattered, cascading down in glittering shards. Without *Laevateinn* in her grasp, Frigg's magic was weakening. The barrier wouldn't hold much longer.

I shoved Frigg down, pinning her against the stone. The knife hovered at her throat. My hand shook with exhaustion, with rage, with everything she'd stolen from me. Beneath me, her chest heaved, pulse racing visibly at her throat where the blade pressed. How many times had I dreamed of this moment? How many nights had I lain awake, imagining her death?

Her eyes narrowed, jaw set with defiance. Her gaze never wavered from mine.

"Do it," she said. "Kill me."

"You caged me, cursed me, broke me, hurt me..." My voice cracked with centuries of pain, each word torn from somewhere deep and raw. "You killed my children. And you killed Odin."

My grip tightened on the knife.

I would end this. End her. End the nightmares. End the fear that she would hurt them again.

Behind me came a tremendous crash of shattering ice as Frigg's barrier finally gave way. I heard my family's footsteps racing across the bridge, their shouts carrying on the cold air. But this moment was mine. This choice was mine.

My knuckles whitened on the hilt as the blade edged closer to her throat. Heat trickled from my core, down my arm, into the steel, as if my rage itself was feeding the weapon. The metal glowed, first a dull red, then brighter, hungry for blood. I was hungry for vengeance, for justice, for some way to make the pain stop.

Frigg's eyes widened. A bead of sweat rolled down her temple.

My muscles tensed. I inhaled sharply—

"Stop!"

His voice cut through the haze of rage and adrenaline.

Balder.

47

THE PRICE TO BE PAID

Laevateinn glowed against Frigg's skin. Steam hissed where metal touched flesh. Her breath came in short, panicked gasps.

"Stop!"

Of course, Balder would choose now to intervene. Perfect, precious Balder and his endless mercy. Perhaps I was too fast in destroying that dart of mistletoe. Because right now, I really wanted to ram it through his temple.

"Now isn't a good time—" I shifted my stance, pressing Frigg harder against the frozen stone.

"Let her go," he said, picking his way around an overturned car. "Skadi is at Asgard's gates, and Mother must break the curse. She has to. Please. I've already lost too much time."

Wind howled across the Rhine, drowning out the crackle of dying fires around us.

"Don't think so," I said.

I moved to slice into Frigg's trachea, but a force yanked me backwards. Fenrir's arms clamped around mine like iron bands. Sigyn pried the dagger from my grip as my son strained to drag me away, muscles trembling with effort.

"Papa, stop!" Fenrir grunted as I thrashed against his hold.

"Are you serious right now?" I snarled, twisting to break free. "Fenrir, I swear. Please, at least let me break her spine. Her face. Something. Anything."

Balder placed himself between us. But instead of sheltering her, he gripped her arms hard. The sight was actually a little jarring. Golden boy Balder finally showing steel. I didn't think it possible.

"End this," he demanded. "Break the curse. Or have you poisoned everything you claimed to love?"

"Have you forgotten your duties as my son?" she asked. "Everything I did was to protect—"

"To protect what? Your power? Your control?" His voice carried an edge I'd never heard before. "I've taken command of Hel's army. They're pushing Skadi back from Asgard's walls right now."

In all my millennia, I had never seen Balder stand against his mother like this. Absolutely fascinating.

"You did what?" She staggered back from his hold, one hand gripping a nearby car's crumpled hood for support.

"I made my choice." Balder advanced on her, frost crunching under his boots. "I won't let Asgard burn while you obsess over destroying Loki. I won't let you destroy us because you're too proud to admit you were wrong." His hands trembled, but his voice stayed steady. "Break the Salvation Weave. Now. Before it's too late."

I felt Fenrir's grip loosen slightly, his own worry clear in the way his muscles tensed.

"What madness is this?" Her voice rose to match the howling wind. She pushed off from the car. "This is how you repay my sacrifices? After everything I've done for you, you side with monsters?"

"The only monster here is the one who poisoned her husband and cursed her people." He gestured at the surrounding destruction, at the twisted metal and shattered glass. "Skadi broke through the wall. We need the gods to fight her. We need Jormungand and Fenrir's strength to drive back the Frost Giants. Now break this curse."

"I can't break the curse," she said. "Once cast, it's impossible."

"Remove Sigyn's spell then." Balder crossed the distance between them in two quick strides. "Let her translate the incantation. Father could still—"

Still?

"Odin's still alive?" The words burst from me before I could stop them, raw with an emotion I didn't want to name.

Wind whipped Balder's hair, carrying pine and frost and woodsmoke. He pulled a crystal pendant free at his throat.

The gem pulsed with dying golden light, each flash slower than the last. Like a failing heartbeat.

"Barely," he whispered, tucking the crystal away. "But fading. Every moment we waste...Hel will be here soon to take us back to Asgard."

Frigg laughed.

"Oh, my sweet boy. You think your father would have the power to break my curse at this point? After the poison? After the curse has fed on him so long?"

Even if we got the translation...I'd seen what it took Odin to remove Surtr from Sigyn's veins. The raw power that had left him gasping, drained. Breaking the Salvation Weave would require even more.

He wouldn't be capable of it.

This truth must have also settled over Balder as he slumped against a car.

We'd failed. His desperate gambit with Hel's army, seizing control...all too late.

And Odin was dying alone.

Fenrir's grip on me loosened further, but I no longer had the energy to break free.

Balder turned back to Frigg. "An act of love can break any curse. Tell us what the act is."

She chuckled.

"Do you know what it's like?" Frigg's voice dropped low as she paced through the wreckage. "I believed in Asgard. I believed in peace. And what did your father and Loki do? They corrupted it all with their *sentiment*." She kicked aside a broken headlight. "Our people were in danger. Other realms were in danger. And for what? Love?" She spat the word.

Balder pushed himself up, armor scraping paint. He gripped her hands, but there was no more pleading in his touch.

"Your anger has devoured everything, Mother. Even your chances of redemption." He released her.

"Perhaps...perhaps you're right." She reached up to his cheek. "But someone has to restore balance."

Frigg plunged her hand into her pocket, pulling out a small stone. My stomach dropped as I recognized the carved rune stone from the rooftop—the hex she'd bound with the killing power of Dwarven steel. The one I thought she'd dropped."

She hurled it at me. The stone cut through the air, trailing wisps of green light as it arced towards my heart. I tried to dodge, shoes sliding on the ice, but too slowly. The hex whistled towards me, promising an agonizing death.

"No!" Balder shouted.

He launched himself between us, armor flashing, that perfectly coifed blonde hair whipping in the wind. The hex meant for me struck him head-on with a painful flash of green that sent us both staggering backwards. He took the full force, his body jerking as the magic slammed into him.

Smoke coated his armor from the impact of the spell, the acrid scent of burning metal filling the air. The runes on the stone glowed an angry red, searing themselves into Balder's chest plate.

Frigg's scream shattered the air. She ran to Balder, her feet pounding against the bridge, slipping on the ice.

He stiffened, muscles locking, then crumpled to the pavement with a clang of armor on stone.

"You can't die, you can't die!" She cradled Balder's head in her lap, her fingers trembling as they brushed his hair. "Balder, please forgive me. It will all be alright. I'm so sorry. You can't die—"

Balder's back arched off the ground, spine bending at an impossible angle as he let out an agonized wail. Glowing ropes materialized around him, writhing as they wound tighter and tighter. Where they touched his skin, they sizzled and burrowed deeper, leaving smoking trails. His flesh bubbled and blistered beneath the magical bonds.

"Do something!" I scrambled closer, almost falling in my haste. "It's your hex, stop it."

I dropped to my knees beside his convulsing body, the scent of blood so thick I could taste it.

She shook her head, tears streaming down her face as she kept stroking his hair, faster and faster.

"I cannot stop this hex...Once it takes hold..." she said, her words nearly lost under Balder's gasps. "It was supposed to be for you."

Pain filled Balder's eyes. Spasms jerked his body. Foam flecked his lips as he gasped for air, each breath a ragged struggle. The veins in his neck and temples bulged, pulsing an unnatural green as the curse wormed through his system.

And then blood.

Blood flowed from deep lacerations where the magical tendrils carved into his flesh, staining the ice crimson.

Jorg crashed to his knees beside us, hands weaving complex patterns in the air over Balder as he tried to shred the parasitic bonds. But for each tendril his magic severed, two more erupted from the wounds, burrowing deeper into Balder's thrashing body with wet, sickening squelches.

Blood ran across the street in rivulets, seeping between the cracks in the ice and dripping into the river.

I joined Jorg, working to unravel the hex eating into Balder's flesh. The magic felt wrong—twisted and hungry, pulsing with Frigg's hatred.

Sigyn slid through the blood to kneel beside me, pressing her hands over the worst of Balder's wounds. The steady flow of crimson soaked into her sleeves.

Fenrir stood over us, his voice rumbling a prayer.

"What's happening to him?" Sigyn asked, her voice tight. "Tell me how to help."

My magic flickered as I struggled against the hex. Against the Salvation Weave still gulping me down. Jorg's face gleamed with sweat. Balder slipped away fast, each breath rasped. Jorg's eyes met mine, and he shook his head, confirming what I already knew.

Balder was dying, and we could not prevent it.

We stopped our magic, and the absence of its hum engulfed us in the echo of Fenrir's prayers. Sigyn clutched Balder's hand. Blood continued to spill from him.

Balder's death would have once brought me the most sublime joy. But now, cold dread gripped my heart. If Balder died again...When had I started caring? When had his life become something worth saving?

It was not meant for the laws of death to be defied twice. A second death could shatter his soul, scattering it beyond Hel's grasp. Or worse, the darkness lurking between realms could devour his essence. I'd seen what lived in those spaces between worlds.

The thought of Balder facing that alone...

The thought of Hel suffering at his complete loss...

And was I partially to blame for the fact he faced a second death at all because I slightly killed him the first time? Not important. Though that guilt gnawed at me, too.

But what was important was stopping it. Saving his soul. Making right what I'd once made wrong.

But how to stop it?

Hel's words rose in my mind like ghosts.

This coin grants passage through the underworld's gates—no matter the circumstance, no matter the magic. As long as you possess the coin, you'll materialize in my throne room whole and unscathed, even if your soul gets blasted into a million pieces."

I couldn't stop his death, but maybe I could guide him through it so he'd find a way home to Hel.

"Sigyn, *Laevateinn*—quickly!" I extended my hand.

She hesitated only a heartbeat before placing the hilt in my palm. I yanked down the waistband of my trousers and slashed at the stitching of my underwear where I'd hidden the coin.

"Sorry for the impromptu striptease," I muttered, hastily pulling my trousers back up with one hand while retrieving the coin with the other. I handed *Laevateinn* back to Sigyn with an apologetic grimace. "Yes, definitely the proper use for that dagger. Nothing says 'legendary blade' like cutting open one's underthings."

The coin pulsed against my fingertips, a steady rhythm that matched the failing beats of Balder's heart. How had we come to this? Me, saving Balder? The irony wasn't lost on me.

I forced the coin into Balder's cold hands and clamped my fists around his.

"Hold tight," I said. "Don't let go, even in death. It's your lifeline to Hel."

Magic erupted between us, crackling and spitting. The moment the coin touched his hand, the Salvation Weave seized me like a hook through my chest, dragging me towards oblivion. Reality blurred to shadow as every muscle screamed, fighting to keep our hands locked together. One slip, one fraction of an inch, and I'd lose him. The coin had to stay pressed between our palms.

Sigyn drew *Laevateinn* across her palm. Blood welled up like rubies. "You said my blood would help," she whispered, letting crimson drops fall onto the blade. "Let it help."

The faith in her eyes nearly broke me. How could I tell her? That all of this—the blood, the sacrifice, the hope— was for nothing now?

"Let it help," she pleaded, tears cutting tracks through the grime on her cheeks. Blood pooled in her palm.

I smiled, memorizing every detail of her face. The stubborn set of her jaw. The fierce light in her eyes. The love I didn't deserve.

"Please don't forget me," I said. Not 'goodbye.' That would make this too real.

Sigyn's face crumpled, fresh tears falling to mix with blood and dirt. "I will find you. I will come after you."

I gripped Balder's hands tighter, drawing strength from

her promise while praying she wouldn't keep it. She deserved better than chasing my ghost through darkness.

The Bifrost split the night like lightning, spilling bitter cold across the bridge. Hel strode through, her black cloak billowing behind her, frost spreading beneath her boots.

"Who is ready to help me put a stake through that Skadi wrench's heart—" Her voice died in her throat as she took in the scene, faltering mid-step. "Balder!"

My arms shook holding the coin. Just a few more seconds.

"Hel, we tried all we could..." Jorg stumbled back from Balder's body, hands dropping to his sides.

Her eyes swept over the blood-stained ice, the magical bonds cutting into Balder's flesh, crimson pooling beneath him...

When she saw Frigg cradling his head, something terrible crossed her face.

"You did this," Hel snarled, crossing the distance in three quick strides. "Get away from him!"

She ripped Frigg away and slammed her into the railing. The impact rattled a nearby SUV as Frigg crumpled, gasping.

Hel dropped beside us, sliding in the bloody ice. As she traced the carnage, hovering her fingers over Balder's wounds, her face might have been carved from stone. Then her eyes caught on the coin pressed between our hands.

"Father?" Her voice broke as she reached for me. "What are you—" The words died as realization hit fully. "But you won't come back."

"That's okay." I forced a smile as the curse pulled me apart. "You said this was your failsafe, so you could always find each other."

"No." Hel's voice hardened as she grabbed my shoulder,

fingers digging in desperately. I heard the echo of my own stubbornness in her tone. "You can't do this. I won't let you—"

"You know what happens if we don't," I ground out as the Salvation Weave clawed at my bones. "His soul will shatter. Nothing will remain for you to save. I've never been much of a father to you. Let me be one to you now."

Balder's breathing stuttered, each gasp shallower than the last. His skin had gone waxy, tinged with blue. Blood no longer pulsed from his wounds. His heart was failing.

Hel touched Balder's cheek, and in that moment she looked terribly young.

Balder's breathing stuttered, each gasp shallower than the last.

"Please find your way home to me," she said to him.

Balder's hand slackened in mine, fingers uncurling.

The coin flared with white light as death took him. The curse roared through me like a tempest, reality splintering at the seams. Through the chaos, I saw Hel press her lips to Balder's still-warm mouth, tears falling onto his face. Light erupted from the point where our hands met, where their lips touched, where Sigyn's fingers gripped my shoulder.

Sigyn screamed my name as darkness swallowed me.

The Rhine's rush faded.

The wind's howl died.

Blood and magic gave way to the musty dank of the Underworld.

And I fell.

Into darkness.

Into void.

Into...

Light.

Light burst outward, searing through my vision. The

magic started where Hel's lips met Balder's, rippling outward in rings of blazing gold. Each wave slammed into me like a summer wind, melting the ice that had crystallized in my veins since the Salvation Weave took hold. Overturned cars rocked on their wheels. Shattered glass danced across the pavement. The very air seemed to vibrate with power, humming a note that made my teeth ache and my bones sing.

I snapped back to full consciousness. The pull of the underworld vanished, replaced by solid ground beneath my feet. My senses sharpened, the world around me coming into crisp focus.

Frigg clasped her hand against her mouth. Jorg and Fenrir stared wide-eyed as Sigyn gripped my arm, anchoring us both against the tide of power.

The light continued to pulse, each wave breathing life back into Balder. Color flooded his cheeks as his wounds knit closed. Hel cradled him closer, their forms nearly one in the magic's intensity.

As the last wave dissipated, Balder's eyes opened—clear, alert, alive. He blinked rapidly, focusing on Hel's tear-streaked face above him, a smile spreading across his blood-flecked lips.

He pushed up on shaking arms, swaying as he found his feet. Hel wrapped her arms around him. He drew her closer, hands spanning her waist as she buried her face in his neck, shoulders heaving with silent sobs. His fingers trembled as he stroked through her hair.

Seeing perfect, precious Balder holding my daughter like she was the most precious thing in all the realms. The tenderness in the gesture made my chest ache, and my stomach churn slightly. Of all the men in the Nine Realms she could have chosen...

What the hell just happened?

And, more importantly, why was I still here? The Salvation Weave should have...oh. *Oh.*

I blinked.

Now this was interesting...

I patted my arms frantically—solid. Pinched my side hard enough to make me wince—definitely real. Inhaled deeply—diesel and frost filled my lungs, not the musty rot of the underworld.

This was *very* interesting.

Before I could process what it meant, Sigyn slammed into me from behind, arms locking around my chest with enough force to drive the air from my lungs. I spun in her embrace, pulling her closer, afraid this dream might shatter if I loosened my grip. The rosemary in her hair flooded my senses as she pressed her face into my chest, her warmth against me like coming home.

"Loki," she breathed against my skin. "I...I remember everything! I love you."

My breath caught in my throat. I drew back enough to take her hands in mine, our fingers intertwining. I gripped them hard enough that it had to hurt, but she held on tighter.

"Sigyn?" My voice came out rough, heavy with disbelief and desperate hope. "And I love you, too. This must mean the curse is—"

"No. No, no, no..." Frigg's voice cut through our moment as she struggled to push herself upright, one hand braced against the blood-smeared railing. Her eyes darted wildly between rage and relief as she stared at Balder. "Do you know the work I put into this curse? I bound it with the essence of a dying star, forged in the depths of Niflheim— and you just...You ruined everything!"

"Is it really broken then?" Fenrir walked closer.

"And I don't understand how," she said. "It was impenetrable."

I laughed.

"But it wasn't," I said, savoring the look of confusion that crossed Frigg's face.

She lurched away from the railing, wincing as she pressed a hand to her bleeding temple. Her boots rasped against the icy pavement as she stumbled towards us, eyes fixed on Balder with horrified wonder.

"Balder." Her voice cracked. "You must believe me—I never meant to hurt you—I do love you."

She stretched out her hand, but Hel threaded her fingers through Balder's, holding him close. Frigg froze mid-step, arm still outstretched.

"I don't want to hear another excuse or explanation or reason from you ever again," Balder said, steel beneath his quiet tone. "You're done. I'm sure now that Thor is free, he won't appreciate having been cursed. None of the gods will."

He tugged the crystal pendant free from around his neck —the one that now pulsed with a steady golden light.

"Father's heartbeat is growing stronger by the minute. The breaking of the curse must have purged the poison from his system, too." A grim smile crossed his face as he let the pendant fall back against his armor. "I expect he'll have quite a lot to say about all this."

He was alive. Relief doused me, raw and incredibly irritating. I squeezed Sigyn's hand harder, my heart racing with a thousand thoughts I didn't want to consider, because each upset me more than the last with their truth.

But he was *alive*.

The color drained from Frigg's face as realization seeped in.

"The gods," she whispered. "They are all free, and that means—"

The Bifrost flared, its energy making the bridge tremble as it deposited a squad of Hel's warriors onto the snow-covered stone.

"It means you and Freya and Mr. Ragnar are going to spend a whole lot of quality time together." A cold smile touched Balder's lips as he stepped forward, armor glinting in the portal's light.

I couldn't help imagining Frigg and Freya imprisoned together, bickering over who would apply Mr. Ragnar's rectal prolapse cream next. Now, this was the kind of deviousness that made me almost proud of Balder. Maybe this was a better fate than death.

Frigg's composure shattered. She lunged forward, reaching for her son. "No, please, Balder—"

"Take her away," Balder commanded.

Hel's guards seized her arms. She thrashed, her screams echoing across the bridge and over the rushing Rhine below. I gripped Sigyn's hand tighter as we watched Frigg disappear through the portal, her cries cutting off as she disappeared into the Bifrost.

A weight lifted from my shoulders. The nightmare was finally over.

Fenrir moved closer, running his hand through his dark hair.

"So was it Hel's kiss that broke the curse?" he asked. "True love's kiss and all that?"

"No..." Jorg's expression hardened. "The magic was far more complex than that. Did you feel it? The way it came in waves?"

I nodded, remembering how the power had surged through us. "Like streams flowing together into a river."

The residual energy still made the hair on my neck prickle.

"And it didn't just break the curse," Jorg added, crouching to examine a patch of ice where magical residue still glowed. He gestured to where Balder stood. "Whatever that pure magic was, it seemed to burn away all corrupt magic it touched. Including your mother's hex."

"Which explains why I'm still breathing," Balder said dryly, rolling his shoulders as if testing that everything still worked. "She built her magic on hatred. It wouldn't have stood against..." He paused, looking troubled. "Against whatever exactly happened here."

"Father only said it would take something nearly impossible," he continued. "A precise combination of circumstances he'd found theoretically but claimed would be harder than catching a fish's breath."

I glanced between Balder and Hel, then down at my own hands, still warm from gripping the coin, then to Sigyn. Something nagged at the edge of my thoughts, like a half-remembered dream. We'd done something tonight, something supposedly impossible, but I couldn't quite grasp what.

Fenrir leaned against an overturned car, arms crossed.

"What I don't understand," Jorg said carefully as he stood, brushing ice from his knees, "is how Frigg never saw it coming. She designed the curse specifically to resist any act of love, no matter how powerful..."

"So, you're telling me we accidentally stumbled onto the one solution Odin theorized?" I sighed. "He's never going to let us hear the end of this. I can already picture his smug face as he explains every excruciating detail."

Maybe I was too hasty in celebrating his survival.

Whatever. I had more pressing matters than magical

theory. Like the way Sigyn's hand felt in mine. I tugged her closer, away from the others.

"Now, I believe we have some lost time to make up for..." I pulled her closer, drinking in the sight of her. The lamplight caught in her hair, turning the dark strands into silk. I traced up her arm, savoring the shiver that ran through her.

"Oh?" Her eyes sparkled with mischief as she pressed against me. "And here I thought you would be more interested in unraveling the magical mystery of the age."

"Some mysteries are more enticing than others," I murmured, tilting her chin up. Her breath caught as I leaned in, our lips inches apart—

Balder cleared his throat loudly, shattering the moment. I turned to him slowly, not bothering to hide my irritation.

"I'm afraid we first have Skadi to deal with."

Ah. That little chestnut. In all the excitement of not dying and breaking unbreakable curses, I'd almost forgotten about the Frost Giant army at our doorstep.

Hel's eyes gleamed as she spun her spear, the weapon humming through the air.

"I've been wanting to properly stir her bowels with my spear for an age," she said.

Rainbow light blazed across the bridge and over the contorted metal and splintered glass. The Bifrost's energy hummed in my bones, calling to the violence still singing in my blood. After the day I'd had, killing some Jotnar seemed just the treat, especially now that I had my chaos back.

I leaned close to Sigyn, my breath stirring her hair. "You know, a battlefield is a wonderful place to have some alone time. Nothing gets the blood pumping quite like—"

She pressed her finger against my lips, silencing me. That simple touch sent shivers down my spine.

"After the battle," she whispered, her voice full of promise that made my heart race faster than any fight.

48

FINALLY

Asgard

The roar of the ocean drifted through the open terrace, mingling with steam rising from the tub where Sigyn and I shared a decent bottle of wine. Candle flames coated the marble walls and coffered ceiling in wavering golds and shadow. The most glorious battle I'd ever experienced left blood caked on my knuckles and wedged beneath Sigyn's fingernails.

"It was kind they gave you back your old rooms." Damp tendrils of honey ginger hair clung to the graceful curve of her neck.

Memories seeped in like poison surrounded by the familiar walls.

"I suppose." I relaxed back against the curved edge, letting the heat seep into my bones while trying to ignore how the shadows still knew exactly where to fall. "Although I wish the gods would have provided a better vintage. After the battle we just fought, after we saved all of their asses, it would have been the least they could have done."

I reached for her wrist, gently washing away streaks of dirt, grateful for the distraction.

"I hope we didn't cause too much of a mess tracking in all this mud over the floors," she said.

I chuckled, remembering how we'd slipped and slid all over the battlefield like children playing in the rain. But then again, most children didn't leave trails of giant blood in their wake.

"The servants have cleaned worse. That time Thor brought home an entire dragon carcass, the stench lingered for weeks." I stretched lazily. "Besides, defending Asgard comes with certain housekeeping allowances."

Sigyn quirked an eyebrow.

"Defending Asgard? I seem to recall you suggesting we let that one Frost Giant through just to see the look on Thor's face."

"Well, can you blame me? His expression when things go wrong is absolutely priceless." I grinned. "And speaking of priceless expressions...did you see Skadi's face when I conjured that illusory avalanche? I thought her eyes would pop out of her head."

Sigyn leaned back against the opposite side of the tub, stretching her legs alongside mine. Her eyes danced.

"But what really finished her was when Fenrir in wolf form shook and flung slobber all over her boots. I thought her shrieks would burst my eardrums."

The image of Skadi running away in tears flashed through my mind, quickly taken over by Sigyn's fierce grace as she cut her sword into a Frost Giant's leg, her hair whipping in the wind. The image sent a jolt of desire through me.

"I have to say, I never thought I'd ever be back here, especially sharing this tub with you." I admired her naked body as she took a clean cloth and dabbed the gash still healing on my collarbone. Wounds from Dwarven weapons always took longer to heal, even for a god. "Life changes so fast. You think I'd be used to the flip-flop of circumstances, but..."

Truth was, it felt like being stabbed with a thousand tiny daggers, being back in these rooms after, well, after *everything*. But I also couldn't deny the charm this place still held. The rush of the surf and the best views of Asgard in the entire palace. So, when Odin offered, I accepted...for her. Because I wouldn't let her sleep in those shit rooms overlooking the gardens, where the stench of roses was overwhelming even on a good day. But gods, how the walls remembered. They whispered of betrayals, both given and received.

And then the thoughts marched in like those Frost Giants, eradicating every good thing, eating me from inside, forcing me to face all the million possibilities of how I nearly lost everything. Again. How I could still lose everything. Again.

Again.

What if...

She laced her fingers through mine beneath the water, giving a gentle squeeze. The warmth permeated deeper into my core as more steam scented with vanilla and almond filled my breaths, bringing me back to the surface. Gods. I was acting like a human. But I wasn't human, and I couldn't stay upset over this. Wouldn't give the past that satisfaction.

"Where did your mind go just now?" she asked. "Please don't tell me you're still sore about Skadi's snowball to the face?" Sigyn smiled, eyes crinkling at the corners.

"No, it wasn't that, it was just..." The words died in my throat, caught between centuries of shoving my emotions deep, deep down, and this new, raw honesty thing I was trying.

Sigyn moved closer. Rivulets of water ran down her bare shoulders, catching the candlelight. She was everything I'd yearned for and everything I'd feared losing again.

"It was just what? Tell me." Her voice held that gentle persistence that could crack even my best defenses.

I breathed in steam and candlesmoke, searching for courage. I still hadn't gotten used to all this *talk about your feelings* stuff. Gods weren't exactly known for their emotional literacy, and I'd spent millennia perfecting the art of deflection.

But I had to start somewhere, and now seemed as good a time as any.

"It was like drowning, being without you," I said, the words scraping my throat like shards of glass, each syllable drawing blood. "Every day without your memory of me, carved another piece from my soul. To see you look through me, to have lost your faith in me. Your love..." My voice cracked, the horror of it all finally breaking free like a dam bursting.

Sigyn's hands found my cheeks, her touch making my every cell ache for her. Droplets from her bath-dampened palms traced down my skin. Our faces drew closer, and I fought the urge to close the last whisper of space between us, terrified that even now, she might slip away like smoke.

"My faith in you, my love for you," she whispered, her eyes searching mine with an intensity that made my heart stop, "was never lost. It lived in my bones even when my mind forgot. You must know that you always have my love. Even when I'm not here. Even when I'm gone."

Her steadfast conviction, her fidelity, pierced my soul like a blade of pure light, shattering the shadows that had haunted me for so long. I pulled in a shuddering breath, my chest constricting at the unconditional love and acceptance radiating from her eyes.

She saw me. Truly saw me. Every jagged edge. Every scar. Every bit of darkness I'd tried to hide. And still, she looked at me as if I held the stars themselves. As if I were worthy of such devotion.

Love and grief and wild, desperate joy tangled in my chest until I couldn't breathe. I leaned in and captured her lips in a kiss that held everything I couldn't say. I poured myself into those seconds that stretched into the bone-deep relief of being known again, and the crushing gratitude of having her back, having her mine, and it threatened to bring me to my knees.

I lost myself in her taste, in the warmth of her skin beneath my fingers. In this moment, even the ghosts of my past seemed to retreat to their corners.

When we finally parted, breathless and clinging to each other, I rested my forehead against hers. The hollow ache that had carved its home inside my chest these days began to ease, filled by her presence, her touch, her love.

And as I held her tighter, another kind of yearning stirred, chasing away the last shadows of melancholy.

Seriously. I'd had enough melancholy to last me entire lifetimes.

"Remember what we attempted back at Fenrir's cabin?" I asked, letting mischief creep into my voice.

I moved my finger down her chest, tracing a path around her collarbone and over the soft curves of her breasts.

"Yes—" Sigyn's breath hitched as I continued to move slowly downward, trailing my fingertips along her skin. A spark of desire glinting in her eyes that matched the hunger rising in mine. Her nipples hardened under my touch as I teased them lightly.

"What if we tried again?" I whispered, my voice dropping to a rough velvet that made her shiver against me.

"You can't be serious," she breathed, though her pupils had dilated with want. "I still have Frost Giant blood crammed beneath my nails."

Something dark and hungry flared in my chest at those words.

"Even better," I growled, sliding my fingers up her back, savoring each shudder I drew from her. "Now that I'm a god again, my shoulder is fully healed, and I'd like to *thoroughly* test that everything is working properly." I pressed closer, letting her feel the heat radiating off my skin. "I think it's time for a proper do-over. If you're willing, of course."

A slow smile spread across Sigyn's face. Her breath came faster, chest rising and falling against mine. She wound her fingers through the waves of my copper hair, nails scraping lightly against my scalp in that way that made my blood sing.

She leaned in, and her lips brushed the shell of my ear, sending electricity down my spine.

"I think you're absolutely right," she said. "It would only be prudent to make sure everything is back to usual."

My heart thundered against my ribs as I drew her closer, her wet skin sliding against mine like silk over steel. The bathwater had left glittering droplets across her shoulders, and I watched as they traced paths down her body. The heat of her breath feathered across my skin, and when our eyes met, the raw intensity there nearly undid me.

"I'm going to make you understand how much I missed you," I said.

I captured her lips with mine, drinking her in like a

person dying of thirst. Our tongues met and slid as I deepened the kiss, becoming something wild and desperate. This was pure need.

She wrapped her fingers around me, sending a shock of pleasure through my body. My head fell back as a moan escaped from deep in my throat, each stroke sending sparks exploding behind my eyes.

"Sigyn, I...if you don't stop...*gods*—" I ground out.

"I need you inside me," she whispered, working me faster. "Now."

That finished me.

I wasn't ever a three pumps kind of person, but I couldn't stop losing myself in her hand. My vision blackened as pleasure pulled me over and under.

"Oh. I apologize," I said, deeply embarrassed, catching my breath.

She laughed.

"And you always say I'm the impatient one."

I chuckled against her cheek, the last spark of my end fading, and being replaced by a new heat as I already hardened for her again.

"I love you," I said, pulling her against me, fresh arousal coursing hot through my body.

"And I love you." She straddled my hips, guiding me as she sank down. "And I think we've had enough of patience, don't you?"

I would have agreed if I still had a voice.

I slid into her, filling her, and the world stopped. Shattered. Splintered. Gods, she felt so good. My hands found her hips as she moved, each slow rotation filling her further. Waves of pleasure consumed me surrounded by hot velvet.

She moaned, moving faster, taking me in deeper, her

warmth thrilling every part of me. And that coil inside me tightened, ecstasy driving me further towards that edge.

I dug my fingers into her hips, guiding her movements as we crashed into each other. Water splashed over the tub's edges as our pace quickened. Our eyes locked and more heat doused me, reality breaking at my edges as pleasure mounted through my body. I loved the way her lips parted from me moving in her, loved the flush spreading down her neck...

I skated my hands upward, caressing her breasts, and I delighted in how she gasped and whimpered from my touch, each thrust bringing her closer to that precipice we both chased.

She cried my name as she let go, and her body tensed around me as waves of pleasure shuddered through her. And it took everything in me not to lose myself as that coil between my legs pulled taught to snap.

I slowed my movements in her, pulling every ounce of pleasure from her I could. Relishing every breath, every sigh.

And as her breathing evened, a wicked smile curved my lips. I wasn't nearly done showing her exactly how much I'd missed her.

Standing, I lifted her from the water, rivulets streaming down our bodies. I pressed open-mouthed kisses along her shoulder as I carried her into the bedroom, each taste of her skin threatening to undo me.

I pressed her back into the cool silk sheets of the bed, drawing a gasp from her lips that turned into a sigh of pleasure as I pushed into her again. I loved how she stretched around me as I rocked my hips against hers.

And I took control, moving in a languid and unhurried

rhythm, savoring each slow roll of the hips, each tender caress. I loved her.

She wrapped her legs around my waist, drawing me deeper, and her element washed over me like spring rain. Gods. Her hope flowed into me, intoxicating and pure, and I wanted to lose myself in her forever.

She moaned as I surged my chaos through her veins, like liquid flame filling her to the brim with me. And still she drank me down, needing more. As our elements thrummed through each of our every cells, we moved faster.

Her nails dug into my shoulders, her movements frantic as she begged for more. And that coil in my depths tightened more than I knew possible as another rush of her hope rippled through me like a cool balm. I slammed into her, our hips pounding. She shuddered around me again, and my own pleasure tore through my entire body as I finally let go.

Gasping for breath, I pulled her closer, her lips finding mine in a kiss that tasted of devotion as traces of my chaos danced beneath her skin, as her fidelity continued to sing in my blood.

When our breathing finally steadied, Sigyn drew back enough so I could see her smile, her skin glowing with sweat in the moonlight that streamed through the archways. The gauzy curtains billowed in the night breeze, carrying with it the crash of the Asgardian Sea far below.

"Well," she said, her voice still husky. "I suppose that was worth the wait."

She stood from the bed and wrapped one of the silk robes around her body. Her hair fell in damp waves around her shoulders, and the sight of her all disheveled was enough to send another rush of heat between my legs again.

I stood, the marble cool beneath my bare feet, and

reached for the unopened bottle of wine that sat waiting on the bedside table.

I walked to her, curling my arm around her waist and pulling her close. When I pressed my lips to hers, I could still taste the lingering sweetness of that first bottle on her tongue.

"We have another bottle," I purred against her lips. "If you're up for another round or five?"

I gestured towards the bed with its layers of purple silk sheets, raising an eyebrow. Gods, I loved how she laughed, how it sent shivers racing down my spine.

She plucked the bottle from my hands, eyes glinting with that perfect mix of mischief and desire. The cork came free with a soft pop.

"Only five?" She took a deliberate sip, letting a drop linger on her lower lip. "And here I thought you wanted to test your restored godhood thoroughly."

Heat rushed to my cheeks.

Gods, I loved her.

I loved my life.

49

REUNITED

Victory filled the feast hall, rumbling the beams overhead. Torches blazed in iron brackets, washing the carved knotwork in gold. Musicians in the gallery pulled bows hard down strings, and pounded on drums, weaving melodies through the din of the celebration below.

I lingered beneath a shadowed archway, smoothing down my dark green silk tunic as I waited for Sigyn. I traced the Elven embroidery along the hem—gods, how I'd missed proper needlework.

Bragi belted out off-key songs about how the gods now owed their freedom to me. Funny how quickly they'd forgotten their "You're the Destroyer and we hate you" nonsense. Still, the fact I could rub their noses in this for the next three centuries almost made up for Bragi's awful lyre playing.

His fingers fumbled over another series of chords, each note threatening to split my skull.

Maybe I should have let them remain cursed...

But worse than Bragi's drunken caterwauling was how

my gaze kept drifting to the head table. I'd been doing so well, keeping my eyes on my mead, on the dancers, on literally anything else. But I looked.

Odin sat alone, his russet hair covered in golds from the firelight. The gray of his tunic seemed to emphasize the weariness in his shoulders as his fingers traced the rim of his goblet, that familiar gesture making my chest tighten with memories I'd rather forget.

Something dangerously close to sympathy stirred in me. No—worse. Something that made me want to close the distance between us, to—

I took a long drink of mead, trying to drown whatever that feeling was. Completely disgusting, this newfound inability to properly hate him. I blamed that moment with the poison, when I was forced to admit...well. Better not to think about that.

Instead, I watched him sit there in his quiet dignity, and tried to convince myself I wasn't watching at all.

"You're doing it again," Sigyn's voice came soft beside me, her fingers finding mine in the shadows. I hadn't even heard her approach.

"Doing what?" I asked, though we both knew exactly what she meant.

The silver embroidery in her lavender gown glinted in the torchlight.

"That thing where you look at him like you're trying to solve a puzzle, then look away like you've been burned." She squeezed my hand. "You haven't spoken to him since the curse broke."

"There's nothing to say." I took another drink, but the mead had lost its taste. Just like these halls had lost their warmth, their familiarity. Everything felt...off-kilter. Changed. Or maybe I was the one who had changed.

"Isn't there?" Her eyes, knowing and gentle, searched my face. "I saw you that day, when you thought you'd lost him. And you told me what you finally admitted to yourself—"

"Don't." The word came out sharper than I intended.

"Loki," she said, resting her free hand against my cheek, turning my face to hers. "The heart doesn't follow rules or reason. It certainly never listened to pride. You don't have to choose between loving him and loving me."

I stiffened. "I don't want to be with him."

"I know." Her smile held centuries of patience. "But you don't have to pretend you feel nothing either. We're immortal, more or less, with hearts that have room enough for many kinds of love, in many shades. You can forgive him. Move forward. Stop running from what you feel."

"I'm not running," I muttered, but even I didn't believe it.

She laughed softly, the sound warming me more than the mead ever could. "You've been hiding in this corner all evening, watching him while pretending not to. If that's not running, I don't know what is."

I leaned into her touch, exhaling. "When did you get so wise?"

"One of us had to be." She pressed a kiss to my temple. "Talk to him. Or don't. But stop torturing yourself with all these unspoken words. You're allowed to feel, Loki. Even the complicated things. Even the things that scare you."

I looked at her then, this remarkable woman who could hold my chaos and still choose to stay. "What did I ever do to deserve you?"

She smiled, then grew serious.

"Love isn't about deserving. It just is. Remember that."

She pressed another kiss to my cheek before pulling away. "I should fetch that ledger of damages before Freya tries to write off her apricot harvest massacre as a battle necessity. Again. It will be good for the trial."

I watched her go, her words echoing in my mind. My gaze drifted back to Odin, still tracing that damned goblet with his fingers. Something pulled at me, drawing me forward before I could think better of it. One step. Two. Unspoken words sat heavy on my tongue.

Thor's booming voice cracked through the hall like lightning. "You should have seen Skadi's face when that bolt split her glacier!"

I flinched and retreated to safer ground, letting my attention wander the feast hall instead. Tyr and Njord were locked in what appeared to be their fifth arm-wrestling match of the evening.

Heimdall gave me a slight nod from his position near the door, though he still kept one hand on his sword. Old habits, indeed.

Thor's enthusiasm threatened to take out half his table mates as he gesticulated wildly, Mjolnir crackling faintly at his side. "Split that Frost Giant's skull clean in two!" He pounded his fist on the oak table, making the platters jump.

The great doors groaned open, and my pulse quickened as Hel swept in, her brothers at her sides. Jormungand moved with his usual cool grace, while Fenrir walked beside them, brown hair tied back and stubble darkening his jaw. The purple of their tunics marked their new status in Asgard, though Hel had insisted on black silk instead.

Fenrir broke away first, walking to where I stood.

"Papa," he said, glancing around. "Where's Sigyn? I thought I saw her with you earlier."

"She's fetching the ledger of damages from the coup," I said. "We need to account for everything before the compensation begins. Apparently, Freya single handedly destroyed an entire apricot crop for her face masks."

Fenrir shifted in his shoes. He scratched his chin.

"Ah. About that. I...may have accidentally crushed Farmer Byggvir's barn while I shifted into the wolf." He fidgeted with the end of his sleeve. "It wasn't intentional."

It took everything in me to bite back a smile at his earnestness. I patted his shoulder.

"Though, I suspect Byggvir's tales of the giant wolf who apologized profusely for property damage will be far less dramatic than he'd hoped. Hard to paint you as fearsome when you're fretting over vegetables."

"But, all of those poor cabbages. I squashed every one."

Fenrir was too gentle for his own good.

"We've already discussed this three times. Enough with these cabbages—"

"Your father is right," Tyr said as he approached us, his remaining hand raised in greeting. The sight of them together—my son and the god who had sacrificed his hand to help him escape—filled me with gratitude I still struggled to express. They embraced like the closest of friends. Maybe even closer.

"Listen to him," Tyr said, clapping Fenrir on the shoulder. "Sometimes you have to trample a few garden plots to save someone's life." His eyes met mine briefly, twinkling. "The farmers will survive. You did good today, Fen."

"That's surprisingly wise, coming from someone who once thought the best solution to everything was hitting it with a sword."

Tyr laughed.

"And that's surprisingly gracious coming from someone who once turned my sword into a stalk of celery during treaty negotiations."

Gods. He'd never let me live that one down.

"The celery improved your negotiating skill significantly," I pointed out. "Though I notice you're still keeping your distance from the mead."

"Some lessons stay learned," Tyr said with a grin, the silver arm rings on his blue ceremonial tunic gleaming as he turned to Fenrir. "Now that this curse business is finally over, I can actually come try these *smoothie* things you've been taunting me with. Do you still have that honey and blackberry one you told me about?"

"Of course! Though..." Fenrir brightened, his earlier worry about the cabbages forgotten. "I can make you something special. The Crushed Cabbage Catastrophe, in honor of poor Byggvir's garden."

"Finally turning property damage into profit?" I couldn't help but say. "I've taught you well."

Tyr laughed. "I've been waiting months to visit *Kalehalla*. Though perhaps we skip the cabbage—"

A flash of blonde hair and ceremonial purple disappeared through the archway that led to the high balcony.

The feast hall would be too crowded, too loud for Jorg after all that time trapped in the dark.

I followed him, knowing how isolation could become habit. How it could envelop you like a second skin until even welcome company seemed strange.

The balcony stretched before me, ancient dragon heads snarling from weathered stonework above. Below, waves crashed against the cliffs, sending up plumes of sea spray.

Jorg stood at the balustrade, cigarette smoke curling around him. His shoulders were rigid with a tension I recognized from his childhood, when he'd try so hard to be brave, to not let anyone see him cry.

"Room for one more?" I asked, hating how small my voice sounded.

Jorg studied me with eyes too old for his face, and I knew he searched for the trick, the hidden barb he expected from me. I exhaled when he nodded.

I settled beside him at the railing, close enough to talk, far enough to give him space in case he decided to change his mind and punch me in the face again.

The ocean winds tugged at his hair, carrying with them the tang of brine and distant storms.

"Thank you," I said. "For helping save our family. And I suppose those other self-righteous idiots too, though they were more of a bonus, really." I paused. "When you had every reason to let them rot."

"Don't," he warned, but there was less venom in it than before. His fingers tightened on the railing.

"You showed tremendous strength today," I said. "Not just in battle, but in choosing to fight alongside those who once..." I trailed off, my failures as a father dragging us down.

"Alongside my betrayers, you mean? Alongside *you*," Jorg's voice was rough, but something in his rigid posture had softened.

"Yes," I said. "Alongside me."

He took a drag from his cigarette, the ember flaring bright against the darkness. After a moment's hesitation, he extended it to me.

I accepted this token of peace. The harsh smoke filled my lungs.

"I wanted to watch them all burn," Jorg said. "For centuries, that's all I dreamed about in those depths. Their screams. Their suffering." He laughed, but there was no humor in it. "And now here I am, celebrating their salvation."

"Jorg—"

"No, let me finish." He took the cigarette back. "I'm still angry. At them. At you. For leaving me there. For not—" his voice caught. "For not coming for me."

The words hit like physical blows. Each one deserved.

"But today, watching you try to save everyone, even them..." He shook his head. "Maybe there's something to be said for choosing to be better than what was done to us."

Jorg was quiet for a long moment, watching the waves below. "I don't know how to stop being angry," he said. "But I don't want to drown in it anymore, either."

"Perhaps we can figure it out together," I offered carefully. "If you'll let me be there this time."

Footsteps neared us, Fenrir's boots accompanied by the click of Hel's heels as they walked onto the balcony. The living half of Hel's face held all the sharp beauty of Angrboda, while the other side revealed the elegant architecture of bone and decay. But her green eyes were mine.

My smile flattened as Balder appeared behind her, and I instinctively dipped to the dagger at my hip.

Oh, right. Balder good.

I stopped my hand and forced it back calmly to my side. The familiar urge to stab him battled with the memory of Hel's face when she thought she'd lost him. Damn him for making my daughter happy.

Balder good.

"I see you're still alive," I said, leaning against the balustrade. "Unfortunate." The word lacked its usual bite, though I'd never admit it.

Balder's brow flattened into annoyance as he stepped closer to Hel. His navy blue tunic was embroidered with such fine gold work it could only have been Elf crafted. The bastard always did dress well.

"This is what I'm talking about, Hel. He won't accept us being together," Balder muttered, pushing his hand through his annoyingly perfect hair.

"Why are you getting so upset? I think I'm being rather magnanimous here, not stabbing you," I said, pushing off from the railing and circling him with a predatory grin. Though watching him stand against Frigg, choosing to save us all despite knowing what it would cost him...well, it had been surprisingly not awful.

Hel rolled her eyes and stepped between us.

"Father," Hel said, placing a firm hand on my arm, her tone warming with, what was that, affection? "I wanted to thank you. For saving Balder."

I arched an eyebrow despite the warmth coating my insides from this rare display of thanks, forcing myself to stand still under her touch.

"Well, I could hardly let him die again. The paperwork alone would be atrocious."

Balder shifted in his overly polished boots.

"Yes, well. I appreciate your intervention, all the same," Balder managed, struggling with the words as he played with the cuff of his sleeve.

The feeling was mutual. I wasn't used to this either, this awkward dance between old enemy and potential family. Oh gods. He was going to be family.

Balder. Good.

Hel sighed and moved to stand at the railing, and in that sound I heard centuries of weariness. Of standing between two stubborn gods who'd both rather nurse ancient wounds than try to heal them.

No. Enough. I wouldn't be the reason my daughter kept

sighing like that. And if being the bigger person happened to give me bragging rights over Balder—no, wait. That's not how this works. Why was being good so boring?

"Come now, Balder. Surely we can be civil, for Hel's sake? After all, we've moved well past the whole me-orchestrating-your-death thing. And you choosing to betray your mother to save us all rather evens the score, wouldn't you say?"

I extended my hand to him, enjoying how he took a small step back.

"Please don't hurt me," he said, flinching away from my outstretched fingers.

I rolled my eyes.

"I gave up that coin to save your perfect, poetry-inspiring face from that hex. If I wanted you dead, I'd have saved myself the trouble and let it happen."

He considered my words, his weight shifting from foot to foot.

"I know, it's just, well...friendly isn't like us," Balder said, though his stance relaxed slightly, shoulders lowering. "We spent millennia trying to destroy each other. It will take some time to get used to this."

I grinned, remembering the time I'd replaced his favorite mead with fermented fish juice right before an important speech to the Elves. Or when I'd enchanted his perfect golden hair to turn an alarming shade of green during the summer solstice feast. Though he'd gotten me back for that one, somehow convincing Thor that I'd stolen his hammer again, leading to a very undignified chase through the gardens that ended with me face-first in Freya's prize rosebushes.

And despite it all, my eyes softened as I regarded the man who had finally stood against Frigg.

"True," I said, drumming my fingers against the stone railing. "But times bring change to us all. And, I suppose, I also want to—" I gagged on the words. "—thank you for making the right choice."

Balder took my hand, his grip tight on mine.

"You saved my life," he said. "Even after everything between us. I won't forget that."

I edged away slightly, maintaining my grip on his hand while creating distance. The words stirred something uncomfortable in my chest. I'd saved him because it was right, because Hel loved him, because something in me had changed enough to want to do good. But admitting any of that was like swallowing thorns.

"You mean after breaking your oath to my daughter?" I couldn't resist giving his hand an extra squeeze. "Though I suppose we covered that thoroughly during the battle. Saving Odin's life, giving us a chance to break that wretched curse...well, at least you broke it for a halfway decent reason. Better than I've managed, most times."

We both realized we were still gripping each other's hands. We let go at the same moment and stepped back. I wiped my palm on my tunic while Balder flexed his fingers as if ensuring they were all still attached. But something had shifted. The old hatred seemed...hollow now. Like a well-worn coat that no longer quite fit.

"Father," Hel said, a warning in her tone, though her lips twitched.

"What? That was practically a compliment," I said. "I didn't even mention the time he tried to have me executed."

"That was one time," Balder muttered, but there was something almost like humor in his voice. "And as I recall, you had just turned all my ceremonial armor into snakes."

I found myself almost smiling at the memory.

"Yes, well," I cleared my throat, all this gooey sincerity choking me. "I suppose if my daughter had to choose someone insufferably noble and heroic, at least she picked one with a decent jaw."

The real truth, the one I'd rather die than speak aloud, was that he'd proven himself worthy of her. Not because he was perfect, gods knew I'd spent centuries cataloging his flaws, but because when it mattered most, he made the right choice.

"So you approve?" Hel asked, but I caught the slight upturn of her lips. Something flickered in her green eyes. A shadow of the little girl who once sought my approval for everything from her first spell to her choice of weapons.

"Your mother would say I'm in no position to approve or disapprove of anyone's life choices," I said. "But yes. You have my blessing."

She lifted her chin, though she held herself as if my words might shatter something fragile within her. "Not that I require it. I would have married him anyway, even if you'd thrown one of your legendary tantrums about it."

"Of course you would have." I reached out to cup her cheek, thumb brushing the hollow of her dead cheek. "You are my daughter, after all. Stubbornness runs in our blood."

Fenrir snorted and pushed off from the stone dragons.

"Speaking of stubbornness..." He crossed his arms and stalked towards me, fixing me with a suspicious glare that was pure Angrboda. "What's really going on here, Father? You're being...thoughtful."

Looking at my children gathered here—truly looking at them—I saw echoes of their mother, of myself, of all the years lost.

And in that breath, a need took root. To let them know.

"I am capable of the sentiment from time to time. I have layers," I said. "Just as I'm capable of *this*."

I stepped forward with open arms. Balder, showing a rare moment of tact, quietly retreated to the far end of the balcony.

Jormungand actually gagged. "Oh gods, no. We're not doing this."

Hel took a swift step back. "Father, really, this is hardly—"

"Come on," Fenrir said, his eyes bright. "When's the last time we had a family hug? Never?"

"There's a reason for that," Jormungand muttered, but Fenrir was already pushing him forward.

"If I have to suffer through this display of sentiment, so do you," Hel said, grabbing Jorg's other arm as he tried to escape.

I pulled them all in, probably too roughly judging by their collective grunt of protest. Jormungand went rigid as a board, Hel seemed to be trying to touch as little of us as possible, and Fenrir, bless his gentle heart, was the only one who actually hugged back.

"This is awful," Jorg complained, his face mashed against my shoulder.

"Completely horrible," Hel agreed, though she'd stopped trying to maintain that careful distance.

"Just shut up and hug," Fenrir said cheerfully.

In those seconds, all my mistakes crashed over me like a tide. What a dumbshit I'd been, thinking I could simply write off years of absence with clever words. A father should have been there. Should have fought harder. Stayed closer.

"I love you," I said. "I know I've given you little reason to believe me, but I love you all so very much." My voice cracked slightly on the last words.

Jormungand's stiff posture finally softened. Fenrir's arms tightened around us all, and, to my surprise, Hel's tears dampened my shoulder. My children. *Gods, my children...* who had survived every horror the worlds could throw at them, who had grown strong and fierce and beautiful despite my failures. We couldn't erase centuries of pain in a single moment, but I felt real hope that we could begin to heal.

"If anyone mentions this to another soul," Jormungand mumbled into my tunic, but his arms had found their way around us.

"Don't worry," Hel said, her voice thick. "No one would believe it, anyway."

I held them tighter, memorizing this moment—Fenrir's steady heartbeat, Jormungand's reluctant surrender to the embrace, Hel's fingers gripping my tunic. I wanted to be better. Needed to be better. Not just for them, but because watching them now, I finally understood what it truly meant to be a father.

50

WHAT IF

The feast's victory songs still echoed through the halls as I slipped away. Sigyn's words followed me, refusing to be silenced by the click of my boots on stone. I needed air. Space. Anything to escape the truths I could no longer deny.

Stars still dotted the sky as I walked, but hints of purple bled into the black horizon. The path to the beach wound between the cliffs, worn smooth from centuries of use. Salt air filled my lungs, growing stronger with each step. Waves pulled at the pebbles below, their endless whisper too familiar.

I shouldn't have come here. This beach held too many memories, too many moments that still burned. But my feet kept moving, drawn by something stronger than sense.

The waves came into view, gray in the pre-dawn light. Cliffs rose on either side, dark pines clinging to their faces. A figure stood at the water's edge, his plain gray tunic billowing slightly in the sea breeze.

Of course, he was there. My heart did that thing where it

made me want to fall to pieces. To face something dangerous—forgiveness.

Odin's arm arced as he threw another stone at that same damned boulder we'd aimed at for centuries. Something raw and fierce clawed at my chest, refusing to be buried again. No point fighting it anymore. Not after almost losing him. Not after finally admitting the truth to myself.

Fantastic. Nothing like a nice chat about feelings at dawn. Truly, my favorite way to start the day.

"Your aim always was shit," I said, because it was easier than saying what I'd come to say.

He turned, sea spray catching in his hair as sunlight touched the silver at his temples. The weariness in his bearing made that thing in my chest claw harder.

"Couldn't sleep either?" he asked. He tightened his hand briefly on the stone he held before deliberately relaxing.

The pebbles shifted under my boots as I walked closer, the gold embroidery on my dark green tunic catching the first rays of dawn. I deliberately kept a few feet between us as I picked up a smooth stone, grateful for something to do with my hands. The words I needed to say lodged in my throat, choking me.

And that damn familiar scent of sage and clove drifted from him on the breeze, stirring memories I'd tried so hard to bury. Each one was a knife twisting.

"Too many thoughts."

"About?"

I opened my mouth. Closed it. The stone was heavy in my palm. *I almost lost you. I still love you. I hate that I still love you.*

"Is this what you do now you're reinstated to the throne?" I asked instead. "Riveting. Glad to know this is what I almost died for. You to throw rocks."

He shifted his weight.

"I suppose I should have known you'd be insufferable, especially since I have you to thank for helping me reclaim my throne. For saving me. As I've already said now a million times, Asgard and the worlds are in your debt."

"Yes, I wanted to have a little chat about that, if you think about double crossing me—" The words tumbled out, taking us further from what I'd meant to say.

He chuckled, and something in that familiar sound made my chest ache. He bent to retrieve another stone, the waves hissing against the pebbles at his feet.

"I gave you my word, and I have kept it," he said, straightening. "I want things to be better between us. I've already told you, now Frigg is gone, you're free to go where you please. The Southern Isles, Midgard, or to stay in Asgard." Something flickered across his features too quickly to read as he turned back to the water.

Dawn had fully broken now, turning the cliffs golden and catching in the spray of each wave. Stay in Asgard. *Please*. However...I glanced at the palace rising above the cliffs. There was something to be said about the views here that even California couldn't compete with.

I tightened my fingers around the stone until its edges bit into my palm. The real words pressed against my tongue. Instead, I swallowed them back.

"Oh, I know what this is about," he said, moving closer to the shoreline. "You're here to collect the apple I promised."

"I don't think the apple is necessary anymore, don't you?" The stone felt heavier in my palm with each passing heartbeat.

He chuckled softly, turning another stone over in his hands.

"Since your chaos has returned along with your godhood, probably not," he said.

The waves crashed against the shore, filling the stretching silence. My heart hammered against my ribs. *Say it. Just say it.*

"You told me I'd be mortal forever," I said, throwing the stone into the water, an inch from its target. Better than his, that landed two feet away. "I guess this just teaches me once again to not believe a single word out of your mouth." I let the corners of my lips quirk, so he got the jest. "However, I wouldn't mind some clarification."

And it would let me put off saying the other things bubbling beneath the surface. The emotions churning in me were giving me a headache.

"Finally asking for one of my explanations instead of rolling your eyes? I'm touched," he said.

"How do I still have my chaos?" I asked.

He smiled in that way that meant a lengthy explanation was about to be hurtled my way. Damn. I should have known better than to ask. But at least while he talked, I wouldn't have to.

"Your chaos isn't only power, Loki. It's woven into the very fabric of who you are—fire and chaos incarnate," he said. "When you bound Surtr into the amulet, we thought you had given up all of your element. But I now realize that even such a sacrifice couldn't completely extinguish your own nature any more than it could stop the stars from burning." His voice softened. "And then, when you and Sigyn bound yourselves together..."

I scoffed. This was the most ludicrous thing I'd ever heard.

"No, it was gone, I felt—" I had felt a hot prick of a needle afterwards when Sigyn and I bound ourselves to each other. "Why didn't you tell me this was a possibility before?"

His gaze dropped to the waves.

"I believe that binding with Sigyn did more than connect yourselves in marriage. Her fidelity, her unwavering hope... they became like air to your suppressed chaos, helping it slowly rekindle within you. I didn't want to get your hopes up, and truth be told, I thought it quite impossible your power would return. But you've always defied what's impossible." He turned the stone over and over in his hands.He could say that again.

"So, all my symptoms—"

"The growth pains from your returning chaos," he confirmed. "And regrowing an element would never be pleasant. Think of it like a flame that can never truly die, your true nature fought its way back. Yes, Surtr diminished your element, your fire and chaos, but who you truly are could never be fully extinguished."

And it all clicked. The constant stomach aches I'd blamed on Fenrir's smoothies. Those aggravating hot flashes that followed. The tingles in my palms when my emotions ran high. The doctor's baffled expression when I'd recovered from the lackerli incident. Even that night in Sigyn's apartment, when rage had burned through me and the candle had flared to life...

I'd dismissed them all. Called them coincidence. Adrenaline. Anything but what they really were. My chaos, slowly growing back, refusing to stay buried.

Huh. Interesting.

And infuriating.

"It would have been nice had you mentioned that theory earlier when I had my head in a toilet after eating an olive," I said.

"As I said, I didn't want to raise your expectations, and then, you know, I got a little distracted when Frigg cursed me."

Excuses. Excuses.

"There is one thing I don't understand...what in the deepest fires of Muspelheim was the act of love that broke the Salvation Weave? I recall you using the words 'impossible' at one point."

He chuckled.

"I did, because the deeper I researched, I learned it was more intricate than I ever imagined," he said, his voice taking on that familiar tone that used to put me to sleep in five seconds flat. "She designed the Salvation Weave with a twist. She wove in failsafes, contingencies, so that a single act of love would not break the curse."

I let out a sigh of extreme relief.

"Oh, thank gods." I said. "I knew I didn't owe Balder and Hel's love to breaking the curse, this is wonderful news—"

"Well, actually..."

"Odin, do not tell me I owe my life to Balder and Hel's love," I said.

He shook his head, a rueful smile playing at his lips.

"What broke the curse wasn't just their love, or any single act. It was a convergence—like streams flowing into a river until it becomes powerful enough to break through a dam."

"Come again?"

"Think about that moment on the bridge. Balder willing to die for you—"

"Disgusting."

"You using the coin to save him, knowing it might trap you in the underworld—"

"Don't know what I was thinking."

"Sigyn's unwavering faith, promising to find you even as you were being dragged into darkness, giving her blood without a single memory, choosing to believe in you when all seemed lost. Your sons refusing to leave your side." His eye met mine. "Hel's kiss at Balder's death. Each act of love alone would have barely scratched the curse. But together, in that precise moment..."

Understanding dawned. "They amplified each other."

"Exactly. Pure magic building upon pure magic, each wave making the next stronger, until it created something powerful enough to burn away any corruption it touched." He picked up another stone, turning it over in his hands. "Frigg built her curse to resist any single force, no matter how strong. But she never considered what would happen if different kinds of love—sacrificial, romantic, familial, unconditional—all manifested at once."

"The impossible combination you theorized," I said, remembering how the light had rippled outward from where Hel's lips met Balder's, each wave burning brighter than the last.

"Love in its purest forms," he said. "Not just sensed, but proven through sacrifice. Each person choosing love over their own safety or survival, creating a cascade effect that even the darkest magic couldn't withstand."

I stood in silence, his words sinking in. Behind us, seabirds wheeled between the cliffs, their cries mixing with the endless pull of water against stone. It wasn't just Hel and Balder's love that had saved us all, but the collective power of our bonds, our willingness to sacrifice for each other.

The ooey gooeyness of it all was enough to make me hurl.

"I do hope Frigg is fuming over this, although I wish you

had imprisoned her somewhere other than the dungeons. Fleas and rats are far too nice for her."

He grimaced and threw another stone into the churning water.

"It's only temporary until the trial when it's decided what's best to do with her," he said. "She has many supporters in the Nine Worlds, and that carries certain ramifications."

The casual way he discussed her fate made something crack inside me. After she nearly took him from me, after I was forced to confront how much losing him would destroy me...My fingers dug into the stone I held until my knuckles went white. I paced along the beach, pebbles crunching beneath each step, trying to contain the storm of emotions threatening to spill over.

"How can you be so calm about this?" My voice came out rougher than I meant it to. I spun to face him. "She tried to—" The words stuck in my mouth as Frigg's admission echoed in my mind. I knew exactly what that poison would have done to him, eating through his veins, slowly destroying him from within. The thought of him suffering that fate, choosing that fate rather than betray me...

He turned to look at me then, and something in his expression made the last of my walls crumble. All the love I'd never quite managed to kill, no matter how hard I'd tried, surged up with crushing force.

I hurled the stone, watching it arc into the waves.

"You were going to die. For me." The words came out raw, wrenched from somewhere deep inside where I'd buried every tender feeling I'd ever had for him. "After once choosing the death of that King's son over..."

"Loki—"

"No." I drew a shaky breath, the salt air burning in my

lungs. "You were ready to let her poison eat you alive rather than tell her about my mortality—after once betraying everything we had because you feared death so much."

His eye met mine, filled with such pain. "I learned something, losing you all that time ago. There are worse things than dying." His voice broke. "Living with knowing I was too much of a coward to love you properly. That was worse than any death she could give me."

"Odin..."

"I won't fail you again," he whispered. "I know I have no right to ask for your trust, not after everything. But I swear to you, Loki, I will never forsake you again. Even if it means—"

"Don't." The word came out sharp, desperate. "Don't you dare finish that sentence. I spent centuries telling myself I hated you. And then she told me you were dying, and I..." My voice cracked. "I couldn't lie to myself anymore."

He took a step towards me, then stopped. "Loki..."

"You were dying," I whispered, "and all I could think was 'please don't go, not before I tell you...'" I laughed, the sound raw. "The great Liesmith, and my biggest lie was pretending I didn't still love you."

Something shattered in his expression. He reached for me, then let his hand fall.

"I don't deserve—"

"No," I cut him off. "You don't get to decide what you deserve. You finally chose me. You chose me over your own life."

Tears spilled down his cheek.

"I should have chosen you the first time. Every time."

I closed the distance between us, pebbles shifting under our feet. I touched his face, brushing away his tears with my thumbs. Surprise bled from him. The cliffs caught the sound of the waves, throwing back their endless rhythm.

"We can't change the past," I said. "But maybe...maybe we can stop letting it poison the future."

I held his face between my palms, holding him there, memorizing every line and shadow. For a heartbeat, his expression was so raw, so vulnerable. And beneath, was that melancholy I always wanted to chase away.

He leaned into my touch, his eye closing as his hands came up to cover mine. Tears spilled beneath my thumbs. We stood there, foreheads nearly touching, sharing the same breath, the same heartbeat. Both of us standing on the edge of something we couldn't name.

Then I drew him closer, letting my fingers slide into his hair, and kissed him. Not with passion or heat, but with something deeper—an ache, a tenderness that had survived centuries of hurt. He made a broken sound against my mouth, his hands coming up to frame my face with a gentleness that undid me. The kiss tasted of salt, tears or sea spray, I couldn't tell. Sage and clove filled my senses, and beneath it all, that familiar warmth that was purely him.

When we finally broke apart, I kept him close, our foreheads pressed together, both of us taking shaky breaths. My fingers still tangled in his hair, his hands still cradling my face, neither ready to let go of this fragile moment.

"Did we just..." he started, his thumb tracing circles on my cheek.

"Forgive each other? I think we did."

He laughed softly, the sound thawing something long cold inside me, his breath warm against my skin. "Well, that's unsettling."

"Isn't it though?" I pulled back just enough to meet his gaze, though my hands lingered on his shoulders, not quite ready to break contact completely. "Just don't expect me to make a habit of it."

He bent to pick up a stone, the movement putting a gentle space between us that felt right, necessary. When he straightened, he offered it with a smile that held more questions than answers.

"What now?" he asked.

I took the stone from him, feeling every jagged edge of our past pressed into my palm, tracing its rough edges with my thumb, like running fingers over old scars. But stones could be polished smooth, given time and patience.

"We begin again."

EPILOGUE

Six Months Later

Malibu, California

I browsed the racks and racks of Versace and Gucci that lined one wall of my large closet. December sunlight poured through the floor-to-ceiling windows, warming the teak dressers and polished chrome. Beyond the glass, the Pacific stretched endless and blue, white-capped waves pounding the Malibu cliffs in a steady rhythm that filled our home.

"Sigyn, I need your opinion," I called out, pivoting on my heel. I held out a deep emerald velvet blazer and a black and gold jacquard print that screamed delicious. "Which one says 'yes, I'm attending a formal family function, but also I am the main event?' Though I must say, even Alexander McQueen's embroidery pales in comparison to what the Elves can do."

Her laughter echoed from the bedroom before she

appeared in the doorway, honeyed-ginger curls spilling over one shoulder as she leaned against the frame.

"The velvet," she said without hesitation, crossing to take the blazer from my hands, her fingers brushing mine. "Especially with that silk shirt that's just this side of indecent. The Aesir won't know whether to be scandalized or impressed."

I grinned imagining Thor sloshing his mead in jealousy when he realized the collar and cuffs were embellished with black pearl beading. Apparently, ever since that wedding incident with the tulle dress, he'd developed quite the taste for couture.

"The perfect combination," I said.

We walked from the closet into our bedroom, where luggage lay open on the dark hardwood floor. Clothing waited in neat piles across our white duvet. While Sigyn slid the blazer into a waiting garment bag by the bed, I folded the silk shirts we'd chosen, smoothing each crease.

Through the windows, a pod of dolphins arced through the waves, their sleek bodies gleaming silver against the deep blue. I smiled, remembering why we'd chosen this beach house in Malibu. We could have returned to Asgard, or finally visited those Southern Isles I'd dreamed of during my banishment. But somehow, this place had become something else entirely...a home of our own choosing. These quiet moments beside Sigyn, with just the sound of the ocean and the soft rustle of clothes being packed, felt like the greatest triumph after everything we'd been through together.

"The workshop at *Kalehalla* went well last week," Sigyn said, placing her navy sweater in the suitcase.

"Surprisingly well." I folded another pair of trousers for the pile. "Though I still maintain that smoothies are an affront to proper beverages everywhere. But I suppose that blackberry and honey concoction wasn't completely terrible. Even Tyr seemed impressed, once he got over his suspicion that I'd enchanted the blender."

"You have to admit, that outdoor meditation garden Fenrir is adding is inspired." Sigyn said, moving another stack of clothes from the bed to the suitcase. "Those carved stone benches overlooking the Animas River Valley. And the way he sources those rare Norwegian herbs for his signature blends...it just sets everything apart from the competition."

"At least it's better than that spirulina nonsense. I still maintain that stuff tastes like pond scum scraped off a kraken's back." I shuddered. "However, what I'm most curious about is how long before Jenn figures it out? The girl's sharp. She's bound to notice something's odd about why a one-handed Norwegian businessman keeps showing up to 'consult' on their wellness programs."

"Fen says she just thinks they're all really committed to the Nordic wellness aesthetic." Sigyn laughed, tucking her hairbrush and toiletry bag into the suitcase. The scent of amber and jasmine drifted up from the perfume I'd found for her in Paris. My favorite on her. "Though I suspect *Kalehalla* isn't the only thing catching her attention..."

I chuckled and slipped past her to the antique writing desk by the windows where we'd set up our gift-wrapping station. I picked up the obsidian skull pin I'd had commissioned for Hel. Finding a proper Yule gift for her had been a challenge. I'd originally wanted to get her the actual skull of her enemy, but apparently those were harder to come by these days. And rather illegal here in Midgard. I hoped she appreciated the rubies set in the eye sockets regardless.

"While we are on the subject of my sons," I said, carefully wrapping the pin, working the delicate paper. "Jorg actually answered my text yesterday. He's been traveling, making art. I found this absolutely gorgeous set of charcoals for him."

I didn't mention how my heart had leaped at seeing his name on my mobile, how carefully I'd worded my response, deleting and rewriting each sentence until it felt right. Some wounds healed slower than others, but each small step forward felt like a victory I hardly dared to celebrate.

Sigyn left the suitcase on the bed and crossed to the writing desk where I worked, finding my hand and squeezing gently. "I'm so happy to hear this," she said. "He's trying. You both are. And one day, you'll see it will all work out."

"Yes, well." I cleared my throat, busying myself with the gifts, methodically aligning the corners of the wrapping paper. "At least Balder's proven tolerable enough these days. Though I still have to fight the urge to punch him at least once per visit."

I smiled, setting down the wrapped pin and reaching, with only minimal grimacing, for the vintage Krug champagne I had chosen for him.

Sigyn had insisted that since he and Hel were together now, I needed to include him. The rare 1928 bottle seemed appropriately extravagant for the God of Light and Goodness, though I'd never tell him I'd actually enjoyed hunting down this particular bottle.

"But he makes her happy," I said. "I suppose that's worth enduring his particular brand of nauseating existence."

She smiled.

"You're actually starting to like him," Sigyn teased, settling on the edge of our bed beside the half-packed suitcase.

"Now don't get too ahead of yourself, there," I said,

flicking a bit of wrapping paper in her direction. I picked up the envelope I'd wrapped for Fenrir—proof that I'd finally paid back every penny of those bank "loans," plus a sizable donation to the Red Wolf conservation project he'd been supporting in North Carolina.

She laughed, catching the paper and letting it drift to the floor. She glanced at the small pile of remaining gifts.

"Speaking of difficult relationships...did you decide what to give Odin?"

I stilled, the ribbon in my hands suddenly very interesting.

"The first edition Hemingway. From that bookshop in Venice, near where we have our coffees." I tried to keep my voice light, but Sigyn knew me too well. "Though I will admit, having the whole family in Asgard for Yule...it's both terrifying and..." I trailed off, unable to voice the hope that threatened to choke me.

"Wonderful?" she said.

"Something like that." I set down the ribbon and walked to one of the windows, pressing my palm against the cool glass, watching the waves beat the shore and rock. My thoughts drifted to those careful meetings in Venice, the way Odin and I would sit at that little cafe, both of us trying so hard.

"It's strange, building something entirely different from the ruins of what was. We'll be talking about nothing important. The weather in Venice, a particularly good espresso, some ridiculous mortal fashion trend...and suddenly we're both so careful, treating each word like spun glass. Sometimes I catch myself wanting to make a cutting remark, but then I see something in his eye. A similar struggle, a similar hope...and I choose differently. If one wrong word might shatter this fragile peace we've found, then perhaps the right ones might strengthen it." I smiled faintly, dropping my hand. "So far, no one's been stabbed, so this whole friendship thing may be working out."

Sigyn rose from the bed and padded across the room and wrapped her arms around me from behind. She rested her chin on my shoulder, and I felt her exhale softly against my neck. "You've come so far," she murmured. "We all have."

I leaned back into her embrace, finding her fingers where they rested against my chest.

The afternoon sun shifted, growing long shadows across the wood floor. She slipped her one hand free and brushed a strand of hair from my face. Something about the tender movement, about watching our shadows merge and stretch across our bedroom, made my chest ache with a familiar mixture of love and loss. All these mending relationships, all these careful new beginnings, with Odin, with my children...

They stirred up older wounds, deeper hopes.

I turned in her embrace, studying her face...the face that had seen me through darkness and light, through loss and redemption. I traced the line of her jaw as I struggled to find the words. "Do you ever think about..." I hesitated, the weight of memory heavy between us. "About trying again? Having another child?"

Her eyes softened, holding all the grief and hope we shared. She stepped back slightly, taking my hands in hers. She brushed her thumbs over my knuckles in that soothing way.

"I think about Narfi and Narvi every day," she said quietly. "They're part of who we are, part of our story. And if someday we decide to add another chapter to that story, we will. But right now, I'm happy just being us. Building these relationships with your children. Finding our way forward together."

I pulled her closer, sliding one hand up to cup her cheek as I drew her into a kiss. Her lips met mine with that perfect blend of tenderness and need that still made my heart race. She sighed against my mouth, curling her fingers into my shirt, and I deepened the kiss, tasting deliverance.

Her body melted against mine as I traced her cheekbone with my thumb, her other hand coming up to tangle in my hair. We'd shared countless kisses, but each one still felt like a gift, like a reminder that we'd survived, we'd found each other, we'd built this life together.

When we finally parted, both a little breathless, I couldn't help but grin.

"I wouldn't mind spending more time finding our way together," I murmured, drawing her back for another gentle kiss.

She swatted my arm, laughing, and returned to the bed where our half-packed suitcase waited.

"Pack your outfits, Loki. We have a feast to attend."

"And mead," I added, crossing to the organized mess of our gift-wrapping desk to pluck my favorite green silk tie from where I'd set it aside. "Lots and lots of mead. I'm going to need it to survive an entire week of familial bonding."

I joined her by the bed, stuffing the tie into the suitcase.

"It will be perfect," she said. "Chaotic and messy and absolutely perfect."

I caught her hand, pulling her close again. The steady crash of waves outside vibrated through the floorboards as the warmth of the setting sun painted our bedroom in gold and amber.

"I love you," I whispered against her hair, breathing in rosemary. "Even when the world burns down around us, even when destruction comes kicking in our door...I will always love you. You are the calm heart beating steady beneath all my storms."

"And I love you. Chaos and all," she said. "Now, again, seriously, we really need to get these bags packed before Fenrir's flight lands."

I folded another shirt beside her as she organized the suitcase, and the weight of our history settled around me. From 16th century Basel to modern Malibu, from godhood to mortality and back again, we'd fought our way back to each other across centuries and realms, through darkness and light, and even through Ragnarok itself, until we'd finally found our way home.

Watching her now, I knew with absolute certainty that I would choose her again. Over immortality, over power, over everything the Nine Worlds could offer. Because she didn't just love the god or the mortal, the chaos or the calm. She loved all of me, every fractured, healing piece. And it was her love, her unwavering faith even when I'd lost faith in myself, that had made all of this possible—these mending relationships with my children, this fragile peace with Odin, this second chance at being not just a god, but a father, a friend, a better version of myself.

The sun dipped lower towards the horizon, painting the clouds in shades of rose. My phone buzzed on the night-stand. Probably a text from Fenrir that he'd landed, or maybe another message from Jorg. He promised, after all. Across from where we packed, Hel's thank you gift hung over the dresser. A framed butterfly mounted with her characteristic precision, its dark wings edged in silver. I'd suggested she find a less morbid hobby, but this was who she was, death and beauty intertwined, and I loved her for it.

Five centuries ago, I wouldn't have believed this life possible. This wholeness filled with family dinners and hesitant reconciliations. Perhaps that was my greatest trick. Not the lies or chaos or cheating death, but finding peace without losing myself. Learning that the most rebellious act wasn't burning everything down, but letting something new grow from the ashes.

What we had was better than perfect.

It was real. It was earned. It was ours.

And that was everything.

The End

EXCERPT FROM "THUNDER, BLOOD, AND GOATS"

Eons back, long before Thor had his hammer, and Loki was still new in Asgard...

Alfheim

"You just *had* to take the goat drawn chariot," I yelled over the crack and snap of splintering pine branches.

Thor ground his teeth beneath his fiery beard and tugged the reins of his two goats, jerking us left, avoiding a tree limb hitting me square in the chest by an inch.

"Shut up and let me concentrate on steering," he said.

Another yank and we swung right, skimming the tree-tops, stripping them bare of their pine needles.

"MAAAAAHHH!" the goats screamed.

"You consider this steering? You have the navigational dexterity of a slug." I ducked, grimacing at the whoosh of another branch grazing the top of my head. "Give me the reins."

Laughter burst out from Thor's lungs.

"Trust you with driving my precious Tanngrisnir and Tanngnjóstr? I'd sooner share a pint with a frost giant and spend the afternoon chasing butterflies," he said. "Only I know how to handle these goats properly."

We jolted up higher over the forest, glimpsing the Whispering Mountains to the South. Thor wrenched the goats' heads back. We plunged into the darkness of the packed pine, my stomach remaining somewhere high in the night sky.

Yes. He handled them splendidly.

This would have all been great fun if it didn't come with the risk of ripping half my face off my skull. I was rather fond of my face, with its sharp points and angles and excellent bone structure.

If I lost it in a freak goat chariot accident...Thor would pay dearly.

Branches smacked the sides of the chariot, scratching deep into the paint and whacking us back and forth. Each strike produced a thousand more plots to swim in my mind of ways to get back at him for this mess.

"Had you not taken that wrong turn at Mount Erbis, we would be there by now," I said.

"Had *you* not kept chattering about trivial things like east and west and everything in between I wouldn't have missed."

Always my fault.

"We would have been to Afethemar by now, decidedly less cold, and with fewer splinters wedged into our cheeks." I pulled a sliver of wood out of my flesh and rubbed away the sting. "That dragon has probably eaten half the village by now."

Thor growled and snapped the reins, urging the goats faster. More enraged cries followed, but from the goats or me, I wasn't sure. I gripped the edge of the chariot harder, digging my nails into the woodgrain.

This dragon was supposed to be a quick jaunt.

The Elves had been entreating Asgard for our assistance for weeks with their little dragon problem. Apparently, the monster had grown quite the taste for sheep. And cows. And Elves.

Of course, I immediately volunteered to lend a helping hand to our Elvish neighbors.

I was a beacon of generosity.

...And the fact it presented the perfect opportunity to prove myself, freshly arrived in Asgard and a new god, didn't hurt either.

I'd wipe those sneers off their smug Aesir faces. They'd learn chaos was not to be underestimated. And not to brag, but I knew my way around a blade. Killing one measly dragon wouldn't be a problem.

The problem was Thor, who also found a spot of dragon killing a fine idea, and just like that, I found myself in a goat drawn chariot, being struck by every pine tree from Asgard to Alfheim.

Thor clapped the reins again.

And again, the chariot bobbed and swayed, rising over the forest. A river glistened near the horizon, cutting through snow-covered hills and a patchwork of fields and clusters of trees. Moonlight swathed the soft landscape in blues and grays and shadow.

We coasted through cold air.

Down we sped.

Down faster, heaving around trunks and through crackling twigs.

Out we popped into a clearing, aiming straight for a woodcutter's shed.

"Thor..."

The shed drew closer.

"I know what I'm doing."

But did he?

We went faster, feet from the shed.

"Thor! SHED!"

"Just let me land in peace!"

The chariot bumped and ground into a foot of snow. Thor twisted and wrenched the reins, making the goats bleat, swinging us around and skidding us directly for the shed. My future sped past my vision, a future of splinters and pain and broken bones.

I closed my eyes and braced myself, grinding my fingers until numb on the edge of the chariot.

The reins squealed in Thor's grip, stretching and twisting.

The chariot tapped the shed with a gentle *plink* and we came to a stop.

I cracked open my eyes.

Had I survived?

The shed creaked. I looked up. I tried to leap out of the way.

Piles and piles of snow sloughed off the roof and dumped on my head and lean frame, crushing me beneath a mountain of wet, cold bullshit.

I clawed my way through the snow, cursing in every language I could.

Thor laughed, shaking the forest with his thundering baritone.

"You look ridiculous," he said, shaking a bit of frost off layers of furs draping his bulky shoulders.

He chuckled, grabbing me by my collar and hoisting me out of the snow.

"Let me go," I snapped. "You'll stretch my tunic with your big, oafish hands."

He laughed louder.

"You are a prickly one," he said. "I thought Father insane when he brought you to Asgard and told us what he did." He pointed at my arm, where a scar hid beneath my sleeve. "But you are hilarious!"

This again. Why was everyone so surprised by Odin and my blending our blood and swearing an oath together? I might be a trickster, but I was quite capable of upholding a promise.

Especially to someone like Odin.

He offered me a chance.

More than I ever got in Jotunheim, rotting away. My talents wasted. Sure, I kept busy with the odd assassination or some light thievery, but I was so much more, and Odin saw my potential.

I slapped Thor away and pulled pine needles and twigs from my red, copper hair that fell in waves just past my shoulders. I brushed clumps of snow from my cloak and furs.

"There are better modes of travel." I picked a pinecone off my backside. "Ones that smell far less."

I threw the goats a nasty look.

The goats looked back, growling from deep within their bulbous bellies. Tanngnjóstr ground his harness between his teeth, not breaking eye contact with me. He tugged and stretched at the leather as if determined to make me eat my words. Cantankerous, hateful things.

Thor stomped over to them and removed the harness from Tanngnjóstr's mouth. The goat continued to stare daggers—or whatever goats fancied murdering you with— into me.

"There, there." He pushed his thick fingers through their fur, caressing their necks and sides. "Loki didn't mean it. He doesn't understand how special you both are. Yes. Who are good boys? Your daddy loves you!"

Gods.

I turned away from the cooing and looked out at the forest, gauging where we were. My toes were already ice.

Jumping on a boulder, I looked out into the dense pine and rocky forest floor. There was a lot of land to cover, and we were at least ten miles off course from our target. Finding this dragon would be like finding a needle in a haystack. A very angry needle.

My enthusiasm about this mission surprised me, but then, this wasn't just about proving myself to the gods and giving them the most sublime of middle fingers. It was also about proving Odin right in choosing me.

Ever since I arrived in Asgard, I inspired nothing but glares and whispers and barbs. As if judgement had been passed and I was declared the ultimate fiend.

I thought me a pretty cheerful fellow, myself.

I had to show the gods how wrong about me they were.

I owed it to Odin.

Fat flakes of snow fell faster.

Thor plodded towards me, ice crystals clinging to his red beard, covering it in silver.

"Where is this blasted dragon hiding?" he said.

Sucking in a breath, I looked down. I smiled.

"Don't move," I said, putting out my arm to him.

He stopped, one knee bent, shaking and trying to keep balanced. I dragged my hand down my cold face.

"You can lower your leg," I said. "Look under the rock."

I pointed.

He inched closer.

His small eyes grew twice the size and filled with mirth.

Dragon tracks as wide across as I was tall trailed to the right, heading into the forest.

I jumped off the boulder, the snow crunching beneath my boots.

"This is perfect," Thor said, swinging his massive axe over his massive shoulder. "I can't wait to bury my blade into its skull."

He started off, nearly skipping into the forest.

Say what you will of Thor, but I did appreciate his love of adventure, although I sometimes wondered if he knew what death was. I think he believed death was just something that happened to other people.

* * *

THE MOONLIGHT MADE the forest glow a vivid blue as we trekked several miles over slick rock and along snow-packed paths. We grasped onto bushes to keep from sliding down slopes and yanked on tree branches to fight our way up steep hills.

Then there were the surprise cliff edges, which mixed well with slippery trails.

I already couldn't feel the tip of my nose, and the thought of plummeting fifty feet was something I really could do without.

The snow thickened, filling in the tracks hour by hour. I could barely make them out through my frost coated eyelashes as time and weather worked against us.

If we came all this way for nothing...

We trudged on, the hard winter silence only broken by the squeal of snow against our boots and the hoot of a snowy owl somewhere in the distance.

I breathed in cold air mixed with moisture from the Cartha Ocean that lay to the north, and it gave the air a nasty bite that burned my lungs.

Just as my calves burned, lifting my legs high to pass through the snow.

Thor groaned.

"Why are we doing this at night?" Thor said, wiping his nose on his sleeve. "Wouldn't light make this easier? And warmer?"

I forced my leg out of the snow and shoved it back in, achieving one step forward.

"Yes, but if you'd know anything about dragons, this particular kind sleeps at night in its den. That makes it easier to find if it isn't roaming about. Plus, irritable things are better to kill while they are asleep."

He scoffed.

"But not as fun," he said.

He had a point there.

But this wasn't about fun.

I stopped.

A slice of black cut through a mound of rock and roots of trees twisting between crevices and stone.

A small cave.

And the dragon tracks led right inside the mouth.

Thor bounded towards it. I grabbed his steak of an arm and tugged him back, which took every ounce of my strength to keep me from flying off my feet.

"What?" he said. "Let me at it!"

"And wake it up?" I said. "No thank you. This requires *finesse.*"

Thor scratched his head.

I forgot that word was not part of his vocabulary, or his

being. Thor was more of a smash and, well, smash type of personality.

"We need a plan," I said. "If we approach the cave quietly...*gently*...from the right, I can...Thor?" I snapped my fingers in front of his wandering gaze. "Hey, eyes on me."

"Huh. Oh. Right. *Plan*." He yawned.

His brain always overpowered anytime the word *plan* was mentioned.

"I will approach from the left. It will be surrounded. Then—"

He eyed the cave mouth again.

"Thor, pay attention. Then—"

A twig snapped, echoing through the silence.

"Dragon!" he bellowed. "Die foul creature!"

He flung his axe towards the sound. The axe spun, hurtling through the pine and lodged itself neatly in a trunk.

SQUEEE!

A squirrel fell out of a branch, landing in the snow with a soft *thud*.

It stood on its haunches, shook itself, and scurried off into the forest, hissing and snarling a litany of squirrel curses at us.

I rolled my eyes.

"Good job, Thor," I said. "You sure showed that big, bad squirrel who is king."

Thor grumbled, walking to his axe to retrieve it.

"Stupid dragon. Lousy axe. I need a better weapon. One that comes back to you after you throw it. Damn tedious this is."

The wood groaned and bark crackled as he wiggled the axe head, trying to dislodge it from the trunk.

Something growled.

Deep. Warning.

The ground rattled beneath my feet.

"Thor, please tell me that was you," I said.

Thor yanked out the axe.

"I thought it was you."

A puff of hot breath saturated with the stench of a hundred rotting sheep corpses blew out of the cave, blowing my hair straight back and flapping my cloak around my arms and legs.

Red eyes opened in the darkness.

* * *

**Enjoy more adventures with Loki in
"Thunder, Blood, and Goats"**
(Tales of the Nine Worlds)

Available here

THANK YOU!

I sincerely hope you enjoyed reading this book as much as I enjoyed writing it (and trust me, wrangling Loki's chaos into coherent sentences was quite the adventure). If you did, and even if you didn't, I would be eternally grateful if you'd consider leaving a review on Amazon or your favorite book website. Reviews are an author's lifeblood. They're like digital high-fives that help others find our stories. Even just a few words or stars can make a huge difference. Thank you!

ACKNOWLEDGMENTS

I should probably thank Loki first, since chaos clearly wanted to make sure I was living authentically while writing this book. Between health adventures, house renovations gone sideways, THREE hurricanes (because one wasn't dramatic enough), floods, and general Life™ shenanigans, it's been quite the journey. But like any good story about our favorite trickster, we made it through!

First, endless gratitude to Rafi, who created an oasis of peace in our hurricane of a year (both literal and metaphorical). Your support means everything, especially when I'm deep in Norse mythology rabbit holes at 3 AM.

To my parents, who continue to enthusiastically support my obsessions—I promise I'll write that Hallmark movie someday. (No, I won't. Sorry not sorry.) Thank you for always being there to listen to my endless Norse mythology rambles.

Hannah, you magnificent editor-slash-voice-of-reason, thank you for saving me from myself more times than I can count. Your "are you sure you want to do THAT?" always comes at exactly the right moment. And yes, you were absolutely right about "the horse" incident—that ledge was definitely not worth walking over. Also, your continued insistence that naked scenes are always the right choice has yet to steer me wrong.

Jenn, you absolute champion. Who else would read a 700-page tome THREE times without batting an eye? Your love for these characters (especially our precious Fenrir) shines through in every piece of feedback. May there always be blueberry smoothies in your future.

Cait, thank you for helping me navigate the delicate waters of romance. Your insight helped make those scenes sing (or should I say, sizzle?).

Casey, my partner in chaos, your enthusiasm for Loki's suffering gives me life. Thank you for helping me make the crucial decision about Loki's most despised footwear. History will remember that a notorious foam clog (not naming names) was the only choice. These are indeed the weighty decisions that keep authors up at night.

To my readers, you beautiful, patient souls who stick with me through every twist and turn of this journey. Your support means everything. Without you, I couldn't keep torturing—I mean, writing about—these characters we all love so much.

And finally, to chaos itself, thanks for the authentic research experience. Though next time, maybe we could stick to just ONE hurricane? Just throwing that out there.

ALSO BY LYRA WOLF

The Nine Worlds Rising

Novellas

Thunder, Blood, and Goats

Novels

Truth and Other Lies (Book 1)

The Order of Chaos (Book 2)

That Good Mischief (Book 3)

The Fire in the Frost (Book 4)

ABOUT THE AUTHOR

Lyra Wolf is a Swiss-American author of fantasy and mythic fiction.

Raised in Indiana, home to a billion corn mazes, she now lives in Central Florida, home to a billion mosquitoes. She enjoys drinking espresso, wandering through old city streets, and being tragically drawn to 18th century rogues.

When Lyra isn't fulfilling the wishes of her overly demanding Chihuahua, you can find her writing about other worlds and the complicated people who live there.

Lyra has earned a B.A. in History and M.A. in English.

* * *

Sign up for the **Lyra Wolf's Substack** for exclusive content, updates, and other delicious goodies.

lyrawolf.com